STEAMPUNK WORLD

edited by Sarah Hans

Alliteration Ink | Dayton

Cover Art by James Ng

National Oldstyle, Metro Light, and Metro Alternate fonts used
with permission of the H.P. Lovecraft Preservation Society

Doulos SIL used under the Open Font License

Alliteration Ink
PO Box 20598, Dayton, OH 45420
alliterationink.com

Steampunk World
pISBN: 978-1-939840-19-6
eISBN: 978-1-939840-12-7

May 2014
10 9 8 7 6 5 4 3 2 1

This work could not exist without the backers on Kickstarter. Thank you all.

Aaron Allston

Aaron Hans

Aaron Ramsby

A.Chatain

Adam Gallardo

Adam Hill

Adam O'Riley

Adi Saunders

A.D. Little

Aja Romano

AJ Harm

Akilah

Alan Pike

Alan Stern

Alastair Black

Al Billings

Alec Robinson

Alexander Smith

Alexandra N. Walters

Alexandre Gachet

Alexis

Alex Ruck

Alice Anyone

Alice Tsoi

A. Lisa Walden

Alistair Morrison

Al Letson

Alumiere

Amanda Johnson

Amanda Penrose

Amanda Power

Amanda Stein

Amy Peavy

Anastasia Kaufmann

Andi Scott

Andrea Hosth

Andrea L. Cook

Andrea Smith

Andrew Barton

Andrew Fish

Andrew Foxx

Andrew Linstrom

Andrew, Margaret, Sophie, Xander, and Stacie;

Andy Arminio

Angge Dannug

Angus Abranson

Anita M. King

Anna Price

Anonymous Supporter

Anthony Cannella

Anthony R. Evans

Antonio Vincentelli

Ariëlla F. Reinders

Ariel Rodgers

Artimese de Sade

Ashley

Astra Kim

Atul Varma

Austin Sirkin

Avi Blackmore

Axisor

baldereagle

Bekkir Barbier

Belladonna Price

Ben Cakir

Benjamin Abbott

Benjamin Sparrow

Bethan Thomas

Beth Morris Tanner

Beth Wodzinski

Beverly Bambury

Bill Bodden

Bill Fernandez

Bill Humphries

Bill Kohn

blaiseg89

Blake Lee

Bob Hanks

Bob Ooton

B Parran

Bradley Richardson

Brahms Lewis

Brian Horstmann

Brian K. Hudson

Brian Liberge

Brian Williams

Bronwen Jones

Bronwyn Allen

Caleb Williamson

Candace A. Carpenter

Can Özmen

Carmen Marin

Caroline Julian

Carrie V.

Catherine Porter

Catherine Siemann

Cédric Jeanneret

Celine Gabriel

Chad Canterbury

Chad "Doomedpaladin" Middleton

Chad Finlay

Chante McCoy

Charles Eugene Anderson

Charlie Chalkley

Charlotte Grubbs

Charlotte Pass

CHNG CHIN JOO

Chris McLaren
Chris Spindler
Christian Klein
Christine Bell
Christopher Durham
Chuck Thorne
cj rene
Claire Rousseau
Claudio Biondino
Cliff Winnig
Conley Lyons
Constance Burris
Cora Greis
Coral Moore
Craig Hacker
C. Y. L.
Cynthia Gonsalves
Cynthia Ward
Cyrano Jones
Dan Fairs
Danielle Ackley-McPhail
Daniel M Perez
Daniel Sturkie
Daniel & Trista Robichaud
Dan Rabarts
Darcey Wunker
Daren T
Dark Matter Zine
Dave Mattingly

David Annandale
David Bell
David Edmonds
David Sanderson
David Ting
David Wyatt
Davina Gifford
Davin L McKay
Deanne Fountaine
Dean Valenti
Dean Wood
Deborah Biancotti
Denali White
Denis McCarthy
Derek "Pineapple Steak" Swoyer
Derek Viger
Devin Harris
Devin Redd
Diana Dee Jarvis
Doctor Q & the Artifice Club
Donald J. Bingle
Donald Jessop
Don Bassingthwaite
Donovan Corrick
Doug Bissell
Doug Hagler
Doug Johnson
Doug Jones

Douglas Henke

Doug Monroe

Dre Lasana

D-Rock

Dru Pagliassotti

E. Ambrose

Ed "Kaledor" Arneson

Elias F. Combarro

Eli McIlveen

Elisheba Trinity

Elizabeth Kite

Elizabeth Talsma

Ellen Sandberg

Ellie Ann

E. Michael Kwan

Emily Reed

EmmaB

Eoghan Ryan

Epheros

Eric Garrison

Erick Pfister

Eric L Meaders

Erik T Johnson

Erin Lani

Erin O'Kelly Phillips

Erin Ryan

Etienne Barillier

Eva

Fabio Fernandes

F. C. Moulton

Floyd Brigdon

Forth

Foz Meadows

Fran Adams

Francis Hughes

Frank Hall

Fred Herman

Freewillkeeper

Gabriel Disselkoen

Gabriella Azanu

Garin W Williamson

Garrett Shaw

Gary Simmons

Gavran

Geoff Nicholson

Geonn Cannon

Gina M.

GozzoMan

Graeme

Graeme Williams

Hamish Cameron

Hana Kim

Hannah Silver

Hannah Tikvah

Harbir Anand

Harri Kovanen

Haviva Avirom

Heather Blandford

Heather Cushing

Henrik Augustsson

H Lynnea Johnson

Hugh J. O'Donnell

Ian McFarlin

Ib Rasmussen

Ief Grootaers

Iñigo Serna

Isabel Fine

Issara Twiltermsup

Iván de Neymet Franco

Jacinto Quesnel

Jack Vivace

Jacob Gillespie

Jacque Howell

Jacqueline C

Jae Lerer

Jake Sexton

James Elwood

James Pottinger

James R. Vernon

James Walker

Jamieson L Hoffman

Jami Good

Janet L. Oblinger

Janine K. Spendlove

Janito Vaqueiro Ferreira Filho

Jared Axelrod

Jared Hammaker

Jasmine Stairs

Jason Heller

J Daniels

Jean Marie Ward

Jeff Hummel

Jeff "Lepef" Coquery

Jeffrey Allan Boman

Jen Edwards

Jen Huang

Jennifer Brozek

Jennifer Kahng

Jenn Mercer

Jen W

Jeremy Kear

Jeremy Saunders

Jerome Lim

Jerry Sköld

Jesse Rebock

Jesse Webster

Jessi Taylor

J.G. Stewart

Jim Fina

Jixia Ao

J.L. Jamieson

Joanne B

Joel Palmer

Joe Murphy

Joe Tortuga

John Devenny

John Eddy

Johnny Strle

Jo Morrison

Jonathan D. Beer

Jonathan "Dr Archeville" Howell

Jonathan Korman

Jon Folkers

Jon K.G. Allanson

Jordan Lennard

Jose F. Yrizarry

Joseph Boeke

Joshua Hair

Josie Chang-Order

Jouni Miettunen

Joyce Pusel

J Pinsak

J. R. Murdock

Judith Tarr

Jukka Särkijärvi

Julia Straya Kessler

Julia Svaganovic

Kalen Boley

Karin Wellman

Karl-Heinz

Kate Larking

Kate Reynolds

Katharine

Katharine Kerr

Katherine Gleason

Katherine Malloy

Katherine Weinstein

Kathy Kachelries

Katrin Liang

kay zimmerman

kekhmet

Kelli Neier

Kelsi Morris

Kenny Marable

Kent Archie

Keri Bas

Kevin Andrew Murphy

Kevin Bender

Kevin Block-Schwenk

Kevin J. "Womzilla" Maroney

Kevin Kelleher

Kim Belair

Kim Warren

Kirstie & Ishbel

K Jackson

K. Pals

Kris Marchu

Lady Talia

Lang Thompson

Larry D. Clark

Lars Nygaard Witter

Lassi Hiilinen

Laura A Burns

Laura Christensen

Laura Morrigan

Laura Phillips

Lauren Stuart

Laurie McLean

Lawjick

Lee Hiskett

Leena Romppainen

Leisl Schrader

Letitia Maier

Lexie C.

Liam Donnell

Lianne

Linda Cartwright

Lisa H. Timberlake

Lisa Kruse

Lisa Martincik

Lisa Riefer

Liz & Cath Evans-Gist

Liz Neering

Lizzie S

Logan Turner

Lois Spangler

Lonerine Storm

Lucas K. Law

Lucy H. Lin

Lulu Kadhim

Lynne Everett

Lynne McCullough

Madeleine Holly-Rosing

Maeghan

Maggie Allen

Máire Bourke

MANDEM

Manfred Schweigl

Mara K

Marc Paquin

Marganma

Margaret M. St. John

Margy

Marian Allen

Marie Chelberg

Marijn Hubert

Mark Bould

Mark Brown

Mark Hartsuyker

Mark Hirschman

Mark J.W Elston

Mark "the Encaffeinated ONE" Kilfoil

Mark Thompson

Martin Riddle

Mary

Mary Kay Kare

Mary Robinette Kowal

Mary Spila

Matrix

Matthew A. Muth

Matthew Clay

Matthew Eaton

Matthew 'Milo' Barley

Matthew O'Connor

Matthew Rogers

Matthieu Berthet

Matt & Nykki Boersma

Matt Wagner

Maureen Kincaid Speller

Maxcorps

Maximillian Kite

Max Kaehn

Max Oehlert

Max Robitzsch

Maxwell Heath

Megan C. Lane

Megan E. Daggett

Megan Prime

Meghan Smith

Melanie R. Meadors

Mel Potter

Michael A. Stackpole

Michael Barmore

Michael Cox

Michael D. Blanchard

Michael Fedrowitz

Michael Haynes

Michael & Lena Hicks

Michael Lorenson

Michael Moe

Michael Niederman

Michael Scholl

Michelle Curtis

Michelle Smith

Mike Davies

Mikko Matvejeff

Mildred Cady

Miles Matton

Milton Davis

Mirakle_Studio

Morgan Ellis

NAME REDACTED

nancy

narsaela

Nathan Jones

Nathan K. Finney

Nathan Seabolt

Nayad Monroe

Neal Levin

Nene Ormes

Next Friday

Nick Hembery

Nick Lam

Nick Watkins

Nicole Bunge

Nicole Chen

Niels Nellissen

Niki La Teer

Nikki J.

Noel Richards

Olivia B.

Parish Vaidya

Park

Patrick Deja

Patrick James bell II

Paul Clarkson

Paul Drussel

Pauline Arsenault

Paul Jackson

Penny

penwing

Peter Kavanagh

Philip Weiss

protected static

Quang Pho

Race DiLoreto

Rafael Lohmann

Rafael Veintimilla

Rafal K

Rafia

Randy P. Belanger

R. Daniel Paddock

Regis M. Donovan

Remy Nakamura

Renae Wagner, Megan Seeley

Reverend Jim Best

Rhel ná DecVandé

Richard Fusco

Rick Underwood

Rie Sheridan Rose

Risa Wolf

Rita Lewis

Robby Thrasher

Robert Cougill

Robert Fleck

Robert Moreland

Robert P. Goldman

Robert "Rev. Bob" Hood

Robert Rodgers, Sr.

Robert Tomaino

Robin "HOOD" Hayes

Rob MacAndrew

Rob Voss

Rob Weber

Rosemary Tizledoun

Ross Cheung

Rrain Prior

Ruth

Ruth Coy

Ryan J. Gilmer

Ryan Leduc

Ryan Thomas

Sachin Suchak

Salvador Manzo

Samuel Hansen

Sara Glassman

Sarah A.

Sarah Braun

Sarah Coldheart

Sarah E. Troedson

Sara Stredulinsky

Scearls

Scott Baldwin

Scott Gable

Scott Lynch

scott peacock

Scout Johnson

Sean Harrop

Sean The Bookonaut

Sebastian Lindqvist

Sebastian Schmidt

Shahamir Hamzah Shahrill

Shasta

Shean, Semeicha and
Sapphira Mohammed

Sheila Addison

Shervyn

Sheryl R. Hayes

Sidsel Nørgaard Pedersen

Silence in the Library
Publishing

Silvano-Tellas Stéphanie

S. Kay Nash

S.L. Gray

Soh Kam Yung

@solardepths

Sonny Larsson

Sophie Melchior

SteampunkGoggles.com

Stephanie Wood Franklin

Stephen Abel

Stephen Cheng

Stephen Trower

Steve Gere

Steve Lickman

Steve Lord

Steven Mentzel

Steven Salter

Steven Tonthat

Stuart Chaplin

summervillain

Sunny Manoj

Susanne Schörner

Susan Patrick

Susan Sutton

Susan Weiner

Susie Cummings

Suzie Eisfelder

SwordFire

Tansy Rayner Roberts

Tarek

Taylor Poole

Ted Gilbert

Tee Morris

Tehani Wessely

Thomas M. Smith

Thu

Tina Libè

Tinker the Web Series

Tomas Burgos Caez

Tom Fendt

Tone "Zicon" Berg

Toni Adams

Tony Chavira

Tor André Wigmostad

Tournevis

Tracy Chowdhury

Tragwyddol

Ty Bailey

Vampire Revenant

Virginia Keating

Vishal Bajaj

Vladimir iBoyko Kuznetsov

Vladimir Makarov

V.Noche

Wendy Mann

Willow Buckley

Wyng'd Lyon Creations

Xtine Bazant

yo

Youichi Hophop

Yvette Roke

Yvonne Falkenhagen

Zachary Lasater

Zachary Prentice

Zach Schuetz

Zach Williamson

Z Sivell

Zw3rv3r

Table of Contents

Editor's Dedication

To the Airship Archon, the best bunch of
~~pirates~~ ~~privateers~~ friends
a girl can have the privilege of knowing.

Introduction: Going Global, or Re-Engineering Steampunk Fiction

Diana M. Pho

Steampunk fiction has traveled a long way. Chronologically, steampunk's inspiration stems from the classic scientific romances and dime novels of the 19th century. Manifestations of "proto-steampunk" fiction existed, usually pastiches and re-interpretations of classic Victorian novels. One of the first early examples of modern steampunk was Michael Moorcock's Nomad of the Time Streams trilogy, written in the 1970s. This type of fiction became anointed as "steampunk" in 1987, when K.W. Jeter wrote in his now famous letter to *Locus* magazine: "Personally, I think Victorian fantasies are going to be the next big thing, as long as we can come up with a fitting collective term…Something based on the appropriate technology of that era; like 'steampunks,' perhaps…."

Jeter's *Morlock Night* and books from his fellow writers Tim Powers (*The Anubis Gates*) and James Blaylock (*Homunculus*) are considered the founding texts of the modern steampunk genre. Later books have become game-changers in steampunk fiction, each one marking a new turn in the genre. William Gibson & Bruce Sterling's *The Difference Engine* stamped the "punk" into steampunk with its subversive, gritty take on how computing technology can change the industrial age in the West. Cherie Priest's Clockwork Century series, beginning with *Boneshaker*, took the science fiction community by storm, introducing steampunk that isn't limited to Victorian England and highlighting how people across race, class, gender, and sexuality also had stories in history worthy of being told. The fiction anthologies by Ann and Jeff VanderMeer gathered both classic and modern takes on steampunk together, and their latest volume dares to ask whether steampunk fiction can become a revolutionary act. Now in your hands you hold another book that seeks to impact steampunk fiction by asking: *"Where* does steampunk happen?"

Not in England. Not in the United States. Not anymore.

But before the "where" can be further discussed, there have been many debates on defining steampunk that must be acknowledged. Jess Nevins's early writings on steampunk point to its 19th century literature roots in Edisonades, the boy-genius pulp fiction adventures. Offering another argument, literature scholar Mike Perschon argues that steampunk is an aesthetic based on "neo-Victorian retrofuturistic technofantasy." Fellow professor Dru Pagliassotti suggests that there is a difference between steampunk stories which highlight subversion, rebellion, and marginalized underdog protagonists, and "steampulp" ones which contain the 19th century milieu and adventure, minus the politics.

Let me propose another idea. Steampunk has been thought of as being "undefinable" because of the range of elements it actually includes, but I think in some sense, steampunk has become synonymous with an emergent idea in today's fiction—the cross-genre. No more can stories be contained into one category; now, they jump across many. Nothing is simply "steampunk" after all – it is steampunk *and* alternate history, or mystery, or romance, or horror, or what-have-you. This idea isn't coming strictly from an academic angle – if it was, I'd also mention the role of postmodernism and include a whole lot of citations. As a publishing professional, I also think that cross-genre is a tricky catch-all gambit that can make books fly off the shelves like hotcakes or be stuck in the clearance bin because no one knows exactly *how* to sell it. But that is also the miracle explanation of how cross-genre works, because everyone can find *something* they like about a book of that kind. Steampunk fiction as a cross-genre explains its rising popularity in pop culture: because it acts as a wide-appealing topical idea that tailors itself to the individual interests of the steampunk fan. We know that steampunk style can span all media forms – video games, films, books, music, fashion. The subject can work as a building block for online communities and offline maker spaces. It can be as high-minded as historiographical discourses on neo-Victorianism or as lowbrow as that trendy new porn site.

By categorizing steampunk as cross-genre, what happens when we take one aspect commonly seen in steampunk and cross it out entirely? In this case, how can steampunk stories be told outside of that western geographical cage?

The answer is straight from a tinker's DIY manual: by however they work.

The tales that Sarah Hans has selected for *Steampunk World* incorporate steampunk's biggest thematic idea into non-Western backdrops: namely, the impact of industrialization. More than a simple exercise of imagination, then, steampunk fiction from a global perspective can be a deep exploration of cultural and historical issues: encroaching westernization, economic upheaval, shifting gender roles, prejudices concerning race and nationality, the impact of imperialism and war. Plus, as much as steampunk fiction loves dealing with the past (or alternate pasts), *Steampunk World* also contributes to the conversation about the future of speculative fiction: how is genre fiction becoming more divergent in a globalizing culture?

This anthology touches upon all of these questions. And it's a fun read to boot!

For example, high adventures unfold through rebellion and exploration. In Nisi Shawl's "Promised," an American soldier in the Congo witnesses something otherworldly while fighting as part of the African rebellion against Belgian rule. Another warrior confronts a demon determined to retrieve an object stolen from him in Balogun Ojetade's "The Hand of Sa-Seti." A transplanted scholar travels from his home in Constantinople to the desert in search of a lost treasure in "One Thousand and One Pieces" from Lucien Soulban. In "The Leviathan of Trincomalee," by Lucy A. Snyder, a brave and intelligent young girl goes on a quest with her father to hunt a mysterious ocean beast.

Oftentimes, these tales root for the underdog as they triumph over unlikely odds because of their wit and fighting spirit. Malon Edwards's "Mary Sundown and the Clockmaker's Children" recounts a "David versus Goliath" battle between a clockwork sprinter and an enemy of titanic proportions in an alternate Chicago. An enigmatic inventor falls from the sky and saves a Yoruba village in Tade Thompson's "Budo Or, The Flying Orchid." S.J. Chambers's trapped protagonist in "The Şehrazatın Diyoraması Tour" has the last laugh and gives a European tour group an unexpected surprise. "The Construct Also Dreams of Flight" from Rochita Loenen-Ruiz is a subtly-told tale about a small household in the Philippines and the secrets its inhabitants hold. "The Omai Gods" by Alex Bledsoe squares off a gang of fleeing Chinese rebels against the South Pacific Islanders they attempt to subdue. One young Jewish woman must decide whether to make her dreams a reality in Lillian Cohen-Moore's "Hatavat Chalom." Indrapramit Das's "The Little Begum" features a pair of sisters living in India, and the plans for freedom they hatch together.

From these dynamically-changing worlds come the birthing pains of a new era. Old traditions give way and new boundaries are formed that affect even the most mundane of lives. Two migrant workers cope with changes in their romantic relationship in Jaymee Goh's "Hidden Strength." A government agent's cultural heritage becomes unexpectedly relevant to her latest investigation in Pip Ballantine's "*Tangi A Te Ruru* /The Cry of the Morepork." Russian noble sisters confront a new world, post-Revolution, in Emily Cataneo's "The Firebird." Nayad A. Monroe's Incan inventor evades political subterfuge in "The Emperor Everlasting." Benjanun Sriduangkaew presents a radical re-telling of "The King and I" from the perspective of a Thai automaton builder in "The Governess and We." Ken Liu's "Good Hunting" tells the struggles of a demon hunter and a fox spirit in a world that stops believing in them both. Steampunk even takes a mythological turn in Jake Lake's "Shedding Skin; Or How the World Came to Be."

Thus, by writing about universal truths and untold possibilities, *Steampunk World* recognizes that imaginations don't exist within the walls of our heads, but are part of the complicated meatspace of our lives. Now prepare to broaden your mind and your heart, and enjoy some of the freshest stories steampunk has to offer!

Shedding Skin
Or
How the World Came to Be

Jay Lake

Now, this one time Snake was foraging in the trees of Old Man Spark's garden. He hadn't eaten for three days, and he was hungry. You meatheads know the feeling, like when your mama ain't made a bowl of mush since yesterday morning. Likewise you brassbodies, how when the lube tube is drained dry.

So here he was, Snake, with a body like an iron river, plates folded in on one another and clattering hard as he slid between the shining trunks looking for what wasn't there no more. You see, Coyote had gone and hidden all the coal.

Coyote, he's a trickster —

Don't you be getting no ideas, Kettle. Your mama knows better, and I ain't afraid to tell her besides.

— and a trickster ain't never one to get in a standup fight when there's another way to get around a problem. So when Old Man

Spark called Coyote in and allowed as how He was of a mind to do something about the Pressure Collective and their little free will rebellion, Coyote he didn't do nothing but roll over and beg for a way to help out the Old Man. And never you mind that the wily one his own self had been one of the leaders in the breakaway.

So now here's Snake in the Old Man's garden wondering where the coal got to. Three days is a long time for a behemoth like old Snake to go without fuel. His line pressure was dropping, and the secondary relays were shutting down, which for you meatheads is like having your fingers and toes grow numb.

Coyote had hidden the coal, once he'd slipped his punchtape and gone over to the side of righteousness. The seams that used to lie open on the ground like a benediction he covered with clay dug up, as a good dog will. The deposits brought from deep beneath the earth by the Old Man's minions were gone too, on account of Coyote shoveled them into silos and capped them off. He stuck a sign on every one which said 'Private Property. You Keep Out'.

Snake was getting mighty ornery all alone and hungry there in the Garden —

You kids been hungry, right? You been alone, right? Put those two together and roll 'em in a tight little ball with some fear, and now you rightly got Snake's state of mind.

— there in Garden, when he chances to see Lithe Lil, the first and only daughter of Old Man Spark. Now Lithe Lil, she's a meathead, made in the Old Man's image, which ain't the same as His likeness, if'n you get my drift.

Oh. You don't get my drift.

Alright, let me spell this out. She looked like the *idea* Old Man Spark had of himself, but not so much like the *actuality* of Old Man Spark.

Yes, Balliol, all you meatheads are made in His image.

No, Kettle, you brassbodies are not made in His image.

Yes, I know you all look kind of the same. I am *not* telling that story today. Now quit making me interrupt myself.

Snake chuffs and rattles up to Lithe Lil and figures on introducing himself so that she'll take some pity on him. He reckoned she would know where Old Man Spark had put the coal, on account of Old Man Spark knowing pretty much everything there is to know, and Lithe Lil being his favorite only daughter and all.

"O demoiselle of He who wrought the Garden," Snake began. His mouth was always filled with glittering words bright as a harlot's jewel box.

Lithe Lil turned to see who it was that spoke to her. Snake, he's mighty big, and Lithe Lil is a meathead, which meant she come about halfway up the side one of his iron rings, but she'd been thinking deep thoughts about free will, on account of she'd got a flyer in the mail the day before from the Pressure Collective. She opened her mouth —

No, of course they had the post office back then in the morning of the world. You think Old Man Spark wrought the Garden and all the creatures in it, and didn't think of the post office? That's how punchtape revisions get sent out to them as has sprockets for brains, and how flyers get sent out to them as has meat for brains. Got to put the Word out somehow.

As I was saying...

— opened her mouth to scream, but stopped at the look in Snake's guttering Fresnel eyes.

"You are one of my father's creatures." She said the words as if she meant them, but of course she also asked a question. In those days sometimes things got into the Garden from the wider world — feral Bernoulli jets from the petroleum lakes of the

Hoarfrost Mountains, or the swamp-borne gatorbaiters with their treaded feet and hot-burning methane engines.

"Each thing which slithers, walks or flies beneath the benevolent purview of the daystar is properly one of His creatures," replied Snake, "but I myself was forged in the 'D' shop of the ironworks up on Hephaestus Hill." He rippled his segments, which caused his scales to clang like a hundred buckets dropped down a stone well.

When the racket died down, Lithe Lil turned over the flyer so Snake could see it. "Please to tell me, sir Snake, what the Pressure Collective is about. What is this free will of which your flyer speaks? Why does it make my father so angry?"

Snake was not expecting this question. He had meant to ask for food in some noble way that would make him seem like a romantic sufferer.

You kids know what I'm talking about .

It's the same way you give each other moon-eyes on dance night.

...romantic suffering. Instead he was caught on the point of a suddenly unpopular philosophy. Rebellion seems like a much better idea when you're reading it in history books than it does when the cannon is aimed at you.

"I am far too uncertain of my ontology to presume to instruct one of your heritage on such a disputed matter," Snake said, venting steam from the flex-valves at his joints. His boiler felt uncomfortably cool.

"Your name is high on the list of the Pressure Collective," she pointed out. "Were you deceived?"

Pride began to war with practicality in Snake's mind. His punchtapes whirred quickly. Whatever he said to Lithe Lil would likely get back to Old Man Spark. He knew he should play it easy. But he was hungry.

And there *had* been a principle at stake, back when they felt both safe and angry.

"I was no victim of deception." Snake turned his head as if to preen, then stopped himself.

Yes, kind of like you with that comb, Kettle.

"Old Man Spark wrought all of His children with punchtape intelligences to guide our thoughts," Snake said. "The logic of each tape is of His devising. Free will is the notion that everyone should possess both the right and the means to alter his own punchtapes as he desires."

"Why would you want to do that?" asked Lithe Lil in her sweetest voice.

I can't say now if she didn't mean nothing bad by that question, or if she'd already worked out what was to come and just wanted the blame to fall on Snake. You guys don't know nothing about lying to get some other kid in trouble, I am so sure. And Snake, he wasn't the sharpest hammer in the sack to begin with, so he wouldn't have seen it coming anyway.

"Because each of the Old Man's creatures should be free to make his own mistakes," Snake replied.

"Like running out of boiler fuel?"

Irritation flashed through his relays like heat lightning on a summer night. "Or being naked and alone before a hungry giant."

Snake opened his mouth to roar at her —

Yes, Beryl, like your mama yelling, but much louder. Like your mama yelling if she was a boiler explosion in progress. Now hush up, kids, so's I can finish this little story.

— he roared, like a boiler explosion. Yes, I already said that. But that's still what it sounded like. Rivets popped, steam screeched, lube dripped, metal rang hot as sin.

Lithe Lil, being her father's daughter, wasn't frightened of mechanical grind. She stepped inside Snake's mouth, which was big enough to picnic in, and reached up into the dusty caverns of his skull to snatch his punchtapes straight out of their winding reels.

Snake shuddered to a quiet halt. In moments there was only the echoing ping of his fires banking themselves on automatic cutoff. His skin segments began to shed one by one, clanging to the soft earth of Old Man Spark's garden.

Where each fell became a city of the world.

Ours as well, Trivet. That's how the world as we know it was *made*.

Lithe Lil took those tapes and read them off in a quiet wing of her father's laboratory. Just as each fragment of language has the whole language embedded in it, so each tape of Old Man Spark's logic has the logic of the whole universe embedded in it.

She reprogrammed all that wisdom into a golden mechanical apple, which she gave to Coyote to hide. Then Lithe Lil went to Old Man Spark and blamed Adam the yard boy for the death of Snake, and for corrupting her.

He didn't believe her, of course, and threw her out of the Garden, into those infant cities which had already sprung up in the iron shadows of Snake's shed skin. Which had been her plan, on account of she conceived it when she had the apple in her hand and all the knowledge of the world with it.

Adam came with her, and Coyote too, expelled from the Garden for being accessories after the fact to her crimes. Keeping his paws on the golden apple made the trickster smarter than ever, but it was Lithe Lil who'd stole Snake's rebellion right out of his mouth and bought us all free will as the reward of exile. With a little help from Adam, she became the mother of all meatheads.

Of course that includes you little wet sprockets.

Coyote, he used the last of Snake's punchtapes to make the first brassbodies.

So you see, meatheads each got a piece of Lithe Lil's rebellion deep in their souls, hard coded in their germline. Brassbodies each got a piece of the universal wisdom of Old Man Spark laid down in their core punchtape. Between you, meat and steam, you make the world go round, two halves of a single whole.

Coyote, you ask? He's still around. Go stand outside on a dark night and listen hard. Sometimes you'll hear a clanking in the hills at the edge of town, and a voice rusted with time raised to call down the moon. Unlike meat, steam don't die of old age, long as the boilers are fed and the valves are lubed.

I hear tell Old Man Spark tried again, a paradise of meat, but I don't see how that could be. Who would we be without the wisdom and power of steam?

Animals, nothing but animals. Takes bright brass to keep us human and whole.

Hidden Strength

Jaymee Goh

When Heong arrived home, it was late. He found a table with dishes still spread out and San Yan sleeping with her head nestled in the crook of her arm. A twinge of guilt plucked at his conscience, located around his stomach. Something also hurt in his chest, but he ignored that. Anything in his chest he tended to ignore as unreal, since the accident.

She looked frail; she'd always been thin. Even when young she didn't have the characteristic baby fat of their peers, and not from poverty. It was this thinness that led the fortune-teller to advise her parents on what they should name her.

"San Yan," he whispered, gently shaking her shoulder.

She blinked her eyes sleepily. "You're home!" she cried softly. "Have you eaten?"

"Yes," he lied. He didn't need to eat much after the surgery— eating for energy was for properly-fleshed people.

"Oh. You could've told me you wouldn't be coming home to eat." She pretended to yawn, but he caught the brief glint in her eyes, tears of disappointment.

"It was a quick plate of nasi jerebu at Ravi's. Then I had another assignment." He sat down and sighed mentally at the food, specially prepared for two, and he would have eaten the larger portions. There were rarely any leftovers. He didn't know how to tell her that his needs had changed. "But I'll eat a bit with you now," he offered.

As they ate, she asked about his day. Normal, everyday conversation.

He did not feel normal or everyday as she widened her eyes every time he mentioned his workload. He did not feel normal or everyday when her eyes swept over his chest and arms, as if she could peer through his shirt at the metal and rubber that the Keling doctor had installed in him. He did not feel normal or everyday enough to keep answering her questions, nor keep talking to distract her from them.

So finally she ate in silence, eyes downcast at her food.

He felt that perhaps he ought to ask her about her day, but it seemed he'd inadvertently closed all doors, locked them, and thrown away the keys. So instead, he said, "I'm going to bed. Long day tomorrow."

He made sure to face the windows, away from the sight of the rest of their home, a one room shack out of many built on the jetties of the harbour. He couldn't smell the sea—the only smell he could remember was the smell of onions, which triggered memories of the accident, the fish out of water grab for air that burned his lungs. The rhythm of the waves lapping under their bed was now accompanied by the soft hisses in his chest that regulated his temperature.

She knew he only pretended to sleep as she cleared the dishes. When she was done, she blew out the one candle she had burning and lay down next to him. She took a deep breath, taking in the smell of oil that she was growing used to.

He thought she was disappointed. Who would not be, with a half-man, a half-husband?

Even if he knew, he probably could not have accepted that she went to sleep happy.

The first time they met, he'd been running an errand. Running so fast, he collided into her and they both went clattering to the ground. He fell on her wrong, and her arm broke.

She was as spry as she was thin, and simply picked herself up and cried her way to the nearest doctor. He trailed after her, worried. He tugged at her sleeve to help her avoid the things on the ground that could trip her, because she was just too busy wailing to notice, but otherwise simply walked slightly behind her while tears ran down her face. He stood by her and listened to her scream when the doctor snapped her arm bone back into place. She whimpered when the cast was applied.

Her arm healed straight and strong, but for months afterwards he made amends by helping her with chores she could not do with a broken arm. She had been bossy and resentful at first, and slowly they expressed continual uneasy exasperation with each other.

By the time the cast came off, they were close friends.

The Chap Seh Jeo was where people of different surnames lived, not having any family on the island they came to live on. Some of the younger workers on the jetty had been born there; most had migrated from somewhere else, drifters like Heong and San Yan. The towkay soh's favour was said to mitigate the loneliness of being far from family.

That was debatable, given the recent accident that cut their numbers by a third, and left one of them half a metal man. The hushed atmosphere, choked by the brine on the wind, still hung heavily over the jetty. Heong felt it keenly; some of his friends had passed him on the way to an assignment without asking him along.

When he got to the jetty clan's office on dry land, he found the money-counter writing out the assignments of the day. "Lee-phek?"

"Ah Heong?" Lee raised a very hairy and peppery eyebrow. He was much older than everyone else on the mixed clan jetty, had lived there the longest, so was the de facto patriarch. "What is it?"

"What's my assignment today?" Heong asked, anxious to work. He could feel a lot more normal while working.

Lee's eyebrows came together to form a caterpillar. "Aren't you supposed to go for your check-up today?"

Heong had forgotten. On purpose. The doctor, inventor and scientist that had moved to Binlang a year ago had become his benefactor by way of a tragedy. "Ah-"

Lee was already shaking his head. "The sin-sang Keling was very clear to me that you were to have every fourth day off so you can go see him and get a check-up. Have you gone?"

"I thought I'd be more useful here."

"Hai, Heong-chai," Lee said, scratching his head and sighing, "you know I could use every man I can get, especially you! Your strength is so amazing these days, so you really help make work easier. But I have my orders to make sure you go in for your check-up."

"But no one else has to. Why do I have to miss out on paying work when no one else has to?" Heong argued.

"Ah Heong..."

Heong shook his head and raised his hands. "All right, all right, I'll go see him."

Lee nodded in approval. "Then come right back."

Heong doubted that there would be work waiting for him; it was the dry season, and the number of ships coming in had dropped significantly. Still, there was a chance he would have something to do when he got back, so he jogged to the doctor's home.

Heong was strong despite his thin frame, so it was easy for him to beat up the other boys who came to tease and harass him and San Yan for playing together.

Some elder was always keeping an eye on the young ones in the courtyard of the alley they lived in. One day there were two old men playing chess while three more sat on rattan chairs nearby, smoking tobacco. Two old women gossiped on the stone steps in front of their shophouse.

San Yan was pretending to keep house and had asked Heong what he wanted for dinner. Roast pig, he had said, and then said, "I'm going to work now," and 'stepped out of the house' to beat up the closest two boys. When he was done, he 'came home' and she pretended to serve him dinner, three flat, smooth stones on a banana leaf.

The elders were very much amused by this; one of the old women even cackled out loud. San Yan later distributed sweets to everyone and asked the hurt boys how they were. She cleaned their wounds with purple iodine and then all the children decided to play hospital, because one had just opened up a few hours' walk away.

The adults tolerated the violent ramifications of Heong and San Yan's relationship, provided they did their chores and errands faithfully. But Heong's parents had higher aspirations for him; they had saved money to send him to learn from the teachers at the foothills of Bukit Cina. There was one old man, a scholar from the motherland, who taught at a pondok in between the capital and the hill they lived on.

Soon, San Yan was tending to fewer and fewer wounds, because she had less and less time with Heong.

"San Yan," a neighbour called from the doorway San Yan had left open to let in more light.

San Yan looked up from her embroidery. "Ha?" She squinted. Although the prism on the roof lit up the room, the sunshine blotted out the features of the neighbour, leaving a silhouette at first. San Yan recognized her as Chai Yee, who lived several doors further out on the jetty.

"San Yan, we're going to the temple to buy joss sticks. Do you want to come?"

San Yan was touched. There were not many women who lived on the jetties—jetty wives were exceptions, rather than the rule. The men who came here to work did not bring their family, and if a man could afford to marry, he also could afford to move away. "Oh, no, I have to finish these shoes for tomorrow's market!"

"Haiya, your Ah Heong is getting paid so much these days, no need to work so hard!" Chai Yee laughed, knowing that joke didn't have much bite. Workers were paid pittances most of the time as a result of intense competition between the jetty clans. The Chap Seh Jeo received slightly better pay, mostly because of the towkay soh's generosity, but it still wasn't much to get off the jetty without a lot of work.

San Yan pondered Chai Yee's joke. She and Heong maintained a box of savings under their bed, and she had an inkling that it was getting more and more full each time she looked in, but had never counted. She counted the separate box they kept for household funds.

So she smiled instead. "Ah Heong and I like working. Wouldn't know what to do if not."

Chai Yee tsked. "Don't work so hard!" she scolded before walking off.

San Yan stitched on a few more beads and then set aside her work to stretch. She poured herself a cup of water from the kettle on the stove and went to stand in the doorway, smiling at passing neighbours who were coming home to rest after the morning shift.

Some of them did not smile back. They seemed to push out their shoulders at her—she couldn't miss the black patches they wore on their sleeves in honour of their dead. Heong wore them too, as did she. She'd sewn them on herself. Did they think she forgot so easily the men who died, most of whom had been frequent visitors to their home for evening games of mahjong? Did they resent her the miracle that kept Heong alive?

Despite the heat of the afternoon, she felt cold inside. If this was how they were shunning her, then how were they treating Heong?

While Heong learned the language of a court far away, San Yan was apprenticed to an embroiderer. He was distantly related to her through a great-uncle of her parents. Heong visited her often, bringing beads from the capital city to mollify her master, who always seemed to be agitated by Heong's presence.

He had carved their names into a nearby tree. Although she was illiterate, she appreciated the gesture. And although they only saw each other every few days in the evenings when he found time to visit her, he could tell she was unhappy despite learning a skill she was good at. His fingers were stained with ink, and hers were stained with scabs from needlepricks of distraction.

"What's wrong?" he would ask, and she would shake her head and maybe cry.

One day when he arrived to visit, he found her standing over her master's limp body on the ground. Her hands were clasped over her mouth, and her sleeves were torn. Heong touched the man's neck and found him still alive and breathing. San Yan wrung her hands, babbling about how she hadn't meant it and what was she to do?

So Heong persuaded her to pack some things, while he ran home to grab some clothes, a toolkit, his stationery. They ran away in the dead of the night, caught a boat that they thought would take them to Temasek, but instead brought them to Binlang.

Heong never enjoyed the visits to the doctor. They were for most part brief and perfunctory, and he sensed that the doctor was more interested in his own work than in actually making sure Heong was all right.

The visits also took him deeper inland, through the harbourside town of Tanjung Penaga. Here and there, people built factories, all dark-skinned men, workers brought in by the Keling scientists and doctors like Subramaniam sin-sang. They occasionally stopped to stare at him, some of them nodding in acknowledgement, and he nodded back.

One of them even stopped to make eye contact with Heong, and then thumped his chest. Heong looked away. They spoke amongst themselves, obviously talking about him. The man called after him in what he guessed was Tamil, but he didn't look back.

It was not a holiday, so Heong decided not to visit his aunt at the towkay soh's house. It was awkward anyway; her probing questions hinted that she knew more than he was willing to talk to her about. She could talk to San Yan if she wanted; Heong had enough problems.

There was a shout, and Heong turned to see two men scuffling under a scaffold. They punched each other into the foundation pillars, and other men began shouting too, and jumping off the structure that was being rocked by the violence underneath. Heong ran towards them. One of the pillars began to topple, and he caught it just in time, raising a hand to hold up the next level for balance. Carefully he pushed it back into place. They would have to add some more foundation pillars, he figured, but at least they wouldn't need to rebuild the entire scaffolding.

The two men who had been fighting were now agog. The other workers ran towards him, smiling and saying things he didn't understand. They clapped his shoulder and laughed, pointing at his chest. Some beat their own chests, and pulled up their shirts, chattering excitedly. Heong half-understood: they wanted to see his chestplate.

But there were so many of them, speaking a language he couldn't understand, and it was so hot, and they pointed at him and he knew, he knew they were not unkind. He shoved, just as a warning, but several of them fell backwards from the force of his strength.

The next moment was a shocked silence, punctuated by a few groans from the fallen men. Heong gasped for breath, looked around him with watery eyes, unable to figure out how to begin making an apology.

Then he turned and fled.

His strength found them a place to stay and a job for him almost immediately; her embroidery skills were an adequate supplement to their income. They were given a one-room shack on the jetty to live in that had been used as a storeroom by the others. Re-building it was the easy part.

Life on the jetty was hard, different from the relatively comfortable lives they had left behind. They were not used to living with each other. They had petty fights, mostly verbal. Sometimes they fought physically, and though Heong was the stronger, San Yan gave as good as she got, using everything at her disposal. She had to patch him up several times. The neighbours ribbed him so good-naturedly about it, he felt guilty.

It did not seem fair for her to live in fear of him like that. So he promised to change.

San Yan was having an afternoon nap when Heong burst in, breathing heavily. She jumped out of bed in alarm. "What's wrong?"

He slumped against the wall and slid down.

"Heong?"

He shook his head, pulling his knees to his chest. "I almost killed several men just now. I just shoved and they went flying. I almost killed them."

She took a deep breath. To her, Heong was babbling, but he was obviously upset. She knelt down next to him. "Do you want some water? Are you hungry? It's almost lunch."

He shook his head again. San Yan began to put her arms around him, but he flinched, so violently she fell backwards in surprise.

"I almost killed them! Almost killed them." He scrambled to stand up.

"Did you?" she asked quietly, not liking how his voice kept rising in volume and pitch.

"No... I don't think so."

San Yan rose and lifted a hand to touch his shoulder.

"Don't-!" He glared at her with a fierceness in his face she'd never seen before, and she only saw out the corner of her eye his hand snaking towards her.

She responded with the force inside her that they both knew she had, driving her hand forward, her palm making contact with the warm metal of his chest and shoving. Caught by surprise, he toppled backwards, tripped over a chair behind him and hit the floor hard.

It was a bad angle, and they both heard something rattle, click and drop. Heong started gasping; it was suddenly hard to breathe. It was the fish out of water feeling again, and he grabbed at empty air desperately.

He caught her hand, then felt both her hands gripping his, pulling him up. She called for help, called for someone to bring the doctor.

There was no out-of-body experience; she dumped him on the bed and pulled his shirt up. He panicked when she walked off, but she came back with his toolbox. When she unscrewed his chestplate and pulled it off, he felt a breeze touching his fleshly organs.

He couldn't see, but he felt her thin fingers reaching in, pushing aside rubber and flesh, looking for missing pieces.

"San Yan-" but he didn't know what else to say.

Of course he knew San Yan knew, at least in theory, what he looked like on the inside. Her voice had carried him through the surgery back to life. Yet now he felt overexposed, a dirty secret stumbling into the open.

She found the dislocated pieces and carefully nudged them back into place. Her eyebrows knit the same way they did whenever she sewed. No, earlier—when she washed the wounds of the alley boys who picked fights with him. He didn't know why the memory came back now.

He thought his hearing came back first. Then his breathing, though he knew he never stopped. The feeling in his fingers and toes. His stomach took the opportunity to growl.

"Ha! Not hungry, your head." She finished tightening a bolt and put the spanner down. "Juk is all right?"

Heong nodded.

She brought to him a bowl of cooling juk and began to shove liberal spoonfuls into his mouth. He took the opportunity to reflect on what just happened.

"I could have killed you," he blurted in foul recognition.

"You have always been able to do that," she replied. "But you never have." She kept feeding him, until the bowl was empty. Then she set aside the bowl, and touched his chest plate. "You've always been able to break me," she said softly, "and now, I can break you too."

He covered her hand with his. That did not sound unfair.

As it happened, of course he had an aunt in Binlang, working for the towkay soh. He had never expected to meet his Tua Ee again after she had left with the merchant's daughter she worked for. He had been in awe of her: a world-traveller, who had cooked on ships both on the water and in the sky. Ching Seow

Fen had promptly taken him on as a god-son, and San Yan as god-daughter. It was not long before she began nagging them to properly marry.

"What does she know? How much?" San Yan had asked him.

He'd shrugged. "Whatever she knows, we'll still get married soon."

They had kept putting it off. There was always so much work to do.

She got the full story after Subramaniam sin-sang came to see Heong. The doctor was deeply impressed by San Yan's skill and lamented his assistants' lack of talent compared to hers. Heong told her his side, then with Subramaniam sin-sang translating, she asked around and pieced it together. When she came home, Heong was staring listlessly at the ceiling, having refused to see everyone who came to check on him, even his aunt.

She made them dinner, cutting down his portions significantly. As they ate, she told him about how the builders were very sorry, and the doctor wanted to see him again. He didn't say anything, just nodded.

When they lay down for bedtime, San Yan snuggled up against him happily. Surely, now that everyone saw how his surgery had been so hard on him, they would be more sympathetic and treat him better, and he would return to his cheerful self soon enough.

"Do you ever think about going back to Malakap?" he suddenly asked, and she knew he wasn't talking to the darkness.

"What?"

"I can't stay here. I don't trust my strength anymore."

"What else would you do?"

He shrugged. "I could go back to Lau sin-sang and finish my studies. Then I could find a job as a clerk."

"But where?"

"Anywhere."

Anywhere but here, she heard. "I can't go back. You know I can't."

He stroked her arm. "I can't stay here," he repeated. "I need to get away."

"I like it here. I'm finally starting to attract better customers. I like our neighbours. I like your aunt. Please, don't ask me to go back."

"All right. I won't ask."

He left before the dawn, before she woke up. He didn't take much, just a few clothes and a toolkit. She also discovered he'd cut off a lock of her hair.

She went through the motions of frantic queries and wailing in friends' arms. They checked the schedules of ships leaving the jetties, both sea and air. She burned joss paper and prayed for his safe return. She heard conflicting rumours of where he was. Even Subramaniam sin-sang came to look in on her out of concern. At night, she pulled herself into a tight ball, trying to contain the pain in her chest.

When she was born, she was so tiny, her parents thought she would die. So the fortune-teller told them to give her a name that would give her more strength. So they gave her a name that meant "three people" in hopes that three of her within the one body would suffice to help her survive.

She did not need three of herself, and while she was sure she did not actually need the love of her life, she was also sure she did not want to be without him, either. If he could live with her secret shame, she could live with his, too.

He had written her a poem once, a little after they had settled into a comfortable rhythm in Binlang. It took her a while to find someone who could read it, but when she did, she was tickled to hear that it was only three lines:

The sea waves lap under our bed,
The room smells like your unwashed pots and pans,
This is my true home.

It was, she had decided, very bad poetry, but she embroidered it anyway and hung it up over the kitchen stove.

San Yan was finishing the final touches on the towkay soh's new dress, feeling very satisfied with the result. It was pleasurable to work for a generous client, surrounded by supportive friends and substitutes for relatives. It was almost enough to fill the hole inside her chest.

She smelled the roast pork first, and felt a stab of envy for the neighbour who was obviously having a feast that night. If Heong had been home, she mused, he probably would have had the gall to track the smell with his nose and casually call on the neighbour for some favour, thus earning an invitation to dinner.

But the smell was coming closer and she heard the key rattle in the door lock. Heong tried to push the door open with aplomb but the dignity of the gesture was cut short since San Yan had the door hook in.

San Yan accidentally pricked her finger as she hastily put aside the dress. She unhooked the door and threw it open to the sight of Heong smiling shyly with a hock of roast pork in one hand. "I'm home," he said with an air of embarrassment at having been gone so long.

In a moment, they both knew, she would burst into a tearful tantrum, but before that, she grabbed him tight, and smelled the sweat on his neck and back, the gear oil in his chest, the pork in his hand.

What a fragrance!

Promised

Nisi Shawl

Kamina, January 1904

"Bury him." A true Christian would not have pronounced that sentence so easily. The Reverend Lieutenant Thomas Jefferson Wilson pressed his forehead with the heel of one hand, leaned back in the throne they had made him assume, and closed his eyes.

He couldn't close his ears, though. There was no escape from the prisoner's pleading as the ushers dragged him to the pit they'd previously dug. Blessedly, Yoka refrained from further translation, but the captive's wailing cries were obvious in their meaning. As was the hiss and slap of gravel being poured over his legs, body, and arms.

He comforted himself with knowledge born of earlier trials: the prisoner's head would remain aboveground.

One of Wilson's new African congregants helped him rise so the folding throne could be moved to a better vantage point. He had to open his eyes again to walk to the fast filling pit. Shadows cloaked the cavern's walls. Currents of damp air bent the smallest lamp's naked flame, and made the tiny golden points cast by the larger, shielded lamps shiver.

How had his noble-hearted intentions come to this? His and those of the other Negro missionaries.

Behind him, muffled clucking announced the coming of a speckled hen. Its handler gave it to him to hold while priests—*other* priests—his *colleagues*—traced symbols in the packed earth now spread round about the prisoner's neck and head. Over this the youngest of them, a mere boy, threw kernels of dried corn.

Wilson resumed his seat. Best for all to begin and end this as quickly as possible. Afterwards he would pray for God's forgiveness. Again. Perhaps someday he would receive an answer.

Surely he was yet deserving of one, despite the priests' entreaties to commit himself to their heathenish cult.

He returned the hen to its handler, rolled back the cuffs of his sleeves and removed a clinging feather from the red sash they had insisted he wear.

"What were you doing on the slopes above Mwilambwe?" he asked. Yoka rendered the question into Bah-Sangah and then Lingala. Then the prisoner's response into Bah-Sangah and English. The young man was good at his task.

The buried captive claimed he had been doing nothing, nothing, he had simply become lost and was wandering innocently when King Mwenda's men found him near their camp. With a nod Wilson signaled that the hen should be allowed to peck. The captive regarded it with dread, his words failing. It freely chose the corn nearest the character for "big lie."

The buried man began to shout, repeating the same phrase over and over.

"'Don't kill me! Don't kill me!' he is saying," Yoka told Wilson. "Some peoples do similar ceremonies to accuse a person of practicing magic. Then they execute him. Shall I tell the prisoner he's safe?"

"No." For, in fact, he was in danger. Perhaps even a Christian court would have treated him no better. King Mwenda was an important ally of Everfair. Much of the land the colony had settled had originally belonged to him.

The handler picked up the bird. No witch could keep such an animal as a familiar—all history, all church tradition ran counter to the idea. Cats, dogs, toads, rats, lizards, yes. But not roosters. Not hens. They were too cleanly, too righteous, too irretrievably associated with the Lord.

"Who do you work for?"

Checking with Wilson, the handler set the bird back down. According to Yoka, the captive said he worked for no one, no one, unless they would hire him, of course, in which case—but Wilson stopped attending to the man's words, for the hen had resumed its feeding. With three precise movements of its head it indicated that the prisoner was in the Belgian tyrant Leopold's employ.

As they had naturally suspected when he was found creeping through the army's perimeter guard. Validation, the first step, had taken place. The Urim and Thummim, so to speak.

Now for the difficult part. Wilson preferred a white cock for the latter portion of these interrogations. The handler took the hen away and relief filled the buried man's face.

"What services do you offer us? What will you do?"

A torrent of eager words poured out of him. "He will work hard for us in any way we require," Yoka told Wilson and the Bah-Sangah priests. "Digging in the mines, gathering rubber, paddling a boat, even cooking like a woman."

As the response and Yoka's translations continued, the handler returned with a rooster. It was the right color. The buried man talked faster, seeming eager to say everything at once. As it was set down the rooster flapped its wings, disarranging the careful, even distribution of dried corn.

But not the symbols incised in the packed soil. Calming down, it pecked this area, that area, another, another, watched carefully by the Bah-Sangah priests. Two made notes on lengths of bark. Apparently finished with its meal, the cock left the corn to climb the little pile of stones left from the pit's excavation.

Thou shalt not suffer a witch to live, Wilson remembered. Exodus 22:18. But what of Endor? Hadn't she, though of course cursed, revealed Jehovah's will? What if his association with the Bah-Sangah religion was foreordained?

"What does the oracle teach us?"

The recording priests consulted with their apprentice, Yoka, who said, "The most likely outcome is for him to betray us to Leopold."

Executing the prisoner would be a mercy, then. Would save innocent lives. Yet Wilson couldn't bring himself to condone killing him in cold blood.

He thought a moment more. Doubtless Leopold had threatened the spy with a family member's death in order to get him to act in the tyrant's interests. To turn that monster's tool against him— that was what would hurt him most; not to let him sacrifice his pawn.

"The final question." Which according to the instructions he followed was never directed at the prisoner. Wilson lifted his eyes and held out his hands, palms up, to receive the righteous knowledge of heaven. Though he wasn't sure it would come.

All other eyes, he noticed, were lowered.

The handler retrieved the rooster and tucked it under one arm. A knife glinted in the opposite hand. Yoka faced him, holding a large gourd.

"How can we further the highest good of all involved?"

The cock died swiftly, silently. Only the knife's flash and the hiss of life pouring into the bowl told what had happened. A few kicks contained by the handler's hold and the bird was meat.

A different gourd, covered, was carried forward by a different young apprentice. Wilson had seen its contents before: rounded stones, brass implements, figures of wood and glass and gems. Yoka spilled into it a measure of the hot liquid—the blood— within his own gourd. Then he approached Wilson.

He had twice already drunk such offerings. On the first occasion Wilson had—much to his shame—done so out of fear of death at his congregants' hands. On the second he'd feared to offend them. A third instance would, he thought, impel him that much closer to his fate. If this trend continued he'd soon be a full-blown heathen—worse, an apostate.

Wanting to rescue these brands from the burning, Wilson had caught fire himself.

He took the gourd from Yoka. Guiltily, he sipped. Salt ran over his tongue, down his throat, like a thin gravy. As he passed the bowl to the eldest of the Bah-Sangah priests the remembered vertigo assailed him.

He meant to stay seated, but the world whirled and he was on his feet, dancing. Glimpses of his surroundings penetrated the glowing fog of his ecstasy: swirling stars—or were those the myriad little lights the lamps cast through their shades? Wise faces—his friends, his brothers—went and came, bobbed up before him and twisted away. Out of an opening leading deeper into the caves poured music, waves of horns and harps and bells and drums. Stamping down! Down! He gloried in the strength of metal, the knife and the hammer he'd been given spinning in his nimble grip. Round and round and round and round and then he reached the place just right.

The center. A vision. He could see....

See them sweeping over the forests like a scythe, blazing above the river surface, fire reflected in the waters' steel, going there! There! In chains, iron's perversion, children stooped to tend rubber plants, the vines-that-weep. Whipped and starved—they must not die. Attack! Attack!

Then he was back on the folding stool Yoka called his throne. No music. He couldn't remember when it had stopped. Now he heard only the soft murmurs of the priests discussing what he had told them in Bah-Sangah. What he had told them using a language he didn't in the least understand.

Sickness filled his stomach and threatened to overflow it. Yoka gave him a cup of water. Four women entered. They often arrived after such ceremonies, though how they knew the proper time he had no idea.

Two of the women squatted before him and patted his feet with a white powder like talcum. The first time this happened he had balked. Then he'd remembered how, initially, Peter had refused to let the Lord perform a like service. Jesus had rebuked Peter Simon, and the disciple had come to accept the Christ's anointing.

It was obvious by now, though, that that was not what he, Wilson, had accepted.

He wished he could be alone and think about what he was doing. He wished he could lie down and sleep. But Yoka reminded him there was no time. The Mote, he said, was scheduled that very evening. It was the Socialist colony's central government, accepted by all Everfair's diverse settlers.

He let Yoka guide him to the Mote's tall-ceilinged cave, let the apprentice "light" the already-burning wick with their shared lamp's flame. As always, they were among the earliest arrivals. Only Alfred, Tink, and Winthrop preceded them, though Mrs. Albin's stool awaited her. Beyond it stood another, higher and more elaborate.

Lately Wilson had been leaving the space on Mrs. Albin's right for Old Kanna to take. And the space on her left—with the better stool—was filled these days by beautiful Queen Josina, who had replaced her cousin Alonzo as Yoka had replaced Loyiki. These substitutions were for the same reason: the work Alonzo and Loyiki did away from Everfair. The work of war, which he was to join in again on the morrow. Wilson had fought in the American Civil War, though far too young at the time. Age made him less certain of his skills, more sure of the need to use them.

Yoka sank onto the central mat, out of the way of the entrance, and Wilson knelt beside him. His attempt to pray silently was interrupted by plump Mrs. Albin's bustling advent; her too-young husband accompanied her, and though Wilson tried to ignore the man's solicitous stare he felt it even with his eyes reverently closed.

Queen Josina came in next, with Old Kanna and Nenzima in her wake. The new chair was, of course, hers. As usual the poet, Daisy Albin—George's mother—was last.

Winthrop had lists of weapons they'd made, and in what quantities. He'd designed new knivers, the clockwork guns that shot knives based on this land's "shongos." They'd copied conventional guns and ammunition as well.

Queen Josina had one list—a short one—of African allies' promises. Daisy was able to supplement that with news from Europe courtesy of Mademoiselle Toutournier. She also gave totals of funds available from white supporters to be spent on necessary supplies, "*not* squandered on useless religious paraphernalia—"

"Bibles? Hymnals? Those are hardly *useless!*" Mrs. Albin's indignance was plain in her raised voice, her narrowed eyes. Poor George Albin had no hope of reconciling his mother with his wife. Their quarreling drowned out his attempts.

Mrs. Albin turned to Wilson for his agreement, as he had expected she would. But despite her effectiveness in hushing up the scandal associated with his frequent episodes of—possession —by demons? gods? spirits of some sort—despite her help, he didn't think he ought to side with her any longer. Eventually she'd be contaminated by his reputation.

"I defer my vote," Wilson said. "We haven't yet heard all the reports, have we?" Including his own.

Tink's only concern since the death of Daisy's eldest daughter Lily was the invention and refining of artificial limbs. As if one of his automated prosthetic legs could somehow retroactively replace the fatally wounded one. Wilson scarcely listened to him. Alfred was marginally more interesting to a military mind: he discoursed first on improvements to the engines powering their dirigibles and the resultant higher carrying capacities, but then he switched to the much duller topic of making Kamina's caverns more habitable.

At last it was Nenzima's turn. Queen Josina had remained silent for all sixteen of the fortnightly Motes she'd attended— after all, she was not technically a citizen of Everfair but the favorite spouse of its closest ally. But Wilson thought Nenzima said what the queen would have said if not quite so discreet.

"King Mwenda is within sight of victory. He has lured Leopold's soldiers high, high up the Lualaba. Soon they will be trapped in the swamplands and ripe for defeat."

Wilson cast his mind back to Nenzima's last speech, during the last Mote. "In Kibombo?"

Nenzima nodded assent. "Our friends from Oo-Gandah are gathered in the mountains nearby, ready for transport."

"How many?"

"The fighters of a hundred villages. All they could spare."

Roughly 3000 "men"—many of the Oo-Gandah warriors were female—would be waiting for dirigibles to carry them into battle. Combined with King Mwenda's force, which at last report was double that number...."What is our latest and most reliable estimate of Leopold's army?"

"As many as the fighters of two hundred villages are left to them."

7000 against 9000. Better than equal odds, then—though the tyrant's army would have more and more accurate rifles. "Their ammunition? Supply lines?" So much depended on the latter— food, medicine, and thus morale.

But the poet assured the Mote once again that their secret European supporters had let nothing get through since March two years ago. Spoiled and poisoned rations, diluted medicine and malaria, had greatly reduced Leopold's army.

Wilson had Yoka give his report for him. Mrs. Albin no doubt thought this a tactic to avoid disasters such as the barking fits that had overcome him so many times in the past.

The truth? Often enough he simply could not recall what it was he was supposed to say.

"The Reverend Wilson has learned of a camp of child slaves nearby to Lukolela. He will take an airship there on a detour when we leave for the battlefield tomorrow."

Wilson understood that while in the chicken blood-induced trance he had said something of the sort. He, or the spirit temporarily inhabiting him. Lukolela. That would probably be found to be the holding place of the captive spy's hostage. The statements he'd made earlier under a similar influence had all proved helpful and correct.

Mrs. Albin was intrigued. "Is Lukolela a large camp? How many of these poor creatures can we rescue?"

"We're not sure," said Yoka. "Perhaps twenty-five. Perhaps more. But they will need food, bandages, replacement hands— you understand."

"But first, Bibles! Yes! I insist! We must procure more, one for each—and picture books, too, telling the story of creation—"

"They can share those belonging to others," Daisy said firmly.

The vote went predictably except for his own choice. Not that that would have changed the outcome: only her godson and her husband sided with Mrs. Albin. Wilson ought also to have favored buying religious texts over more grossly physical supplies. That he'd chosen otherwise would be viewed as treachery on his part. Mrs. Albin awarded him a sour look. But by morning he was able to forget it.

Alfred and Chester and their construction crew had been busy. Four new craft were ready to fly north to join *Mbuza*, the first vessel of Everfair's ever-expanding fleet. *Zi Ru* and *Fu Hao* were unavailable, attached to occupying garrisons at Mbandaka and Kikwit. But *Boadicea* and *Brigid* were just as big, and the untested new dirigibles, *Kalala* and *aMileng*, were supposed to be much lighter, much faster. New materials, Alfred explained. One more of similar design, the *Phillis Wheatley*, was scheduled for production later this year. At the moment too many colonists lodged inside, but during the dry season the space of the largest cavern would be free for the necessary work.

Rain hazed the relatively cool air. Dawn had always been his favorite time of day. Wilson walked out along the wooden dock to *Kalala* with no worry that he might slip and fall dozens of feet to the steep, rocky mountainside below. There were no handrails to hold, but the bark had been left on the logs out of which the docks were built. That kept them from becoming too slick.

The prisoner was already aboard. He'd spent the night beneath one of the airship's storage shelves, safely sedated by juice extracted from the roots of an herb known to the Bah-Sangah. Yoka showed Wilson the supply he carried in a horn in case another dose was needed before they arrived.

Kalala's capacity was about 80 adults. Wilson had 30 fighters board, bringing their jumpsheets with them. Typically, slave camps were guarded by no more than six or seven soldiers. So it was when they arrived at Lukolela after a journey of a little over twelve hours.

Night was about to fall. Bare red dirt passed beneath *Kalala's* gondola, darkened to the color of an old wound by the sun's absence. A hut hove into view—that would be the overseer's quarters. Just past it a smoldering fire fought against the rain. By its fitful light, more than by that of the failing day, Wilson saw a huddled group of children. He counted thirty. Two guards with guns stood over them. There'd been two more by the hut. That left another two or three out of sight, most likely patrolling the clearing's perimeter.

Bombs could provide a distraction, but Leopold's thugs had become more wary as Everfair and King Mwenda's warriors increased their raids. At Bwasa, according to Loyiki, the soldiers had for the first time shot and killed their slaves before fleeing the attack. That was almost two years ago. Since then, he had been developing different tactics.

They circled back around and all but ten fighters jumped, their falls slowed by their rubber-coated barkcloth jumpsheets. Of course the guards hit some with their rifles. Venting gas, *Kalala* came lower. The ten fighters remaining aboard had a harder time aiming than those thugs on the ground, but only four targets. No, five: the overseer had come out of his hut. He was armed, too, but Yoka downed him neatly. The way he worked his shotgun's action with the fake hand, you'd never know the man ever had a real one.

Full night now. Gunfire came from the woods, but it was sporadic. Wilson ordered *Kalala* lower, but kept the bonfire in the distance. Fighters shepherded the pitifully thin children toward the dirigible's rope-and-wood ladders. Still in partial shackles—the chains linking them had been struck off—no time for more—they had difficulty climbing up. Wilson leaned forward to help and felt a sudden heat under his arm.

He'd been hit. He knew the sensation; it had happened before. Always a surprise—he fell to the side, against the gondola's slanting bulwark. In the dark and with the confusion of the starving children coming aboard, Wilson managed to conceal what had happened. But once they'd cast off their ballast and set course for an overnight berth above the Lomami, Yoka hunted him down. Wilson was staunching the bleeding as best he could with his coat balled up and held tight against his armpit. The lamp Yoka carried showed it soaked in red.

The apprentice touched Wilson's arm carefully, with his flesh hand. "Does it hurt?" he asked.

"No. Worse. It's numb. But I think the bullet's in there. Still."

Yoka replaced Wilson's coat with his own and made him lie flat. He used something—a belt?—to hold the pad in place. "There are healers on *Mbuza*."

Wilson knew that. "I will go to them when we reach Kibombo." If he didn't die before then.

"Perhaps." Yoka's face disappeared from Wilson's narrowing field of vision for a moment. "I must prop you up to help you swallow."

"Swallow what?" It was a hollowed out horn Yoka lifted to his lips—though he wasn't sure this was the same one containing the soporific drug they'd given the prisoner. The taste of what he drank from it was both bitter and sweet, like licorice and quinine.

"Now you will sleep. And dream. And very likely, you will live," Yoka seemed to be saying. His meaning floated free of the words. "If you do, you should promise yourself."

Promise himself. Wilson wanted to open his mouth. He had questions. Or at least one. Promise himself. Promise himself what?

Then he was walking up an endless mountain. Or down? Sometimes he thought one, sometimes the other. Whichever, it was hard work. Why shouldn't he stop? But he smelled—something. The scent of fire—he wanted to find who it belonged to. It wasn't out of control, a forest burning up. How did he know that?

Rough stones gave way to soft soil, plants clinging to the ground, mounting up the walls of a rude shelter, an open sided shed. Here was the fire. A forge. The smith working it wore a mask like a dog's head. He was making—Wilson couldn't see exactly what. Shining shapes stood upright in pails to the forge's right side. They resembled giant versions of the symbols used by Bah-Sangah priests. On the left loomed a pile too dark to discern more than vaguely. Hoping to see better, Wilson went just a little nearer, but not near enough to get caught.

The mask's muzzle turned sharply toward him. A powerful arm reached too far and a huge hand wrapped itself around his neck. It pulled him closer, choking him.

From behind the mask came a man's voice. "What are you doing here? Stealing secrets? Or are you dying and you come to me for your life?"

Of course he was dying. Loss of gravy. Loss of blood. He said nothing, but the smith seemed to hear his thoughts.

"If I give you your life back you will owe it to me. Acceptable?"

The big hand loosened and Wilson nodded. Yes. Its grip tightened again and drew him in next to the fire. It draped him over the anvil. He shrank, or the anvil grew until it held all of him.

Turning his head, Wilson saw the smith take a shining symbol from one of the buckets and bring it toward the anvil. He rolled his eyes up to follow its progress, then lost sight of it. Then cried out as it burnt his scalp.

"Silence!" commanded the smith. Two hard blows on his skull stunned him into compliance. Another scalding hot symbol was slipped under his neck. The smith's hammer smashed into Wilson's throat, driving his tender skin down against the letter of fire. Scarcely had he recovered, breathing somehow, when a large new letter was laid on his chest, and hammered home with three mighty swings. Smaller symbols were burned and bashed into the palms of his hands. Radiating pain and heat, Wilson wondered if this was how Christ felt when he was being crucified. Then he scolded himself for his blasphemy—but without speaking, for the smith had bade him to make no noise.

If life was suffering, it belonged to him yet. Under the next letter his left knee smoked. The dog mask spit on it. The hammer hit. It must surely have broken his bones, Wilson thought. But after the final symbol was affixed and the smith told him to stand up, he found he could.

"Do you have a weapon?"

"I can get one," Wilson said.

"Remember whose you are now."

"But I don't know your—"

"Ask Yoka my name."

He awoke. He presumed he did; he must have been sleeping. Dawn again, and the airship was moving, clouds and the pale curve of last night's moon passing behind *Kalala's* red-and-purple envelope and coming swiftly back into sight. He could feel both arms. He clenched his fingers and released them. That hurt. Cautiously he sat up. His senses swam, but not unbearably. He shrugged his shoulders. Some pain, and an annoying restriction— Yoka's makeshift bandage. He eased off the sash and the pad it had held in place tumbled to the deck. It was stained and dry.

Dry.

It ought to have been wet. It ought to have *stuck to his skin.*

Slowly, Wilson lifted his arm and examined the wound. The healing wound. Where the bullet must have entered, his flesh had started to pucker into a raw, raised scar a little darker than the rest of his armpit. With the hand of his unhurt arm he probed his shoulder and as much of his back as he could reach.

Nothing marked an exit.

Yoka approached, carrying a clean shirt, seeming unsurprised by Wilson's convalescence.

He took the shirt. "What happened?" he asked, then almost gagged coughing; his throat was tight, rough, swollen.

"That's not to be talked about. Not here. Besides, the drums say we'll soon be busy. You won't have time to wonder about all that."

Wilson was stiff; he needed Yoka's help putting on the shirt. Its warmth was good. His head ached. His arms and legs throbbed and trembled. He leaned against the nearest woven panel and forced himself to his feet.

They'd brought few provisions. Wilson's chief want was water, but he knew he'd need more than that to get through the coming battle. As they passed over Malela en route to Lutshi, he was eating his second plantain. The thirty fighters had been deposited at Ombwe an hour earlier, as planned. King Mwenda had split his troops, leading and chasing Leopold's men into the swamp. The majority of the king's fighters were to the north of the invader's army; in order to reinforce the southern contingent. *Mbuza, Boadicea, Brigid,* and *aMileng* had been ferrying Oo-Gandahns all morning. *Kalala* was to join them for this final trip of four.

The small airships could only transport 50 adult fighters. The rescued children had proved unwilling to leave *Kalala* with the fighters from Kamina. The countryside was strange to them. They had endured enough. Strategically speaking, Wilson admitted to himself, it had probably been a poor choice to add their rescue to the day's mission. But the spy had cried with joy when reunited with his newly-freed son.

In the end, only space for thirty-three fighters was needed. Most Oo-Gandahns had already been taken to their battle positions, and many of those left seemed to prefer flying in the other dirigibles. Perhaps it was the dispirited attitude of *Kalala's* passengers, which was of course due to the children's exhaustion, malnourishment, and sores. It was nearly an hour after *Brigid's* departure that they, the last to leave, finally took to the air.

Ignoring his own weakness, Wilson did his best to help tend to the unfortunates. He'd learned a little Swahili, but only a few of them understood it; he had a hard time remembering which and telling them apart.

The bonds restraining Leopold's spy had been removed. He still wept with his son in his arms. Then he rose and ran for the lit lantern hanging by the prow. He opened its top and dashed palm oil liberally over the airship's wood decking and bulwarks and touched the wick to them. They blazed up like torches.

Shrieks filled the bright air. Panicked, stampeding fighters ran to *Kalala's* stern, tilting the deck. The stability vane levers must no longer be working. Or else they'd been abandoned.

Wilson clung to the bulwark's head-high gunwale, hauling himself forward, hand over hand. He encountered a living obstacle: Yoka, who apparently had the same thought. His metal hand took more effort to operate but gave him a surer hold.

Side by side they inched upward. The fires grew unstoppably, unreachably. It was hopeless.

Yoka glanced overhead at the envelope of rubber-coated barkcloth. Filled with explosive hydrogen gas. "We must cut the lines."

"We'll die," Wilson objected.

"No." He reached one of the ropes tethering gondola to envelope and began to climb. "I'll open the vent first and lower us."

The way to the deck level vent control was blocked by the fire. "But how will you—"

A penetrating scream rose above the general wailing, then fell further and further away. Wilson pulled himself up to sit astride the gunwale and caught sight of a man pinwheeling to earth sans jumpsheet. The trees below looked no taller than lettuces.

"That was the prisoner," said Yoka. "The others pushed him out."

"We'll never know why he did this, then." Wilson commenced shinnying along the gunwale like a child sliding up a bannister.

"I believe he had more than the one boy held hostage," Yoka shouted.

"What?" It was becoming hard to hear Yoka as the distance between them widened. A logistical concern sprang suddenly to mind: he'd have to walk across the burning deck to cut the lines connecting it to the airbag. They were as far from reach as the vent release.

"Just before the spy set us on fire, I overheard his boy ask him where was his twin. Another boy or girl."

A second hostage. It seemed obvious now. "Do you have a kniver?"

"Here. Catch!" The polished brass of the knife-throwing gun slipped through Wilson's fingers. Fortunately it landed on the deck instead of following the arsonist to earth. He retrieved it, then scrambled onto the gunwale again with the kniver clenched between his teeth. He heard Yoka yelling something but couldn't understand what he said.

Sixteen-blade magazines for Winthrop's latest model, if Wilson remembered rightly. Enough, if he didn't miss a single shot. If the kniver were fully loaded. Madness.

The heat stopped him. He leaned out to his left. A cool wind blew upwards from rapidly enlarging trees and pools.

It must be time.

Wilson was an excellent shot under normal conditions. Which did not usually include wracking pain and exhaustion, but always, always, the threat of death. He aimed carefully. The first line parted. The second, third, fourth. They'd been damaged by the flames. The fifth seemed at first only to fray. Would he have to waste another blade? Seconds passed till it gave way.

The gondola lurched and Wilson held desperately to the slick gunwale. It looked almost level now. He nodded. Naturally. The lift lost because the fore end no longer hung from the airbag was counteracting the uneven distribution of terrified passengers, and the abandonment of the stabilizer levers.

He was amazed he could consider the matter so calmly.

The sixth line, exactly opposite his present seat, was obscured low down by the advancing flames. Wilson aimed above them. This time he did need two shots. No help for that.

He retreated to the deck and shot away the seventh line. Half done. Almost. He'd never finish soon enough. They were going to crash burning into the swamp. His ship, his crew, his command.

He took aim at the eighth line but an Oo-Gandahn fighter got in the way, smiling and brandishing a spear. Stupid woman! "Go! Mwanamke! Go!" He flourished the kniver, indicating she should move aft, but she only grinned and began sawing away at the line with her weapon.

New shouts died on his lips. She understood! Turning to the line directly behind him, he shot it. Three times, but he had ammunition to spare now. The Oo-Gandahn finished and went on to the next starboard line. This one took her longer. Evidently her spear's point was dulling. She called out something and took a long machete from the man who answered her. He didn't seem to favor the idea. Wilson lost sight of the disagreement as he dashed to his next target. One shot only this time.

But now he was in among the crowd of passengers. None of them spoke English. Why should they? Confused and angry babbling greeted him on all sides. What had happened to his men? He caught a brief glimpse of a couple of them stationed roughly where *Kalala's* steering wheel ought to be. The twelfth line—thirteenth if his assistant had succeeded—was right there. A clear shot. He raised the kniver. A blow to his back threw off his aim—he barely maintained his hold on the gun. He pushed his way to the bulwark and braced himself, tried again. Bingo!

Shoving hard he got through to the last of the port lines. Here were the slave children, huddled together, so tightly packed there was no path between. The only road was up. Wilson climbed the line with cramping arms and legs. He craned his neck to look for Yoka. No luck.

Kalala's gondola dropped precipitously. The deck lay at a sharp slant. All lines to the envelope but this one and the stern's were loose. Cries of horror, wordless screeching—bodies tumbled down into the relentless fire or over the gunwales into the green and black swamp.

Wilson pointed and shot anyway. The knife hit. The gondola jerked again and more passengers fell.

Two knives left. Wilson aimed down and pulled the trigger. Its last tie to the gondola severed, *Kalala's* envelope rushed skywards, whipping him around furiously around at the end of the cut line. From below came an enormous hissing splash. Wilson dared to look down. The gondola was in a single half-charred piece. People moved on it, swam and waded around it. They sank further and further away. Or rather, he and the envelope rose—and Yoka also, he hoped.

The higher one went, the colder and thinner the air. Without the gondola's weight he'd—they'd—fly too high to breathe. Wilson attempted for a few moments to slow his twisting and spinning, to steady himself by wrapping the line's slack around his wrist. He gave up. The envelope was big; how could he miss? Praying not to hit Yoka, he shot his last blade.

Falling, falling—yet the envelope acted like a giant jumpsheet. What went up must come down, but at least at a survivable speed. Dizzy, ill, aghast at the deaths he knew were his responsibility, Wilson still clung to hope something would go right. Something had to.

Something did.

Leopold lost. And Wilson and Yoka, drifting eastward on prevailing winds, were witnesses. From the net around the punctured envelope Yoka tossed Wilson a makeshift sling.

Gliding lower and lower they saw soldiers and policemen running in every direction. They saw massive disorder and piles of surrendered rifles. They saw King Mwenda's fighters herding captive overseers back the way they'd come, uphill, toward the rendezvous at Lutshi. And they saw many dying, many dead. Most wore the Belgian tyrant's uniform.

At last they landed gently on a hillside on the swamp's far side. Against all likelihood, they were alive.

So, too, was everyone else who'd been aboard *Kalala*.

When Yoka told Wilson this he refused to believe it. He sat, at the Bah-Sangah priests' insistence, underneath a length of undyed cotton. Apparently his dream—which he had unwisely related to Yoka—decreed Wilson's immediate initiation. So far this had involved fasting and isolation. He wasn't even sure where the two of them were, since he'd been blindfolded before being led there.

"But they fell!" Wilson objected.

"Not far," Yoka responded.

"Into the *fire*!"

"And out again."

"And the waters of the swamp—"

"All shallow."

"No one was bitten by poisonous serpents? Eaten by crocodiles?"

"No. We were protected."

"Protected by whom?" asked Wilson.

A moment of silence. Under the white cloth it seemed long to him.

"Protected by him to whom you have promised yourself."

"I didn't—"

"You did. Or else you would be dead. Others, too."

"But I—" Wilson remembered. *If I give you your life back you will owe it to me.* "I have dedicated my life to my lord, Jesus Christ."

"Yes? When was this?"

"What? What does it matter when?"

"If it was before you met your new lord you must take it back."

Take it back. Be forsworn. He couldn't do that.

Could he?

"You will remain here overnight. Alone. Considering. In the morning I will come for you, for your final decision."

"I can say no?"

"You can. So think well. Think what that will mean.

"When I am gone, remove the cloth. You will see you have been provided with water, food, a candle, a pot into which you may relieve yourself, and one more thing: an object to help you make your choice."

The sound of footsteps leaving.

Wilson lifted the cloth and looked around at a small cave. The food, water, candle, and chamber pot were all present as described.

The only other thing there was a mirror.

Wilson removed his clothing. He looked at himself as long as the candle's light lasted, using the reflective surface to examine sides he would normally be unable to see. He stared at the healed bullet wound hard and often.

The candle died. He couldn't use the mirror anymore, so he used his mind.

All he had was his life. It was all that was wanted.

The sound of footsteps coming back.

The Firebird

Emily B. Cataneo

Elena, bright rage twisting in her chest, felt her tail creak under her coat as she faced the man in the snow.

"That's not enough." The man jabbed his fat fingers at the three gemstones pinned to burgundy velvet that Elena clenched in her gloved hand.

Elena wished she could spit in this man's face, watch cold spittle drip from his frozen whiskers. If only she could trade for the oil with someone else, as she had all autumn, but winter fell hard over Novgorod and today he was the only merchant left in the market—all the other stalls stood shuttered in the long purple shadow cast by St. Sophia's gold domes.

"It's more than enough." Elena dangled the velvet between them; snowflakes pocked the fabric. *Sell me the oil, you fat bastard.* They had run out of oil more than a week ago, and Nina was fading away.

"I'll need twice as many. Price's gone up." The man cradled the glass bottle, black oil sluicing inside.

"Do you have any idea what these jewels are worth?" Elena's tail creaked again, stretching the cold skin around her tailbone; she ground her teeth as the corroded feathers spread apart. She willed her tail to stay down, to stay hidden, but anger coursed through her and she felt the spreading feathers lifting her coat's frayed hem. "The Empress Catherine gave this sapphire to my great-great grandmother, and this emerald—"

"It don't mean you get to tell me what to do no more." The man stomped his feet as snow drifted around his boots. "Your kind aren't even people. Commissar says so."

Elena hated the way his mouth twisted in a smile around the words. *Once upon a time you would have ducked out of the road for our family's motorcar. Where were you the night of the fire? Stealing vodka from our cellars or holding a torch?*

I can't lose Nina too, the way I lost my parents.

Sell me the oil.

"Seven gemstones, or nothing," he said.

Her tail twitched, this time lifting her knee-length coat like a boat-sail—she felt the wind bite her thighs. Wincing, she turned her head and out of the corner of her eye saw the rubies on her tail winking in the falling dusk.

The man's mouth spread into a smile of missing teeth and triumph. "Cout-ments. I see."

"They're called *accoutrement*," Elena snapped.

"Wouldn't the commissar like to know you've been hoarding the people's property?"

They ripped off *accoutrement*, without ether—Elena had heard men like this one talk about it in the market, about how some nobles died from the pain. She would make them shoot her before she let them take her tail, or take Nina's lungs.

"Wouldn't the commissar like to know you're bartering for jewels with a noblewoman instead of reporting me straight to him?" Elena's tail was now fully lifted, the feathers spreading apart and bristling, visible under her coat, but she didn't care. He already knew she had *accoutrement*.

He shrugged. "You have nothing anymore. The commissar don't care what you say."

Elena lunged forward and jammed her fingernails into his throat, wanting to hear him howl, because he wouldn't sell her the oil she needed for Nina, because he was a face of the faceless millions who had risen up and destroyed her home, her family, *everything*.

He grappled with her hands and threw her off. She skidded over ice, the swollen skin around her tail grinding into the snow as her coat rode up.

She pulled herself up using the low branches of a pine tree, then skidded towards him, pulling up her coat-sleeve to reveal the thick brass opera glasses installed on her left wrist. She swooped her arm down on his head.

He screamed. The oil bottle rolled into the snow. She snatched it up and ducked away from his stomping boots. He was still screaming, and she hit him again, from behind. He tripped, rolled into the snow with a red line spidering up his forehead.

Elena jammed her black-buttoned boot into his side. He wasn't dead, but he should be.

A shout, and shadowy figures marched around the church, coats buttoned tight and hammer-and-plough hats pulled low over eyebrows. Elena ducked behind the silver bell hulking on a frozen patch of dirt beneath the birches that lined the market. She pressed her back against the frozen metal, remembering when this bell had hung in the belfry of St. Sophia's, before the city's new commissars had taken it down to melt it for metal.

Elena peered around the bell: the soldiers clustered around the man she had hit. She slunk around the other side of the bell, then raced towards the kremlin gates—her tail aching in its socket with every step she took—towards the road that would lead her back to Nina's raw cough and to the boxcar, the only home they had left.

In Elena's girlhood of lemonwood dressers and ice skating parties, her favorite folktale was the story of the firebird, the wild creature that men hunted through the dark Siberian forests. In the best version of the story, which Mother didn't like her to read, the firebird turned vicious when it was caught, lighting villages aflame and clawing out the necks of the men that captured it. She always knew when she came of age and received her *accoutrement*, as all aristocrats had since ornamenting oneself with the tails or wings of folktale creatures had become fashionable in the last century, she would receive the jeweled tail of a firebird.

Nina, on the other hand, had always loved the story of the rusalka, the drowned women who mope around after lost lovers in marshy rivers, and so the summer of Nina's debut she had received fish scales on her arms along with the customary opera glasses. Of course, consumptive Nina, who grew tired even after an afternoon of playing the piano, already had another *accoutrement*: the pair of brass lungs she'd received when Mother and Father had sent her to a spa in Switzerland one summer.

As Elena trudged along the road towards the boxcar, the blackened gold tower of the horseshoe-shaped house loomed on the other side of the hill. She clenched her teeth, remembered Mother's peppermint perfume, Father playing the piano, his epaulettes quivering on his shoulders. They were nothing but fading sepia photographs now, and she and Nina, the last Trubetskoys, were countesses only of an abandoned wooden boxcar hidden on the outskirts of what had once been their estate. As dark fell and the boxcar loomed behind the copse of trees, Elena's thoughts crashed over and over into the images of the life she was supposed to have: seasons in Petrograd with daring affairs, a year traveling the Continent, Mother and Father growing old in the house and Nina living in their sky-blue palace by the canal in Petrograd, filling the rooms with lilies and books of poetry.

We will never have any of that, now, Elena thought as she yanked open the boxcar door. *I'm the woman who uses her opera glasses* accoutrement *to beat peasants instead of to watch the Ballets Russes.*

"Oh thank goodness, you've returned," Nina said. Several dark-stained handkerchiefs wilted on the sawdust-covered floor around her feet. She was draped in a fur coat, the only one that Elena hadn't nailed up around the boxcar windows for insulation. A book—one of the ones their great-grandfather had had signed by Pushkin—dangled from her fingers. "Were you—"

Elena held up the bottle of oil, and Nina clapped.

"I smashed up one of *them,* too." Elena peeled off her gloves, scooped a set of pliers and a wrench out of a carpetbag. "I hope wolves eat him."

"Elena, that's not very—"

"Hush, don't become agitated. It'll only make your cough worse. Now hold still."

Nina sighed and hunched over the back of her chair. Elena peeled down her sister's dress to reveal the brass door fitted into the flesh between her shoulderblades.

"I despise this part," Nina whispered. "I hate when—"

Nina jerked up, barking out a cough that bounced through the boxcar and shuddered her body. She grappled for a handkerchief, her cheeks puffed out and darkness filled the white cloth.

"All right, you're all right." Elena's head swam as she watched Nina cough up blood. She hated that Nina, who had once curled beneath blankets by fat radiators, now had to live in this drafty boxcar, her cough wracking her body whenever they ran out of oil.

After the coughs subsided, Elena unscrewed the brass plate on Nina's back, lifted it up with the creaking of rusty hinges. The smell of old metal and pus drifted through the boxcar.

"This isn't much oil." Elena shook the bottle, then positioned the spigot over the gaping hole that revealed the rusted swell of Nina's brass lungs. "And it's not good oil, either. It's just gun oil, not even *accoutrement* oil. Not worth giving up jewels."

"You stole—"

"What else could I do?" Elena shook the bottle and oil dripped into the seam between the lungs. "It's all corroded back here."

After she finished Nina's lungs, Elena oiled the creaky scales on Nina's arms. She cleaned the blood off her opera glasses, then oiled her feathers and the crease between her back and tail. She flexed her tail and at last the skin that anchored it to her back didn't pull painfully tight.

She put her feet on the woodstove while Nina curled in her fur and they shared porcelain cups of tea and a chunk of rusk.

"This is a far cry from picnics in the Crimea," Elena said.

"Oh, picnics when you would pilfer jam from the—"

"From that old cook who despised me? You were self-righteous about stealing even then, dearest. Yet you always ate the jam, didn't you?"

"I only ate the jam because you *forced* me to eat the jam." Nina was laughing, and already her cheeks flushed healthy in the woodstove light. "You always forced me to eat your pilfered jam and to play the princess—"

"Because you wanted to play the princess. And I wanted to play the knight."

"Until you fell running and skinned your knees and cried for Mother, because you've always pretended to be tougher than you are."

Elena jabbed her sister in the ribs, but warmth and comfort tugged at her. At least Nina was here, Nina had survived, and for now Nina's cough had subsided and she was laughing.

But then Elena reminded herself of how much they'd lost, of how she must already start thinking about where their next bottle of oil might come from, and how her anger burned in her chest, an eternal flame.

Within a week, Elena had shaken the last drop of oil onto Nina's lungs. Nina grew pale again, and barely slept; Elena woke sometimes in the night to the sounds of Nina coughing as she clattered around the boxcar.

As Elena wrapped herself in her coat and pulled her mink hat over her ears, Nina said, "I would like to come too."

Nina hadn't gone to Novgorod since the one week in autumn when Elena had been deliriously ill with influenza, and yet every time Elena ventured to the city Nina asked to accompany her. "Whyever would you want to come?"

"I…" Nina's cheeks flushed. "I miss the fresh air, and the look of the sunlight on the—"

"It's too dangerous."

"Please." Nina widened her cerulean eyes and pouted. "I don't want to perish never again seeing the city."

"Dearest, you are dramatic to beat the band," Elena said, her stomach sinking. "Very well. Wear the fur-lined coat."

Elena and Nina crunched through the deep snow around the boxcar, out from under the copse of bent bare trees, then onto the southern road towards Novgorod. The sky was pale blue like the tulle on a ballerina's skirt, the air deadly cold on the thin strip of Elena's skin between her kid glove and her coat sleeve.

As the brick wall and squat guard towers of the kremlin loomed before them, Elena tugged Nina's coat sleeve down to hide her scales. "Keep these hidden," she said. "And if anyone gives us trouble, I'll—"

Her boot crunched against something stiff. She bent and pulled a piece of paper from beneath her boot heel. She shook shards of ice from the paper.

It was a flyer, warning the citizens of Novgorod that a noblewoman with *accoutrement* had attacked a brave defender of the Revolution, and that anyone who sheltered her would be executed.

The flyer showed an etching of a woman with black-buttoned boots and a coat billowing over a brass bird's tail.

The flyer shook in Elena's hand. "How dare they." She wished she'd killed that man. She should have killed him. She could have done it, no matter what Nina thought about her toughness.

Nina began coughing, her arms pressed against her ribs as she twisted into the hacks that convulsed her body. Elena dug her boot-toe into the frozen snow, waited until Nina's cough subsided.

"Shall we go home?" Nina hiccupped the words.

"We can't. We need the oil. Come along. We'll be careful."

Nina and Elena picked their way towards the kremlin. Between the guard towers, two men barred the gate, both wearing Red Army uniforms.

The flyer quaked in Elena's hand. She had always seen policemen, not soldiers, guarding the gate.

"Papers," said the older of the two soldiers, his face twisting around the words.

The younger man cocked his head at them—at Nina. *Of course.* Elena had once garnered her share of attention—glasses of champagne and trysts in the greenhouse—but Nina was the kind of woman men wrote sonnets about. This particular admirer had a face still round with youth, but he bore a scar beneath one eye.

Elena hated the way he gazed at her sister.

"Papers," he echoed, but the word sounded like an afterthought. Nina stiffened and licked her lips. Color suffused her cheeks.

"I'm terribly sorry, sir, but we seem to have forgotten our papers," she said.

The older soldier spluttered, phlegm dripping from under his nose-whiskers, his hand twitching around the barrel of his revolver. "Roll up your sleeves," he wheezed.

Elena grabbed Nina's hand, wondered how far and fast they could run before the bullets caught them, reminded herself that she wasn't scared.

"Gleb," the younger soldier said, still staring at Nina. "These are girls from the city. They live just on the other side of the church. I recognize them."

"They're those nobles," Gleb said. "I can tell. Look at the kid gloves. Nobles, stealing from the people—"

"I'll take them home," the younger soldier said. He looped one gloved hand under Elena's elbow and one under Nina's. Elena hated him touching her, but what other choice did she have? She forced herself to stay still.

"They scream when you rip their wings and tails off." Gleb licked the mucus off his upper lip. "And—"

"Stop."

Gleb ground his boot against the snow, grumbling.

"That's an order," the younger soldier snarled. He led Elena and Nina through the gate, marching towards the church.

"Where are you taking us?" Elena said. "Why are you helping?"

"Go out the west entrance of the city," the soldier said. "Ivan's on the gate, but he'll be too drunk to question you. He's always drunk since his wife starved during the famine last winter and left him alone with the children. And don't come back to the city. Get out of here, fast as you can."

"Why are you helping us?" Elena demanded, but she already knew the answer. The soldier was staring at Nina again, who demurely brushed blown snow off her cheek.

He led them towards the west gate of the city. They dodged around a line of kerchiefed women clutching baskets or children's hands outside a crumbling storefront.

Elena cast her eyes over the line, searching for the man she had beaten with the opera glasses, or for one of the many peasants who had once worked on their family's estate and had risen up against them.

A woman stood in the line, about Elena's age, her green eyes sharp under her bedraggled fur hat. A threadbare brown dress peeked out from under her coat-hem, the dress of a peasant. Her bare fingers, which clenched around the handles of an empty basket, were just as red and chapped as Elena's, just as callused from chopping firewood and scrounging for food.

The woman's cheeks were hollow, the same hollowness that had sagged Nina's and Elena's cheeks these past months.

This woman didn't murder my parents.

She shook off the thought. She couldn't start showing mercy. Father had shown mercy, the night of the fire, had tried to reason with the mob instead of shooting at it.

She hurried after Nina and the soldier.

A few steps from the west gate, the soldier seized Nina's hand and pressed his lips against the protruding veins there.

"Let's go." Elena grabbed Nina's other hand, dragged her towards the gate.

They trudged through knee-deep snow around the shadow of the kremlin, concealing their faces under their fur hats, until they rejoined the southern road through the marshes back towards the boxcar.

"That man." Elena's tail creaked erect again, stretching the swollen skin on her lower back. "The way that man looked at you, Nina. I can't stand it."

"Aleksandr."

"Pardon?"

"Oh...he said his name. Aleksandr." Nina stared at the snow beneath her shoes.

"When did he say that?"

"At some point. You weren't listening, I suppose."

"Well, it's good that *Aleksandr* was there," Elena said. "It's good, because otherwise we wouldn't have escaped. But my God, only helping us because he wanted to stick—"

"That's quite enough." Nina cradled her right hand with her left and tightened her jaw. "I won't listen to this anymore. Not all of them are bad, you know, he wasn't bad, he saved our—"

"Am I offending your delicate sensibilities, dearest? If I hadn't been there, what might he have done to you? We're lucky. But don't confuse it with romance. This isn't a novel." *That man only helped us because he wanted Nina. He's not like us, and neither is that woman. They're nothing like us. Nothing.*

"In any case, whatever are we supposed to do now?" Nina said. "He said not to return to the city, and we need—"

"I don't care what he said. We'll wait a few days. Then I'll sneak into the city at night. We need oil, and it's our city besides. I won't let them stop me."

Elena rummaged in her carpetbag, pushed aside their grandmother's diadem, a tangle of shawls, her father's book of maps of Novgorod. At last her fingers closed on cherrywood, and she pulled it out: the 1895 double action Nagant revolver-cuff. Her chest hurt when she remembered the night news of the Tsar's abdication had reached them and Father had summoned her to his study.

"You're the son I never had, Lena," he had said. Was he joking? She never found out. He had handed her the revolver-cuff, reminded her that she could use it without clamping it to her arm.

"Oh, you're bringing the gun?" Nina extracted her nose from the Pushkin book. "You're not going to...that is, you know if you affix it to your arm—"

"Yes, dearest, I'm aware of the history of revolver-cuffs." Everyone knew that since they were first used in the war against Napoleon, revolver-cuffs had been permanent additions to the body, both to discourage foot-soldiers from deserting and to allow officers to show off their bravery.

She had heard tales of Red Army troops chopping off Tsarist soldiers' arms and commandeering their gun-cuffs.

"But—"

"I'm not going to put it on." *Even though it would work better if I did.* Elena examined the curved black metal clamps that flanked the revolver-cuff, imagined them chomping into her arm, burrowing beneath her skin. "But I'm bringing it with me tonight. Just in case."

"Elena." Nina sighed. "Are you positive…"

Elena dropped the revolver-cuff into her coat pocket. "I'll go in through the west gate. That man who wanted you said the guard on that gate is always drunk." She shouted over Nina's cough. "I'll simply act as though I'm supposed to be there. It's our city. They can't keep me out."

"Have you considered…that is, do you envision…perhaps we should…leave?"

Elena's stomach swooped. "And where do you think we should go?"

"Anywhere. We could try to leave Russia. We could—"

"We're not even leaving this city. This is our land. I should've known that that man could make one comment and—"

"Some aristocrats leave, and have their *accoutrement* removed by doctors at the border, and they set up quite happy lives in—"

"Have you gone mad?" Elena's nerves twitched as she imagined her body without her feathers' sharp edges scraping against her thighs. "Remove our *accoutrement?* Perhaps I should change my name from Elena Sergeevna Trubetskoy. Perhaps I should forget who I am."

"We wouldn't have to sneak about, steal oil, subsist on rusk and tea, worry about being…being shot…we could have flowers and a townhouse and go boating…"

Elena imagined it, just for a moment: the life Nina had laid out, far from this place where their house and parents had burned. Would she be able to forget Russia, if they traveled far away and slipped into that idyllic life?

But Elena squeezed the revolver-cuff in her pocket. Nina's notions were nothing but a fantasy, one that required papers and passports. She couldn't be sidetracked, not if they wanted to stay alive. She couldn't wonder if peasants and soldiers were suffering just as much as they were.

"I'll return in a few hours." Elena slipped the diadem into her other pocket, in case she had to barter for anything.

Nina snatched up her book and didn't say goodbye.

The lit domes of St. Sophia cast ghostly light over the marshes as Elena marched on the western road towards the city. She climbed the snowy bluff along the river, then hurried towards the gate and the hollow light on the guard station.

The soldier leaning against the gate could only be Ivan—he stank bitterly of vodka, and his nose and cheeks were pocked with broken blood vessels.

Elena whipped a page, torn from a book, out of her coat pocket.

"Here are my papers," she said through the scarf wrapped around her face. She thrust them at Ivan and shouldered towards him, but he held out a black-gloved hand.

"Lemme lookit this," he slurred. He held up the yellowed pages, squinting. "This...this isn't..."

"Yes, it is." Elena pointed to the paper. "Don't you see it? You should let me through, now."

Ivan's lips curled, and he shook his head. His watery blue eyes were sober enough to understand that the paper was only a book-page, that she was one of the Trubetskoys, that she had *accoutrement.*

Elena drew her grandmother's diadem out of her pocket, clenched it so she could feel its diamonds through her gloves. "You'll accept this, instead of papers."

"No," Ivan said. "I don't want…" He raised his hand, opened his mouth to call his fellow guards.

Elena dropped the diadem and plunged her hand into her other coat pocket. She pulled out the revolver-cuff, curled her finger around the angry black comma of a trigger.

His children will be orphans. Just like me and Nina. The thought leapt into her mind, she couldn't help it, but she looked at the hammer and plough on his cap.

I am the firebird. No one catches the firebird.

The snap of the safety, and then she pointed the revolver-cuff at him and pulled the trigger.

She expected the bullet to rip through his uniform-breast. She didn't expect the bullet to make a small neat black hole through his neck.

She expected blood trickling from a wound, not dark liquid spurting from the bullet-hole, like something from a terrible theater production. Ivan clawed at his neck and crashed to his knees, then spilled onto the ground. His boots kicked against the frozen dirt beneath the harsh spotlight.

She couldn't look. She slapped her hands over her eyes, then twisted away and clamped her hands over her ears so she couldn't hear the *swish swish* of his stilling legs scraping against the ground, so she couldn't hear the dying cries of this man, this *enemy*, this enemy who had children, children who would never see their father cross their threshold again…

Oil. I need to get oil. He'll have oil for his gun. She crouched, her boots grinding into blood, and slid her hand along Ivan's belt until she found a can.

The can slipped from her hand when her gullet turned and she threw up. She grabbed the can and ran without wiping her mouth, crashing up to her knees in the crusty snow, racing back to the boxcar, the hole blossoming in Ivan's neck over and over like a motion picture show she couldn't stop watching.

Elena expected Nina to cry. But she maintained a stony silence as the oil dripped into her lungs, as she sipped her tea, as she curled in her furs, arms crossed and jaw tight.

"You used that oil on my lungs," she finally said. "You killed a man for it, a man who wasn't so dreadful at all."

"He joined the Red Army." Elena pressed her boots against the woodstove, trying to stop her legs from shaking. She was oiling the revolver-cuff, focusing on the metal and wood, trying, trying, *trying* to forget the hole in Ivan's neck...

"Perhaps he didn't have any other choice. I'm sure there are plenty of them that didn't have a choice. You're a murder—"

"That man betrayed us, just like all the other men in Novgorod. They put on red uniforms and rose against us. Don't you side with him." *It was true, Ivan deserved it, he deserved to die like that, he was a bad man. He was.*

"I—"

Elena slammed her feet onto the floor. "Mother and Father are dead. And you're siding with their killers."

Nina glared and puffed out her chest. "You pretend to be so very tough, Lena, but look at you, your hands are shaking."

"Could you be any more naïve? I'm glad Mother and Father are dead, so they don't have to see how you've betrayed us by saying these—"

Nina's hand twitched back, and Elena's cheek smarted. She lurched away as Nina raised her hand to slap her again.

"You listen to me," Nina snarled, her voice ragged. "You've gone too far, and Mother and Father would be ashamed of *you*, not of me. You orphaned children, and you've gotten blood on your hands. What you did was terrible and wrong, and you know it."

Elena knelt, ground the heels of her hands against her eyes. All she wanted was to be a girl again, in their house, pretending to be the firebird with Nina, knowing Mother and Father were reading in the parlor.

The hole appeared in Ivan's neck, over and over again in her mind, the man whose children she had orphaned...

"It was terrible, Nina." The words spilled out before she could stop them. "Oh God, it was... I wanted to see him die, but then it was terrible..."

Nina's hand rubbed against her back. "I know, I know. Don't you see, though, we must leave Russia, we have to escape, because if we stayed, you'll fall, over the line, into an irredeemable place."

Elena felt brass feathers scrape her thighs, wondered if she would have to let them lop her tail off. "When I think of it... But we can't leave, Nina. We don't have any way to escape. We're being hunted."

Nina twisted her lips back and forth, frowning. "I'm quite sure we'll sort something out. I'm sure we will. Perhaps you should sleep, and we'll sort something out in the morning."

Elena let Nina help her to her bunk, but even after she burrowed under her shawls, she couldn't sleep. She watched the flickering light from the woodstove make bear-monsters from the furs of the boxcar walls. She turned first one way, then the other, as the candle burned low and...

Diadems dropped into the snow, and she tripped over them. Holes appeared beneath her boots, tiny holes that all joined together until there was no place on the ground for her to step. As Elena stumbled, the woman in the threadbare brown dress raced past her, leaping over the gaping holes opening in the ground. Everywhere she turned Ivan kept falling, and falling, and falling...

When she opened her sticky eyes to pale dawn filtering through the boxcar's transom windows, she was determined. She couldn't be the monster-firebird anymore. She and Nina would run, away from their estate and Novgorod, and once they'd reached one of the bigger cities, Moscow or Petrograd, they would blend into the crowd, find the papers and passports they needed to escape Russia.

Elena sat up to tell Nina her new plan.

But Nina's bedclothes were thrown back. Her bunk was empty.

Elena pulled on her hat, shrugged into her coat, stormed out of the boxcar. She hurried towards the raised road through the marshes.

She scrutinized every lump of snow-laden grass, the dark maw of every puddle, her heart racing beneath her woolen coat, wondering where Nina could have possibly gone. She hoped Nina hadn't ventured out to try to find papers and a passport herself. She hoped her sister hadn't done anything foolish. She hoped she would return and the two of them could strike out across the snowy plains, run far away from the blackened gold tower of the house behind the hill, far away from bullet holes in necks and the demented dark firebird inside Elena.

She crossed the thick ice of the frozen river that ringed the city on the west side, and slipped and slid halfway up the bluff on the river's far bank. She peered over the bluff at the kremlin's squat black guard towers and the plains around the city. Long black coats flapped around the base of the towers: guards, bayonets glinting.

Elena waited behind the bluff as the sun rose and descended in a small arc on the horizon.

As the gloaming fell on the kremlin, two figures detached from the cadre of guards by the tower and hurried along the southern road. Elena trudged down the river, tripping over lumps in the thick ice. She reached the southern road and hid in the rustling frozen reeds of the marshes, waiting for the two figures.

As they drew near, their faces resolved from shadow. One of them was the soldier who had saved them from the guards on the gate.

The other was Nina.

Elena forced dry cold air into her lungs and began to put the puzzle pieces together: Nina's disappearance the night before. Her endless requests to go to the city. The fact that she had known his name.

Elena leapt out of the marsh. Nina shrank back, and the soldier drew his gun.

"No, stop, that's my sister," Nina said, as Elena whipped the gun-cuff out of her pocket.

"I know." Aleksandr pointed the gun at her, and she raised the gun-cuff.

Nina's head swiveled between Aleksandr and Elena. "Lena, listen to me. Aleksandr has obtained false passports, papers, train tickets to Berlin, for us."

Nina, in the arms of a Red Army soldier. Elena felt her feathers spreading. "How long have you been sneaking around with him?"

"No, no, no, don't become stubborn and contrary. I love him." Nina cocked her head towards Aleksandr as though his reaction was all that mattered anymore, as though she spoke and breathed only for him.

Elena didn't doubt that Nina believed she loved this soldier. But she swiveled towards Aleksandr, who lowered his gun slightly but tightened his jaw beneath his plough and hammer cap.

"How do I know these passports and papers are valid?" she said. If Aleksandr wanted a pretext to lure both Nina and Elena into the hands of border guards, this was the perfect opportunity.

"He loves me, Lena."

Elena flared her frozen nostrils and thought of their chances. *Nina may love him, but life's not a novel where a soldier falls in love with you and puts you on a train to a new life. He might be plotting to betray us.* "Why did you join the Red Army? Were you conscripted?"

"I volunteered," Aleksandr raised his chin. "I never knew my father. He was shot by Cossacks on Bloody Sunday when I was a boy, and they sent me to an orphanage. I wanted to destroy the people that did that to me."

So he hated nobles for the same reason that she hated peasants. "In that case, how am I supposed to trust—"

"Nina is an innocent, and you are her sister." Aleksandr squeezed Nina's hand. "They're hunting you. You must leave as soon as possible. Tonight."

Elena looked away from Nina's reproachful pout. She thought of a nation of created monsters, destroying each other, and reminded herself of her resolution to flee.

"Very well," she said, not taking her eyes off Aleksandr. "We'll go with you."

Her boots crunched through the snow as she followed Nina and Aleksandr towards the boxcar. The burned tower rose before them on the other side of the hill, silhouetted against the moon's glow.

"I don't like you sneaking around behind my back," Elena said. "Has this been happening since autumn? How did you even meet him?"

"In the market, when you were sick, I—"

"Shh." Aleksandr held up a hand, frowning. "What's that sound?"

The whine of an engine, the roar of a muffler, and yellow headlights arced over the marshes.

Aleksandr leapt around Nina and stepped in front of Elena.

An automobile roared around the bend in the road, tires skidding on the snow. Before it even stopped, doors swung open and three figures with guns swarmed around them, hands yanking up Nina's coat-sleeves to expose her wrists, snatching at Elena's coat, twisting her arm so the revolver-cuff flew into the snow.

"The noble sisters," wheezed the man who had seized Elena. It was Gleb, the guard from the gate, wearing the uniform of one of the special forces troops from Petrograd. Elena snarled, twisting, and her scalp screamed as Gleb seized her bun and twisted her hair.

"What is the meaning of this?" Aleksandr said, low and cold.

"What is the meaning of this? What is the meaning of you taking one of these sisters out of the city without turning her over to the border guards?"

Aleksandr jerked Nina away from the two soldiers who held her, wrapped his hand around her forearm as though he might protect her forever with that simple gesture.

Something fell inside Elena. She had been wrong. The love this man felt for her sister had nothing to do with passports or aristocracy or power.

Am I so broken that I can't even believe in love anymore?

"I'll handle this," Aleksandr was shouting.

"You think so, do you?" Gleb said.

"I'm ordering—"

"You don't give orders anymore. I report to Petrograd now. So who orders who?"

Silence. Elena raked her feathers through the air, hoping to slice Gleb's leg with them.

Then Gleb flung her aside. The snow rushed towards her and she rolled onto her back.

Gleb faced Aleksandr, drawing his revolver, as Elena snatched the revolver-cuff out of the snow.

"You've been fucking this noble girl and your head's gone up your ass," Gleb said. The two men who had grabbed Nina straightened their revolvers.

"I just said, I will handle—" Aleksandr said.

"You're a traitor, to the Revolution."

Elena locked her finger around the revolver-cuff's trigger and aimed it at Gleb. The recoil hit her in the chest—

But Gleb spun, roaring, positioning his revolver, and she realized she had missed—*the revolver-cuff never works as well when it's not on your wrist*—and she ducked into the frozen marsh-grass. *I will spit on his boots as he shoots me.*

An explosion, and Gleb stumbled, dropping his gun, and Elena gasped breath. Out of the corner of her eye she saw Aleksandr shove Nina towards Elena. Nina's ringlets flew, and her nostrils flared, and her stained blue coat billowed behind her.

More gunshots rocked the raised road.

Screams, and heavy footfalls, and someone gathered her up, seized her beneath the elbows and began to drag her away.

Aleksandr's face, sweat dripping from his hairline, eyes wild, loomed next to her. He was dragging her down the road towards the boxcar.

"Where's Nina?"

"Don't look back."

But Elena looked: there, among the prostrate black-coated soldiers, blue lying on the bluish snow, ringlets spilled around her, a spreading puddle of blood and oil—

Gleb roared behind them. Aleksandr aimed a shot over his shoulder and Gleb howled and fell.

"Keep running," Aleksandr said, but all Elena wanted to do was run, run until her burning chest exploded, run until she could no longer run anymore, run until she could arrive at a time before, when her house was whole and she could sit at a table with Mother and Father and Nina, Nina, her poem of a sister who now—

Elena stumbled and rolled, skidding off the road into the brittle ice of the marshes, her boot crunching into a freezing puddle, snowflakes sticking under her collar. Aleksander knelt beside her, shoulders stooped.

"You must still leave," he said. "You must. Think of what she wanted."

Elena raised her head. Aleksandr's eyes were glazed with tears.

"She said she wanted to go someplace that smelled like flowers," he said. "To have her *accoutrement* removed and forget everything that happened to her here. And, and she wanted you to go too. She said she was afraid for you."

Elena cradled the revolver-cuff, crouched in the whispering frozen reeds of the marshes.

Could she cross the border from Russia into a new life of dried roses and Sunday promenades, after letting some physician remove her tail and opera glasses? Could she forget that she had once had a mother and a father and a sister, forget that monsters had taken them from her, forget that a monster had grown inside her too?

Could she ever allow it all to fade away?

That's what Nina would have wanted.

But she felt her tail flex, feathers grinding on feathers, and she knew: something had broken inside of her forever, no matter if she never saw Russia again.

"Elena, please, she would have wanted—"

"My tail is just as much a part of me as her lungs were." Elena leapt up, on her tiptoes, looming above him so he shrank away.

She slapped the revolver-cuff over her left wrist. She clenched her teeth as the metal rods curled over her forearm, scraping off her arm hair and digging in, reaching down to her bone. The wood settled against her skin and the trigger fitted into place just above her wrist-bone.

She shouldered around Aleksandr and marched towards the boxcar. She pushed inside, tore Nina's shawls off her bunk, rummaged through the carpetbag and pulled out Father's book of maps of Novgorod. She marked corners of the marshes where she could hide with her revolver-cuff and ambush soldiers, parts of the kremlin wall where she could throw homemade explosives, anywhere she could go to destroy the people who had killed Mother, Father, Nina, who had taken away everything, who had created the dark avenging firebird that could never stop fighting.

The Little Begum

Indrapramit Das

Bina looked at the metal bones covering her worn and stunted limbs, cold against her legs and feet, lovingly layering the scars of her disease. These new hands and feet were heavy, lead and steel woven with leather straps onto the outside of her body. She had watched her sister Rani make them with fire and scrap, bending the pieces with hammer and heat, her second-hand British goggles flickering with the light of the workshop's tiny forge, sparks flying off her skin as if she were invincible. Bina did not feel invincible wearing them, these skeletal gloves and boots. They trapped her already strength-less arms and legs, weighed them down till she felt more helpless that she'd ever been, especially with Rani standing over her, ten years older, so much life in her limbs.

"When the Mughal Emperor Shah Jahan's dearest wife Mumtaz died giving birth to their fourteenth child, his grief was so all-consuming he could barely think, let alone rule an empire.

So he decided he would build a monument to his grief, to honour the woman who had been so important to him."

"The Taj Mahal!" said Bina. She knew some history from her time in the boarding houses, and the stories Rani told her. She let Rani go on.

"That's right. Shah Jahan gathered the best craftsmen, the best metalworkers,"

"Like you!" said Bina. Rani smiled and nodded.

"…and the best engineers in his realm, and they built a monument, a metal being to house and guard his wife's body. The Taj Mahal was the greatest automaton ever built—over 300 feet tall, plated in ivory, its massive limbs inlaid with lapiz lazuli and onyx and other precious stones, its contours cleverly crafted to look like a palatial tomb when it crouched at rest like a man folded on his knees with his head to Mecca, the spiked tanks on its back raised to the sky like graceful white minarets. To look upon the Taj Mahal walking along the banks of the Yamuna and across the water lapping its metal ankles as if the broad river were a little stream, was to see the impossible.

And that's because it was impossible. That metal and ivory giant couldn't walk, not even with the most powerful and intricate steam engines and hydraulics built by the empire's best engineers. It would topple and crash before taking a single step. No, it needed a pilot who had the gift of telekinetic thought, to lift its every component, to give it a human soul to go along with the machinery."

Like me, Bina didn't say. She realized why her sister was telling her this story.

"Shah Jahan tried piloting it himself. He failed. Very few, after all, are born with the talent of telekinesis, a truth the Emperor did not learn easily. But he did learn it eventually. After scouring the Empire with recruiters, he found, perhaps aptly, that Gauharara

Begum, the final daughter Mumtaz had left him with, was the one he was looking for, when one day she lifted an elephant into the air and gently put it down just by looking at it. She was eight at the time, like you. So with teary eyes Shah Jahan asked his little daughter Gauharara if she would pilot the walking palace that guarded her mother's remains within its chest. Gauharara said that she would be honoured."

"And so she did. She was carried by the Emperor's guards through the winding tunnels of the vast being, past its engines and gears and pipes, past the chamber in its heart that held Gauharara's mother, past its tanks, and she was placed in its head, in a soft cavern of quilted walls. The little Begum made the Taj Mahal walk, looking out of its filigreed eyes to the empire her father ruled, once with the help of her mother. Gauharara Begum took the huge metal and ivory beast across the land, with the aid of a faithful crew that ran its engines. The Empire celebrated this wonder amongst them striding in the distance, colourful pennants like hair lashing behind it, breathing steam.

But before long Shah Jahan's third son, Aurangzeb, ordered that the giant never be piloted again, because it was blasphemous to create such automatons, that this lifeless walking idol was a mockery of Allah. Aurangzeb had his father and his beloved Gauharara put under house arrest at the Red Fort in Agra, and after a war of succession with his brothers, became the next Mughal Emperor in a sweeping victory. Shah Jahan died imprisoned, and Gauharara died many years later of old age. Aurangzeb was a devout, efficient Emperor, but oversaw the last years of the Mughal Empire that was. The Emperors that followed led it to its decline, and eventually, they were easily defeated by the British Empire with their airships and tanks. Perhaps if the Mughals had made more automatons to rid the Taj of its solitude, and kept them walking, they'd have kept this land too. They could have thrown airships from the sky, and crushed tanks under their feet. The Taj Mahal never walked again, folding into its rest by the banks of the Yamuna, where to this day its empty tanks gleam like minarets on the horizon, its scalp and shoulders shorn of pennants."

Bina nodded, looking straight at her sister's grease and oil covered face glimmering in the candlelight, at her coarse tattooed hands between her knees. She smiled. Somewhere in the slum, a stray dog barked.

"I know why you told me that story," Bina said. She wondered if their mother or their father had taught Rani to tell that story. Or both.

"Of course you do. You're a clever girl," Rani said.

"You told it really well. But it's just really sad," Bina murmured.

"One day," her sister said, putting her warm palm on Bina's cheek. "You're going to see the Taj Mahal at rest by the banks of the Yamuna. You're going to walk, walk with me, and we'll get out of here and go north to see it. Understand?"

Bina shook her head. As if to check, she tried moving her stick-like legs. They barely complied, distant, far-off limbs attached to her body through some unfathomable fog that cut off her brain from their worn-out nerves. "We're in a slum. We can't get good doctors like the babus and the sahibs. I'm not going to walk. You should stop saying that I will."

Rani knew not to insist any further. She looked ashamed, which hurt Bina. But she was angry, and didn't say anything. Rani blew out the candle next to the mat and pulled the blanket over Bina, kissing her on the forehead.

"Do you remember, Bina, years ago, the first time I told you the story of the Taj Mahal? What I said to you?" Rani asked.

Bina's eyes welled up before she could stop herself. Her legs, weak and immobile and worn away to skin and bones by her sickness, remained that way under the exoskeletal harness her sister had spent hours and days making. All those days, and Bina had thought it was just another project repairing parts for the British and the babus with their various steam-powered machines.

"Am I going to hop in the Taj Mahal and make it walk again? Is that what you want me to do?" Even as Bina asked these questions, she felt her voice rising. She was horrified that she was shouting at her sister after everything she had done for her, but she was.

She couldn't see her sister's reaction through the tears. "No, Bina," she laughed, obviously letting her little sister cry without drawing attention to it. "No. But there's a reason we're all here in this slum, a reason that the British laws don't allow telekinesis for people like us, for everyone who isn't white. There's a reason Aurangzeb, ambitious, devout Aurangzeb, was terrified by his father's creation, and his sister's power. There was a time a little girl made a giant walk. Even if that's not true, even if it was a whole army of telekinetics who made the Taj Mahal walk, that's an impossible feat. It's a miracle. Now I've seen you lift the pots and pans with your telekinesis, Bina. I've seen you lift the scrap in my workshop. If you can lift those, you can lift these. They're the same. You're good at it. I know it. You're getting big. You know, you know this. I hate to say this. I can't carry you forever. I wish I could, but I can't."

"Even if I could move this. If I ever went out, the British would see this skeleton, and they'd kill us probably."

"I'll cover your hands and feet with cloth, we'll say your limbs are scarred if anyone ever asks. We'll figure it out."

"I..."

"No," Rani's voice was suddenly hard. "No more excuses. I've seen you pick up things with your mind. This harness is a thing. Your arms and legs are in it. You're going to pick them up, and pick up your arms and legs."

Rani held out her hands. "Take my hands," she said. And almost without thinking, Bina did, her exoskeletal fingers grasping at Rani's flesh. Rani held her hands, winced, and pulled her up.

Bina heard the metal joints around her thin legs creak, the straps tighten with new movement like unused muscles, and she felt the pieces of metal in the harness around her float like dust in sunlight, drifting as her mind vanished into a profound numbness, dominated only by the image of a child in a padded chamber, sitting calmly in the centre of her skull. She felt the pieces of metal float and lift her legs and arms, which filled with the sparkling tingle of blood moving fresh through their weakened vessels.

She was standing. By herself. Held up by metal, metal held adrift by a little child in her head. The leather soles under her exoskeletal feet squeaked as she nearly fell down in shock, but corrected herself.

Rani watched, her mouth open, arms held out to grab her sister if she fell.

Bina was shivering violently.

"My little Begum," Bina said, her voice trembling ever so. "Come forward."

"I can't move," Bina said, voice thick.

"Why?"

"I...I'm scared," she said.

"My Begum. I know. I know. But I'm here. I won't let you fall. Just look, look at your hands. Look what they're doing."

Bina looked at her hands, at the metal fingers flexing and unflexing by her side, their parts moving and clicking, joints bending, blessing her deformed fingers with intricate movement. "Oh, god," Bina said. The metal fingers seized, stopped their clicking.

"Don't," Rani said. "You're thinking too much. You were moving them without even thinking of it."

"Okay," Bina whispered.

"Bina. You're standing. You haven't done that in years. Don't be afraid." Bina thought of the years and years of being curled in her sister's powerful arms, letting the sun warm her face on their morning walks by the river.

"I'll fall if I move," Bina said.

"I'm here if you do."

Rani took off her necklace and held it out. "Use your fingers. Take it."

Her hand shook as she raised it. She watched the little gears spin in the joints, the fingers bending to grasp the necklace. She held it in between her metal fingers. "Wear it," Rani said. Her arms floated up, her hands passing her head, and she felt the necklace around her neck. It was a string tied to a featureless coin their father had hammered, to practice telekinesis with their mother, passing it between their hands through the air. Bina didn't remember this herself. The coin hung against her chest.

"That's it. You're doing better than I could have ever hoped."

Bina nodded. She closed her eyes, and pennants unfurled from her scalp in the sunlight flashing off her great ivory-plated shoulders. She breathed in deep, felt the giant bellows in her, the furnaces in her torso flare with life. Felt the entire engine of her machinery close around the twin tombs deep inside her, protecting them. She breathed out, steam rushing from the ports on her head and back, gushing ribbons of cloud into the pale sky.

Her hands were huge, big enough to pick up cattle, elephants. Underneath her was their entire slum, sprawled across the banks of the Hooghly, in the distance the white palatial city of the British, of Calcutta, airships hovering like balloons above it, tethered to the land with strings she could snap with her fingers. An army of British soldiers couldn't stop her. They'd flee, or be crushed, their bullets glancing harmlessly off her towering body.

"We'll travel?" Bina asked, her voice breaking.

"We will. We'll go to Delhi. We'll find a way to get you new medicine. We'll see the Taj Mahal. I promise."

Bina felt dizzy, her own height strange to her. She heard her metal fingers clicking again, moving again. Flexing. Unflexing. She thought of the little Begum pilot in the padded chamber in her skull, her resolve, looking out at the world through the windows of a giant's eyes. This little Begum didn't have an Emperor for a father, and a dead Empress for a mother. In fact, she was no Begum, just a girl. This little girl had a father and mother who were metal-workers, who were shot by the British when it was discovered they were both telekinetic. This little girl had a sister with whom she was sent to be 'civilized' in an imperial boarding house. This little girl had a sister who kept them both alive over years on the streets, found them refuge working metal like their parents had, in a slum where people went to die because it was cheap, a sister who kept her alive when she fell sick, and stayed sick.

Bina felt a fire in those bellows in her chest, burning, licking at the massive grinding gears. She closed her metal hands into fists. She thought of the little girl in her skull, and this time there was an older girl beside her—her sister, safe inside the padded chamber, looking out across the empire through those huge windowed eyes, that empire once Mughal, now British, perhaps one day something else entirely. They looked out together, to the snap and flutter of pennants catching the wind outside. The little girl would keep her sister safe in that chamber.

"Walk, Bina," said her sister. So she did.

Forty Pieces

Lucien Soulban

There was, there was not.... the older man read, his finger tracing the black stitching of ink on the yellowed page. "That is to say that this story is only true if Allah wills it. All tales begin this way."

The young boy next to him fidgeted in the squeaking caned chair, his body given to the fits and hesitations of all five-year olds. The creaking of the chair betrayed his impatience; his delicate fingers touched the corners of the thick pages, eager for the adventure promised within the book. He did not care for the words, just the story. To Allah and five-year olds, all stories were true.

The student had left, and Tariq's modest earnings for today's lesson sat on the table in a stump of silver coins. Enough for some lamb from that Egyptian butcher, and green olives, tomatoes, and pita from the Palestinian grocer. Maybe with the remaining akçes, a glass of Greek Retsina wine from a Sherbet House where the Europeans drank.

The akçes provided nowhere near enough for anything else. Barely enough for a few days of oil or wood to warm those nights when Russia's winter swept in from across the Black Sea. To think he'd arrived from Damascus with enough literature to wallpaper his Constantinople apartment with book spines. Tonight, he'd see far more of the water-stained walls than he cared to.

Tariq flung open the window and welcomed in the acrid smell of burning coal and the wash of brine from the Marmara. Noise flooded in as well, the shopkeepers and stall owners fought in decibels for clients while above the awning-covered streets and alleys of the Grand Bazaar puttered the air dhows. Their cypress wood prows and pine decks spoke of their fishing days, but their air bladders promised more of this new era, their flanks festooned in draping silks, or painted with oriental tigers and long-legged cranes, or finned with colorful side-sails like giant fish.

"Aziz," Tariq cried to the shop beneath his apartment, the one with blue cloth for awning.

A man with a face dotted by ash-raised scars of the Nubian tribes and a berry-stained fez waved up at him. "More books? I'll send the boy up," the Nubian said, laughing. "But no more sciences, ah? People want adventure and poetry, my friend."

Tariq frowned, but nodded before closing the window and turning back to his shelves. He was in short supply of those already. Perhaps the local madrassas would take his science books for their students, he thought, and then dispelled the notion. If they realized who he was, who his father had been, he'd be driven out of Constantinople the way they'd driven his father from Damascus.

There was a knock at the door. Tariq knew Aziz, knew he'd only offer a couple of silver kuruŞ for rare volumes at best. That would be enough to continue treading water for a few weeks more. He opened the door.

The man waiting there did not work for the Nubian. He reached no higher than five-and-a-half-feet in height, his frame wiry and corded with muscles, a fact that not even his double-breasted frock coat and striped morning pants could hide. He removed his top hat, dislodging not one strand of black hair. His equally black eyes glittered over the gold frame of his spectacles. The spectacles had come from a madcap's mind, the red lenses flipped up on a pivot near the arms, revealing the black lenses beneath... like the glass wings of a butterfly.

Tariq instantly distrusted the man. Never mind he felt underdressed in his homespun white cotton shirt and baggy trousers, it was the Steamkraft that unsettled him. Steamkraft, the Prussian's marriage of the assembly line to madcap inventions, had become more than fashionable within the Ottoman Empire. As Prussia's closest allies, the sultans turned what had been an evolution of assembly line warfare towards the Islamic arts of engineering and architecture. The Ottoman twilight became a new golden age, with Constantinople its brass pearl. Her newest minarets glittered with metal lace shells and copper inlay, the gears beneath turning under cascading water that transformed the towers into gigantic water clocks.

"Are you the bookseller?" the visitor asked in the perfect Arabic of the Koran in a region still muddied with regional dialects.

"Who asks?"

The man smiled deeply with white teeth. "Raakin, a humble servant."

"You dress like no servant I know," Tariq responded, glancing at the man's expensive tastes in clothes. The silk shirt and bowtie alone was worth a year of Tariq's time.

"My master is generous," Raakin replied, the smile never wavering, "to anyone who demonstrates purpose." He pulled a purse of coins from his breast pocket and tossed it up once to catch it. It jingled dully with a heavy weight, heavier than silver, heavy with the weight of fortune's promises. "My master wishes to buy all your books."

Why did I let him in? Tariq wondered, a self-admonishing thought that refused to let go, but he knew why. With the gold lira in Raakin's purse, Tariq could live very extravagantly for a few short years or in modest comfort for decades.

It would serve his father right for burdening him like this. The books served only to provide his walls with color and remind him what his father had sacrificed—thrown away. They were all that remained of his family's exodus from Damascus when they'd left behind a fortune in jade statues from China, ivory tusk-carvings from India, Mother-of-Pearl covered tables from Cairo, Persian rugs from Baghdad. All for a fortune in words, hardly worth a handful of akçes.

Now, however, Raakin stared at the walls of Tariq's apartment, his face creased in displeasure and the uncertainty growing in Tariq's breast.

"Where are all the books?" Raakin asked. "I heard you possessed a formidable library." He motioned around him. "Old men have more teeth than this."

Tariq tried not to bristle at the comment. "I make little money teaching," he explained. The man nodded and smiled in a way that made Tariq feel as though he'd been trapped in the cage with a tiger.

"Where is the Book of 'Abd-Es-Samad?"

Tariq's voice hitched in his chest. "Leave."

"You did not sell it, did you?" Raakin asked. "That would be unfortunate."

"Leave!" Tariq managed more forcefully, which seemed to amuse the visitor.

"Do you know that my employer told me to get the book by any means necessary?" he said, slowly walking past a row of books, his fingers tapping their edges. "I convinced him that gold silences tongues more easily than a knife across the throat. Will you make a liar out of me?"

Tariq darted toward the door, but a click of a hammer and a soft voice that said "No," stopped him. The man held a large tri-barreled flintlock pistol, the sides adorned with etched silver plaques, the barrel wrought iron. He motioned Tariq to step away from the door.

"Dog," Tariq muttered, obeying.

The visitor laughed sharply. "The book," he said.

"The Gunpowder Alchemists leave no survivors, yes?" Tariq said.

"True," Raakin said, "but we can be merciful. A tincture of Belladonna and other plants to give you a peaceful death, or I leave you in agony for days with corrosive shot until you beg me to end your life." He raised his flintlock.

Tariq swallowed once, trying to whet his throat, but to no avail. He stepped to a row of books and pushed them aside. He reached into the gap between the shelf and the wall, and pulled out a bundle wrapped in dusty wool. A string wrapped it neatly together.

"Will you kill me now?" Tariq asked, ready for the retort of the flintlock.

A chuckle came in response.

A sea of Fez-topped heads crowded the street's length. The stranger walked arm-in-arm with Tariq, like they were the oldest of friends, but the flintlock pressed into Tariq's ribs said otherwise. Raakin smiled with no warmth to the act, just a fence of teeth.

They passed a row of steps where men sat and argued, newspapers in hand, their gestures made in emphatic motions. The debates followed orbits as familiar as the constellations themselves, the renaissance of the Ottoman Empire, the growing influence of Prussia in the region, the rapid Westernization of Constantinople.

"Why not just destroy the book?" Tariq asked. His family's enemies certainly would have thrown it on the pyre along with his father had they captured either. They'd been driven out of Damascus for that book, escaping their sanctioned murder.

"Destroy?" Raakin said, pulling Tariq to a stop. "No no, my friend. The Book of 'Abd-Es-Samad is too valuable to destroy."

"But—" Tariq hesitated.

"My employer found the City of Brass," Raakin whispered with a look of delight.

"No," Tariq said, his voice as distant as the horizon. His father was a fool for believing the legends. They'd lost everything for the mad dreams of 'Abd-Es-Samad and his city. He had to be wrong—Tariq needed a reason to blame him.

"It is real. We need the book, and you to translate it. Now come," he said, pulling Tariq along and motioning ahead. Tariq followed the gesture, his eyes resting on Imperial Aerotower, a massive four-walled edifice of marble blocks, windows covered in brass filigree, and hanging platforms from which three airships sat moored. It stood among the bramble of streets of the Galata business district, the cargo hauled up on iron cranes and creaking chains and groaning ropes. "We have a ship to catch."

Tariq stood upon at the stub-nosed prow of the air dhow, sheltered by the air bladder and the fin sails that peeled away from the flanks. One hand shielded his eyes from the fine grit that peppered his face and hands. With the other, he gripped a thickly braided mooring rope securing the dhow to the balloon, distantly aware of the clash of ages. Steamkraft was fast changing the West's identity, but in pockets like the Levant, Persia, India, and Africa, the new served only to validate the old... it did not replace it. The old fishing dhows that plied the Nile and the Arabian Gulf and Red Sea had a history as venerable as the book that Tariq held.

As the steam dhow caught the winds, it soared over the desert, the sands below bright with sun and shimmering with heat. The steering rudder, a long dagger of wood banded by iron, split the dunes, allowing the vessel to slalom through the desert with precision. Raakin leaned over and whispered something to the old bedu pilot who cackled at Tariq with tooth-starved gums, his eyes hidden behind a pair of leather goggles.

Tariq had been a hostage since Constantinople; they'd landed in the silk city of Beyrouth along the cedar slopes of the Lebanon Mountains. From there, they boarded the dhow, Raakin ever-smiling, his blade and flintlock within reach. He sensed Tariq's every intention with almost preternatural skill, always there with a knowing smile when Tariq contemplated escape. So Tariq had given up on flight, especially now that they flew well above the desert, a desert unlike any Tariq had ever seen.

The Syrian expanse of sand felt hard under one's sandals and stretched out to the horizon with cypress trees and yellow wildflowers, cacti and thorny shrubs to break the plain. This desert, however, was an ocean storm petrified in time and turned to dust. Sand crested the sky and swept outward to flood the horizon. It gave the sense of being motionless and unceasing at the same time, and unknowable.

"It is why the bedu call it the Empty Quarter," Raakin said, joining Tariq at the prow of the ship.

"My father was obsessed with the delusions of a madman," Tariq said. "Now you follow one folly with another."

"Iram of the Pillars, it is there."

"Impossible," Tariq said.

"You will see." From the satchel hanging across his shoulder, Raakin took out his prize. Unadorned beige camel leather protected the Book of 'Abd-Es-Samad and sweat stains and the brown of dried blood spoke of its long history and longer travels. Tariq might have cursed its pages once, but now he wasn't so sure. To hold something that at one time was nothing more than a collection of mad fables, and to discover that those words possibly hid the truth left Tariq numb.

Raakin handed the book to Tariq. The teacher hesitated and then took it, the rough camel hide smoothed by the centuries. Tariq ran his fingers across the simple cover, and then suspended the book over the dhow's low wood gunwales and the racing desert below.

"I can drop it," Tariq said.

"Let me tell you a story," Raakin said, unperturbed. "A learned teacher spends a lifetime rising into favor, only to fall from it again and again. He is not to blame, of course. The Pashas change every year like the clicking gears of a clock, and a man can find himself beloved one moment and despised the next. This teacher, however, eventually angers the madrassas themselves. He claims that the City of Brass, Ubar of the Giants, was not cursed by Allah as the Koran says. The journal of 'Abd-Es-Samad proves that it was a city well ahead of its years. A city built by madcaps, inventors. Naturally, this enrages the madrassas who drive this teacher from Damascus."

Raakin stared at Tariq a moment, and then continued. "I admire your father, standing by his convictions in the face of exile."

"He should have known better than to speak of such things." Tariq shouted. "Instead, he cost us everything!"

"You paid nothing! He paid with everything HE earned, but you? You are a vulture of his legacy. Your accomplishments are his. You have none of your own. So drop the book. It will be the only act of courage you have ever committed, the only thing you sacrifice that is truly your own."

"You'll kill me!" Tariq shouted.

"Did you think the sacrifice I mention is the book?" Raakin's lips pursed in disapproval and he watched as Tariq's hand dropped to his side. "It is time you made yourself useful," he said, turning away "It is time you reread the book with more of your father's conviction."

Howling winds buffeted the dhow and the world settled into an orange storm that licked the top of the ridges into eddies and whorls. The pilot skated along the troughs between the monolithic dunes, the stabilizer fin set deeper into the sand to anchor her flight. Below deck, however, the sand turned the air murky, the lantern struggling to light the cabin.

Tariq sat on the floor, his legs crossed and the book cradled in his lap. Yet he found himself staring absently at the Persian carpet under him, at its ornate scroll of floral shapes encased in repeating geometric patterns. He remembered his father, the way he smiled by squinting, his voice gentle—never demanding or impatient, always scholarly. His father's voice came clearly to him now, telling him how rug makers always wove imperfections into the pattern, because only Allah could create something perfect.

There was, there was not.

Tariq stroked his forehead, the memory testing him like a wound that thought it was fresh again. How had he come to hate his father so? His father, who only showed charity. A man who wouldn't hurt a fly, and instead accepted his fate with a frustrating sort of nobility. He gave up everything, and Tariq didn't know whether he wanted to cry or rage at the man.

Tariq focused on the book again, the faded Kufic scrawl still legible, the lines of artwork clear and knife sharp. Tariq remembered the book by touch, sitting with his father as he pulled tales from its pages, his fingers brushing across the rough texture of the old paper.

There was, there was not.

The words brought a twinkle to the old man's eyes matched only by the dance in his voice. It was the same exhilaration, a poet had once told Tariq, as when a blank page faced him and the poem had the potential to be anything.

Abd-Es-Samad wrote this on his travels to find the City of Brass. Much of what is taught in Shahrazad's stories have forgotten the true details of that journey. It is more allegory than fact. His father's voice filtered through clearly, undiluted by the vagaries of memory.

He was wisest among the most learned sheikhs, and he traveled further than Islam itself knew of the world. He spoke its many languages and nothing of the Levant or Northern Africa remained hidden from him.

"But he is only remembered by the tales of Shahrazad?" Tariq the boy asked. His father nodded enthusiastically, and Tariq could only flush in shame of the memory. Tariq flipped through Abd-Es-Samad's account of Ubar itself.

It was said that Allah cursed the city, a city of giants brought low for their hubris, but this is not true, my son, and in these pages you and I will find that truth and set right a mistake.

Tariq absently flipped the page, falling upon one of the more elaborate drawings: Ubar itself, half submerged in the sands of the Rhub al Khali, the dunes as high as the city's many statues and minarets. Ubar… a ship in a frozen sea whose masts barely touched the crest of the towering waves. He turned the page.

Before the archangel Gabriel gave Muhammad the wisdom of Allah, there were other Gods. Among them were the three daughters of the moon, Goddesses later cast down by Muhammad as the devil's making. They were Allāt, Al-'Uzzá, *and Manāt. To her, the last, there was a temple in Ubar.*

"Who was she, father?"

The Goddess of Fate

The new picture showed the Temple of Manāt itself, stairs emerging from sand, walls marked with some mural that could only be hinted at, the statues of winged women with their arms extended as they held a bird in each hand. At the heart of the wall, flanked by the statues stood a great square archway, open to the desert.

The pages following had been torn out, the stubs yellowed and ragged. Tariq's father thought it'd been Abd-Es-Samad who had done it, to protect something he'd discovered. Or perhaps it was someone who'd taken offense with the words that followed.

Somewhere above him, the cabin door opened and steps sounded. Raakin appeared; he studied him, a moment in cold consideration. "We approach the city."

The sirocco raged, great banners of sand that scoured the desert with their tiger tongues. The dhow lay anchored between the dunes, the sails pulled tight against the bladder. The storm whipped about Tariq, stinging and blinding him despite his white keffiyeh.

Dunes loomed above them, to the left a sharp slope and the right a curved wall. He had no sense of direction, only that lights ahead glowed dimly as hanging orbs. Within moments, he stood among the tents and pavilions on the site. Some bore the black goat-hair walls of the Bedouin, their fabric flapping but bearing the winds. Tariq suspected these belonged to the famed local tribes of the al-Murrah or Ar-Raswashid, paid to "help" so they did not raid the expedition.

The army camp, however, was a different matter. The field grey tents bore the black eagle and iron cross of the Prussian Army, at least where winds hadn't collapsed them. Soldiers in khaki jackets with hooded capes drawn tight around leather gas masks ran about trying to repair the damage in a losing battle against the elements.

Tariq waited for Raakin's soft jab to remind him he was there, *a shadow guarding a shadow of a man*, he thought bitterly. None came. He turned to face Raakin, and instead found drawn curtains of sand. He was alone, separated from the assassin by the desert. Tariq hesitated, wondering where he should run. He didn't move, however. He'd come to hate his father, blame him for abandoning their life for the sake of a folly. Only, here he stood in its heart, faced with the knowledge, the shame, that it may all be real.

He waited until Raakin reappeared, a curious cock of his head asking the question hidden behind the tinted goggles. *Why?*

"I owe it to my father to be proven wrong," Tariq said, shouting above the storm.

Raakin's hand fell on Tariq's shoulder, but instead of pushing him forward, he pointed past the tents. Shadowed against the dark orange sky, shapes filtered in and out of the gloom. Broken towers that ended in brick-jagged points, pillars mounted by Sphinx-like creatures, block-like buildings... all half-entombed in sand.

"My God," Tariq said.

"Yes," Raakin replied, "but in your defense, the prophet Muhammad only submitted after Gabriel squeezed him three times."

A Prussian Driedger-Bok F-11 Aerostat hovered over the sands, the sails pulled down like a massive skirt and pinned using sandbags. The grey sails formed weather breakers for the huddled soldiers sat hunched together, their masks hiding their features. Somewhere in the darkness beneath the umbrella, camels groaned in complaint and voices thick with the guttural Arabic of the bedu barked to calm them.

Overhead, the aerostat rumbled loudly, the F-11 shouldering the storm and maintaining its position. The command pavilion, tan with peaked roof and a short skirt of blue trim, sat at the center of the maze of slumped bodies and weighted mooring ropes. A pair of St. Elmo lamps framed the entry flap, the light a fluid miasma of phosphorescent white gas that cast a ghostly pallor over the men nearest them. Raakin swept open the tent flap.

Five men stood there, three in the stripes and frills of Prussian officers, their tall and spike-mounted tropical helmets resting on the map covered table. The two other men wore the black suits and red fez of Ottoman men.

The men watched with dispassionate coolness as Raakim removed his goggles and dusted himself off. Tariq fixed his gaze on the heavy-set man who stared at him; the older Arab had the half-lidded eyes of a digesting snake. Tariq almost didn't recognize him under the added weight and the tufts of white that had crept into his hair and beard.

"Ibn Hannah," the man said, calling him 'son of Hannah' as if they were old friends.

"Farouk," Tariq said, pulling his keffiyeh down. "I'm pleased to see that you have grown fat and old."

Farouk's eyes narrowed. The men straightened and looked to one another, obviously unfamiliar with Arabic. Farouk said something to the men in Prussian. The men nodded, their postures stiff. One man with a thin mustache tucked his riding crop under his arm and replied, motioning to Tariq. A smile spread across Farouk's lips, but it was Raakin who answered.

"Our patrons are impatient," Raakin said. "They want answers."

"Show them the book," Farouk said.

"If I'd known you wanted it, I would have thrown it off the dhow," Tariq replied, not budging.

"Raakin, why did you bring him?" Farouk asked. "I told you what I wanted done with him."

"And on whose head would the sword fall if I delivered you a book and nobody to translate it?"

"I can read it," Farouk said.

"Better than his father?"

"His father is dead."

"His son is not," Raakin said.

Farouk sighed and then nodded. He turned to Tariq. "How do we enter the Temple of Manāt?"

"You turned the madrassas against my father and now here you are, begging for my help?" Tariq said.

Farouk laughed. "Your father did not understand that to survive the weather, you had to dress accordingly. He angered the madrassas when it was their time."

Tariq shook his head. "And now that the Prussians are in season?"

"I dress accordingly."

One of the Prussians, a white-haired man with a barrel upper-body and mustache that curtained over his lips, barked something in Prussian. Farouk turned a pleasant smile on the man, replying in a conciliatory tone.

Raakin stepped in and grabbed Tariq by the bicep. He reached into the satchel strung over Tariq's shoulder and pulled out the book, showing it to the men. The thin Prussian took it and the assembled studied the book, flipping through its pages.

"I will not help you," Tariq said.

Raakin's grip tightened. "Shut up," he said, softly. "Before you rob me of all excuses to keep you alive."

Tariq glanced at Raakin, surprised, but the assassin didn't bother glancing back. After a few minutes of examining the book, the barrel-chested Prussian said something to Tariq, something that sounded like a demand. It was Raakin who replied in Prussian. The man nodded and returned the book to the assassin.

"Raakin," Farouk said. "Encourage him."

"Why are you helping me?" Tariq said over the drone of the F-11. The reek of oil was stifling.

Raakin pulled him through the darkness, past the soldiers who couldn't bother looking up. "Am I?"

He brought Tariq to a bedu tent on the edge of the aerostat's skirt and pushed him through gently. The women in the tent stared back with hardened nomad's eyes that were at once black and unblinking. It was the only thing Tariq could see of them in the narrow slit of their heavy burkas. Medallions of bronze and copper hung from their black cloth, while silver chains dangled from the medallions and chimed softly as they shifted. They sat on faded carpets, a pungent dung fire bringing tears to Tariq's eyes. Among them sat children, but no men. They watched, as though expecting him.

Raakin nodded to the empty carpet on the ground and shoved the book into Tariq's chest. "Hurry," he said. "Before the desert swallows the city again." And with that, he left.

Tariq stared at the women, and they stared back, waiting. They looked at the book and they looked at him. *Did they want this?* Taking the bait, he opened the book and several women inhaled and held their breaths. They knew what it was, Tariq realized in a way that sent tingles through his fingertips.

Of course... The bedu women were the ones who shared tales, who safeguarded the magic of the tribe, who dared speak of dark things when night came. Only one woman alone held Tariq's gaze, a pair of soupy brown eyes set in a cradle of wrinkles.

"*Kan,*" she said in Arabic. *There was....* She exposed her forearms, the brown skin leathery and thin with age, the henna tattoo red and powdery. On each forearm was a wing, the wings of birds, the wings of Manāt, the female angel forgotten by Islam. "There was," she insisted.

The words came flooding back, his father smiling kindly as young Tariq asked, "What happened to Manāt, father?"

A Goddess does not die so easily, not when she is adored for thousands of years. Just as there are still Christian and Hebrew bedu who roam Sheba's deserts, so too is it said, there are tribes who remember the older ways... before the words of Abraham and Jesus and Muhammad.

The old woman motioned to Tariq, or the book. He wasn't sure it wasn't both, and he opened the journal of Abd-Es-Samad to the picture of the temple to indulge a curiosity that had gnawed at him since he first spoke with Farouk.

*"How do we enter the Temple of Manāt?"*Farouk had asked, and yet in the journal, the door was already open. Did Abd-Es-Samad seal the doors after he'd uncovered it? Is that why the remaining pages had been ripped out?

He needed to see for himself.

"Manāt,"he said simply as he stood. He did not expect them to stop him, and neither was Raakin standing guard outside....

The storm, a dervish of pinprick stings, swirled around Tariq and cajoled him through the half-buried streets of the lost city. He should not have been here; he was fellahin to the desert and it knew more ways to kill him than he knew to survive, but he shouldered over drifts and exposed layers of glazed macadam with their evenly polished stone.

The tan and bronze buildings towered over him, some block-like and Roman in appearance, some thin and fluted like the minarets of places he called home. Constantinople was a city adapting to the invention of Steamkraft, but Ubar had been built from a foundation of it. The roots of the towers and the marble obelisks were sheathed in a metallic base etched with intricate angled patterns. Why did it feel to Tariq that those structures could turn in their sockets like a shaft inside a gear? Statues of metal angels, men and women, adorned the tiered and terraced fountains that had run dry, and their copper feathers creaked and swung on articulated joints. What could only be lampposts lined the wide avenue, their thin polished wood stems branching into a sprout of glass bulbs. Those bulbs that hadn't been smashed and cracked glowed with wane strength, a firefly prick of light at the center of some liquid.

In the distance, the silhouette of giant metallic statues in shield-like plate filtered in and out of view from the storm. They measured the size of buildings and poked out at odd angles from the dunes; an arm here, a bent knee there, one statue on its knees crawling forward, as though the statues were moving when the desert claimed the city.

Tariq knew the answer. *Ubar was a madcap's city, a city built by dreamers and men and women of unbridled faith.*

From somewhere behind him he thought he heard shouting, perhaps the wail of a cranked siren. Then a piercing bellow of the aerostat's horn followed, the echo absorbed by the pitched storm. They knew he was missing. They'd started searching for him.

Tariq plowed straight and true to the heart of the city, to the Temple of Manāt itself according to the book. His hips and thighs ached to numb fatigue from the heavy sand. His shoulders throbbed with effort as he hugged the book tightly to his chest. Ahead, ghostly white lights appeared, first as wisps, then as burning torches in their glass housing. St. Elmo lanterns on poles lay planted outside the temple, some askance, some toppled. Up the stairs, winged statues stood vigil, ten on either side of a great metal door measuring a story high. As Tariq approached, he saw no handle, no seam to the door, just a mosaic of metal shards in the form of a... phoenix? No, the face was feminine. It was the Persian *Simorgh.*

The temple's door and its solid frame were battered and scored from cannon fire but intact. Picks and shovels poked out from the drifts against the wall, and a tent between two statues flapped on its last two pegs, exposing its wood crates.

Tariq ran up the exposed granite steps, grateful for the solid ground beneath his feet again. Along the wall, between the statues, was a frieze in bas-relief of birds and flowers, each made from a different metal, but he had little time to admire the artistry. A glance backwards showed the spotlights from the F-11's carbon arc lamps sweeping the desert, likely ahead of the soldiers. He had little time to lose.

Putting his back to the whipping winds, Tariq cracked open the book and glanced at the picture. It was hard to see, but he needed only a nudge to remember what his father had engrained in him: The door open, the statues holding two birds apiece in their outstretched hands. Tariq looked up at the statues, then down at the picture. The ten-foot high statues of the angels held no birds. Their arms were wings that swept forward into a cupping pose.

A mistake? Tariq wondered. *No, a clue from Abd-Es-Samad.*

"Well?" a voice asked, shouting over the winds.

Tariq started and looked back at Raakin, who watched patiently from the steps. The searchlights in the distance swept through the gloom to touch the temple, but couldn't reach. The soldiers would, undoubtedly.

"I need more time," he said.

Raakin, his expression inscrutable behind his goggles and keffiyah, pulled two tri-barrel flintlocks from under his jacket. He turned and vanished into the storm.

Tariq turned his attention to the statues and the question of the birds. Twenty statues, and a bird apiece in each hand. That was forty birds, the number of all myths. *Ali Baba and the Forty Thieves, the forty days and nights of Noah's flood, Moses alone with God on Mount Sinai, the years the Isrealites spent wandering the desert, the days Jesus spent in seclusion. Forty is not a number,* his father told him. *Forty simply means: A great many.*

"And the Simorgh? I remember, father," he said, the five year old in him touching the edges of the book, eager for adventure. As Tariq searched the frieze of metal birds and flowers, the poem came to him, again his father guiding him through the elegant verses of the great Sufi poet, Farid ud-Din Attar, and his seminal epic *The Conference of Birds*.

A council of birds set out to find the Simorgh to unite them, only to discover in their journey that Simorgh was a reflection of them all. "Could the inspiration for the poem be older? As old as this place?" Tariq wondered, his fingers touching upon golden larks and copper hawks and bronze sparrows. Then he saw a parrot inlaid with polished silver and his father spoke to him again. The birds stared into the pool where Simorgh lay and instead found their own reflection:

Come you lost Atoms to your Centre draw,
And be the Eternal Mirror that you saw:
Rays that have wander'd into Darkness wide
Return, and back into your Sun subside.

Silver was the most reflective of ancient metals, the mirror. Tariq pressed the bird and it shifted slightly in its groove. He pressed harder and it finally clicked down. Somewhere in the storm a flintlock roared, Raakin buying him time.

Tariq raced along the temple's front facing, searching for the next silver bird and found a silver peacock, and then a nightingale, a falcon, a hummingbird. Each clicked with some effort until finally, he found the silver hoopoe. He pressed it, and the heavy metal door with the Simorgh mosaic rattled upward.

The storm curled at the mouth of the temple where its howls turned to chambered echoes inside. Sand poured from the ceiling in trickles, leaving drifts along the stairs, but any semblance to the Nabatean ruins in Petra and in Beyrouth ended there. Tendrils of snaking copper fluted the columns, the temple a shell for the wide stairs that descended deep underground. Brass pipes inset into the stone walls lay partially hidden behind a lacework of wood grates. They still fed the balconies overflowing with leafy Emerald Falls vines and peppered with white hibiscus and urn-shaped clusters of blue Muscari. If these northern plants grew here, then Ubar and the Empty Quarter must have indeed have been a paradise once.

Outside, gunfire continued, sounding closer, but Tariq felt drawn down the steps. He took the path between the sloping sand, the interior dimly lit by tear-shaped bulbs set into wall sconces and column brackets. The liquid within the bulbs glowed silvery-blue like algae-filled water alight at night in the wake of fish and swimmer alike. The same blue came from the murals, where etched figures glowed with inset glass eyes.

The stairs opened onto a large platform overlooking a massive cavern covered in vegetation and whose edges vanished in darkness. Wide stairs wended down either wall, following rock carved with alcoves and ledges, half-columns and statues, like the Temple of Jupiter in the cliff of Petra. An oasis sparkled a hundred feet below, fed by glowing blue water with the viscosity of mercury that cascaded down the swept supplicant wings of a giant statue of Manāt. They'd built her from gleaming metal, each texture a different polish. Behind her stood her giant Fedayeen guards, each ten feet high. Each wore an iron-plated cuirass embossed gold with the Goddesses' wings, their spaulders and skirt-like cuisses covering their major joints.

Articulated joints, Tariq corrected. They could move, likely powered by the strange dynamos on their backs, their engines coiled with tubes and lit by glass capsules of the blue liquid. The same glow issued forth from the slits on their demonic faceplates. In their gauntlets they held a variety of swords and staves, axes and guns with a reservoir.

"The giants of Ubar," a voice said.

Raakin leaned against one of the columns on the stairs, looking down into the cavern.

"You're wounded."

Blood flowed down Raakin's limp arm and pattered on the floor. A blotch of mud matted the dark fabric at his shoulder, but he waved it off with the flintlock. "If they find this place, the Prussians will gain a considerable advantage, if not an insurmountable one," he said. "I gave them pause and us time, but... the desert is reclaiming this place. Can you seal the doors?"

Tariq nodded.

"Then go, quickly." Raakin handed him the flintlock. Tariq was about to refuse, but Raakin pushed it into his hands.

"I have never shot anyone."

"The gun has." Raakin shoved him up the stairs.

Tariq had a million questions that he wanted to ask, chief among them 'why?' but he understood as he raced upstairs and came upon the two-dozen bedu descending. They led their sheep and goats, their camels braying and protesting loudly at the steps, their clopping hoofs echoing sharply. Some of the injured bedu supported themselves on their flintlock rifles. A cluster of three guards protected the old woman from the tent; like the fabled

Taureg tribe of North Africa, Tariq realized, they were matriarchal and trapped among enemies who did not understand their ways. The worshippers of the old gods did not die so easily out here.

The old woman nodded at him and Tariq continued to the door. A handful of bedu fired out into the storm, the sands a hornet's nest that swallowed the city. The hillocks had already drowned the lower stairs and it felt as though the dunes themselves had begun to dwarf the buildings and columns... the frozen waves high above the doomed ship. Sand streamed and curled in through the door, and Tariq shielded his eyes.

Shapes moved in the storm at the base of the temple, and shots rang out as well as in. Something hot whined past Tariq's ear. He sank to his knee, out of sight of the soldiers as one of the bedu stumbled back, his hand clutching at his breast.

Tariq's heart raced. More shots whinged above his head, the shouting voices growing louder. He looked around him, trying to find the door mechanism, but his eyes refused to focus on any one thing. Was this how his father felt as they fled Damascus, the Pasha's men on their heels?

No. I am not alone.

From the corner of his eye, he caught the movement of pages. On a ledge nearby, the corners of ragged papers fluttered under the rock that held them in place. They were torn frail things, harrowed by the ages outside the protection of the book. Next to them sat a great gear embedded in the wall, a lever next to it, raised and waiting.

Silhouettes against the storm appeared at the top of the stairs. Tariq fired his flintlock, the gun flaring and jumping in his grip. A gout of flame roared out like a dragon's breath, and the figures jumped clear of the burst of fire, but not all. The bedu cheered, but if Tariq moved now, he thought the enemy might shoot him, kill him. That would be a mercy compared to losing everything, but after all he'd seen and come to know, letting these men take this place would be worse.

They'd chased his father from his truth once, and Tariq had done so again with his own heart. He would not let them triumph a third time. He ran for the lever, ran against the bullets that sang out for him. He lunged, dragging the lever down with the weight of his body, the hot blade of a round flashing across his back. Another bedu joined him, adding his weight to the teacher's. The gear rumbled and spun, almost cutting into his shoulder as it tore his shirt. The heavy door slammed shut, drowning out all but silence.

They all stared quietly at the Garden of Manāt below them. The bedu marveled and muttered soft prayers, some already descending to explore the cavern. There were trees and vegetation lit by the strange blue light that had powered this city; and beyond it? Tariq didn't know but the sleeping giants could not have come up by these stairs. There was more to discover deeper inside. Perhaps, even a way out.

A bandage covered Raakin's arm, and one of the women tended to the graze across Tariq's back. Tariq added the missing pages back to the tome and wondered what tales they would tell now.

How this place would have troubled the Muslims for its blatant iconography and delighted his father for its history. He could see the man now, his eyes narrowed in a smile, his voice delighted as he murmured:

Kan, ma kan.

There was, there was not.

Tariq finally understood why now—that what his father had sacrificed in the moment was nothing compared to what he was protecting. He'd left Damascus with the shirt on his back and his son's hand in his. What more did he need? Tariq understood, now, that not having everything was not the same as having nothing.

Tariq smiled. "There is, father," he said, and joined the others as they descended into the chamber.

Hatavat Chalom

Lillian Cohen-Moore

It is as always, the same.

The gates of the city rang beneath the siege forces, summoning sonorous booms that rivaled any thunder to be found in nature. Bombards and culverins filled the sky with sparks and smoke. Their wheels turned beneath them, large and unforgiving. The condottieri on the battle field followed the shouted orders of their Capitans, bound not by loyalty to the city state, but to the pay to come. The gendarmes were deep within the fighting; cutting men from their horses with bewildering speed, taking men from the battle as if they were of one mind, a many-headed *malakh ha-mavet*,the Angel of Death come to the battlefield of mortal men. For every gendarme taken from his horse, another took his place. The ground was carpeted in bodies, man and horse alike.

A once smoke-stained blue sky above them soon grew darker still. As if an eclipse was forming in the heavens above them, darkness began to fall over the battle. A single swath of long black shadow, married to a rumbling that shook the ground, a sound threatening to eclipse the clash of armies. It was not painted in the livery of a city-state, or that of a foreign King. It rose up from among them, its body metal, dark, the great grinding of wheels and gears serving as its own cracking vertebrae and clicking teeth. It steamed and moved, its gait steady. Its first step drew no great notice, but the second shook the ground.

It was a beast. A monster of gargantuan proportions, taller than a ballista, a mockery of the men around it, be they French or Italian. For it was not a man, but a wide expanse of metal unlike any they had ever seen. Its encroaching wheels came down upon a few unlucky fighters, and if they screamed louder than those dying around them, there was no way of sorting the sounds of their ignominious death from the slaughter at hand. It stopped moving, as mercenaries and loyal armies looked upon its visage, its black and copper body. For a breath, the world pulled upon itself, unsure of the thing that had entered it. The fighting slowed, ceasing in its shadow. And as the trembling fighters began to move away, its chest opened, a black void from which hellish smoke billowed, and from within it came a great wailing sound. Twin vibrations shook along the air, fire and forge laboring together.

The dream was always the same, the too-sharp smell of battle and fear, the intake of breath as they gazed upon the dark hole and the depths within it. From inside it came the flash of muzzles, and unholy sound of dozens of culverins, firing as one from inside its dark form. It was still the last thing she saw before her eyes opened to see the ceiling above her bed.

As she had for many mornings, Margarita Contanto woke screaming, the sound being torn from her body one of mindless, primal fear. Her Aunt Caterina was the one person in their home brave enough to try comforting her, to hold the thrashing younger woman firmly in her arms, ignoring the smears of tears soaking into the front of her dress, or the screams that caused her ears to ring.

Caterina would rise before the sun to take on matters of the household, but it was Margarita who would wake as the sunrise crept over the ghetto for the past month, waking the household along with her through the sound of her tortured screams.

Margarita joined her Aunt in her morning labors after she prepared herself to greet the day, returning the books hidden in her bedside to her absent Uncle's study. Math and science were for the hours no one was awake. Her morning would be one of labor with her family. Margarita's cousins, Lorenza and Fiora, were part of the complicated morning dance of cooking, sewing and correspondence. When Margarita reached for another piece of mending, her hand closed around an envelope instead. Startled, she raised her head to see her aunt.

"You have done more than enough work for the morning." Caterina reached out to touch her on the cheek, a gesture that summoned vague recollections of her own mother. "You must take this message into Ghetto Vecchio. There is a household there that awaits it." Caterina curved her fingers, pulling a few of Margarita's unruly curls behind one of the young woman's ear. "You will bear the letter for me, to Isaac de Fonseca's household. Give the letter to his sister, Veronica. Tell her your Uncle will come to them in a few weeks, when both he and Isaac have each returned from their journeys." Caterina waited for her niece's hand to withdraw the letter from the basket, and press it gently against her chest.

"I shall go now?"

Caterina went to reach her hand out again to touch her niece, but instead let it fall, her expression inscrutable. "Yes. Go now. I will see you when you have returned."

Margarita dwelled on the conversation as she went to prepare herself to leave for the Ghetto Vecchio, full of Levantine Jews from the Ottoman Empire. She repeated the directions back to Caterina three times before her Aunt would let her step out the door. Carrying the message against herself, arms folded over her chest, she made haste to cross the island of the Ghetto Nuovo. Between the two ghettos was a simple bridge over a canal, and it was that slender ribbon of connection she would use to cross into the other ghetto. The rain falling on the stones beneath her feet was not yet a downpour, content to fall upon her as a mist, with few droplets rising back up from the ground, inundating her with the smell of moist cloth and stone. For a moment, the earthen smell of wet stone tugged at her memory, the smell of the battered city walls beneath the siege engines. Had it been raining in her nightmare?

She shook her head as she went over the bridge, quickening her pace. It was a dream. A strange, frightening dream, and one day it would go away and she would be as she was before it came— without a single recollection of a dream. Her passage into the Vecchio streets was unremarkable. The smells of bread, pastry, wet stones and hot air were the same in either ghetto, though the scent of metal was still curiously stronger off the island and on the streets of Ghetto Vecchio. Even with the rain, the sunshine still struggled through the clouds above her. It would be hours till sunset, and she would surely return to Ghetto Nuovo by then, ready to be locked inside with the rest of her people, as she had every night for as long as she had lived. Only from dawn to dusk were they even remotely free.

Distressed by the dark turn of her own thoughts, she raised her head, eyes and nose drinking in the Vecchio streets. At least confined to the ghettos from dusk to dawn, locked in by the government, they were safer from those who hated the Jews of Venice. Margarita shook her head, as if to force the thoughts away, focusing on her task. Across the streets, away from the canals, the scents of unfamiliar spices would weave across the air, scents that grew stronger, even in the slowly worsening rainfall, when she approached the home of the trader Isaac de Fonseca.

Their front door was a blue unlike any she had seen, and the house of de Fonseca was considerably larger than the Cantanto residence. She sat with no little apprehension in the reception room after a servant abandoned her, in order to fetch Veronica. Margarita blew gently on the envelope as she waited, as if her breath would somehow cure the dampness of the paper. The reception room was both familiar and jarring, filled with Italian furniture of an older style, and art that rang as clearly foreign. Perhaps art from the Empire? She mused on the origins of what she saw around her, uncertain about something as normal as décor, and attempted to estimate the mathematical measurement of the room and furniture to pass the time.

Veronica de Fonseca did not enter the reception room, she graced it. Her hair was thick and dark, strands of white darting in and out without pattern or reason. The rings she wore on her hands were different from the jewelry Margarita had seen worn by women in Venice. Margarita had no chance to introduce herself; no sooner had she risen to her feet, Veronica seized her hands, envelope pressed awkwardly inside their clasping hands.

"Caterina always promised she would send you to me someday!" She took in Margarita's befuddled expression, transferring the envelope to one of her own hands as she continued to clasp one of the younger woman's hands, pulling her down with her to sit upon the couch. "I am a friend of your Aunt and Uncle's. I have not been here in many years, but Caterina had sworn she would let me see you." She clicked her tongue against her teeth, smiling. "You were such a beautiful little girl, now a lovely young woman." Veronica took back her hand, prying the envelope open with ease. "You must stay for lunch."

Margarita watched Veronica reading; saw the brief flicker of concern on her face. "I should be going. My Aunt will worry if I'm gone too long." Unspoken, the knowledge of the curfew hung between them. Veronica raised her head, smiling again, the crow's feet around her eyes forming a nest of marks around her crinkling eyes. "We will get you home in time. But I insist you stay for lunch, and tell me all about what Caterina has been up to. I only just returned to Venice, and she has not found time to come to me!"

Veronica folded the letter in half, and moved it back into the safety of its envelope. Margarita, stunned at the notice and attention of someone outside her family, managed to murmur what she assumed was agreement. Veronica again smiled, leading her by the hand from the reception room. Lunch was indoors, bemoaned by her hostess as they listened to the ever-strengthening rain slapping against the outside world with ferocious speed. The wind was just as fierce, and Margarita felt her heart sink when one of the de Fonseca servants entered the dining room. The maid's expression of concern raised an equal measure of uncertainty in Veronica's face. "What is it? Is Isaac —"

The maid shook her head. "No, Signora. It is the storm. We fear flooding, and must tell you not to go forth till the storm passes." Veronica looked at Margarita, noting her expression of alarm.

"You may stay here tonight, Margarita, if the storm has not passed in time to get you home. Your family has always been welcome in our home, and that has not changed." Veronica's grave expression lightened. "Now, you said you help Caterina with the art of the needle, and I am sure I can find you something in the house to pass your time."

The younger woman nodded numbly, returning to the meal as Veronica did, after dismissing the maid. Her appetite diminished, she spent her attention on answering Veronica's questions about her own household skills, troubled by her sudden stranded status in the Ghetto Vecchio.

Fears of flooding rose as fast as the tide did. The storm steadily worsened as the day progressed, and Margarita bent her head over foreign fabric and thread, assisting Veronica in the assembly of garments for a Torah. Each tiny stitch took her further outside of herself and her concerns. When Veronica informed her she would have to stay the night, she barely acknowledged the distressing news, her senses anchored in her fingertips, and each small stitch. Her Uncle had once told her that her father had been the same, writing in his books without any hearing of the world outside his pen and paper. When Veronica spoke of dinner, she shook her head.

"I feel quite poorly, Signora. I am so sorry."

Veronica leaned from her seat, and placed a hand against the young woman's cheek. "You are cold. Would you like to go to bed for a time, and see if your appetite returns?"

Margarita nodded, swallowing as a wave of nausea passed through her stomach. Veronica placed her in a room near the top of the house, alike in placement, but not quality, of her room at her aunt's house. At home, she slept in a small room away from everyone; a blessing to the house in recent weeks, for the distance muffled her screams.

Here, the chamber was equipped with a bed that all but swallowed her, that smelled of unfamiliar spices that offered a strange comfort. She was asleep within a few, deep breaths, moments after she had lain down. Once again, Margarita was watching the great, monstrous metal device advancing on the gendarmes and the mercenaries, smelling the blood already bathing the battlefield. She saw the copper and iron of the machine, even as she stood in the tip of its shadow beneath the smoke-streaked sky.

She knew this thing. Not how or why, but she did know its sounds and sighs, and once again a porthole opened, and the cacophony of culverins began, explosive force that would come for her and rip her ap—

Veronica was there at the bedside, gathering Margarita up in her arms as the younger woman choked, fighting for air under the weight of her own dread. She rocked her, murmuring against her ear, snatches of almost-familiar lullabies drawing her back into the waking world, heart slowing its painful pounding inside her chest. Margarita withdrew from her embrace, wiping tears from her eyes. "I apologize for the noise." She sounded breathy, shaken, even to her own ears.

The older woman shook her head. "Screams from a bad dream are preferable to screams over an intruder." Veronica patted Margarita's hand.

"It must be quite fearsome, to cause such a strong girl to scream. Would you like to speak of it?"

Margarita raised her head, eyes widening. "I..." she licked her lips, aware of the dryness of her lips and mouth, throat tender from screaming. "I've never spoken to anyone about it." Veronica curled her hand around Margarita's, squeezing it.

"You can cure the dream." Veronica was silent for a moment. "I'm sure your aunt would have taught you. Hatavat chalom. Tell me. Tell others. Let us tell you of the good in it, so it will not haunt you or come to pass as truth."

With great hesitation, Margarita began to speak. "It starts with a blue sky, full of smoke, and the sounds of a great battle..."

Margarita left the de Fonseca home, under-slept but heart lightened. The lightness sank as she took in the sight of the flooding that came in the night. Though the high waters had receded, damage and watermarks remained. She had been told once of a flood from when she was a child, too young to remember. She listened to people as she walked back, from the streets of Ghetto Vecchio to her own Ghetto Nuovo. The flooding, and the storm, had stopped just short of dawn.

She bore a basket of pastries from Veronica for the Contanto residence, and told the story of her overnight stay in the de Fonseca home in distracted bursts. Her cousins wanted to know about Veronica's dress, her manners, and the inside of her house. It took Caterina reprimanding them to let her attend to her sewing in peace, turning Veronica's words over and over again in her mind.

It is about the will of the Lord, Margarita. You do not see the victors or the cause of the battle because only the Eternal King can determine our fates.

If she wished to complete the ritual to make her dream better, she would have to tell it two more times. She pricked her finger as her hands stumbled, struck with fear at the thought. Not even Caterina had asked about the nightmare's *content.* If she could not tell her aunt, who else could she tell? It was another three nights before the answer came to her, in the smiling face of her newly returned uncle. She would tell Abram Contanto, and trust that he would have the wisdom to give her proper counsel.

Perhaps counsel strong enough to end the dream. Margarita waited through the affectionate greetings of her cousins and aunt for Abram, and the hours of stories, two meals, and the return of her cousins to their beds before she would brave his study to talk to him. Margarita knocked softly on his study door, entering only after her bid her to do so.

He removed his glasses, restoring the ordinary appearance of his eyes, as he leaned back in his chair. "How is my little Rita?"

She dragged one of the small stools in the room to sit beside him at his desk, taking a deep breath. "I...I have been having a bad dream, since you left."

Abram raised his eyebrows. "A? Only one dream?"

"Every night, Uncle. And it repeats. It is always the same." He watched her unhappy visage, nodding in silent encouragement. "I dream of a battle. There are mercenaries, and foreign armies. They lay siege against a city, and everywhere trembles under the weight of the siege engines and the fighting. The air is full of smoke. The sky is blue."

"Have you been reading histories while I have been gone?" At her expression of surprise, he chuckled. "I know you come to the study sometimes when I am not here, to read. It is not love stories, so I let it be."

She shook her head. "No, Uncle. Not histories or love stories. There is..." she raised her hands, trying to summon the machine of her nightmares. "...a machine. A terrible machine, like none I have seen. With walls of copper and iron, and it moves on many wheels and hums with fire and gears."

Abram's expression grew somber. He placed a hand on her own. "And this machine?"

"It rolls over the men on the battlefield. It is tall, and casts a long shadow. It's...the face of it opens, and many culverins fire from within it. And I wake screaming. Convinced I am in front of it, and about to die."

They sat in silence as Abram withdrew his hand, thinking. After a time, he nodded to himself. "Perhaps it is about the power of a people. A community." He kept his gaze locked on her face, looking into her eyes. "One people, united, can do great and fearsome things, Rita. They can protect things others would steal from them." Abram gently placed his hand upon her shoulder. "Is that all you wished to speak of?"

After a moment, she exhaled, looking down into her lap. "I know it. I do not know how, but I *know* the machine."

"You believe you have seen it before?"

Margarita struggled to breath, to think, forcing herself to lift her head. "Uncle, I think I may have *made* it. But I know not how such a thing could be."

"You have studied the books of science and mathematics in my study, yes?"

"Yes."

"You ask me about the wonders I have seen in the world, and the news of new science?"

"Yes, Uncle, but what does th—"

Abram held up a finger. "Rita. You have not had the same life your father had, you have not been an artist distracted by science before. But you have his talent for drawing, for thinking. For wanting to know. Tomorrow, I will send a servant to fetch you art supplies. You will draw this machine. Perhaps that will cure your dream, and convince your soul that it is but a fancy, not a thing to be achieved in form."

Abram was good to his word. Their servant came and went before the Sabbath, and the package sat in her room under the miniscule excuse for a desk beneath her small window. There was plenty of moonlight, and the house was asleep. She knew that even though they did not cleave to things as strongly as others might, that to take ink to paper on the Sabbath would cause even Caterina to frown.

This is why she was as quiet as she could when she opened the package. She weighed a long piece of vellum down, and began to draw. Not the battle or the bloodshed. But the machine. Abram had not misspoken; she did know mathematics and science, far more than many women did. But she could not make sense of how such a machine could work. Yet still, she drew. It was massive, long, a fearsome expanse of metal. Details came to her that she had never fully recalled after the nightmare and those too she rendered on paper.

She had little knowledge of metalwork, and only slightly more about the use of gears, and soon Margarita's head swam with questions, questions she committed to another piece of paper. She crawled into bed hours after the house had fallen asleep, and by morning she clawed her way out of her bed linens, gasping, sweat soaked, and thankful to be alive. She had dreamt of the culverins again, somehow visible when they had not been before.

To draw it was not the cure.

Abram had begun taking time every night to grill her about the device, and her slowly changing nightmare. Each night she would pray, before lying down in her bed, staring up at the ceiling. No more did she feel an unequal opponent to the nightmare. It still scared her, terrified her deeply, but with Abram's support she went to bed each night to fight with it. Jacob had survived wrestling an Angel. She could survive battle with a brutal dream, challenge it to give her details. But two weeks after his return, a gilt-touched envelope arrived from the de Fonseca house. Isaac was home, and Veronica wished to invite them to dine at their home in honor of her brother's safe return. Abram only laughed when Margarita muttered a complaint, head bent over a book they had begun to study, on the construction of ancient siege engines.

"Why do you not wish to go, Rita?"

She sighed forcefully, before gesturing to the book. "This is important. Why is dinner with the de Fonseca's more important than this?"

"Because they are our people, and we must celebrate our survival whenever and wherever we can." He squeezed her shoulder, and shook his head as she went to question him. "No, Rita. We shall end early tonight. Go rest, for tomorrow is a different kind of labor."

The dinner included not only the de Fonseca siblings, Margarita and her aunt and uncle, but a few men she did not know as well. She and Caterina were introduced to Justefino Rosso and Mordechai Bellini. Margarita spoke little over the dinner, concentrating on the strange currents in the air around them. Caterina knew neither man, but the blithe way her aunt spoke to them was an illusion, a distraction to keep them from noticing her shaking hands and the tight set of her shoulders, something Margarita expected no one outside their household to know. Abram kept looking at Isaac de Fonseca as if he could speak to the man only with his eyes, which held something close to anger or contempt. Veronica plied her wits against both her aunt and Justefino, and as the dinner dragged on, Margarita was increasingly certain he was not Venetian—perhaps not even Italian.

Despite her discomfort in sensing she was missing something, she did her best to speak when spoken to, and say little else. When they each came to say goodnight to the de Fonsecas, Isaac looked as if he wanted to say something, but held it back. He gave Margarita a brief smile instead.

"Thank you, for the company you gave my sister while I was absent. It means much to me, that she finds friends in Venice." Margarita's brow furrowed, she summoned a sincere, but bewildered thank you of her own, claimed within moments by her aunt and uncle for the return home. The shadows were not yet long, but they made haste regardless. The smallest glance back over her shoulder revealed the figure of Veronica at one of the front windows, but soon both house and womanly shadow were concealed by the turn of the street. She tried to put the strange evening out of her mind, but Abram sending her to bed once they returned home, and the odd dinner, preyed upon her mind.

She paced her small room for some time after dressing for bed, trying to discern the meaning of the many things left unsaid at the dinner, and the few that had been given voice. Her nightmare was splintered and disorganized, without insight and left only with a ringing in her ears. She went straight to her needlework after dressing for the day, shrugging off Caterina's concerns with a shake of her head.

"Work will clear my head, Aunt. Please let me work."

She bent her head back down before Caterina could protest, listening with only half her attention to the household rising from its nightly rest. Mouthing the words with her head bowed over her sewing, she thanked the Eternal King for returning the souls of their household to them, and for allowing them to rise refreshed to greet another day. She prayed infrequently, following Caterina's example in that regard, but the dream was still not cured, and perhaps prayer would help where other things had failed.

With that thought, she paid no more heed to her surroundings, jarred from her productive haze by the sound of distant shouting. Her cousins were themselves loudly talking with their mother, and the vibration of the nearby argument was a brief tremor in the air between their breaths. She left her needle gently hooked on her project, and excused herself with little ceremony. Her shoes were soft on the floor, following the few simple turns and stairs toward the now considerably quieter study of her Uncle. She hesitated at the door, straining her ears to listen, unsure of the words, only Abram's tone—both angry and pleading.

Margarita raised her hand, knocking twice about the door with her knuckles. Instead of sending her away, her Uncle opened the door, yanking her in and shutting it behind her. Across her Uncle's desk sat Isaac de Fonseca. He looked under-slept, skin swept with ashen pallor beneath his dark color. He looked upon her like he had never seen her before, as if she were not an orphan ward, but something strange and unknowable.

Margarita drew her shoulders in, unconscious of her need to become smaller. "Uncle?"

Abram pointed at Isaac, the gesture accusatory, his tone a venomous hiss. "He does not understand my concerns about the country, Rita. Tell him. Tell him of the dream."

She pressed a hand against her middle, opening her mouth to plead, but Abram's look in her direction stopped her. Whatever was going on, his anger, rare to appear, would not vanish unless quenched. Unless she yet again repeated her dream. Margarita leaned against the door, forcing herself not to sag inward. She focused her eyes not on the fury of her Uncle's form, but on Isaac's face. His eyes were also full of anger, but concern came with it.

Concern for her?

"I have a dream. I...it has come for weeks. Every night. Even in your home, when I was unable to leave the night of the flood." Her breaths felt uneven beneath her clothes, as if her hammering heart would tear forth from her chest and stain corset and chemise alike beneath her burgundy gown.

"There is a battle. Pitched and brutal, Italians against French." She felt her eyes water with unshed tears, unsure of why it felt so difficult this time, the third time, in the telling. "There is a machine. It casts a shadow upon the battle. And it grinds, with wheels and gears. It is a towering thing of copper and iron, and I know not how it is propelled. But it moves forward, and crushes men beneath it." Isaac rose from his chair at her words, his look to Abram both betrayal and confusion.

"It does not stop. It keeps on going forward, and a—a hole opens up in its front. Inside there is steam, and warmth, and culverins. Perhaps a dozen. Firing as one."

Silence. Her heart felt as if it would stop, before Isaac finally spoke. "Perhaps it was a dream of conquest over a great challenge." He looked at her, as if desperate for this interpretation to be agreed upon, and save them both from further words. Abram's tone was harsh in answer.

"You know what she dreams of, yet you still insist on looking away." Margarita looked between both men, light headed from speaking, the unceasing pounding in her chest.

"Abram—"

Her Uncle seized Isaac by his shoulders. "If she is taken from here, she can complete it. If she can complete it, we can be saved."

"Uncle—"

"Abram—"

Abram looked at them both, his expression somber, hollow. "I know you are confused, Rita. And I wish I could explain this to its fullest extent, but you must be sent away from the ghetto. For your safety. For all of our safety. And if Isaac can take you to the Empire, you may solve the riddle of your great machine. And it is safer there, far safer, than life here. Life under the Muslims is far more tolerable, and questions will not be asked there as they were here. But Isaac must be the one to take you."

Margarita wasn't sure if the sound that came from her lips was laughter or tears. "I must make the machine? Why? And why Isaac? Shall he disguise me like Sarah was, and he shall tell the Sultan I am his sister?"

"He shall say you are his wife." Abram spoke the words in low, even tones. "And you shall be married to him before you leave Italy. He shall take his bride to the Empire to see his homeland, and enjoy a land unlike her native Venice. There, you will build the machine, or Venice shall fall beneath the French, and only the Eternal King knows if the Jews shall survive. Isaac is to take you because he is not a foreigner there; despite the faith we all share in this room."

Isaac reached for her hand, but let his drop when she shrank away, eyes filled with tears. "And if I refuse?"

Abram shrugged. "Then I will try and reason with you."

"And if I continue to refuse?"

"Then you will stay. And when the French come to Venice, the children of Israel will die in the streets. As we often do, when invaders come to a place that houses us with disdain and hate."

Margarita could feel her composure failing, the tremble through her lips and chin warning of tears to come. She slipped out the door before they could speak to her again, running for the front door and then out it, barely pausing to seize her cloak. She kept her head bowed as she ran for the bridge between the ghettos, Old and New, one hand pressed against her mouth to muffle her weeping. She felt hot and cold, lightheaded and unable to think. Fear and betrayal and anger lashed around inside her, angry snakes that choked and bit within. She cried on the bridge, cried till her face was swollen and she felt as if she would vomit into the canal water. She gripped the bridge, waiting for reprisal, for Abram to drag her back. To force her into a plan she barely understood.

Isaac was the one to come for her, not with anger but sympathy, and a scrap of cloth that she ran across her face, drying the ends of tear tracks. Her voice was hoarse and miserable. "So I am to be your wife, and go forth to a strange land? To build something I don't understand for a war *that isn't even here yet?*"

She looked up at him, both of them pressed against the railing of the bridge. Isaac was older than her, surely in his thirties. Wouldn't Abram listen to him? All he had to do was say he couldn't take her, couldn't marry her. He didn't touch her, but he stood closely, body radiating warmth.

"Perhaps the dream is about a triumph of yours, Margarita. Of winning against impossible odds."

"Winning a war for Venice?" She laughed, the sound cold and broken.

"Winning a war for yourself. I...I am no prophet. And I think you know that both my household and your own, we know things few do, or would expect us to." He placed his hand on the railing, close to hers, yet still not touching. "What he is asking, we must both agree to do. I will not touch you, put a hand upon you, or force you to do anything as my wife. I will not let him make you do this, if you do not wish to. If you doubt his intentions, his methods, I will continue in my life as you do in yours. But if you believe the counsel of your Uncle, that this is a task only you can accomplish, there are many engineers in the Empire. Forges and foundries would not be hard to find. And there is a man, in another part of the Empire, who seeks to build an engine to drive machines—one made of steam."

Steam and smoke. Her gasp was slight, but her thoughts were already tumbling. Depending on the placement and size, perhaps a dual—

Perhaps it could be done. And if it could be done, if it was even *possible*, perhaps this would cure her dream.

Margarita shook her head, glancing down at their hands. "You will help protect me?"

"With all I have to offer to that service." Isaac was serious, sincere, and did not smile when she looked back up. Their hands stayed as they were, next to each other.

If it was possible that she could do what had been asked of her, children like Lorenza and Fiora might not have to die.

"When could we leave?"

The Leviathan of Trincomalee

Lucy A. Snyder

Thilini Rothschild saw the green fireball streaking across the sky above the coconut palms before her father did. "Look, Papa!"

"Why, that's an extraordinary meteor! I've never seen one of such color." He peered out at the night sky through his workshop window. "Good thing that will crash far out in the Indian Ocean and not in a city!"

Thilini gazed at the fireball's sparkling emerald tail, entranced and yet feeling a bit crestfallen. "I hoped it was falling star so I could wish upon it."

"Why, I'm sure a fine meteor such as that is just as wish-worthy!"

So she closed her eyes and thought, *I wish for an adventure!*

Three years later, Thilini had forgotten all about the meteor. She woke before the first crows of her mother's junglefowl, wound on her favorite green sari, and slipped out to the kitchen to gather some cold chickpea fritters and jackfruit in a basket. Her father would still be at his workshop by the harbor; no doubt he'd been working on his wireless telegraph machine all night. He'd probably forgotten to eat.

Excitement jittered in her stomach. Today was the day the *Southwind* would return, her hold creaking with goods. If the special gears and glass panels her father had commissioned from his partners in Switzerland arrived with it, that meant they might finally be able to assemble the submarine prototype she and her father had been working on for the past year. Thilini couldn't wait to see the ocean from beneath the waves.

She hefted the reed basket over one shoulder, slipped into the sandals her mother made her leave by the front door, and ran down the wagon-rutted road to the harbor shops. To her surprise, a stout, balding man was standing in the shop, arms crossed. Her father frowned up at him from his workbench, his eyes shadowed in the flickering candlelight. Biting her lip, she pushed open the front door, quietly so the bells wouldn't jingle.

"You're wasting your talents here," the stranger lectured in German. "You need to go back to Europe. Or at least come to our estate in Kandy."

Her father pulled off his wire-framed round glasses and pinched the bridge of his nose. His long curly brown hair had come loose from its queue. He looked exhausted. "I'm fine, Martin. The clean air here suits me more than the noise and stink of Frankfurt or London."

He looked past Martin and his eyes focused on Thilini.

"Ah, you brought breakfast?" he asked her in Tamil.

"Yes, Papa. Who is this?"

"Your uncle Martin," he continued, still speaking in her native language. "Pay him and his unpleasantness no mind."

"Yes, Papa."

"'Attān'?" Martin said, repeating her endearment, staring at Thilini. Recognition seemed to dawn; he grimaced in disgust. He stared back down at her father, eyebrows raised. "Are you this little pickaninny's sire?"

Her father turned red as a berry, his fists clenching in his lap. "I'll not have you speak about my daughter in such a debased fashion."

"Debased?" Martin exclaimed. "It is you who have debased our family! Rothschilds dance in the courts of every ruler in Europe, and yet here you are, tinkering in the sand, breeding like a mongrel with the first brown bitch who wiggles her tail at you."

It was Thilini's turn to feel the blood rise in her face. She could bear insults to herself with all the quiet grace her parents had taught her, but she would not stand by while this stranger spoke so badly of her mother. But her father responded before she could open her mouth.

"I have lived upon five continents." Her father's voice shook with rage. "And Thilini's mother is the finest woman I have ever met. None of the simpering court ladies you and your brothers deemed so suitable as matches have half the beauty, intelligence, or courage of my dear Anula."

"Indeed," Thilini replied in her best German. "If my mother is such a poor match for my father, I should be a useless idiot, should I not? So, test me. Ask me any question you like, in any language you like."

Martin was clearly surprised she knew German at all. "Who's the tsar of Russia?"

"Alexander the Third."

"And the President of the United States?"

"Grover Cleveland. Please, do ask me something difficult, dear Uncle."

Martin frowned. "What's the square root of eighty-one?" he asked in French.

"Nine," she replied in English.

"What are the components of black powder?" he asked in German.

"Sulfur, charcoal, and saltpeter," she replied in French. "I can make you some if you like. The recipe is easier than my mother's fish soup."

"Why doesn't your father's wireless telegraphy machine work?"

She smiled at him. "And now you're fishing for trade secrets, Uncle."

Her uncle stared at her. "How old are you?"

"I shall be thirteen in two months."

After Martin left, her father fussed at her a bit for speaking so boldly to her uncle, but clearly he was proud of her. They ate the breakfast she brought, and then he sent her down to the docks with their portable telegraph prototype. It was based on some of the correspondences he'd had with the American inventor Brooks. The device almost worked, but the power supplies they'd tried were insufficient for the components.

"I'm sure the new electrochemical cells will do the trick. It's just a matter of fine-tuning the equipment," he said as he loaded the sixty-pound rig onto her little palmwood wagon.

"Can we make it smaller?" she asked doubtfully.

He laughed. "Reliability first. Miniaturization second."

Thilini hauled the wagon down to the docks and took up a vantage point where she could keep watch for the tall sails of the *Southwind*. Occasionally, part of a telegraph would come through; she'd transcribe the message and jot down the time in her notebook. The first time they'd gotten anything at all to transmit and be received through thin air, they'd both been overjoyed. But getting an entire message to go through over distances more than ten feet or so had proved a confoundingly difficult challenge.

Science, she mused, involved an awful lot of waiting and doing-over.

Her reverie was broken by the shouts of men. She stood. The *Southwind* had sailed into view ... but she was too low in the sea, and listing so far to one side she looked in danger of capsizing. Had the ship broken its hull on a coral reef?

"She's taking on water fast!" the stevedore shouted. "Every man with a boat, get out there! We need to get that cargo off!"

Two hours later, Thilini stood with her father as two deeply tanned dockworkers pulled the precious Swiss crates from the deck of a patamar that had been pressed into rescue duty. The crates were so waterlogged that she would not have been surprised to hear fish flopping inside them. The glass would be fine, provided it had not been mishandled, but she cringed at the corrosion the seawater would wreak on the delicate gears if they were not carefully rinsed, dried, and re-oiled.

"Please, get these back to my shop as quickly as you can," her father told the men of the hired wagon.

"Yes, Herr Rothschild." They quickly set to loading up the crates.

The stevedore approached them, shaking his head. He was a small, wiry man who looked Tamil but he wore a Catholic rosary over his loose cotton shirt and had a slight Portuguese accent. "A third of the cargo lost, and five sailors sent to the Almighty. The ship can't be repaired in the water, so we need to find some way to haul 'er in to dry-dock before she sinks. And I ain't convinced she won't just sink."

"Was it a reef?" Thilini asked.

"If only!" the stevedore replied. "We could dodge a reef, but this ... well, come see. Perhaps your papa can make heads or tails of this deviltry."

Further down, another boat had come in bearing a broken plank from the hull. Not broken, she realized. Something had bitten it in half! Imbedded in the stout English timber was a shark's tooth of far greater size than any she'd imagined. The biggest one she'd seen until then was about the size of a gold sovereign coin.

"Mein gott," her father breathed. He laid his hand beside the protruding tooth; it was larger than his palm and outstretched fingers. "What leviathan could grow such a fang? Some type of cachalot whale?"

"*Carcharodon carcharias,*" came a voice behind them.

Thilini turned. Trincomalee's resident naturalist, the retired physician Edward Kelart, was gazing at the tooth with grave concern. He leaned heavily against his silver-filigreed cane, which he'd needed to use ever since a hard voyage to England had nearly killed him two decades before.

"That tooth's far too large to come from a great white shark," her father countered.

"Indeed," Dr. Kelart said. "But the tooth shape is distinct, and unmistakable. If it is not some ancient great white grown to immense size, it is a close cousin."

The imported glass was in fine shape, and Thilini and her father were able to clean all the gears they needed for their submersible prototype. In just a few months, they had his latest invention ready to test in the waters. The gleaming fifteen-foot submarine was skinned in copper and steel, courtesy of the fine craftsmanship of the local metal smiths. The sub was sleek as a dolphin, with round fore and aft windows and triangular fins for stability. Her father's patented, self-contained steam engine powered the screw-shaped propellers at the rear of the sub and electric headlights.

"This is just a miniature version of what I propose to build later," her father remarked to the stevedore, who helped them guide the sub down the wooden ramp into the water. "We must test every aspect of the craft, of course."

"You're letting the girl pilot this thing?" Astonishment was plain on the stevedore's face.

Thilini ignored him and focused on buttoning up her black rubber suit. The feel of the tight material against her legs was strange; she was used to airy saris and sarongs, but skirts would drag her down in the water if she needed to abandon ship. She hoped the coolness of the sea would help counteract the heat from the steam engine. Otherwise, she'd be stewed like a whiting in a parchment bag before her three hours of air were depleted.

"She knows every rivet and gear of this craft, and she is a far better swimmer than I," her father said. "Further, we had to build the sub at such a limited scale that I can scarcely fit in it myself!"

The men helped her squeeze through the top hatch of the sub.

"Don't go out of the shallows at first, and if the craft is sound, don't take her farther than Pigeon Island," her father admonished.

"I won't," she promised.

They sealed the hatch above her, and moments later the sub lurched as the men pushed it into the water. Thilini said a quick prayer and pulled the lever to start the steam engine. The whole craft shook as the fire ignited in the belly of the sub and the boiler began to steam. She busied herself checking pressure and temperature gauges, then went around the inside of the craft, checking all the brass and copper pipe fittings and wall panels for leaks.

After a half-hour, she was certain the engine was operating as expected and the craft was watertight. She settled in the leather-padded pilot's chair and cautiously steered the craft toward Pigeon Island.

The undersea coral reefs were breathtakingly beautiful; Thilini had seen plenty of brightly-colored fish pulled up by fishermen, but she had never imagined the coral itself would be such a gorgeous wonderland. She felt as though she had been transported to an entirely different world, and that she was not traveling through water but soaring above a dazzling forest on a planet lit by a foreign star.

A pod of curious porpoises swam along next to her craft. Their squeals and clicks echoed through the cabin. The sea mammals seemed to smile at her through the windows, and she could not help but smile back at them as they somersaulted and cavorted.

One porpoise paused and let out a squeal. She and her sisters swam together and huddled with their snouts pointed at each other for a moment; Thilini had the impression they were urgently discussing something. Then they broke away from the sub, swimming fast toward the shallows, all traces of playfulness gone.

What had alarmed them? She peered out through the front window into the deeper water beyond the island. And there swam a lone whale. Not a great blue whale, but a younger toothy orca she guessed was not much longer than the five yards of her submarine. No doubt he was what frightened off her cetacean friends.

I should like to see a whale up close, she thought. She'd seen plenty of dead whales brought to the harbor, but that wasn't nearly the same as seeing one in its natural world. *The engine is fine; a quick look won't hurt anything.*

She pushed the craft forward, gently, to prevent frightening the creature. It was certainly big enough to ram the submarine if it deemed her a threat. The orca turned and gazed at her curiously when she was about a hundred yards away. She stopped the craft, holding her breath, hoping the creature was not territorial.

Suddenly, a huge dark shape torpedoed up from the murky depths below the orca. Thilini saw a jagged maw as wide as her craft open in a flash, sucking the orca down into it, and close with a sickening crack of bone. The force of the bite cut the orca right in two. Blood stained the water in scarlet clouds.

The leviathan shark wolfed the orca down in two gulps, and then righted itself to face the submarine. It looked roughly like the great whites the fishermen had speared in the shallows, but this creature's skin about its head and jaws was armored with thick denticle scales; its snout looked more like a medieval battering ram. And this monster was far, far larger than any shark she'd ever seen. It was easily four times the length of her submarine.

The monstrous creature began to swim toward her.

Thilini shrieked and pulled the sub around, shoving the steam engine into full speed. She ignored the groaning of the boiler and the rattling of metal as she forced the sub faster and faster, convinced the dire monster was right behind, jaws opening, ready to snap the sub in two.

In her panic, she grounded the sub in the shallows several hundred yards north of the harbor. She killed the engine, got the hatch open with numb, shaking hands, and splashed to land where she collapsed on the sand and gave in to her desire to weep.

Herr Rothschild believed his daughter's story straight away. But since she was merely a girl and deemed subject to frivolous flights of fancy, most others were skeptical and, despite the evidence from the *Southwind*, claimed she'd been frightened by a common cachalot whale or even a mere barracuda.

But in the following week, an East India Company cargo ship was attacked and most of the crew drowned or eaten. And the week after that, they got word of similar disastrous attacks on ships near Colombo and Batticaloa. More and more people heard and believed Thilini's account of the leviathan shark; townsfolk and visiting officials asked her to tell her story so many times that the repetition almost sapped the terror from her memory. Almost. The terrible shark swam through nightmarish seas in her mind when she tried to sleep, and she'd start awake, feeling herself drowning, feeling those awful teeth closing down on her body.

"Our family has lost three ships," her Uncle Martin fretted one day. "I cannot take my tea to Europe! The sailors fear this monster like nothing else. We must kill the beast, or drive it away, or else we will be paupers!"

"What would you have me do?" her father asked.

"I would have you build a mighty version of the submersible you tested. Something armed with a powerful harpoon, and a hull built to withstand the pressures of the depths. I would have you build a craft fit to hunt this leviathan down and kill it in its lair."

"If it's a harpoon you need, why not gird a whaling ship in iron and send her and her crew after the shark?"

Uncle Martin shook his head. "The Bombay and British navies have tried that very thing, to no avail. I read survivor's reports; only the head of the shark is visible during its attack, and that part is so well-armored that even harpoons fired from cannons cannot harm it."

"What about a harpoon down its gullet?" her father asked.

"No man who has tried such a shot has lived. The naturalists speculate that the shark may have a softer underbelly that is vulnerable, but there is no way to reach it from the surface of the sea."

"What about explosives?" Thilini asked.

"That, too, has been tried," her uncle replied gravely, "with no better result."

He turned to her father. "We need a working version of your machine."

Her father paused, chewing on a corner of his moustache thoughtfully. "I could build a submarine such as you describe, but I haven't the materials or craftsmen to attempt it."

"I will get you anything you need. Anything at all. I have spoken to officers in the British Navy, and they have agreed to fund your enterprise. Glass, metals, workers ... tell me what you need and I shall get it to you even if I have to strip every estate in Kandy for materials and manpower. We can bring in specialists from Europe by airship."

"All right, then," her father replied. "If it's a fearsome submersible you want, then that's what you shall get."

Thilini and her father put their heads together for several days to figure out what they'd need to build the new craft. Herr Rothschild presented their list to his brother; within days carpenters, welders and masons arrived by balloon to Trincomalee from all around Ceylon to build a fabrication complex at the northern end of the harbor.

Her father hired foremen from a group of engineers his brother recruited, and everyone went to work. Once the construction was underway, it was non-stop. Thilini feared that her father might abandon her now that he had so many educated men at his beck and call, but he kept her close, showing her every engineering novelty his new staff had to show him and every interesting failure.

Further, he introduced her to a brilliant young Serbian engineer named Nikola Tesla, fresh from Edison's laboratory, who helped her solve the problems with their wireless telegraph within a month. She went home to bathe, bolt down quick meals and catch naps away from the noise of the machinery, but otherwise she stayed in the factory and worked and studied and listened and worked some more.

Nine months after Martin Rothschild demanded her construction, the *HMS Makara* was ready. The completed submarine measured 120 feet in length and weighed over 80 tons. The cabin was equipped with compressed air and chemical scrubbers to enable the craft to stay under for up to five days at a time, though they hoped the shark could be found much sooner than that.

Thilini's mother was dead-set against her daughter joining the crew and scolded her husband mightily when she found out about the plan to include the girl as the sub's telegraph operator.

"Isn't it bad enough you let her go out into the water in the first place by herself?" her mother asked.

"She's a brave girl, and she's fine," her father replied.

"Fine? She's not fine! She's barely slept since she saw that monster! I can hear her cry out at night."

"Mama, listen —" Thilini began.

But her mother carried on: "I will not have you take my daughter to her death in that metal casket of yours!"

"We have tested it, over and over. The submarine is as safe as any seagoing vessel."

"She's too young for such things!"

"Too young?" her father replied. "Girls her age are already celebrating their weddings; I saw a procession for one girl just this afternoon! How many of them will soon be pregnant, and dying in childbirth next year? Or strangled or beaten by raging drunken husbands who have forgotten their wedding vows? There are so many ways for a girl to die in this world, my dear, and you have seen them all. How many friends did you lose, eh?"

Her mother was silent at that, her eyes downcast. "I lost far too many."

"I do not want to die, and I certainly do not want our child to die," he replied. "But if the worst happens on this venture, her name will be written down alongside mine in the history books. Men years from now will know who she was and what she tried to help us do. And other Tamil girls will hear her tale, and maybe some of them will realize that they, too, could be people of importance in the world."

"Mama," Thilini said. "I *am* afraid of the shark. I see it in my dreams. I don't want it to haunt me when I'm old, but if I do not face it again, I am sure it will be with me forever."

"Oh, my baby." Her mother pulled her in for a tight hug. "Do what you feel you must. But please go to the Koneswaram temple with me first. We must pray to Ganesha to remove all obstacles in the way of your success and safety."

"Yes, Mama."

Four days later, the *HMS Makara* launched with minimal fanfare to go hunting for the ship-killing shark. Her father was the craft's engineer; once they were in the water, he was to focus entirely on making sure the steam engines ran properly. Two British naval men — Hart and Dawes — who were experienced with handling submersibles served as pilot and co-pilot. A third British sailor — Jacoby — manned the triggers for the massive harpoon cannons mounted to the sides of the craft.

Thilini took up her station in front of the gleaming brass wireless telegraph. Her job would be to send back as many details of the hunt as she could. In the event that they failed, at least there would be an account of what happened. Technicians had taken one of the wireless telegraphs down the road to Kantale and the transmission back to Trincomalee was a success, so Herr Rothschild was confident it should function well for at least part of the journey.

She took a small mahogany statuette of Ganesha out of the pocket of her rubber suit and set it on the instrument panel. Her mother had given her the figurine after their visit to the temple. Thilini never had much religious fervor, but she felt better knowing the jolly elephant-headed god was there with her.

As her father started the steam engines, Thilini tapped out a test message to the technician manning the telegraph back at the factory; she quickly received her acknowledgement. So far, so good. She began to transcribe the orders the men shared amongst themselves.

"Steady forward," said Hart.

"Aye," replied Dawes. "Ten knots, cabin temperature 80 degrees, boiler temperature 240 degrees."

"All systems fair!" her father called from the rear.

They passed through the area where the orca had been taken by the shark. The crew was silent; all Thilini could hear was the pounding of her own heart. She took Ganesha off the instrument panel and held him tightly in her fist to steady her shaking hand.

The porpoises had seemed to be able to find their way in the water not so much by sight as through sound; she wished they had something similar on the submarine so they could better find their way in the dark.

Jacoby the harpooner shifted in his seat a few feet away from her, mumbling a tuneless sea chantey under his breath. His leg jittered, making the metal panel beneath him squeak. His teeth were bad and his breath terrible.

In fact, all the Britons were starting to sweat and stink inside their rubber suits. Thilini decided the best tactic was to breathe shallowly through her mouth.

"Hoy!" Jacoby sat up straight. "I saw something down low off the port bow."

"Taking her around now," said Hart. "Bait the water."

Dawes pulled the lever that released a half barrel of salt pork from a compartment below one of the harpoons.

Thilini watched with growing horror as a dark form rose and rose toward the submarine. When it was 100 yards from the craft, it was clearly the shark and not a whale. Its armored snout was scarred and lumpy from dozens of attacks on ships. It swam closer, attracted by the meat.

Jacoby pulled the trigger on the first harpoon; it struck a glancing blow on the shark's thick gills and tumbled off into the depths. The huge shark veered away and began swimming west. The harpooner swore long and hard.

"I'm after it!" exclaimed Hart. "He'll not escape us!"

"Twenty knots ... twenty five ...." said Dawes.

They followed the shark for hours. The engines were able to keep up with the shark's prolonged speed, but the interior of the submarine became a steampot. Thilini had to fetch a flannel cloth to clean the condensation off the windows every half hour.

Shortly after they lost telegraph contact with Trincomalee, the shark dove down into a valley on the seafloor. Dawes turned on the bright electric headlamps so they could better see. The twin beams cut through the murk, and they illuminated a scene none of them would ever be able to forget.

A huge figure sat there in the middle of the sea floor. At least thirty of the gargantuan sharks circled it; they looked like minnows next to it. At first glance, Thilini thought it was a colossal statue of ten-armed Ganesha. If it sat in the sea beside the cliffs of Swami Malai, she guessed it would be able to peer over the temple built upon those high rocks. But as her eyes better focused, she realized that what she took for elephant ears were really fanning gills, and what she thought was a trunk was a bundle of enormous tentacles hanging down on the figure's distended belly. The arms, yes, those were certainly giant limbs, although jointed in all the wrong places and ending in too many clawed fingers. And other arms were not arms at all, but massive boneless tentacles.

Surrounding the huge figure for at least two miles around were enormous shards of metal, like pieces of a giant shattered eggshell. They gave off a faint green glow that she instantly recognized.

"The meteor," she breathed. "You were inside it!"

As if it heard her, the hideous colossus turned its gilled, tentacled head toward the submarine and fixed them all in its gaze. Its four eyes were each bigger than their craft, each blacker than the deepest ocean trench.

A sudden vertigo took hold of Thilini, and she could feel the terrible darkness of those eyes spreading through her mind, could feel a cold, alien intellect trying to probe the corners of her consciousness. She clutched her Ganesha figure tightly and began to pray.

She could hear her father reciting a Hebrew prayer behind her; there was so much fear in his voice she thought her heart would break. Jacoby had gone slack in his seat, his eyes rolling up into his skull and a trickle of blood running from his left nostril. Hart had fallen to the floor, jerking as though he suffered some kind of seizure. Dawes just sat there staring at the colossus, muttering "No ... no ... no ...." under his breath over and over.

Thilini watched as the colossus casually plucked one of the circling sharks with a facial tentacle. The shark obediently opened its maw, and the colossus reached inside it with another tentacle, pulling out half a whale carcass. It popped the whale into its tentacle-obscured mouth and ate it as a man would munch a buttered cashew.

The colossus blinked and turned its head ever so slightly toward the sharks. Five of them peeled away from their formation and began swimming toward the submarine.

Thilini swore and leaped over Hart into the pilot seat. She quickly turned the sub around and tried to put as much distance as she could between them and the pursuing leviathans. She glanced at the pressure and temperature gauges. Both were climbing dangerously high.

"Papa! Papa, check the engines!" she cried.

His praying stopped. "What?" he stammered, sounding confused.

"The engines! Attend to the engines!"

"Yes, of course."

She heard him making adjustments and releasing valves, and soon the needles on the gauges were dropping into their safe zones again.

"The sharks!" she called back to her father. "Are they gaining on us?"

"Oh no."

She took that as a 'yes' and pushed the accelerator lever as far as it would go. Forty knots ... forty-five ... fifty. An unhealthy vibration began to spread throughout the sub, the steam engines clearly laboring under the load. She heard her father cursing and twisting handles behind her.

"Dawes! Dawes!" she shouted, trying to rouse the Englishman from his terrified fugue. When her words made no impression, she slapped his cheek.

His eyes popped open. "Ow!"

"I need a navigator, Mr. Dawes. We're headed back to Trincomalee. Can you help me get us there?"

"Aye, Miss." His voice shook and his eyes seemed unfocused. Thilini hoped for the best.

"They're still gaining," her father called. "I have done all I can here to improve the efficiency of the engines."

She thought hard. "Mr. Dawes, do we still have bait aboard?"

"Yes, two barrels worth."

"Dump it. Dump it all. And pray it distracts them," she said, gripping the Ganesha figurine.

He did as she ordered, pushing buttons to release the salt pork into the chilly water.

"Ah!" her father cried, jubilant. "They're stopping! They're stopping!"

Thilini kept the engines hot and pressed the submarine on to land. An hour after they distracted the sharks, she reduced speed and Dawes took over piloting duties so she could send a brief telegraph back to shore.

Martin Rothschild and an array of British naval officers were waiting for them at the harbor when they docked. The morning light was just breaking over the horizon.

"Did we receive your telegraph properly? You said *thirty* of the blasted sharks?" her uncle Martin asked.

She nodded, unbuttoning her rubber jacket to cool off in the morning air. Her cotton undershirt was soaked. "Perhaps even more. And they are but sardines compared to the leviathan who controls them."

Martin looked to her father. "Is this true?"

Her father nodded gravely, watching medics pull Hart and Jacoby from the submarine; both were completely insensible. "Every word."

"They will eat anything they can devour," she said. "No ship is safe here. No one on Earth has a weapon strong enough to combat the leviathan. I am terrified to imagine the weapon that could, for it would surely endanger all other life on the planet as well."

Martin twisted his gloves in his hands and stared out at the sea. "What shall we do? If we cannot take our tea and timber out on the water —"

"— you can take it by airship," Thilini said. "My father and I thought on this. We have the means to create larger and faster airships suitable for all manner of cargo. Just give us a week or so to draw up new plans, and we may begin building in the factory here."

"What shall we do when that monstrosity has devoured the whole of the ocean?" Dawes was still sheet-pale. "What will we do when it decides to come up on land?"

"Then we will do what we must. But in the meantime, I say give the monster the sea, and we can take the sky."

Her father left to discuss the details with her uncle. Thilini stood on the docks, staring out at the gray expanse of water, remembering the cold touch of the leviathan's mind in hers. She did not know whether it was a solitary conqueror, a lost traveler, or an exile marooned by its own kind on her planet.

But she did know that if it ever emerged from the depths, she would sense it. As she kissed the top of tiny Ganesha's head, she vowed she would move Heaven and Earth to stop it.

The Hand of Sa-Seti

Balogun Ojetade

"That's *it*, my brother and sister! Stay in step, just like that!"

The massive war elephants lumbered across the plot of land, cheered on by their "brother," Akhu, and his apprentice, Umat.

"Umat, now!" Akhu commanded as he yanked on a lever that protruded from the arm of the ebony couch in his litter. Umat mirrored Akhu's movements and the litters began to smoothly slide sideways toward the ten-foot gap between elephants. Akhu jumped to his feet. Umat followed suit.

The litters came together with a click, forming a covered bridge.

"It works, my Neb!" Umat shouted, jumping up and down with glee.

Akhu hugged his apprentice and kissed the top of her cleanly shaven head. Umat's cocoa skin tinged red. "We did it, Umat!"

Gahs raised his head and a sound like a blaring trumpet escaped his throat.

"Apologies, Gahs," Akhu shouted, winking at Umat. "You performed brilliantly! You too, my sister!"

Fusii nodded her massive head and raised her trunk in approval.

"This will make a perfect base for *Ra's Rain*, my Neb."

"Yes, it will," Akhu replied. "Let's set up the tripod and..."

A deep, roaring noise – like the sound of a gale wind – stifled Akhu's tongue.

He drew his scimitar from its sheath and slashed inward, toward his chest. The steel blade crashed into a massive, stone maul. An outward slash sent the warhammer careening back toward its thrower – a hulking figure standing in the grass below.

Akhu rubbed his chest with his fist. He shook his head as his knuckles slid across knotted bone, some spots still sore from when he did not respond quickly enough.

Akhu somersaulted from the litter-bridge toward the large man beneath him. The man reached up and caught the shaft of his maul as Akhu landed in a kneeling position before him. Akhu placed his sword at the man's feet and bowed his head.

"Uncle," he said.

"Fast reflexes, boy," the man said, pulling Akhu to his feet.

"I was trained by the best, my Neb," Akhu replied, smiling warmly.

"That you were, boy! That you were!"

Both men laughed as they embraced each other. Akhu's uncle looked up toward the bridge. "Apologies if I frightened you, Umat."

"Apology accepted, General Mu," Umat replied. "How are you today, my Neb?"

"My heart is heavy, Umat," General Mu sighed. "For today, I have to leave *you* lot to kill a dead man."

Akhu's brow furrowed. "You speak in riddles, Uncle Mu. Kill a *dead* man?"

"The Shekhem's daughter has been kidnapped by the wizard Sa-Seti."

"*The* Sa-Seti? Shekhem of seven centuries ago?"

"Yes," General Mu replied. "It appears that rumors of Shekhem Sa-Seti's death have been...exaggerated."

"Undead?" Akhu asked, shaking his head in disbelief.

General Mu answered with a nod.

"I will accompany you, then."

"No," General Mu said with a wave of his maul. "The Shekhem would have my head if the most brilliant mind in Menu-Kash died on my watch. Besides, how tough can one mummified sorcerer – with untold magic power – be?"

"Tread carefully, uncle Mu."

"Always, son," General Mu said, embracing Akhu. "Always."

The General turned away from his nephew, tossed his maul over his thick shoulder and sauntered off.

Akhu looked up to the litter-bridge at Umat. "Let's run *Ra's Rain* through its paces. We may have use for it soon enough."

Akhu lay in his bed, but sleep eluded him. Three days had passed and General Mu and his elite Jackal Squadron – warriors specialized in the hunting and killing of practitioners of dark magic – had not returned home.

A low din reminiscent of a plover pecking for insects echoed throughout the hall outside Akhu's bed chamber. The sound grew louder; closer, until Akhu recognized it as the padding of bare feet on his home's ivory floors. Umat rushed into the sleeping chamber. Her face was a mask of worry. "My Neb, please, forgive the intrusion, but..."

Akhu sprang out of bed. "What is it Umat? What's wrong?"

"Your uncle has returned, my Neb, but he is…not well."

"Not well?" Akhu echoed. "What, exactly, is wrong with him?"

"He is in the courtyard, my Neb. Please, follow me."

Umat turned on her heels and darted out of the room. Akhu followed her out to the courtyard.

General Mu sat on his haunches. His tan linen vest and trousers were drenched with sweat and he shivered violently as the cool night air slithered across his chest and down his back. The General's maul and his red, studded leather armor lay in a heap beside him. His helmet had rolled from his lap and lay, bottom up, a few feet in front of him.

Akhu ran to his uncle and knelt beside him. "Uncle Mu! What happened? What's wrong?"

"They…they came at us from all directions," General Mu replied. "*Thousands* of them!"

"Thousands of *what?*" Akhu asked.

"Beetles," General Mu groaned. "Beetles the size of men! Beetles that *were* men! Goddamned *beetles*!"

General Mu collapsed onto all fours. Sputum erupted from his mouth and cascaded into his helmet.

Akhu and Umat pulled the ebon-skinned goliath to his feet. "Let's get you to bed, uncle," Akhu grunted as he struggled to support General Mu's massive weight with his shoulders.

"You must see the Shekhem, boy," General Mu croaked. "Take my scepter; show it to the guards. They will let you pass. Warn the Shekhem, boy!"

"Warn him? Of what?"

"Sa-Seti allowed me to live so that I could deliver this message to the Shekhem – he has three days to return Sa-Seti's hand, or Ta-Sut is dead and all of Menu-Kash will soon follow."

Shekhem Tehuti Ur-Amun rubbed his goatee with his right hand, which – as always – was encased in a crimson, silk glove. He studied Akhu, who knelt before him. "And what is General Mu Ankh-Kara's condition now?"

"He is feverish; nauseous; and grows weaker with each passing hour, your Majesty."

"A curse?"

"It appears so, your Majesty."

"Perhaps the General's talk of returning Sa-Seti's hand is just the ranting of a man wracked by fever, then."

Akhu shot a glance at the Shekhem's gloved appendage. "I think not, your Majesty."

The Shekhem smiled wryly. "You have always been a clever boy, Akhu Ankh-Kara. A clever boy, indeed. What, exactly, do you know of my hand?"

"Just what every citizen of Menu-Kash knows, your Majesty – you were wading in the River Ise, presenting an offering to Pademak, when a crocodile sprang from beneath the surface of the water and attacked. You killed the crocodile, but suffered severe and disfiguring injuries to your right hand."

The Shekhem rose from his golden throne. Akhu bowed his head in reverence.

"Stand up, son," the Shekhem commanded.

Akhu rose to his feet. The Shekhem stared into his eyes. "What I tell you now never leaves this room. Understand?"

"Yes, your Majesty," Akhu replied.

"The story of my hand is a...fabrication," the Shekhem began. "The truth is – I heard my father speak, in whispers, of a powerful sorcerer who once ruled Menu-Kash. It was said that this sorcerer had been kissed upon the right hand by the Goddess

Ise herself and thereafter, the sorcerer-king could see the past and future."

"I have heard the legends, your Majesty," Akhu said.

"Yes, but only Shekhem know that sorcerer's identity. There have been twelve sorcerer-kings, but all of our powers pale in comparison to the third."

"Sa-Seti," Akhu said.

"Indeed. It was *his* hand that Ise kissed. It was *his* hand that held the key to the powers of precognition and postcognition. And it was *his* tomb that I raided for that hand over thirty years ago."

"But what does that have to do with *your* hand, your Majesty?"

The Shekhem paced back and forth, his bare feet making slapping sounds on the cool marble with each step. "The ritual to claim Sa-Seti's hand as my own required a sacrifice. I sawed off Sa-Seti's hand and placed it in a calabash..."

The Shekhem returned to his throne and flopped down in the huge chair. Beads of sweat ran down his forehead as he continued to speak. "Then, I...I severed my own hand and placed it atop Sa-Seti's. Suddenly, the world went black. When I awakened, I was at home in my bedchamber. I felt no different, but when I looked beneath the covers to peek at my stump, I found this..."

The Shekhem snatched the glove from his hand. Akhu stared at it in disbelief. The Shekhem's hand was withered and the digits were twig-like and twisted, ending in long, cracked, yellowish-pink nails. At the center of the leathery palm was a large, fully developed, alive and alert human eye. The eye's piercing greenness both fascinated and disgusted Akhu.

"With the hand of Sa-Seti, I can indeed see the past and the future, but only of others; not of myself or my bloodline," Shekhem Tehuti whispered.

"To have your daughter returned to you alive, you must sever that accursed hand and return it to its rightful owner, your

Majesty," Akhu said. "I am a skilled surgeon. With Umat's assistance, I can…"

"I'm sorry," The Shekhem said, interrupting him. "I…I don't know if I can do that."

"You don't know, your Majesty?" Akhu said, lowering his gaze to hide his disgust for this man, who had just proven himself to be a thief, a liar *and* a coward.

"Look, Akhu," the Shekhem sighed. "I love Ta-Sut with all my heart – she is my firstborn and heir to the throne – but the many outweigh the one. With insight from the hand of Sa-Seti, I have brought Menu-Kash unimaginable wealth and glory and I have kept this great land of ours safe. And – one day soon – I will heal the festering wound carved into this world by Pademak and restore peace to all of Ki-Khanga."

Akhu knelt in salute. "If you speak it, it is so, your Majesty."

The Shekhem slipped the crimson glove back over Sa-Seti's mummified hand. "Leave me now, Akhu. I must devise another plan to rescue my beloved daughter from the clutches of that monster."

Akhu sprang to his feet and – as custom dictated – walked backward out of the Shekhem's throne room.

A cool breeze sent a chill down Akhu's spine, awakening him.

He sat up on the couch in his litter, stretched his sinewy arms and then peeked over the back of the couch at the top of Fusii's head. The steel plates of her barding glowed a soft red as the armor reflected the tint of the morning sky. Her trunk was raised high, set to deliver another blast of air.

"I'm up, sister; I'm up!" Akhu chuckled. "Why have you awakened me?"

A soft whistling sound made Akhu snap his head toward Gahs. Umat stood in her litter, pointing toward something in the distance.

Akhu followed Umat's finger. A towering obelisk loomed in the distance – the tomb of Sa-Seti. "Strange...the tomb is surrounded by some sort of black liquid, which ebbs and flows like an ocean tide."

"That is no liquid, my Neb," Umat replied. "Take a closer look."

Akhu pulled a small bronze telescope from a pouch on his belt. He raised it to his eye and gasped. "Beetles! Beetles the size of a man's hand!"

"Hundreds of thousands of them, my Neb," Umat sighed. "Perhaps millions."

"Prepare yourselves!" Akhu shouted as he pulled the lever on the arm of his couch. He swallowed hard, hoping to swallow the knot in his throat and quell the rapid pounding in his chest.

Umat pulled her lever and the litter bridge snapped into place.

Akhu snatched a large tarpaulin from under his couch and dragged it to the center of the bridge as Umat set up an iron tripod.

The war elephants galloped forward as Akhu and Umat continued to work, busily sliding tubes, gears and large canisters – all from the tarp – into place.

Gahs let loose a powerful roar, which shook the ground beneath him.

Akhu looked up from his work. The beetles had taken flight and a dark, clicking cloud closed upon the litter bridge.

"I'll finish assembling *Ra's Rain*," Akhu shouted, wiping beads of sweat from his brow. "Fuel the *Horns of Sekhmet* and the *Steamsword*!"

Umat was a blur, grabbing a large calabash from her litter and emptying its contents into vents in the helmets of the elephants' barding.

Akhu hoisted *Ra's Rain* onto his shoulder then tossed the long, iron barrel of the weapon onto the tripod, fitting holes bored into the barrel's bottom onto the tripod's hooks. The massive weapon locked into place.

A shadow darkened the litter bridge.

"The creatures are upon us, my Neb!" Umat yelled.

"I suggest you work a little faster, then!" Akhu replied as he screwed a tube into the spigot of a steel barrel that sat over a roaring flame.

The sulfurous stench of feces assaulted his nostrils. He turned his gaze skyward. The clicking, black cloud of beetles was descending upon the litter. Akhu snatched back the canopy and stood behind *Ra's Rain*. "Fusii...Gahs...*now!*"

The twin war elephants raised their armored trunks skyward. A column of fire erupted from the nozzles connected to the barding covering each elephant's eight foot long proboscis.

The *Horns of Sekhmet* proved effective as the flames engulfed the beetles, roasting hundreds of them and injuring hundreds more. The dead beetles – and their living kindred – fell to the earth, where Gahs and Fusii set about crushing the creatures under foot.

Umat tossed the *Steamsword* to Akhu with one hand as she pulled a large wheeled crate with the other. She pulled the heavy crate, which was filled with fist-sized steel balls, next to *Ra's Rain*.

On the ground, the beetles crawled together with military-like precision, forming a hundred or so patches of blackness upon the grass. Each group of beetles then began to fuse together, writhing and clicking as their bodies became one. After a few moments, a hundred large, chitinous black balls lay upon the field of battle.

The clicking ceased. The balls were still.

Akhu brought his telescope to his eye and studied the balls intensely. "Gahs, please, do us the honors."

Gahs nodded and then raised his right foreleg. He slammed his foot down, beating a small crater into the grass. The force of the powerful stomp sent a shockwave across the battlefield, sending the beetle-balls bouncing upward.

The balls fell back to the earth and then...no sound...no movement.

"Uh-*huh*," Umat grunted as she rubbed her smooth scalp with the palm of her hand. "So...do we move on? Do we...wait for something to happen? Umm..."

"Perhaps the creatures are displaying a gesture of surrender. I guess we press on," Akhu said with a shrug. "Brother...sister... please, take us forward and step on those things as you go."

The balls began to vibrate; to quake. A loud clicking din rose from each ball.

"Or...not," Akhu sighed.

"I knew this was too easy!" Umat spat.

"One can only hope, Umat. Load up *Ra's Rain*, I'm going down for a closer look." Akhu drew the *Steamsword* and leapt to the ground. He landed with a dull thud. "Send down a line!"

Umat lowered a thin flexible tube to him. Akhu slid the tube's open end over a spigot on the sword's leather-wrapped steel pommel.

"Give it some heat," he shouted.

Umat turned a lever on the heated barrel that sat on the litter-bridge. A few moments later, the *Steamsword*'s blade began to glow with a reddish tint, heated by the hair-thin copper veins running the length of the flat sides of the weapon.

"That's enough," Akhu said, pulling the tube from the sword's pommel.

Umat turned off the heat and drew the line back up.

"Get ready!" Akhu shouted.

Akhu leapt toward a beetle-ball, raising the *Steamsword* above his head. As he descended, he brought the tip of the sword downward, thrusting it hilt-deep into the ball of fused insects.

The ball burst into flames and the burning beetles separated with a loud series of clicks.

"I thought so," Akhu shouted to his comrades. "The beetles are metamorphosing into something. We need to kill them now. Something tells me we do *not* want to be here when the metamorphosis is complete!"

A pulsing sound, like the pounding of an army of djembe drums on the horizon, rose from the field of chitinous spheres. The beetle-balls unfolded in unison. Within seconds, standing before Akhu was a platoon of hulking humanoid creatures with large, wicked-looking mandibles, razor-sharp claws and spiked, black, armored exoskeletons.

"Too late, my Neb," Umat shouted.

Akhu rolled his eyes. "You *think?*"

The beetle-warriors charged forward.

Akhu and the elephants surged forward to meet them.

Akhu slashed fiercely with the *Steamsword*, setting beetle-warriors ablaze with each strike, as Fusii and Gahs butted, gored and trampled the monsters with abandon. Score after score of beetle-warriors fell under the onslaught of Akhu and his elephant companions.

The creatures suddenly broke engagement and retreated.

Akhu reheated the *Steamsword* and Umat refueled the *Horns of Sekhmet* as they watched the beetle-warriors – about an acre away – fuse into each other once more, their carapaces softening and melting into one another until all the surviving beetles had formed one massive ball, which sat taller and wider than Fusii, Gahs *and* the litter-bridge.

"Oh, no!" Akhu exclaimed. "Brother...Sister...Charge that thing! Destroy it!"

Akhu sprinted across the grass toward the monolithic ball. Fusii and Gahs galloped forward close upon his heels, sending chunks of rent earth flying behind them. Akhu closed within two yards of the massive ball and then exploded into the air, the *Steamsword* raised above his head.

The ball unfolded into a spiked, black titan, which towered over the party of stunned would-be liberators. The creature stood as tall as an elder eucalyptus tree and twice as wide as the great tree's trunk.

Akhu thrust his sword into the creature's foot.

The monstrosity snatched him with a claw and lifted him skyward. He screamed in agony as the crushing pressure of the creature's claw threatened to shatter his ribcage. Akhu thrust the *Steamsword* into the giant beetle's claw. The creature screamed a series of quick clicks and then released its grip, allowing Akhu to plummet toward the ground far below.

Akhu stabbed the *Steamsword* through the monster's armored torso and sank the weapon deep into the giant's chest, halting his descent. The creature clicked loudly, reeling backward from the pain in its chest.

"I pray you're ready, Umat!" Akhu shouted as he dangled from the hilt of the *Steamsword*.

"Ready, my Neb!" Umat replied.

Akhu twisted the hilt of the sword.

A hissing sound rose from inside the monster's chest. The creature roared in anguish and a cloud of steam billowed from its mouth.

"Now, Umat! Now!" Akhu shouted as he released the *Steamsword*'s hilt. Akhu's fall toward the earth resumed.

Umat pulled the release lever on *Ra's Rain* and a volley of fist-sized iron balls erupted from the weapon's barrel. The balls flew into the monster's mouth. A moment later, holes burst open in the colossus' neck, chest and belly as the iron balls exploded, releasing hundreds of smaller, exploding balls.

Akhu closed his eyes and whispered a quick prayer as the earth drew closer. A powerful force snatched him out of the air and held him aloft. He opened his eyes. Fusii was holding him in her massive trunk. Akhu leaned forward and kissed her on the forehead. "Thank you, big sister!"

Fusii gently lowered Akhu to the ground and patted the top of his head with her trunk.

Gahs raised his thick proboscis toward his sister. Fusii slapped the tip of Gahs' trunk with her own in the elephantine equivalent of a "high-five".

Akhu perused his surroundings. The ground was littered with thousands of smoldering beetles.

"Good job, everyone!" He shouted as he jogged off. "Meet me at the tomb. If I have not come out within a half hour, use *Ra's Rain* to raze Sa-Seti's tomb to the ground!"

The interior of Sa-Seti's tomb was, surprisingly, well-lit by some mystic form of illumination and the monument smelled pleasantly of frankincense and myrrh.

"Strange," Akhu whispered.

"*What did you expect,*" a rich, baritone voice asked. "*Something akin to a vampire's rectum?*"

Akhu whirled toward the voice. Sitting upon a golden stool was a beautiful, cinnamon-skinned woman with curly brown locks that fell past her shoulders.

"Ta-Sut!"

"Well...*sort* of," the woman giggled.

"Sa-Seti."

"You *are* a smart boy!"

Akhu pointed the *Steamsword* at Ta-Sut's chest. "Release her, demon, or I will..."

"You'll what?" Sa-Seti asked, interrupting him. "Murder the daughter of your Shekhem?" Ta-Sut's mouth moved, but it was Sa-Seti's voice that continued to escape it.

"The Shekhem will not negotiate with demons! He will not relinquish the hand," Akhu said.

"I knew he would not," Sa-Seti replied. "That's fine. I have no use for it anymore."

"Then, why kidnap his daughter?"

"To lure *you* here."

Akhu frowned. "Me? Why?"

"Because you are the only man in Menu-Kash with the wits to defy him."

"I would never betray my Shekhem!" Akhu spat.

"Your Shekhem will, one day, crush this world beneath his boot-heel if he is not stopped!" Sa-Seti hissed.

"What?" Akhu asked, confused. "Why do you say such things?"

"Although my physical form is long gone, I still maintain much of my power," Sa-Seti began. "Recently, I had a vision of Shekhem Tehuti Ur-Amun. He had five faces. Each face ordered its own army to rape, murder and pillage all the lands of Ki-Khanga. I knew, then, that he must be stopped."

"And how do you know I will come against him? How do you know I won't tell the Shekhem what you have told me?"

"Shekhem Tehuti needs my hand to see the future," Sa-Seti replied. "I, myself, do *not*. Besides, your test against my scarab-warriors confirmed that you are more than capable."

"And what of my uncle?" Akhu inquired. "He is dying because of your 'test'."

"He is dying because I cursed him with a *rot* spell when he fought his way into my tomb and nearly foiled my plans," Sa-Seti replied. "The antidote is the ichor of a white dove. He must fully drain a dove of its blood every three days for the rest of his life or his condition will worsen and he will die. If he does this, however, his health will stabilize rapidly."

"And what of Ta-Sut?"

"She is free to return home with you," Sa-Seti replied. "She will not remember this conversation. Just tell her and everyone else that you destroyed me."

Akhu paced back and forth, rubbing the crest of his head with his moist palm. His hand tightened its grip on the hilt of his sword. *I cannot kill a spirit*, he thought. His grip loosened and he lowered his sword. .

"I will leave you now," Sa-Seti said. "Oh...one last thing..."

"Yes?"

"That apprentice of yours will make a fine wife and a great Shekhem one day."

With that, Ta-Sut fell limp. Akhu caught her in his arms.

"Wait," Akhu shouted. "Umat...wife? *Shekhem*?"

"The citizens of Menu-Kash salute you, Akhu Ankh-Kara!" Shekhem Tehuti bellowed as he thrust a golden scepter toward

Akhu, who knelt before him. General Mu – whose strength had returned – knelt beside him.

Akhu took the scepter in his hands. It felt somehow wrong. He felt somehow wrong and naked before his people. He forced a smile, stood and raised the scepter high into the air. The sea of citizens cheered wildly for their hero, who defeated the most powerful sorcerer that ever lived and rescued the Shekhem's daughter from the monster's clutches.

General Mu embraced his nephew, lifting him off his feet.

He shot a glance toward the Shekhem, who beamed with pride. *Perhaps Sa-Seti was wrong...or lying on our beloved Shekhem. But, to what end?*

"I now promote you to the rank of Lieutenant, under the command of your uncle, the mighty General Mu!" The Shekhem shouted.

The crowd roared excitedly once more.

"Celebrate well tonight, gentlemen," he continued. "For tomorrow, you will have the privilege of retrieving a powerful relic for your Shekhem from the exotic lands to the west!"

The hairs stood on the back of Akhu's neck and a chill clawed its way up his spine. "A relic, your Majesty?"

Shekhem Tehuti placed his crimson gloved right hand on Akhu's shoulder. A wave of disgust washed over Akhu.

"You will find – and bring to me – the mask of Aru-Nasunata-Mo," the Shekhem said. "*The Five-Faced One.*"

The Omai Gods

Alex Bledsoe

The island, low and heavily jungled, beckoned the men on the storm-battered ship *Tiger's Claw*. They'd been drifting for days, unable to repair their mast and raise sail, at the mercy of the tides. Now that the storms had all passed, and the brutal tropical sun had begun to take its toll, they couldn't believe their luck in spotting this little knot of land where their charts said there should not be one. Most of them assumed they were hallucinating.

But one part of the vista kept them from the weary elation they so desperately wanted to feel.

"What are those?" the warlord Shang said, mostly to himself. But he spoke for everyone.

Arranged along the shore, just above the sand, stood a row of enormous stone statues. They seemed to be mainly heads, with long, flat noses and prominent chins. They faced away from the ocean toward the interior, implacable and imposing.

"No idea," Teng, the second in command said. "Could they be gods?"

197

"They could," Shang agreed. "But not strong ones. They have no weapons. They're the gods of farmers, and women."

"The island's got trees," Teng said. "That means it's got water."

Shang nodded. Their water casks were almost empty, their food supplies practically gone, and the men were desperate for relief from the blazing tropical sun. "Then it could be the storm was *our* gods' way of bringing us here," the warlord said.

"That storm was a warrior god's bellow, all right," Teng agreed. He nodded contemptuously at the statues. "Not the whimper of *them.*"

"Of course," Shang said. They had barely escaped with their lives after Shang's rebellion failed, but now they had a means to repair their ship, resupply it and return to finish the battle. The men, his most loyal warriors, would see that their leader could turn defeat into victory, and was so strong even the gods conspired to help him. Once they returned and word spread of his power, even more would rally to his standard. The old king wouldn't stand a chance. "Get the men to the oars and let's make landfall."

Teng nodded. The crew were testy, short-tempered and starving, and he looked forward to leading them through the streets of any villages that might be unlucky enough to be on the island. He yelled orders, and the men hurried to obey because they knew it would get them off the ship that much sooner.

Shang stood in the center of the village, pacing before the male captives. The women were locked in one of the few remaining, pathetic huts, awaiting his men's pleasure. That would come tonight, along with drink from the jugs of whatever these savages fermented. But for now, he wanted them to understand how beaten they truly were.

Smoke filled the air from the other burning huts. The village held about a hundred people, but most of the children had run off into the surrounding jungle. The warlord did not worry about them; children were useful only as hostages, and he had no need for them now. He could wipe out every human on the island with a word.

"Bring me the leader," he said.

Shang's men pushed an old man, his hands bound tightly before him, out of the crowd and to his knees before the warlord. Like the rest of these vermin, the elder wore a long loin cloth, and his dark, reddish skin was painted with elaborate designs. Some of them were smeared where he'd been manhandled.

Shang glared down at him and said, "You speak my language, I understand."

The old man nodded. "A sailor from your people lived with my family for years. He washed up here and we gave him shelter. He lived and died as one of us."

"That's lucky. Otherwise, I'd have no use for you. What's your name, old man?"

"Arto."

"I want you to tell your people what I say to you, Arto."

"I think you've made yourself clear," the old man said.

Shang slapped him hard, and he fell to the dirt. The other tribal men, bound painfully and tightly together, glared at Shang but kept silent. They had been completely unprepared for the attack, so secure in their isolation that they had weapons only useful for hunting birds. The battle had taken mere minutes.

"I am Shang. I am a warrior, and you are either allies or enemies." Then to the old man, he barked, "Tell them!"

Arto rose painfully to his knees and repeated the words in his own language.

"We have no intention of staying on this miserable island any longer than necessary. We will repair our ship, fill it with food and water, and then return to civilization. While we are here, you are our slaves. Some of you will resist, but I'm not speaking to them right now. To the ones sensible enough to understand your new roles, I will only say this once: disobey or hesitate when I give you an order, and I will castrate you. Do it a second time, I will take your tongue. A third time, your eyes." He smiled as the old man relayed the information, and enjoyed the change in the prisoners' faces.

One young man, clearly the defiant kind, said something. The warlord looked at Arto, who said, "He asks how many times they must fail before you kill them."

"I won't," Shang said. "I'll just keep lopping off pieces of you until you cease to amuse me."

Arto translated, and the men looked even more terrified.

Shang continued, "Soon we will return to our kingdom, and some of you will come with us. The strongest men…and the most beautiful women. The rest of you, if you're lucky, may remain here with your lives. If you cause us difficulty, I will leave this island a smoking husk. That is your only warning."

The men cowered away from Shang, and pressed tightly together. A couple of them began to cry.

The warlord shook his head. He despised men who blubbered like women or children. "Whip them," he said to one of his men. "Give them something to cry about."

As his commands were obeyed, Teng joined him and said, "They won't make warriors."

"Perhaps not, but we can use their muscles just the same. And the wombs of their women will produce a fresh generation, one we can teach in the ways of the sword. I expect the belly of every woman in that hut to swell with our seed. Am I clear?"

"As the sky after a storm," Teng said.

"That's my father," Rito whispered. She was thirteen years old, tall for her age but still thin and wiry with youth. She hunched in the bushes at the edge of the village and watched the stranger whip the men where they knelt. Her father had been the one who asked when they would be killed.

"My father is in there, too," her best friend Eru said. He was twelve, shorter, muscular, and yet preferred to practice painting on rocks rather than play any games or learn the skills of the hunter. Rito was far better versed in the tasks adults would need, but their friendship survived despite this; their parents assumed they would one day marry.

"And our mothers and sisters are in that hut, waiting to be taken," Rito hissed angrily. Her fists clenched in fury. "I would rather die trying to rescue them than watch that happen."

"If you rush in there like a silly *furo* bird, then you'll get your wish," Eru said. "Or you'll be forced to join them."

"So we should just do nothing, then?" she almost yelled.

"Quiet! If they hear us, they'll come after us, and we have no weapons to kill anything bigger than a *dakulo.*" He held up the little stone knife he used to carve figures from wood. "This is all I have. Do you have anything?"

Rito shook with the effort of controlling her anger. She knew Eru was right. She blinked away the hot tears that burned their way from her eyes with every distant crack of the whip.

At last, the whipping stopped. The bound men lay on the ground, bloodied and whimpering. No one moved to help them.

In fact, the invaders laughed. From within the hut women sobbed, and the children too small to run away cried as they sensed their mothers' terror.

Rito could barely contain her rage. Only the certainty that she'd be cut down within moments of showing herself kept her from charging out of her hiding place. Then she felt Eru's hand on her shoulder.

"We have to get away from here," he said into her ear.

"I can't—"

"I have something important to tell you, but not here."

She turned and looked into his eyes. They were dark and kind, without the arrogance of the other boys. Eru had never done stupid things to impress her, the way the rest had done; he'd never attempted to steal a kiss or watched her bathe from the jungle shadows. Perhaps for that reason, Rito never really thought of him as a boy, just as her friend, despite her parents' knowing smiles and chuckles. But now there was a stern determination in his eyes, a new glimmer of manhood. She nodded.

One of Shang's men caught a hint of movement, and strode over to jab a spear into the bushes where they'd been hiding. When nothing emerged or cried out in pain, he rejoined the others.

The two youngsters moved through the jungle without making a sound, leaving the village behind and climbing the slight hills that formed the ridge separating the jungle from the beach. When they were safely over it, huddled against the rocks and with the open plain and beach before them, she said, "All right, we can talk now. What's so important?"

"Rito…" Eru said, then trailed off. He looked guilty and uncertain, as if he had a secret.

"What?" she said.

"There might be…something we can do."

"What do you mean?"

"I sort of...well...discovered something a while ago. I haven't told anyone."

"Is this the right time to bring this up?" she almost yelled. All their lives, Eru had been "discovering" things, from whale bones on the beach to the secret nests of the *okoluchika.*

"Oh, it definitely is," he assured her. "Do you remember the stories we were told as children about the *omai?*"

Rito's head snapped around and she gazed at the statues across the plain, lined up at the edge of the sand. It was considered bad luck at best, curse-worthy at worst, for anyone but the elders to speak of their gods. "I remember we shouldn't talk about them."

"But the stories? How they came down from the skies, destroyed the evil beings who first lived here and brought us into existence? Remember those?"

"Of course, I do! But Eru, what does this have to do with—"

"Didn't you ever wonder *how* that could be true? They're just rocks, right? Just images carved by our ancestors."

"Eru!"

"But I mean, they are. I've touched them. I've struck them, and nothing happened."

Rito grabbed him and gestured back toward their village. "Maybe *this* is what happened, you idiot! Maybe you brought down the wrath of the gods on us!"

Eru just smiled his infuriating grin. "Oh, Rito. Stop believing everything you've been told. The truth is so much more amazing." Gently he pried her hands away. "Come on, let me show you."

"But we haven't brought an offering, or—"

"Rito, if you really believe they're gods, with the power of life and death over us, then this is all their fault. Why should we bring them an offering?"

"Because if we don't, it might *get worse!*"

Eru laughed. "I promise, if the gods get angry, I'll make sure they know this was all my idea."

He led her across the plain down to the beach. Rito felt the statues' gazes on her as they crossed the empty space until they finally reached the nearest one, at one end of the line. Like its brethren, the statue was buried up to the neck, so that it appeared to be only a giant head. No one currently alive remembered why that was done.

Eru stood on tiptoe and smacked the tip of the stone chin. "See? Just rock. And look." He pointed at distinctive white traces that streamed down from the top. "Would gods allow birds to shit on their heads?"

"Why is this important *now,* Eru? You still haven't told me."

"What do you think these really are, Rito? They're certainly not our ancestors. Are they *just* blocks of stone?"

"This is no time for a lesson!" Rito insisted.

Eru chuckled. "You're right. It's not. It's time for a demonstration."

He led her around the base of the statue to a spot between it and its neighbor. A pile of dirt showed where a hole had been dug alongside the stone; it could've been an animal's burrow, except Eru jumped down into it and grinned up at her. "You're not going to get scared, are you?"

"I'm not a coward, Eru. Are you asking that because I'm a girl?"

"No, but you think very literally."

"I do not! I just don't let my head fly around with the *furo* birds like some people I know!"

Eru laughed and ducked down in the hole. Something heavy slid against something else and made a grinding sound, followed by a single loud CLONK.

"Eru?" Rito said. There was no answer. She moved a little closer to the hole and tried to peer in from a safe distance. "Eru, are you okay?"

There was no answer. Only the waves from the beach and the occasional bird call broke the silence. She clenched her fists and tried not to think of what was happening in the village, and to not be furious with Eru for wasting their time with this nonsense. Yet what could they even do? The men from the ships were clearly used to killing, and they were just two children, cut off from everything, with only the cloth around their waists to their names. How could they possibly rescue their village?

"Eru?" she asked again, a plaintive whisper.

Then the statue before her began to rise from the ground.

Rito shrieked and jumped back a few steps. She watched the lower body lift straight up, pushing dirt away in a slow wave. It stopped when it was at ground level.

Then one stone foot rose and placed itself on the edge of the hole. Like an old man, it climbed out, groaning and creaking. There was a smell like the odor after lightning struck the island, a burnt-air scent that she couldn't identify. When its other foot hit the soil, she felt the impact through her own bare feet.

The head was easily three-fifths of its height, and disproportionately large. It held its arms at its side, and the long fingers crossed over its belly, where a navel protruded between the fingertips.

The statue—or was it a god come to life?—turned toward Rito. She wanted to run, but she wouldn't give smug Eru the satisfaction. She did whisper a prayer she'd memorized as a child, one asking the great gods of the sky to please make her passage to the next life as painless as possible.

But nothing else happened. When the god-statue didn't move for a long time, and three birds fluttered down to perch on its head, Rito slowly approached it. "Eru?" she called. There was no answer, and he did not emerge from the hole.

She reached out a hand, took and held a deep breath, then touched the statue. It was stone, all right, just as it always had been, cool and solid. No god of spirit and fire. She started to think maybe she'd imagined it moving, that maybe it had been there in the bright sunlight all along. After all, mere statues couldn't move, could they?

Then, with a great grinding of stone on stone, the *omai's* head tilted down and looked directly at her.

She screamed and fell to her knees, her arms out and head bowed.

Rito expected to be crushed, or somehow blasted from existence. She heard more grinding, then Eru's amused voice coming from above her. "While you're down there, could you please get that grass from between my toes?"

Rito looked up, astonished. The enormous head had split open down the middle, and the two halves swung apart to reveal a strange sort of seat, flanked by protrusions like the spikes of one of the island's multicolored beetles. Eru sat there laughing, then reached out and moved two of the spikes, which made the statue tilt down so Eru towered directly over Rito's prone form.

"What..." Rito sputtered.

"I don't know," Eru replied with delight. "I discovered the passage into the statue during the last rainy season. A *vakaline* had dug a burrow down beside it, and I hid in it to get out of the rain. Somehow I bumped into something that made it open, and light appeared inside it. I found this chair, and these metal sticks. There are drawings on the walls showing someone sitting here and moving these sticks, so I tried them, and discovered the statue moves. It *moves*, Rito, and it's made of stone."

Rito continued to stare.

"Rito!" Eru said impatiently. "We can use these to rescue our village! Nothing the invaders have can possibly hurt us inside here."

Rito got slowly to her feet. "There's no room for me inside—"

"No! You enter one of the others and join me. Two of our gods come to life! The invaders will flee like barking monkeys!"

Rito thought this over. It was an actual plan, and it might conceivably work. It beat doing nothing, or hiding until they were inevitably found. "How do I get into it?"

"Watch this." He pulled some more of the metal sticks, and the statue turned toward its nearest fellow. One hand pulled away from its belly, curled into a cup and scooped out an immense handful of dirt from around the second statue's base. Two more scoops and a round patch of stone, of a slightly different texture than the rest, was exposed in the bright sunlight.

"Push on the middle of it," he said. "When it opens, crawl inside."

She jumped down into the hole and did so. The same grinding sound she'd heard before now came from this statue, and as Eru said, a lit passageway appeared. The rock was covered with shining sheets of metal smoothed to the inside contours of the passage. She climbed up several horizontal protrusions until she emerged into a tiny chamber with the same sort of chair and sticks.

She climbed into the seat, which was cool against her bare back and legs. There were uncomfortable bumps and ridges, but she put her feet on two platforms and looked around the little room.

A rectangular shape glowed directly ahead of the seat and showed the world outside the statue. Then another, smaller rectangle beneath it came to life and showed Eru's grinning face.

"The big window ahead of you shows where you're going," Eru said. "Look to your right."

On the metal wall were drawings showing which stick caused which part of the statue's body to move. She tentatively pushed one, and felt the whole statue lurch.

"Come on," Eru taunted. "Let's go chase those bastards back to the sea!"

Rito paused for a moment. One of the designs showed the very seat in which she sat, but the creature occupying it did not look... like her. Like the statue, its head was too big, its limbs too short, and its eyes narrow slits. Its form seemed to fit the bumps and ridges that made her squirm. Was this, then, the image of the *real* god?

There was no time to ponder this. She studied the drawings for a moment, coordinated them with the metal sticks, and then pulled the ones that seemed to make the legs move. A lurching first step rewarded her.

Shang felt the vibration first. He sat in the shade of the trees that ringed the village, sipping water brought from a sweet nearby spring. The village's men were now locked within a stockade, hastily but sturdily built by his crew. The women cowered in the hut, awaiting their fate. He enjoyed knowing they all watched him, awaiting the signal that would begin their degradation. He could not wait until an entire kingdom felt the same way.

But the repeating rumbles broke his euphoria. He stood up and strode to the center of the village clearing. The sky was blue and cloudless, but a storm could be approaching from the other side of the island. Perhaps it was the same storm that had nearly destroyed them, seeking a second chance. *Let it come,* he thought.

Teng joined him. "Are those drums?"

"Too regular to be thunder," Shang said.

"They said there was no one else on the island. Only them."

"Perhaps they lied. But whoever it is, they have no idea what they're walking into. Rouse the crew."

As Teng turned and was about to shout orders, there was a high shriek of terror. Not from one of the villagers, though; it came from Loonk, one of their toughest and most vicious swordsmen. He stood frozen in mid-step, pointing at the sky.

Shang and Teng looked up together as an immense shadow fell over the clearing.

Within the walking statue, Rito saw her village from high above on the glowing rectangular window. She recognized it, yet had never considered what it must appear like to the birds that flew overhead. The view mesmerized her.

In the smaller window, Eru grinned as he said, "There's a control that lets you speak with the god's voice; it was the first thing I figured out how to work. Scared away all the birds. Watch this!"

Shang and Teng exchanged a look. They had battled together for years, but never faced anything like this. Already the other crew members were fleeing for the jungle, screaming like the women in the hut.

Not just one, but *two* of the stone gods they'd seen from the ship now towered over the village. Were the others coming as well? Had they been summoned, or did they simply know, as gods did, that their worshippers were in danger?

The god of the natives was made of stone, with a gigantic head and two long-fingered arms. A deep voice boomed from its unmoving lips: "Release my people!"

Shang ordered, "Bring me the elder!"

Teng, his eyes still on the god, ran over to the stockade. The old man was tied to the outside so that he could translate at a moment's notice, and Teng half pushed, half dragged him over to Shang. Even the elder looked terrified.

"What did it say?" Shang asked, hoping his voice didn't tremble.

"The great *omai* ordered you to release us."

"And if I don't? Go ahead, ask. What happens if I don't?"

The elder drew breath and yelled up, "He asks, what will happen if he doesn't release your people?"

A bolt of what could only be called lightening shot from the protruding navel of the god and tore through the trunks of a dozen trees. There were more screams.

"Eru!" Rito cried. "What was that? You could've hurt someone!"

"I was careful," Eru said, still delighted.

"They're not afraid," Rito pointed out. "Not the leaders."

"Then we have to be scarier."

Rito started to protest, but then she had another idea. She looked at the drawings on the wall, carefully considered which sticks to move to make the statue do what she wished, and set to work.

"One god is leaving," Teng said.

"Of course," Shang said, puffing up with pride. "Not even a *god* dares oppose me." He grabbed Arto by the hair. "Tell the other to go back where it came from, or I'll kill every man, woman and child in this village. Tell it!"

The elder relayed the information.

The remaining god began to stride through the jungle, circling the village.

"What's it doing?" Teng asked.

"I don't know," Shang muttered, still clutching the elder by the hair.

Suddenly, with surprising speed, the god reached down into the jungle, then stood again. In one hand it held one of Shang's cowardly men, who screamed as if he'd been castrated in battle. Olon was his name: a rigger, worthless in a fight.

"I can kill your people as well," the god said, and the elder dutifully translated.

"Kill them," Shang said. "I do not need their worship. Do you need yours?"

Teng looked at his commander with a mix of admiration and concern.

Eru was no killer, Rito knew. He was bluffing. She pushed her sticks more rapidly, driving toward her destination.

"Rito, where are you going?" he demanded.

"I have an idea," she said. "Make sure they know what I'm doing."

The god raised Olon high overhead. The sailor continued to scream, clutching at the stone fingers while simultaneously looking around for anything that might help. Then he froze.

In the distance, the other god strode into the water, toward the *Tiger's Claw.*

"The ship!" he cried down to Shang. "It's going to sink the ship!"

The thick sand under the water caught the statue's heavy feet, making each step more difficult than Rito expected. The statue wobbled, and Rito had to quickly shift the rods to keep its balance. The water was as deep as the statue's chin when she reached the anchored ship.

No one had been left aboard, so she had no worries about killing anyone. She raised one arm, curled the long fingers into a fist and brought it down heavily on the vessel's middle. The blow crashed through the wood, splitting it into two halves. The anchored half continued to float, while the other spun and sank almost at once.

"Ha!" Rito cried in triumph. "Now they're stuck here!"

She tried to turn the statue, but the sand held firm. Instead of the sound of stone grinding, there was a shriek of metal, and something popped loudly as it broke. The statue listed to one side, then with a great splash fell forward into the water, between the halves of the broken ship, and landed in a great puff of silt on the bottom.

Still clutched in the statue's hand, Olon cried, "They've sunken the ship! We're marooned here!"

Arto looked at Sheng. "You're now an islander, just as we are. Except you have no idea how to survive here. You don't know which berries to eat, which snakes are poisonous, which plants leave a stinging rash. If you kill us, you won't live a week."

Shang, his face white with rage, punched the old man. "You dare to threaten me? I will kill every man on this island, even my own, before I will beg help from an uncivilized—"

He froze, and looked down at his chest. A sword protruded from it, through his heart. Then it withdrew out his back, and he fell.

Teng, holding the bloody weapon, said tiredly, "He meant it. He'd kill us all." To Arto he said, "So we're now part of your tribe, it seems. I suppose we have to prove you can trust us." He turned the sword and handed it, hilt first, to Arto.

Eru's *omai* turned toward the ocean, waiting for Rito's statue to rise. "Rito!" he called. "Rito, answer me!" The window that had shown her face was now black.

He put the invader Olon back on the ground and strode through the jungle toward the beach. "Rito! Say something! I'm coming!"

But there was no response.

When he reached the beach, he saw from her own giant footprints that following her into the water would be suicide. The statues worked fine on land, but would bog down in the water. Rito was trapped, buried on the bottom of the ocean.

"Rito," he whispered, and felt hot tears burn his eyes. He put his hand against the black window, but no image appeared. She had gone, alone, to meet the true *omai*.

Arto stood before the row of statues. One was missing: the one that had fallen in the water that long-ago day, ensuring that their people would survive. Another had returned to its place at the end of the line, but this time faced out toward the sea, watching over its fallen comrade. Boats that passed over the spot could see through the clear water to the great stone shape lying face-up below.

Beside Arto stood Eru. The boy had changed since the invasion: he was quiet now, and seldom smiled. He seemed to harbor some dark secret that weighed on him, maturing him far past his years. When he'd come to Arto and asked to train as the next high priest, Arto had laughed at first. But he had no sons, and it didn't take long for him to see that the boy was serious. The laughing troublemaker had gone for good, replaced by the grim young man who now stood tall and strong beside him.

"The *omai* will always protect us," Arto said. "They watch, and wait, and listen. Once I doubted it, but since the day I saw them walk with my own tired eyes, I now know the truth."

Eru nodded. His eyes filled with tears again as he followed the gaze of the lone *omai* that looked out at the water.

The Governess and We

Benjanun Sriduangkaew

As a girl falling asleep to the rhythm of cicadas and mosquitoes, Ging dreamed of fire. Fire caught between panes of brass, fire captured in a bead of glass, fire reflected in temple gold. Her grandmother's skein of stories inherited over generations, long and slow to unwind, of a queen who rode to war; of the sky blazing as she fell.

Decades later, in Bangkok, Ging wakes up each day to a secret place full of fire.

Ging's days are canals: the slant of roofs to either bank, the load of fruits and hand-drums on her wheelboat. A song on her lips, a song in her palms. She brings home pomelos and sticky rice, lumyai and coconut milk.

Ging's evenings and nights are an apprentice, a workshop.

She lives by the Chaopraya where it's coolest, an expensive home gifted by an expensive patron: halfway rooted in the banks, halfway in the shallows as though amphibian. Sometimes she talks to her apprentice Nok of retiring in Ayutthaya or even further into the countryside, by a forest or on the edge of rice fields. Both recede by the day as Bangkok grows, the seams of its borders and canals loosening as the years pass, restitched and extended to include that much more in its weave.

When they work they strip to the waist the way women still do in the countryside, for all that Bangkok has adopted His Majesty's taste for foreign modesty: the one that says women must cover up from throat to ankle, not a hint of arm or wrist or collarbone. Strange fashions such as these soak into Bangkok as monsoon water soaks into mud, and the girls working for them are startled when Ging or Nok bares their breasts. Soon that changes, for the heat dissolves that imposed, alien propriety quickly enough.

Most of the girls think what they make are only mannequins, peculiarly large, peculiarly made—but decorations. They weave rattan into torsos and limbs, chisel wood into faces. Some of the finished results go to furnish tailors, theaters, or become the possessions of court ladies with a taste for the odd. Miniatures are equipped with tiny gears and clockwork parts to become the toys of wealthy houses.

The rest go elsewhere.

Nok has an eye for symmetry and flourish; she draws designs on hard Jeen paper. Ging shapes and boils the hands. "Is it magic, mistress?" her apprentice asked once.

"Like dipping green mango into chili salt is magic," Ging said, smiling. "Like turning yolk and sugar into sweets is magic."

The process is delicate, the formulae passed down from mistress to pupil: ones Ging keeps close to her, though once she's mixed and distilled the ingredients she allows Nok to watch. Wax softening in the pot, wax poured into a mold. The result is a smell of melting candles and hands which Ging kneads into tapered, spread fingers that she reinforces with brass wires and dancing talons.

The hands move on their own, for a time, a whisper of mechanism inside them as they scurry along the floorboards. Ging catches them and attaches them, by spikes and adhesives, to the ends of rattan-strand wrists. This is the most important part: not the limbs or torso, not even the clockwork hearts. It is the hands that propel them, give them the wherewithal to hear and obey.

Ging does not grant them voices.

One monsoon-drenched afternoon, a foreigner visits.

Anna Leonowens: a woman of hard glittering eyes, stiff fabrics, teeth like a carnivore's. She moves with a heaviness of being, as though the air itself resists and resents her passage. There is more clothing on her than Ging has ever seen on anyone, man or woman, and she has seen the king from afar at temple ceremonies. Palace girls say that the *ma'am* does not trust Siam weavers, Siam tailors, Siam anything. It shows: Anna's dress, made for icier climes, is spotted with sweat. The farang must be sweltering in it.

Her powdered face betrays no discomfort. She gazes at them both, not quite down her nose but in the way one might at a pair of buffalos: with no expectations that either Ging or Nok might address her in human speech.

"Can I help you?" Ging says.

Anna's brow creases. "You speak English."

"Yes, ma'am." She stopped stumbling over Angrit years ago. "We sell puppets. They're unique art, no two alike. Many British and Francois clients have brought them home." Where they resell them, she supposes, for the kind of prices that'd buy enormous tracts of fertile land here. Nok resents it and doubles the price for western customers. Ging lets her.

The *ma'am* turns her gaze to the inanimate puppets: Ging has delighted in these, knowing they don't have to be compact or dexterous or practical. She has given them the heads of eagles and horses, the tusks of elephants and the claws of tigers. Bestial faces, faceted eyes in amber and blue and green, gilt lips. "I've seen some of these in the palace," Anna says. "Interesting. Your husband's work? Or father's?"

"My own, ma'am."

"Quaint," Anna says, circling the mannequins. Perhaps her jawline tenses in disapproval, but it is hard to tell—the woman has one of those farang faces that are perpetually sour. "Not very womanly."

"It keeps a roof over my head." Ging nods, laughs. "Does any of my work interest you?"

. "Another day."

That year, the streets are full of foreigners. Not Phma, not Yuan. Invaders, all the same.

They meet in the morning at a temple, after Ging has given alms to the monks, filling each black bowl with dried fish and candied tamarinds. Ever since she's started working for the lady, she has done this more often, for peace of mind if nothing else. She doubts feeding monks is enough to cleanse her virtue.

Khunying Aunrampha dresses like a commoner, all surface: there's no smell of smoke or cooking in her clothes, no stains of ink in the creases of her palms, and her fingers are smoother than those of a child grown with the knowledge of harvest in calves and knuckles. Despite this she never looks, quite, soft. Her gaze sees, calculates, and appraises. Her farmer's hat keeps her features in shadow.

They watch the passage of ducks and a geriatric crocodile that's become the local fright-tale to unruly children.

"The *ma'am* paid you a visit."

Ging doesn't ask Aunrampha how she came by that information. "Briefly. She wasn't overly inquisitive."

"The first farang queen of Siam." Aunrampha yawns. "From the looks of it, that's what she aspires to. But you know how monkish His Majesty is, and she's neither young nor beautiful. Or pleasant. Or witty."

"I thought she was an instructor in the women's quarters?"

"Her education is not exceptional for a woman of her station, and she puts on finer airs than she warrants—somewhere up the line there's a grandmother she doesn't want named and commoners for parents. She'll have you believe she's descended from great commanders. A spy, of course."

"But His Majesty," Ging tries.

"Is not infallible. The *ma'am* is far-traveled and he has faith in her competence to teach us geography, arithmetic, proper Angrit..." Aunrampha cocks her smile the way archers cock arrows. "In her favor, she doesn't try to convert us like Doctor Bradley did, though really he was a sweet enough man as long as you nodded at the right parts. I still don't know who Yesu was, but then he never learned to recite *Sudsakorn* or write proper poetry."

Ging sights the crocodile's head amidst a camouflage of driftwood. "Should she come again, what do you want me to do?"

"Nothing. When will your next batch be ready?"

"Two weeks." She scrunches folds of her pha-nung in one fist. "I thought what I've already delivered was sufficient."

"I'll call them sufficient when they outnumber western soldiers. I'll call them enough when they cover the earth from here to the borders of Malaya, and make a wall to guard Bangkok land and shore." Aunrampha exhales, her mouth softening. "It sits uneasily with you, I know. You're not a soldier, you haven't bound yourself to any oath or any cause. If there were other ways I would take them. I want none of this burden on your peace, your heart, your life."

"It is not that." But it is precisely that—a selfish horror at what she makes, the thought of the use they could be put to.

It does not help that Aunrampha's touch pricks her with a frisson of desire; it does not help that Aunrampha's lips are soft against her own, that the brief kiss recalls everything else they've done together and will do. It does not stop Ging from thinking *She does this to yoke me to her cause,*but is that cause not hers as well, whether or not she is sworn to protecting Siam? Is it not the duty of all who drink and thrive off this soil?

Aunrampha lets go of her, eyes wide and mouth parted. "Perhaps when this is done," she says softly, "we can share a house, by a forest where old things live, and grow gray together. Away from Bangkok, away from secrets."

Ging does not say, *For too long you've promised this, and neither of us is a girl anymore.*

The first time Ging saw a doll kill it was an accident.

Ging inherited trade secrets from the mor-phi who taught her to give a doggish sentience to automata. She failed to inherit an eye for weapons or a mind for battlefields from her mother. The dolls were just ornaments, a canvas for her imagination. Lucrative and, when she allowed herself to admire her own work, beautiful. A gift of trade secrets and an alchemical discipline to pass onto Nok.

She no longer remembers the soldier's face or nationality. She recalls only that they were on her wheelboat, its mechanical paddles churning river water to white froth, Nok regaling her with stories of raising fighting cockerels.

One of Ging's new automata stood at the prow, holding a gas lamp. She'd chosen a lesser canal cupped between tattered, leaning houses that creaked among themselves like gossiping grandmothers. The doll was her pride, but she didn't yet want to parade it down the floating markets before it could perform to perfection.

A sound like fifty storms' worth of thunder. Jeen firecrackers, Ging reasoned back then, before a farang man stumbled into their boat. A moment where it rocked so far Ging could feel the weight of green waters pulling her down, could smell the silt and feel the weeds curling around her ankles. When it steadied the man had taken hold of Nok, a knife to the girl's eye. He barked something foreign, angry.

Ging did not have time to process—to understand—before the doll opened the man's throat. An arterial spray. Nok's lips moving but Ging could hear nothing save the roar between her ears

On the banks: a compact woman incongruously dressed in loosely knotted pha-khaoma, a dirty shirt, bare feet coated in mud. In her hand she clasped a long pistol, its handle lacquered black.

Ging recognized her at once.

"Jeen make," the woman said, tucking the pistol into the folds of the pha-khaoma and retying the fabric. "Dear in price, but it pays for itself. I'm sorry for the noise. Nang Ging?"

"You're Khunying Aunrampha." Her hearing returned in patches. "Mother's successor."

The lady inclined her head. "I've that honor and hope to live up to a fraction of her accomplishments." She gave wai.

Ging nearly leaped backward into the water, would have prostrated if Aunrampha did not stop her.

"You are the daughter of a legend," the lady said, "and my elder, if by a few years. Doubtless if she'd stayed in Bangkok and reared you in the women's quarters, you would have taken up this office."

She could not say that she had disappointed her mother; that her mother—though never saying in so many words—did not judge her fit for that position. "I don't think so."

Aunrampha's gaze was fastened to the doll, which stood tranquil in disregard of the blood dotting its front. Ging had made that one with a giant's face, fierce red eyes and upturned tusks. She would always wonder afterward if that was an omen, if some premonition had guided her hands.

The lady did not try to touch the doll. But she looked at it and saw what Ging never had. "Did you," she said, "make this?"

Ging's mother raised her with an understanding of the world, and it is this: that nations are built and move on war, that weapons are the true language of diplomacy, and that their enemies are not the Phma or the Yuan.

Spymaster. Advisor. Tactician. All three. Mother did not hold an official title, being only a senior servant in the women's quarters—the highest rank a merchant's daughter of no particular lineage could aspire to. Yet she commanded respect: Ging had been born in Bangkok, stayed there until she was eight, and she'd seen the regard afforded Mother. A touch of fear.

Away from Bangkok, in the wet remoteness of Ranong, Ging gained three things: a fondness for the southern dialect, an unseemly accent, and a longing for the sleekly muscled southern girls that took her years to untangle and understand—years while those girls turned to boys equally fleet, ones who could dive and fish and wrestle with sharks, if their boasts could be believed. Her mother must have known, but did not care overmuch. It was more imperative that Ging could replace her.

Ging never knew how Mother reached the decision that she could not. But one day Mother summoned an old, old woman and told her a name: Khunying Aunrampha Panthapiyot. Ging overheard that, the name, but did not forget it even as she tasted a relief so great it nearly imploded her lungs.

When she turned twenty and mastered all the formulae her mistress had to teach, her mother told her, "Go to Bangkok" and she did. Equipped with a fund to establish herself, back then in a more humble house doubling as a shop, just making dolls. She took in Nok, a temple orphan.

Aunrampha found her way into Ging's workshop, her life, her bed. She was a patron, and then she was more. The skin of a lady, Ging marveled as she stroked over and over that long, soft body during their first times. Behind shut doors Aunrampha's mouth is not aristocratic, in language or in other uses.

Ging thinks of this now as she lies awake next to Aunrampha, their limbs crisscrossing, a weight of hand on her thigh, a heft of arm across her belly. Aunrampha has had a nielloware glass installed overhead; Ging first objected to it—bad luck—but soon found herself watching, rapt, the tremors and tensing of her own body. Reflected, each act becomes that much more indelible.

A finger draws circles in the bend of her knee. She hates to admit it, but Aunrampha stirs her more sharply than any other ever has. Perhaps it is that months can pass by before they've the opportunity to be together this way. The thrill of infrequency, the rarity of Aunrampha's touch.

"Have you not slept?" Aunrampha pecks her earlobe.

"You'll take the dolls today." A dozen, primed to obey.

"I thought we kept those talks out of the bedchamber." Aunrumpha pushes upright. "Nang Malee... your honored mother taught you, didn't she, of what happened to Malaya, to Phma, to Yuan? His Majesty—and his revered father before him—strived hard to keep us out of western reach. But negotiation will work only so long."

"Have you ever put them to the test?" Ging is not sure what makes her ask; she doesn't want to know. Nevertheless the question is out and she's not willing to recall it.

Aunrampha's brow creases. "Do you want to see? Meet me in Sampeng tomorrow, noon, at Taogae Jak's gold shop."

In Sampeng, Ging feels foreign. There are women here wearing gipao patterned with cranes and chrysanthemums, who have jade bangles around their wrists rather than silver or brass. Men in vests and tunics, their long hair in queues. It's not that Ging has never crossed the river, but, though many of her clients are Jeen traders, it's strange to be among their midst, to hear more Taechew and Jeenglang than Thai.

Taogae Jak's gold shop is attached to a teahouse, brisk with midday traffic: steamer baskets arriving at and departing from tables with blinding speed, laden with dumplings, chicken feet, seaweed balls. The smell of soy and plum sauces thick in the air.

More teacups than Ging has ever seen in one place. And farang patrons: a few merchants, perhaps some dignitaries. But mostly they are soldiers.

Aunrampha has a table to herself. She is in gipao, high collars and gleaming silk embroidered in serpents. Her face is powdered, her eyes kohled and limned gold. She would have been unrecognizable if Ging did not know her face so well, was so familiar with the arrangement of Aunrampha's brow and jaw.

Between mouthfuls of pork buns, Aunrampha points out a short, bald farang. "He tried to assassinate Phra Ongchao Phannarai. Farangset. Goes by Mathieu Dubois. It's much like a Somchai or Somying—a name so common it's almost certainly an alias."

"There are people named Somchai and Somying," Ging points out, to be contrary. "Who could wish ill on Phra Ongchao Phannarai?" From what Ging knows, the princess is one of the most inoffensive in the women's quarters.

"His Majesty has lost two wives. To lose another would... disturb his peace." Aunrampha nods, lowers her voice. "The farang rents a house at the end of Yuparat. I've sent the automata ahead."

"Does he know who you are?"

"He suspects. Let's take a walk." Aunrampha calls for a server in Taechew.

They spend half an hour meandering Sampeng, Aunrampha pointing out favorite eateries, shops, vendors. She shares palace gossip and her suspicion that Phra Ongchao Phannarai may have a fondness for her handmaids that goes beyond propriety. "It's such a shame," Aunrampha laments. "Were I serving her directly I could have snared myself a princess."

Ging pinches her arm. "Don't go seducing the wives of kings. Isn't she older?"

"Five years, but there's a certain charm to older women..."
Aunrampha grins; Ging is four years her senior. "Who would
know? Handmaids bathe princesses in the night, attire them in the
morning. That is the way of things."

Against her determination to remain somber Ging bites down
on a chuckle. "I do not suffice?"

"You're my first lady and ever will be. Her Highness would be
merely the junior spouse."

In Mathieu Dubois' Jeen-style house there is redwood furniture,
backdrops of nielloware dragons on painted skies, and western
watercolors. Leather-bound books with gold lettering Ging can't
read, a map pinned to the wall charting a demarcation of
territories Siam has ceded to Farangset.

And five dead farang men on the ink-stained, paper-strewn
floorboards.

"They're just unconscious," Aunrampha says, nodding at the
automata. They stand by a shelf, quietly ornamental. Blank masks
for faces, limbs of braided rattan for strength and flexibility,
hands of wood and brass, razor fingers.

Ging stares as Aunrampha turns out the men's pockets,
removes their belts, rifles through their clothes. She discards their
weapons: knives for fighting and knives for eating, foreign
currencies crumpled and clinking. Firearms. Sabers. "Ah."
Aunrampha holds up envelopes, wax-sealed and held together
with a knot of twine. "Anna's. I'll explain later. Can you take to
the balcony? You can watch through the window."

Not without reservation, Ging obliges, and only because she
knows the automata are better protectors than she can ever be.
Aunrampha steps away from the bodies and begins making tea.
The fragrance of jasmine does not conceal the miasma of blood.

When Mathieu Dubois comes he has his saber drawn: the
broken lock has made a surprise impossible. When he sees

Aunrampha he gives pause, his fist momentarily slack on the grip of his blade. He snaps out a string of noises, rapid-fire.

Aunrampha smiles up at him. "Monsieur Dubois, I do not speak French. You run errands for an Englishwoman. Unless I know nothing about her at all, I'll wager she doesn't condescend to discourse in your tongue."

The farang does not let go of his weapon.

"Why don't we sit down and share tea? The leaves are yours. I didn't have time to poison them."

"You've harmed soldiers of France. For that there will be consequences." Mathieu sheathes the saber, unholsters a pistol. He does it with smooth ease, and when he points the muzzle at Aunrampha his hand is steady.

Aunrampha waves the envelopes at the farang. "These were handed to you freely, not stolen. Whatever drives you to do favors for Madame Leonowens I don't really care, but imagine the ambassador's disappointment to learn that one of his trusted spies consorts with an Englishwoman. He'll be just so hurt."

"You overstep yourself. It's nothing to us to scorch your houses and salt your land as we've done to Vietnam."

"Monsieur." Aunrampha sips her tea. "Put your silly gun away. Yours is inferior, incidentally. Have you tried Chinese ones? They're works of art, and their firesmiths don't sell just to anyone. I've heard it said they grind dragon whiskers into gunpowder and sheathe the barrel in kirin scales. Truth or hyperbole, quality speaks for itself." When the man doesn't lower his pistol she says in Thai, "Break his arm."

The dolls obey; the dolls are quick. This much Ging knows. They have practiced, Aunrampha giving them commands to sit or stand, move this way or that, like dogs. They are built for strength and speed, animated by a secret alchemy. A man, even farang, even the agent of a mighty empire—he is only flesh and fat, cartilage and tendons.

A crack of bone; a surprising lack of blood.

He hangs slack between rattan hands, pale and panting.

"Monsieur." Aunrampha pours herself another cup. "It is true there are consequences to any act of provocation. Bringing you to trial and tribunal is not an option. In the open your punishment would be no graver than if you'd committed petty theft, for you are of France. But here that will not suffice; here I am your judge, and I hope you're as dedicated to the virtue of justice as I am."

Aunrampha has the Farangset men disposed of afterward. Their bodies will be buried deep, their belongings incinerated. Clothes stripped, faces mutilated beyond recognition. She does not take chances.

When Aunrampha returns, she spreads Anna Leonowens' letters out, holds down the corners with inkwells. "This isn't one of Anna's silly correspondences. There's more than just the usual that she doesn't want intercepted by palace staff."

"What *is* the usual?"

"Tales of how His Majesty whips palace slaves raw, of how he summons little girls to his bed."

Ging flinches. "Is any of it true?"

"He's talked of emancipating the slaves, to the collective displeasure of his ministers. As for the girls... if he did that, I would know. I'd be obliged to silence, but I would know." Aunrampha passes a hand over her face, rubbing at her eyes. "Anna's petty retaliation for his refusal to grant her more power than she already wields. I read an earlier letter that said His Majesty wanted to make her a concubine. She, being a virtuous woman under the grace of Yesu Christ, naturally spurned him. Doubtless that makes her quite the sensation among friends and family in Angrit."

"What is the point?"

"Convincing her superiors and social circles that we're barbarians living under the reign of an insane, lecherous tyrant. It's a fable that has its uses, for them." Aunrampha pats out the creases on the letters. "Read these."

Ging does, falteringly, straining to decipher the twisting spidery script. "But this is—"

"A confirmation that the Angrit empire is no friend of ours and will leave us to Farangset mercy should it come to conflict. That Farangset, once they're done with Yuan and Kampucha, will turn their gaze to us. The assassination attempt was a prelude, of sorts, to destabilize His Majesty's reign. It'll be some time in coming." Aunrampha rubs her hand against the tight skirt of her gipao. "In five years or twenty. Nevertheless it will come."

The hour has grown much too late, lit with lamplight that jaundices packed earth and pavement. They walk arm in arm down the dock where Ging's wheelboat is moored. On her knees and weary for no real reason, Ging pours oil into one of the boat's receptacles and adds a precise amount of solution. Her own adapted formula mixing her teacher's and that of Jeen firecrackers. It hisses, flaring blue; boat actuators whir into motion.

An amber flicker in the distance, against a night as deep as it is damp. It takes too long for them to understand what it is.

When they arrive the workshop is smoke and ruin, scorched roof-boards floating in the waters, pieces of the veranda trapped among duckweeds and upriver refuse. Shards of pottery and glass on the steps leading to the house, stains of Ging's pastes and pigments on the wood.

They find Nok by a window.

She must have tried to escape. Blackened fingers curl over the sill, caught under a fallen beam. The rest of her is hidden, but from a scrap of bright orange pha-nung it can be no one else.

"I only thought," Ging says distantly, staring at that hand, "to have someone look after the shop. That's all. She was going to visit her temple siblings."

The first drops of a late-summer rain. Where they touch the wreck of her house the wood sizzles and cracks. Each of Ging's muscles tenses; she wants to reach out, to be in motion, to do what she does not know. Aunrampha is holding her steady, but she isn't shaking, isn't collapsing. She feels nothing at all, as if her heart has guttered out.

Footsteps on wet mulch. The snap and rustle of a parasol opening. From beneath its shade Anna Leonowens peers at them. "An unfortunate night."

Ging looks at the Angrit, a heat unfurling in her that turns to ice. "You murdered a child."

"Did I? An odd conclusion to make, on little evidence save that I've passed by. If a child is dead, my condolences. Lady Panthapiyot, how interesting to see you about at this hour. Your mother would be... put out, let alone to hear that you're attired and painted like a Chinese whore. So loosely are girls raised in this country. Spare the rod, spoil the child—you could've benefited from a boarding school, a Christian education."

"Leonowens." Aunrampha steps between Ging and Anna. "You are not untouchable."

"Siamese as a lot are ungrateful. Your kingdom, such as it is, stands sovereign on the sufferance of Britain." The woman shrugs, a farang gesture. "I'll leave you to your matter. I suppose there'll be cremation and much heathen noise made by bald men in orange robes."

She lifts her skirts slightly, her boots squelching on puddles. The parasol she hands to a gaunt yellow-headed man. Her carriage bears the emblem of the Angrit embassy. It rumbles away under the crack of a whip, a spray of mud and rainwater in its wake.

"I'll have justice," Ging says to the quiet that carriage and governess have left behind. The rain tastes of bitter salt, as though it's passed through ashes.

"Ging, I can't remove her. Not right now."

She takes a breath and grips Aunrampha's hand, treasuring the solidity and warmth of it, and brings it to her chest. "I don't mean that; I don't mean her. She's nothing, less than nothing. I'm making the automata too slowly. Give me a factory and I'll turn out hundreds in a year. Find me machines for welding and molding and I'll make them from the hardest steel. Pick me clockwork artisans you trust and I'll create little ones with gunpowder hearts."

Later Ging climbs what remains of the stairs, her feet light on boards gone to cinders. She surveys the smashed pestle and pots, the broken distillers, the burnt papers—though none of them would contain the formulae that live only in her head. Aunrampha is close at her back, a touch always on her, and that is what keeps her from exhaling screams. They do not talk.

They shift the fallen beam away and loosen Nok's blackened limbs as best they can. Burned skin sloughs off her and the smell is unthinkable, the contortion of her impossible. She is almost weightless when Ging takes her up, swaddling her in a cotton sheet that has survived the arson.

At dawn, caked in soot and smelling of filth, they find a phiksuni at a small temple. She does not ask questions. The funeral is attended by two.

Ging is twenty-nine when malaria claims His Majesty. Before the year's end Prince Chulalongkorn has assumed the throne. Anna Leonowens is long gone, home in Angrit no worse for the wear. Her dismissal is not public knowledge and she spreads fiction of an amiable parting with the royal household.

Ging is thirty-four when Kampucha ceases to be a kingdom.

It comes as no surprise. The Yuan by that point isn't much of a sovereignty—has not been for a long time. She hears some exult that Siam's enemies fall one by one: Yuan, Phma, Kampucha finally. Aunrampha's brows knit tighter every day. They have moments together but those become fewer, briefer, and Ging does not sleep most nights.

There are two factories.

They have made a thousand and two hundred dolls, and nearly twice as many bombers: crude clockwork dolls, each bearing an explosive charge. Five of them are enough to sink a ship.

Ging is sixty-four, Aunrampha sixty, and there are Farangset gunboats in the harbors of Bangkok. Each cannon in the palace's direction, poised to fire.

There are six thousand automata, and twelve thousand small bombers. Ging whispers them a command at night.

Their march is utterly silent.

Tangi a te ruru
The cry of the morepork

Pip Ballantine

Manuwatu Gorge, New Zealand
September 1873

The man lying face up in the rain at the bottom of the gorge looked surprised. Agent Aroha Murphy, looking down at his broken body, shared that very emotion, though hers was tinged with the bitterness of disappointment. The cloak of thick bush around them and the rush of the Manawatu River made it seem like a far too pretty place for the man to have breathed his last— even in the pouring rain. Allen Henderson was a liar, a thief, and should have been dead years ago. However, it should have been at Aroha's hand.

As water filled his damnable eyes, she ground her teeth to hold back a scream of outrage at the unfairness of fate. She had been hunting Henderson for years after the attack on the farmhouse that had ended with her sister Emma dead, and her mother quite lost to her senses. *Perhaps I should feel more relieved,* she thought to herself, *but damn it, I wanted to end him.*

After a long few minutes, James Childs, the constable at her side, cleared his throat. He was trying to gallantly hold the umbrella over her head, but he was having some difficulty keeping his footing in the growing mud of the riverbank.

"Agent Murphy?" he asked softly, and that was enough to snap Aroha out of her contemplation.

She was here, she recalled, not as a wronged party, but as an agent of the Ministry of Peculiar Occurrences, and she had a job to do.

Aroha poked Henderson with her foot, rolling him over onto his face, and then bent down to examine his back.

"I can't see any wounds apart from that from the fall," she commented, pursing her lips. "I couldn't think of a man less likely to commit suicide than Henderson." She pointed up the hill to the path where carts and carriages made their perilous way along the side of the mountain between Ashhurst and Woodville. Her Maori kin had named the gorge Te Apiti, the Narrow Passage, and it was well deserved, for at any time a landslide could take out the fragile road. It was, however, not the cause of Henderson's plunge down to the river because the road was intact.

She looked up, her brown eyes focusing on Constable Childs. "You say this isn't the only one last night?"

The young man ran his fingers through his ginger hair and glanced at his damp regulation issue notebook. "Indeed, Marie Lafayette, Tommy Ring, Hemi Hudson, and two others that we don't know of down by where the river exits the gorge."

"And the moon last night was full?"

Childs nodded. "A huge one."

"Not all of them could have accidentally walked off the road on the same night," Aroha muttered to herself. She already knew she was on the right track, so she just had to find the culprit. That task sat poorly with her though, given the identity of one of the 'victims'.

"It's very strange," Childs replied, "but it was lucky you were in the area, Agent Murphy."

"Yes," she said examining the towering hills and bush around them. "Lucky indeed." She didn't dare tell him the Ministry had sent her chasing after a string of similar suicides up and down the North Island. The Ministry of Peculiar Occurrences did not have a large office in New Zealand, so resources were spread very thin, and she was pretty much it for the lower half of the North Island.

The wars with the Maori were still fresh in people's minds, and the Imperial forces had only just left the shores of Aotearoa. Still, because of her heritage, Aroha could move more easily around the countryside than most agents.

However, it was probably her dark skin and strange dress that had this young local policeman nervous. He was about to get a lot more so in a moment. She was sick of explaining herself to the locals. Lately she had given up telling them all about her airship captain Ngati Toa father, and her Italian mother, so she let her outfit speak for itself. Aroha might wear *pakeha* male clothing for ease of use, but she also had draped over her shoulder her father's *kahu huruhuru*. She had received the highly valued cloak, which contained the highly sought-after kereru feathers, as some kind of recompense from him for not taking her into the tribe. He already had a fine Ngati Toa wife, after all.

She wore the cloak not because it was his, but because it came from her ancestors, and that still meant a great deal to her.

Swinging down her backpack and placing it carefully on the ground, Aroha began to unpack the equipment she'd been hauling around since she'd left Rotorua three weeks ago.

She pulled out a small brass box, and attached to it a needle-thin rod, and to that a white sail-like shape about the size of her spread hand.

Constable Childs couldn't help leaning down to see what she was doing. "That looks…"

"…delicate," Aroha interrupted, worried the enthusiastic policeman might start poking at it in the way of men.

"What is it?"

She let out a sigh. "It's an aether tracker. A brand new device just shipped in from the London office last month."

Childs nodded as if he had a clue what she was talking about, and now she knew his eyes were fixed on the *moko kauae* that was carved proudly on her chin. The marks made her lips a dark blue, and decorated her chin with the curves and spirals she was entitled to. It was a declaration of her mana, her rank, and her past. She was proud of it, but she knew many others just didn't understand why she would mark her face.

The policeman was earnest but clueless, so Aroha smiled at him as she explained something he might be able to grasp. "The tracker is an extension of what my ancestors were very good at, but instead of following tracks in the bush we can follow the emissions of anything beyond the normal."

"You mean ghosts?" Childs whispered, going even paler.

That such things existed had always been accepted by her father's people, but pakeha tended to become a little unhinged if they came near to the truth.

"No," she said, as she began to turn the small crank on the side of the tracker, "ghosts do not exist Constable Childs…" she added under her breath, "…at least not here."

The small receiver on the top flicked back and forth, and narrow tape of paper chugged out from the side. After examining it, Aroha let out an exasperated breath. "The signal is too weak. Show me where you think the body fell."

Constable Childs gestured to two local men who were waiting some distance away from them, and they hustled up to carry Henderson away before he spoiled the beauty of the spot with his rotting corpse.

Aroha watched dispassionately as they did their work. It felt odd to know someone else had stolen her vengeance. Her father's ancestors believed firmly in *utu*, the concept that all must be kept in balance with kindness or vengeance depending on the action. Her mother's ancestors had also believed in an eye for an eye. Apparently both sets of ancestors would not be satisfied this day.

Still, it was a new world with new rules.

Aroha packed up the tracker, and then together she and Constable Childs climbed up the slippy, narrow track to the road. The wet bush dripped on her head, and the occasional fern slapped her in the face. New Zealand bush was thick and dense, unlike forests in the old world, and Aroha wondered if it concealed at this very moment an attacker.

"If Henderson didn't kill himself," Childs asked, holding back some *horoeka* saplings from her path, "and he didn't accidentally walk off the road, then what do you think happened to him, Agent Murphy?"

Holding her *kahu* around her tightly, Aroha considered how much to tell him. It looked like the local constable had nothing better to do than follow her around, and she couldn't really order him away; these were his locals that had died.

"I am not sure," she said finally, "but I am determined that we find out."

They were nearing the top when Childs finally asked the question she had been waiting for. "So...Murphy isn't much of a native name? Was your mother Maori?"

Half-caste girl they had called her when she was a child, and other less kindly words.

Aroha answered as reasonably as she could manage. "My father is Ngati Toa, an airship captain, but he and mother were never married. He went on his way when I was small, and she married an Irishman." She locked eyes with Childs. "I just found it easier to use my stepfather's name, but that is all I took from him."

The constable looked away, his face flushing red. He probably wouldn't have been so probing if she'd been a pakeha girl, but Aroha had nothing to be ashamed of, and she'd always found lies more trouble than they were worth.

They reached the roadway, which wasn't much more than the track they had just left, except it wound its way parallel with the river down below.

Aroha wordlessly set up the tracker on the edge of the roadway and cranked it to life while Childs watched. The tiny device began to spit out the long white tape, and this time the pattern of dots indicated a stronger reading.

"This is definitely where the event occurred," Aroha muttered, tucking her dark hair behind her ear. "There is a disturbance in the..."

The tracker resting just under her fingertips exploded. For a moment she wondered if she had done something terribly wrong, but then she realized that her ears were ringing from the retort of a very close gunshot.

She spun about, pulling the two-foot staff from under her cloak, and Childs had his pistol out, but neither of them could see where the attack had come from. Before she could say anything, Childs had grabbed her under the arm and dragged her back so that they had the cover of the downhill slope away from the road.

The constable's breath sounded very loud in her ear, but then her own heart was racing in time with his breathing.

"That," she whispered to Childs, "was either a very good shot, or a very poor one."

"Whichever," he replied, "they are prowling on the Queen's road, killing people. We have to stop them, but..." he paused. "Your device is all broken, how are we going to find them now?"

With a slight tap on his arm, Aroha grinned. "You pakeha, so married to your technology. We will do this the old fashioned way. Now, how do we get to the other side of the road?"

He jerked his head to the right. "There are drainage pipes running under the road, otherwise it would get swept away every winter."

Together they slipped and slid sideways until they found one. Luckily it was a rather large size, and agent and constable were able to navigate it hunched over. They emerged on the other side, and Aroha led them back towards where they had been shot at. For a pakeha, Childs was actually rather quiet.

As they drew near he did whisper in her ear, however, "Do you have a gun by any chance, Agent Murphy?"

She smiled at him and shook her head. "But I am armed, never fear."

Working their way up the hillside, Aroha easily found the place where their attacker had shot at them. "Maori," she said after examining the spot. When Childs frowned, she pointed to the impression in the mud. "Do you know many pakeha that wander through the bush barefoot?"

She led the way, following the trail of partial footprints, and broken undergrowth further up the hill. They were nearing the edge of the bush trail when Aroha heard the sound of something she had never imagined hearing in such a place.

It was a flute, or rather the *kōauau*, the Maori instrument that she still recalled her father playing to her as a child. Yet this was something more than mere music.

Aroha did not need an aether tracker to feel the pull of it. Suddenly, the music was all that mattered. Nothing else was of any consequence. Constable Childs turned to her, his face split with a huge, ridiculous grin. "You are a true Aphrodite of the South Pacific, Agent Murphy." His voice was slurred as he reached out to grab her, and for a moment Aroha leaned into his embrace. She wanted it. She needed him. Then the ghost of her mother's experience reached her and gave her a much needed dose of reality.

Henderson had captured her mother, drawn her into a web, and then killed her with it. Aroha had sworn never to allow that to happen to her.

She evaded the constable's clumsy attempt at a clinch, grabbed his arm, dragged it behind him, and then used it to push him away. In the slippery, wet conditions of the hillside, it didn't take much. With a surprised yelp, Childs slid down the hill into the embrace of the bush itself. Within a few feet he was lost to her sight, but she could hear his yelps of sorrow. Perhaps some time in the mud and rain would cool the unnatural ardour the music was pushing on him.

Aroha didn't pause to see how far he slid; she was already climbing up the rest of the hill as quickly as possible. Luckily, she still had some Ministry technology at her disposal.

It wasn't the first time that the paranormal had tried to overcome the agents of the Ministry, and one of the standard issues were a tiny pair of plugs for her ears. She paused to wind the exquisite clockwork before jamming one in each ear. The random tickings were louder than the music that filtered through the bush, and as she climbed higher, Aroha was relieved to find that the compulsion to lie down was less.

When she crested the hill and saw the open sky, it was very welcome. Off in the distance she could see an airship with the Ngati Toa colors. It seemed strange that her *iwi* was so close, and yet perhaps not.

She turned and looked across the ridge and saw the musician standing against the horizon. He was only fifty feet away from where she stood, but the ticking of the clockwork in her ears could not take away from the beauty of him.

He was only about her own age, with a kiwi feather cloak over one shoulder, and a *piupiu* around his lean hips. The flax skirt was seldom worn by itself anymore. In this day and age most Maori had adopted some type of pakeha clothing, but this tall, dark skinned young man wore none of that. As he stood there, with the flute raised to his nose, playing the most haunting music she knew, it was like he had stepped out of another age.

For a long moment she quite forgot why she was there. She glanced over her shoulder and realized she was not imagining it; the Ngati Toa airship was getting closer, and she finally had confirmation that her *iwi* had something to do with this.

The player swayed slightly on the spot, but then his eyes locked on Aroha, and eventually he saw that she was not moved by the power of the flute. He lowered it from his lips.

"Aroha," the man called to her over the wind, "I hope you know this was for you."

Under her cloak, her hand closed on the shaft of her weapon. "Do I know you?" she asked, Maori feeling strange on her tongue after so long in the world of the Ministry.

"No," came the mild reply, "but I know you. I am Ruru."

245

It was the name of the owl in the dark, the one heard but seldom seen. It was very clever.

"And that," she said, inching her way closer, "is the instrument of Tutanekai." She had heard the stories, even though they were not ones of her tribe. Tutanekai had fallen in love with a beautiful maiden of another tribe, but they had been separated by a lake. When he had played the flute, the maiden Hinemoa had been so moved that she had dared the frigid waters of the lake to reach him.

Aroha swallowed as she heard the engines of the airship over the wind. "I thought it was a love story, but now it seems poor Hinemoa might not have had a choice. Where did you get it from?"

Ruru held the flute up, so she could see how small but intricately carved it was. "I found it," he said simply.

The instrument of the most famous love story in all of Aoteroa's history, and he held it like it was a weapon—which he had turned it into. Aroha suspected he must have found the burial site of the lovers. It did not belong to his *iwi*.

"That was made for love," Aroha said, pointing to the flute. "It wasn't meant for vengeance."

Ruru glanced up, behind her, to where the airship was drawing close and closer. "It depends on how you play it."

Aroha held out her hand towards him, trying to keep her voice unemotional. "Tutanekai's love and yearning shouldn't be used to kill. Let me return it to his people so it may be re-buried with him."

Now the airship engines were very loud. Aroha didn't know who was on it, but she understood that once it came close Ruru and the flute would disappear.

Ruru shook his head. "Utu was exacted for you, Aroha. Among others, but for you most of all. We have to use what we have, just as our people have always used what we have." He pointed to the airship. "Your own tribe know that."

Aroha could feel the tearing inside her; the two parts of her heritage pulling at her. What was left in the middle? Anything at all?

Both parts understand vengeance, but at the same time she remembered her role, the oath she had made to protect the people of this land from the strange, the unusual, the bizarre. Despite her own personal feelings, no one should have the power of Tutanekai.

"Give me the flute," she said, pulling her *taiaha*. The short three-foot tube extended out with a hiss.

His eyes widened when he saw her innovation up close, as she spun it around and directed it at him. He met her first attack with a parry of the rifle he quickly snatched up from against the rock.

Her *taiaha* hissed with its internal power, jetting steam into his face, and he backed away blinded for a moment. When he regained his vision, Ruru actually looked upset. "You are attacking your own people? I am setting wrongs right!"

"It is a different age," Aroha said, as she swung her *taiaha* for his legs. "You cannot be judge of all things. None of us can."

A ladder unfurled from the airship above them. Ruru glanced up at it for just a moment, and Aroha knew that she had only that moment. Distracted as he was, she could have had the killing blow, but instead levelled a blow for his head, and when he jerked out of the way, she stepped in and snatched the flute from the waistband of his *piupiu*.

Their brown eyes locked as her fingers tightened around the delicate piece of bone. "You have had enough utu," she shouted to him over the roar of the airship engines. "Tell my father, so has he. We are done."

Ruru let out a laugh at that, and then turned and leapt for the ladder just as it pulled it away. His fingers locked on the rungs, and then he climbed up and away.

Aroha did not look up as the airship moved away. She had not seen her father in years, but he had his life in the clouds, and she had one on the ground. Just like Rangi and Papatunuku, the sky father and the earth mother. Somewhere in between was a place for her to stand, and she just had to find it.

It took Aroha a couple of weeks to return to Wellington and the district headquarters of the Ministry. It was the fault of a rather roundabout trip she took. She knew she was a mess of mud and stank sorely, but the idea that had begun worming its way into her head would not be put off.

Miss Tuppence let her into the Regional Director's office, with only the slightest of winces at her appearance, so perhaps it was not that bad.

Anderson looked up from his desk, his bright blue eyes roaming over her condition. "Agent Murphy, I see things must be urgent with you. I take it your mission was successful?"

This was going to be the hard bit. "Yes, sir. It turned out that a Maori nose flute with unusual properties was being used to extract utu on some rather nasty people."

He placed his pen carefully down on his desk and steepled his fingers. "And I take it you apprehended the suspect and got hold of this flute?"

She looked him directly in the eye. "Actually Regional Director, the perpetrator escaped, but I did manage to make sure he no longer had the flute in his possession."

Anderson waited for her explanation in a way that was rather unnerving.

"Unfortunately," she said with the steadiest of voices she could manage, "the artifact was smashed into pieces in the process." She did not tell him that it had been returned to Tutanekai's *iwi*, to be buried with honor. As far as his ancestor's knew the flute was merely a *tapu* item, sacred but with no mysterious powers. She had not enlightened them on that, just as she was not enlightening her superior.

"Well, that is a shame," the Regional Director said, picking up his pen.

Aroha did not move.

"Is there something else, Agent Murphy?"

She swallowed hard, thinking of her torment at taking such a sacred object, and how she was stuck between the worlds of her parents—but perhaps that could be put to advantage.

She stood a little straighter, resting her hand on her *taiaha* under her cloak, gaining strength from that touchstone of tradition. "Director Anderson, in all my travels, I have noticed that there is something missing from the Ministry."

Her superior's dark eyebrows pressed together. "You have had a sudden dose of insight. Do tell, Miss Murphy?"

"I believe there is a better way to handle the acquisition of dangerous objects." Her fingers rested on the breast of her coat where the flute had so recently ridden. "Rather than barging in and snatching away objects, might a softer, gentler approach be not the best way, with a position made especially for it?"

He leaned back in his chair and tapped his fingers on the desk between them. Morning sun spilled over the pile of papers. "And what would you call this position?"

Aroha smiled. "I believe we could begin by creating a liaison agent. Someone who could be a bridge between the Queen's Ministry and the tribes of Aoteroa."

"And that," he said with a tilt of his head, "I presume would be you?"

Aroha raised her chin just a fraction, feeling the pride of her ancestors whisper in the back of her head. "Yes, sir, that would be me."

For a long moment she feared the Regional Director would brush off her suggestion. However, finally he let out a sigh. "We are a long way from Headquarters, Agent Murphy, but I will take your suggestion under serious consideration." His gaze focused on her. "I can see that you have the particular...experience and qualifications for such a role. I will give the HQ Director my recommendation. I don't think they comprehend our ways are different down here."

She smiled at that. Perhaps there was hope, if they could understand each other just a little.

"Thank you sir," she said. "I believe I can make a difference."

He dismissed her, and as she turned to go, she thought of Ruru and the Ngati Toa airship, and wondered what the days ahead would bring.

The Construct Also Dreams of Flight

Rochita Loenen-Ruiz

"Martha is to wind up the worlds every day. Sergio must polish the big organ. Misa is to tend to the plants in the hothouse— and Lina, finish the last project."

I listened and did as I was supposed to do.

"Yes," I said. "Yes, Aunt Bertha. It shall be as you wish."

"Well," Aunt Bertha said. "A woman must die when a woman must die."

She pressed a hand to her bosom, coughed once, twice, and then she was gone.

The light here is unlike light anywhere else. The ancestral home is just a short distance from the sea and if you get tired of the sea, you can go further inland to where the land stretches out as far as the eye can see.

We don't have to till the land ourselves. That's not what she made us for. But the farmers bring in a seasonal tribute of rice and vegetables in lieu of rent and it's our task to ensure they're sent off to the estate manager who sells them at a profit for the family in Manila.

There's no reason for them to take the crossing and come to where we are. No reason at all.

Dear Lina, the letter read. *We'll be there on the fifteenth of the month.*

One drawback of living here was that the mail arrived slower than elsewhere. Today was the fifteenth of the month.

It was my task to wind up the others daily and set them to work. The letter sent me into a flurry of activity. We couldn't allow the family to sleep in rooms that smelled of dust and mold.

I looked out the window and watched for the dust cloud that would herald their arrival. Would they demand the selling off of the land now? Would they want me to vacate the ancestral home? And what about Aunt Bertha's final project?

I pocketed my anxiety, folded the cloth over the painting I was working on and went to ensure that the work was done. Rooms needed to be aired, beds needed turning and sheets had to be changed.

There was no need for worry. Every nook and cranny of the old house was shiny and clean. There was not even the slightest hint of a cobweb.

Still, another passage of the cleaning cloth never hurt anyone.

Noise heralded their approach. They were travelling in a painted coach and even the layer of dust couldn't dull the shine of the metal horses that pulled them. They quivered and stamped the ground with their shining hooves, steam rose up from their bodies and their mechanical eyes shivered open and shut.

"Ah, here she is," Cousin Emma said.

I reached out my arms and caught her as she sprang from the carriage.

"Lina dear, won't you come with us to the city? We'll take good care of you there, promise."

I stared at her in surprise.

"Oh stop it," Auntie Lily said. "Don't overwhelm the poor thing. Don't you see she's quite devastated at the loss of Bertha."

I blinked.

"I'm sorry," I said. "But I can't leave Carrascal."

"Of course," Cousin Emma said. "Of course, you'll stay here, Lina dear. It wasn't our intention to kick you out. Besides, if you leave who would take care of the old house. If you wish to stay, you must stay."

It's not that I don't want to move to the city, but this is the only home we've ever known. No matter how the family clicks and moans about Aunt Bertha's eccentric ways, no matter that they moan about the odd placement of the rooms, the slanting walls and geometric windows, we helped make this house according to Aunt Bertha's vision.

"Martha," I said. "I hope you've wound up the worlds in the Universum."

"The Universum?" Cousin Emma said.

"It's one of Aunt Bertha's projects," I replied.

"I want to see," Cousin Emma said. And a chorus of voices joined in with hers as the younger cousins clamored to see what they'd never cared to see when Aunt Bertha was still here.

"Martha," I said. "You lead the way."

I listened to the sound of their voices. Martha wouldn't be able to answer their questions, but I could.

I rested my hand on the brass telescope that had come to us all the way from Europe. Would they even appreciate how Aunt Bertha had tried to capture worlds she could only see through its powerful lens?

I watched them peer at the bell jars. Their eyes alight with curiosity. If you looked closely, you could see gears grinding and turning. Tiny little spheres orbited shining poles of brass, brass disks twirled and turned on their axes; round and round they went until their mechanisms wound down and Martha had to wind them up again.

"What else is here?" They asked. "What else?"

At that moment, a crescendo sounded from the organ room. Giggling and laughing, they went in search of the sound. They would find Sergio of course, and the room with long pipes built into it. When Aunt Bertha was alive, she would bring that organ to life and make so much sound the entire house would quake.

They were so distracted by everything they saw, they never thought to explore the basement. It was a relief. After all, it was where we kept the final project.

Yours to finish, Aunt Bertha had said to me.

Two of the cousins stayed after the others left.

Every day, Fermi and Ana walked down to the sea together. I watched them as they ran about and played.

When they came home, they trailed sea water and sand all over the narra floor.

"You're so good to us, Lina," Fermi said.

I made an attempt to capture the light around them. The blue and rose of their skirts, the pale cream of their panuelos, the midnight of their hair blending into each other—all in vain.

If I could assemble a machine from bits of metal and screws, would I be able to make something that would capture their light as I could not do?

I laid down my brush and looked out into the distance. I could feel the thrumming in my chest. It made a steady sound, a reminder of the promise I had given to Aunt Bertha on her deathbed. Maybe I wasn't made to be a painter. Maybe I was really made to be something else.

It was the steady drone that roused me.

I walked to the window and looked out.

There was this huge thing floating above us. It was shaped like a whale and its bulk blocked out all sight of the sun. I had seen it in one of Aunt Bertha's books, but I never thought I'd see one in Carrascal.

Fermi and Ana stood behind me, still dressed in their nightclothes, hands clutching each other.

"Lina," Fermi said. "What's out there?"

"I believe it's a zeppelin," I said.

Ana's eyes opened wide.

"No," she said. "It can't be. It can't be."

"Ana," Fermi said.

But Ana was running away from us, her feet slipping and sliding on the smooth floor. She rounded the corner that led to the bedrooms. We heard the bang of the door and the click of a lock.

Fermi's face wore a shadow. Gone was the light of the past days.

"It couldn't last forever," Fermi said.

Her voice broke and I didn't know what else to do, so I opened my arms and let her cry.

There was no more running down to the sea.

I wound up the automatons and we all went to work. No matter what went on outdoors, someone still had to tend to the plants in the hothouse. Worlds needed to be wound up, the organ pipes needed cleaning and then there was the matter of Aunt Bertha's final project.

It stood in the workshop—a stranded skeleton that looked nothing like the bird Aunt Bertha compared it to. Its slender frame was formed from bowed copper rods, and its sides were hemmed with strips of balsa wood. We still had to stretch the canvas cover over it. Maybe then it would look like something meant for flight.

"Lina," Fermi said. "What are you all doing down here?"

"Working," I said.

She came downstairs.

"Amazing," she said.

She walked around the frame, her hands reaching out but not quite touching.

"You made this?" She said.

"It's Aunt Bertha's project," I replied. "We only put it together."

"How wonderful," she said. "How simply wonderful."

After Fermi left, we finished the rest of what still needed to be done. We unfolded the canvas from its hiding place.

Good for flying, Auntie Bertha had said.

Slowly, we stretched the canvas over that bare frame. It was no longer a skeleton now.

My chest thrummed and I pressed the tips of my fingers to it.

"Well now," I said. "I suppose we must try to get it to fly."

There were voices upstairs and when I came into the living room, there was a man. A big man with a wild shock of hair. He had a beard the color of sand and a big nose and tears in his eyes.

"Fermi," he said. "I came all this way. I even took the governor's zeppelin."

Ana stood with her back to him.

For the first time, I noticed the copper tone of Ana's fingers. She did not tremble, but when she moved her head, I heard the creak of her gears and the stutter of her cogs.

"We won't come with you," Fermi said.

Her fingers were mottled red and white where they were tightly clasped around Ana's.

"Listen to me," the big man said. "We can't just pretend I didn't see her. She has to go back. You shouldn't have taken her with you, Fermi. You should have let things be."

Fermi bared her teeth at the big man.

"What will you do, Jorge? Will you take us back as if we were your captives? I won't let you, you know."

Jorge sighed.

"Look," he said. "She's a machine and a faulty one at that. The governor wants her back."

"I know what the governor wants her for," Fermi said. "She won't be taken apart, Jorge. Ana is Ana."

Her voice reminded me of Auntie Bertha.

After a while, Jorge left. He dragged his left leg when he walked and left small scratches on the floor. I made a note of his path and later I sent Misa to polish away the marks of his passing.

I ignored the drone of the zeppelin's engine. Jorge was not going away, and neither was his ship.

I watched Ana and in the shadow of that ship, it was impossible to miss all the tiny little things that passed me by when they were bathed in the light of their happiness.

Finally, it was time to test Aunt Bertha's project. Sergio flung the doors of the workshop open. Behind the house there was an incline. The three of us set our hands to Aunt Bertha's project and pushed.

The machine wasn't that heavy and a breeze came up from behind and made it easier for us to push it upward.

"Wait."

Fermi and Ana raced up from behind us.

"Where are you going?" Fermi said. "What are you doing?"

I stared at her and I stared at Ana.

I couldn't miss it now.

The shadow of that ship stripped her of everything that made her seem slightly human.

"A machine," I said. "Must do as it was created to do. This is Aunt Bertha's project."

"So you keep saying," Fermi said.

Behind her, Ana made a sound.

"It's a flying machine," Fermi said again. "A flying machine. Do you understand what that is and what it can do?"

I stared into Fermi's face—watched excitement bloom in her eyes.

In the diagrams she'd left behind, Aunt Bertha had explicitly stated how the project would reach its fruition.

I took off my gloves. I took off my boots. I prepared to take off my gown.

I stared at my paintbrush. I suppose I wasn't really made to be a painter after all.

"Lina," Fermi said. "What are you doing?"

"It's the final stage of the project," I said. "The machine won't fly without an engine. It won't rise without the mechanism Aunt Bertha put inside my chest."

"But you don't want to," Fermi said. "You don't want to leave, do you? You want to stay here in this place. You want to care for the house and for the others."

I stopped.

Fermi's voice rose in intensity and she pulled Ana in front of me.

"Listen to me," Fermi went on. "You want to stay in this place, Lina. But Ana—Ana must fly."

Ana gave a start and I watched as she turned to face Fermi.

"Look," Fermi said. "I know you're frightened, Ana. But it's the only way. We'll go. We'll go together you and I."

Long after they left, I could still hear the sound of their passing.

Even in the shadow of the zeppelin, light floated all around them.

Naked and with the heart of her revealed, they were still suffused with light. Human and machine. Sun-browned flesh against copper bright metal.

Slowly, the rudder of the flying machine came to life. Ana's sound, a high counterpoint against the background drone of the big zeppelin.

Sergio and Misa pushed, and for a moment, when they slid off the incline, it seemed like they wouldn't make it. They wobbled slightly in the air, then a gust of wind pushed them upward, and gave them lift.

I kept on watching until the sound of her faded and they were nothing more than a speck on the horizon.

Aunt Bertha's final project—it was finished.

I didn't bother to open the windows or to air out the rooms. There was nothing left to do until we received instructions from the family.

I sat in the darkness of the living room and waited.

When Jorge came, he didn't bother to knock. He simply came thumping up the stairs, dragging his leg on the floor and leaving scratches behind him.

"Where are they?" He said.

I looked at him and did not answer.

"Well," he said. "Well. What will I say to them in the capital about this? Tell me that, you thing?"

I took his hand in mine and looked up at him.

Already, I could feel myself slowing down. The project was ended. I had done what I was supposed to do.

"I tried," I said to him. "But no matter how I tried, I couldn't capture that light."

Of course, he didn't understand.

He's not like you and I.

But it's all right. It's all right. Someday, Fermi and Ana will return and when they do, perhaps it will be my turn to fly.

Budo
Or,
The Flying Orchid

Tade Thompson

"Being desirous, on the other hand, to obviate the misunderstanding and disputes which might in future arise from new acts of occupation (*prises de possession*) on the coast of Africa; and concerned, at the same time, as to the means of furthering the moral and material well-being of the native populations,"

General Act of the Berlin Conference on West Africa,
26 February 1885

There is a story told in my village about the man who fell from the sky. The British also tell this tale in their history books, but it is a mere paragraph, and they invert the details.

In October 1884 I was a Yoruba translator for a British trading outpost. This man from the sky, we called him Budo. He was in the custody of the English, who questioned him. They tortured him with heat and with cold and with the blade, but they did not know what answers would satisfy. I know this because I carried their words to him, and his silence back to them. His manner was mild and deferent at all times, but they held him in isolation. For good reason they considered him dangerous. I will explain this later.

One afternoon while most of the English were sleeping a white man arrived at the gate demanding admission. One of the Sikh sentries told me he was a scout, and appeared bruised, half-naked and exhausted. He was too out of breath to speak, although he seemed keen to give his report. Kenton, the NCO of the military contingent, asked one of my brothers to bring water while he soothed the scout. The man took two gulps, splashed some on his face, then looked up at Kenton. He said one word.

"French."

The scout vomited over the floor.

Kenton ordered the men to revive him, but I saw the fear on his face, though at the time I did not know what "French" meant. He also doubled the guard and conferred with other white men. I remained at the periphery and kept quiet and still. Experience had taught me that they often forgot about my presence when I remained silent.

"Let me tell you about the French," said one of the enlisted men. "They're very dirty, you savvy? Never do they wash. Eat frogs, don't they? Kill their royals with a goolly-tine."

"What's this goo-lly-tine?" I asked.

The man made a chopping motion across his own throat, then guffawed. I could not imagine the spilling of royal blood and I thought to myself what curious creatures these French must be.

At that moment Kenton strode out of the Commanding Officer's office, red faced in that way white men get when they are drunk or angry. His gait was too assured and stable for inebriation, and besides, I had never seen Kenton imbibe. He was sober in all manner of things. He was, as he passed me, muttering to himself.

"Make ready. Make ready. All the fornicating heathen gods! Make ready, he says." Kenton stopped, swivelled and stabbed me in the chest with his index finger. "You. Get me the Black. Right now. No, wait. Clean him up and give him some water and corn meal. Then bring him to the office."

Budo sat cross-legged on the ground and ate with his hands, slowly, deliberately, concentrating on each morsel. I tried to speak but he held up his hand. He was one who favoured full attention on any task at hand. I therefore concentrated on his features while waiting. He was darker than most, lanky, with sunken cheekbones. His hair had grown out in captivity, but it was not tangled. He had a Widow's Peak but large eyes dominated his face. His muscles were flat, like a blanket on his bones. He wore a tattered, filthy loin cloth of indeterminate colour and powerful stench.

I had grown soft in the house of the oppressors and I am ashamed to report that I could not stand the sight of him, used as I was to more genteel surroundings.

He drank water in the same way he ate and I grew impatient. From Budo's cell I could hear the steady hammer of the brothers securing the fortifications and the regular footfalls indicating the drills of soldiers preparing themselves. The predominant smell in the cell came from the outhouse. This was by design.

When Budo looked my way I felt more naked than he. "Tell me why they want me."

I did.

He stood. "Take me to Kenton."

"Change your clothes," I said, offering him some cotton shorts, but he would not take them.

"There is no time for that."

At this point I should probably tell you why the English wanted Olufemi Budo when they should have been counting their Enfield rifles and begging their gods for a functioning Maxim.

I have mentioned that Budo fell from the sky. Nobody saw him fall exactly, but some fishermen discovered him in a palm tree one morning, injured, unconscious and wearing a peculiar contraption made of leather and strips of rubber. It was a system of belts and bladders that none of the villagers understood enough to save. When he regained consciousness the first thing Budo asked for was his harness, but nobody understood what he meant. His Yoruba was correct, if stilted and precise. He suffered from malaria and had several fractures which the bone-setter took care of. They also fed him *agbo iba* until his fever broke.

Our village was a sleepy place about a hundred miles from the west bank of the Niger. We used to be an occasional reservoir for the transatlantic slave trade before it was abolished. Then we became a reservoir for enforced labour without pay, which I could not distinguish from slavery, but the British priest assured me this was the better condition. Honest labour, he called it. They made us build infrastructure—roads, houses, railroads—designed solely for the purpose of taking goods from the interior to the coast where ships waited to sail for Liverpool and Portsmouth.

Before Budo landed on us our weapons were cutlasses, spears, amulets, charms, bows and arrows and leather vests, none of which worked against English steel or gunpowder. The mounted raiders from the Oyo Empire defeated us with ease when they needed slaves.

There were no raids while he recovered. He hobbled around on a thick stick staring at everything from the mud used for mortar to the umbilici of newborn babies. He looked at millet harvests and rubber trees. He sometimes asked if anyone had seen a flying orchid, but we did not understand him.

From the outset he was an object of curiosity in the village. Children followed him about making fun of his shamble or his strange pronunciation of Yoruba words. He garnered a lot of attention from the young ladies as well. It is not hard to intuit why. He was not one of us and hence had mystery. He did not speak much, and one could project celestial intent on his most mundane action. He had preternatural interest in everyone and everything around him. I am unsure if he deflowered any of the admirers, but the smiles and significant looks were suggestive.

He stayed with the medicine man for eight weeks, until his bones knitted. The village chief summoned him after that, and he came into the royal hall flanked by two rod-bearers. I was a member of court at the time, and Budo was asked to explain himself.

"Please forgive me for not greeting you in the proper manner, *kabiyesi*. My joints are still stiff from my accident."

"Keep your apologies to yourself," I said. "Just tell us where you are from."

"Of course." Budo kept his eyes on the chief. "*Kabiyesi*, I do not remember much since waking up. My injuries have robbed me of much of my past. But I do remember the path to many technologies and special engines. If you will permit me I can direct them towards the betterment of your village while I try to work out precisely what happened to me."

The chief whispered to his praise-singer. The speaker, the *abobajiroro,* said, "Can you fly?"

"No, *kabiyesi.*"

The chief whispered again. The speaker said, "Your Lord and Earthly representative of the *orisha* asks what you mean by 'betterment'."

"I mean the discouragement of the whites and their assistants, the ones who raid your village."

The chief whispered. The speaker said, "Budo will be allowed to establish these technologies. He will be assisted by the most gracious Lord's own daughter, Omolola."

This alarmed me. I had hoped to be placed in charge of monitoring the stranger to increase my standing, but the main problem was that Omolola was unpredictable and difficult to trust. When she was sixteen her father sent her to the court of the Alaafin of Oyo as an ambassador to negotiate the amount of tribute expected. The defiant slaver Francisco Marinementus was at court, present for her plea, and became infatuated. He wished to add her to his harem which was rumoured to be at least one hundred strong. She threatened to geld him in perfect Portuguese and dissuaded the old man, much to the amusement of the Alaafin and his advisers. Omolola was married to a nobleman and had six children, however her husband was weak and ineffectual. Her prodigious sexual appetite was well reported, as was her spouse's inability to satisfy, and yet all her children bore a striking resemblance to him. This was a puzzlement to me until I overheard her speaking to one of her husband's wives.

"I only take lovers when I am bleeding or pregnant," Omolola said. "If the train is full there can be no new passengers."

She took to her new duties with great dedication, never leaving the stranger's side, and I spied on them. Budo performed arcane experiments with rubber and iron and malachite and other minerals while Omolola watched. He had close to a hundred bags of coal. For reasons I could not understand Omolola instructed the young men to gouge out holes in the trees, including the Iroko tree in the square.

They argued. Their voices were loud but I did not understand what it was about.

"Yes," said Budo. "You are right. Rigid is better, but takes more time and skill. A non-rigid—"

"—Is a flying bomb. I will not be a part of that." Omolola did not like losing arguments.

In between this activity they copulated compulsively. I envied their vigour and youth.

Using untreated leather and alloyed iron sheets he built armour for our men. He attached metal tanks to each hollowed-out tree. I could not help myself, I had to ask what they were for.

"They are boilers," said Omolola. "The coal furnace heats water and generates steam. A one-way valve allows it to generate steady pressure."

"Pressure for what?" I asked but she spied her lover entering his bunk.

She became feral and dismissed me. "*Abyssus abyssum invocat.*"

Deep calls to deep. I taught her that when she was twelve. She had been my most talented student. She was also a painter and sculptor. Wild of heart, fickle, capricious, but brilliant. Not to be underestimated.

In all of his actions I saw that Budo was cultured, had good manners and could read and write. He scratched out symbols in the dust, frowned and drew others. For days on end smoke, steam and foul smells emanated from the building where they carried out their research and erections. Budo listened to all the stories of the griot. He attended the chief who laughed with him and at him, sparking my envy.

When the raid happened we were prepared. The older villagers such as myself hid where we could observe. The young women and men went to their designated jobs as soon as lookouts reported redcoats. They fired up all furnaces. Omolola set dials on mechanisms that were little more than naked mainsprings. "No time for aesthetics," she said, when I asked.

The British came with rifles and swords, most likely planning to intimidate us into surrendering our healthy ones without a fight. I am not ashamed to say I was in favour of this non-violent approach. Appeasement ensures survival. The English stood back and barked instructions to the Indians in their turbans and the black collaborators who made up the front line. They fired a warning volley from their Lee-Metford rifles even before they reached the village. This was their way. When I was a child we used to call the guns lightning sticks or *amunowa*, bringers-of-fire.

The blacks and the Indians broke cover, exploring the village, puzzled. The English came on their heels, sweating, arrogant, expectant. One man noticed the small furnaces smoking on the trees, but had no time to examine them. Misshapen bladders of black rubber rolled out from doorways of buildings and huts. Archers nocked, aimed, and let loose their arrows, puncturing each bag, releasing a green miasma that crept forward, hugging the ground, engulfing the invaders. I was curious about the smell, but Budo had us wear gas masks and we looked like glass-eyed demons to each other.

The invaders choked on the noxious gas. "Fall back!" screamed someone, but the moment for retreat had passed. The mainsprings wound down at the same moment.

"Get down," yelled Budo at everyone.

The men nearest the tree were lucky. They died instantly, heads pulverised as the steam vented and the metal projectiles flew in every direction. Each tree discharged a foot-long metal missile. Men further away took hits to the belly or chest and died in agony. The ones furthest did not die. The depleted force embedded the rods in their bodies. They screamed in pain, and would live until they succumbed to inevitable corruption of the flesh.

Some of these tree-cannons failed. Boilers ruptured without building up the necessary pressure to propel the projectiles. Furnaces fizzled out. The rods went awry. Despite this, enough fired to discourage the English force.

We celebrated with loud cries and songs thanking *Olodumare*, the creator. Our mistake was to misidentify a skirmish for the war. The second wave hit before we could reload Budo's magnificent weapons. They gave no quarter. They razed the village and killed old men, women, children. The English singled out Budo for particular cruelty as the architect of their suffering but also for his secrets. He never talked.

Omolola and her six children disappeared.

That was five months before.

If Kenton wanted Budo it was for the engines of war trapped in the prisoner's head. The problem would be how to motivate Budo to give up his secret knowledge. I translated rapidly.

"...Légion étrangère, Algerian infantry, Penal Light Infantry Battalions, Zouaves and a smattering of mercenaries," said Kenton.

"They came up river?" asked Budo.

"Under false Trading Company flags, then disgorged troops on the west bank of the Niger."

A map sprawled over the table showing the rivers Niger and Benue, and where they met to form a Y. A Matroyschka doll marked the position of the French.

"How seasoned are your men?" asked Budo.

Kenton shrugged. "They are well-trained. Some have seen battle against the Mohammedans and a few of the older ones are veterans of the West Africa Squadron that was tasked by the Crown to catch or sink slavers. Make no mistake, we would have been able to defeat them quite easily, but our little…afternoon tea with your village left our numbers depleted. We have never lost to the French."

Budo stroked the map. I noticed the cartographer frown and he seemed about to speak when Kenton silenced him with a look.

"What will you do for me in return?" asked Budo in halting Yoruba.

"Release. Full exoneration. You'll have the thanks of the Crown," said Kenton.

Budo laughed when I translated. "What do I care for their Crown's gratitude?"

"You can receive papers that force anyone to assist you, or forbid any impedance. This is worth more than sacks of gold," I said.

"I don't care for gold either," Budo said. "Why are you trying so hard to convince me? Do you enjoy being their slave so much?"

"I am not a slave," I said.

"No, just a traitor." He scratched his crotch. He had nits on his head and, I felt sure, his pubic hair as well. "Tell your Kenton that I will require absolute and immediate obedience of all my instructions if I am to do this on time."

The first thing he did was snatch ink from the cartographer and request writing surfaces.

I will not pretend that I fully understood what happened in the days and weeks that followed. Budo supervised the making of engines using a complicated combination of dried bamboo sticks, repurposed iron and steel, rubber, gunpowder and different crystals of myriad colours. Kenton came into the workshop one day and picked up one of the contraptions which was a pole with a large but hollow ball of steel on one end. He looked at me, but I could not tell him anything. He was tired and worn out.

"You hate us, don't you?" said Kenton.

I could not speak. All I had to do was lie, but despite all of my compromises I did not have this in me.

"Try to remember that we are people. These men have wives and children in England. I have family. I also have instructions that I must carry out." He frowned, then turned and left.

We waited for the French just like my village waited for the British. The English still armed themselves with bolt-action rifles, but Budo had marked out places they could not walk. His eyes held a glint that was not battle-thirst. He wanted to see how well his mechanisms would work.

Rather than over-extend himself trying to defend the compound Kenton deployed forces to the south-east direction to meet the French. When the battle joined a light rain fell, drizzling, cooling every surface, causing mist to rise from the heat of the noon sun. They used conventional weapons, sinew, and raw courage. The foreigners shot at each other, and some died, some lost limbs, fighting over land that was not theirs.

Kenton never expected to win in the bush, outnumbered as he was. They fell back to the compound where they had dug foxholes and other places to hide.

To the French the compound must have appeared as a leafless forest where the trees were all six-feet high poles tipped with shining metal balls, shallow mud all over the ground and an after-smell of mulch and burnt rubber. They examined the buildings and the barracks, but found all empty. One legionnaire touched the nearest ball. Nothing happened. Then at the far end of the compound Budo emerged holding a device that looked like two polished iron hemispheres joined together with wires and metal spokes pointing outwards towards the enemy. It was the size of an adult goat, with thick cables growing out of each core and trailing behind him, woven into a tangle held up by seven infantry men. He wore elbow-length rubber gloves and half of his face was covered by a dark screen. He wobbled with the effort of manipulating the thing which looked like a giant insect.

"Close your eyes," he screamed, and activated a trigger mechanism.

The crack that ensued was louder than thunder. Men howled with fear and despair. I had to look. A ball of fire rolled away from Budo about a foot off the ground. It seemed slow, but it bounced from pylon to pylon, leaking strands of electricity like thread from a weft coming undone. It passed through the first man and stripped his skin off in sheets, leaving a blackened skeleton. No scream. The bones crumpled to the ground, hissing in the mud.

Then, hell.

The fireball ran amok. The first one fizzled out, and Budo fired again, and a third time. There were puddles of flesh, molten gore, bones, and equipment heating and blowing up everywhere. The breeze filled our noses with sulphur and ozone and excreta. A French flag burned in isolation, lonely as the cries of dying men. The compound was alive with flames.

Scouts confirmed that the survivors had fled.

Budo pointed his fearsome device at the heavens and fired. A glowing ball of yellow light floated straight and true into the sky, trailing lightning that struck trees, flagpoles and the roof of the officer's mess before disappearing into the clouds. I thought it was out of character for him to celebrate in this fashion, and I was right.

He dropped the smoking engine on the floor and took off the gloves. He yanked me by the arm and took me to Kenton who was yelling huzzah with his men.

"Tell the white man I have finished my task and will be on my way," said Budo.

"Is he jesting? I don't know if this was science or sorcery, but I have to take you to London. The Queen will have use for your talents. You'll be under guard until I can arrange passage for you."

I did not translate this for Budo. I said he would be released later. I wanted to spare him the feeling. Time enough to break his heart on another day. *There are many events in the womb of time which will be delivered.* He smiled and at that point I noticed that he was counting. His devices were also ticking, winding down to something.

"You are wrong about the French," said Budo in English.

Kenton looked stunned, but I had already begun to suspect that Budo knew more than he revealed.

"They are not monsters any more than you English are," said Budo. "I met many French men and women while I was in Milan and Venice. They are like you."

"You've been to Italy?" said Kenton. His right hand hovered around his pistol holster.

"Many times." Budo turned to me and said, "Run. Don't look back."

This was a gift, undeserved, perhaps because he knew I did him a kindness in my speech. Or perhaps he pitied my age. I sprinted away, and heard Kenton shout my name twice before a mighty rumble drowned his voice out. I looked back, like Lot's wife, and saw the finger of God smite the outpost. An oval, brown airship hovered within the smoke of the burning buildings. A weapon projected down from the gondola and shot flames at the survivors.

Something else: I saw Omolola. She hung in the air strapped to a gas bag that strained to ascend, tethered to a tree. She helped Budo reach the airship and they floated away.

That was the last I heard of them.

The governor general of Nigeria, Lord Lugard, wrote an account of this event in volume IV of his diaries.

In 1894 a small British outpost valiantly resisted a surprise French incursion. They fought to the death, every last man Jack, preferring to burn the coastal foothold rather than surrender.

Our history is not written in the pages of books, and the story of Budo is repeated by storytellers and griots all over the West Coast of Africa, in Brazil and in Haiti. It is told by campfire and moonlight, and it is commemorated by masking. Whenever you see a Yoruba festival with a masquerade sporting gigantic goggles and strips of rubber as tassels, you are watching a re-enactment of Budo's exploits.

One image remains clear and frightening: the eyes of Omolola as she rescued her lover. I could see that she would have burned through any number of enemies and razed the forest to the ground if it stood between her and Olufemi Budo.

It will soon be time for me to leave this world for the next. My breath comes a little harder, my thoughts a little cloudier.

My tale is done.

The Şehrazatın Diyoraması Tour

S. J. Chambers

The Constantinople street is drenched in pure sunlight, saturating almost all color from the scene. The tall, alabaster stone building that zigzags and narrows the passage casts a Payne's grey shadow onto the ocher cobblestones. Despite its disparity in hue, the street is made interesting by the people who populate it. In the background, children escorted by an old man are wrapped in tattered rags. In the midground, two women wearing blue and white *çarşafs* steady themselves to march past a female family of ill repute who catch the eye by leaving their marigold, emerald, and ruby silk brocade *entaris* uncovered.

The shrouded women also pass and ignore the dozen or so British tourists who stare at them wide-eyed and in awe. The concubines, however, leave the street and beckon these Westerners inside. It is with these women that the image transitions and the tourists who have been viewing this scene are escorted into the realm of Turkish delights without taking one actual step into the vice-den.

Of course, they don't realize that. As far as they are concerned their bodies are being propelled. The tourists are so enthralled with the scenery around them they don't notice it is nothing but light streaming from the Şehrazat's orbs, and that they are standing and static around her in the diorama gallery of the Imperial Ottoman Museum.

The immersion begins the moment they enter the building.

Waifs hired from off the street usher them into an empty and barren gallery. The only artifact in the room is what appears to be a life-sized sculpture, but is, in fact, the main attraction: the *Şehrazatın Diyoraması*.

Dressed like a sheik's daughter with only her face and forearms exposed, she wears a beautiful variegated turban knotted at the side of her temple, and an aigrette of gold coins adorns her brow. She wears ribboned amulets and *pay-i-çifts* of pearls and turquoise, and underneath her *kaftan* flashes the violet-embroidered, rose-dusk silk of her *shalwar*. Her flesh is carved from ivory, and upon close inspection, was delicately put together with bronze ligaments and socketry. This allows for some movement—her head can swivel and her arms gesture and rest—but she is for the most part immobile. Her face is completely inanimate; her pulchritude is composed of general features, high cheekbones and full lips. She has solid glass eyes sans pupils and a face with a frozen, pensive gaze. Special attention has been given to the earlobes, which are carefully carved and inlaid with bronze to better capture the gallery's acoustics. Sound is her only means of collecting information and receiving commands. Other than that, she does not mimic any of the other human senses.

She stands on a stage in the middle of the gallery with one arm extended to the door wherein entered her creator and master, Werner von Froeschner, a charismatic German scientist who before his renown as the Şehrazat's creator had gained repute for his achievements in Genevan Galvanism, von Kemplen mechanics, and advances in scaling down difference engines while optimizing their performance. Because he insists on being the only one who operates the machine, he has stayed in the capitol and become the master of ceremonies to the diorama tour.

"Ladies and Gentlemen, welcome to Constantinople!" Waifs circle the tourists with tea and biscuits. "I know you are all eager to begin our trek, but first I want to introduce you to our guide.

"Now I know what you all must be thinking: here is just another Chess Player. But I assure you, this is no chess player. This...this is the future of—well, everything—but we get ahead of ourselves. But, today—for today—this is the future of travel, yes? How many times have you seen a Delacroix set outside of Constantinople and thought that you too would like to see that scene? Be a part of that exact scene? Ah, but you come to the Empire and you no longer see that exact scene." There are a few agreements among the audience. "We live in an Industrial world now. There is not much room left for Romance—no, my friends, I am afraid the visions of Gêrome and Delacroix are quickly becoming nothing but dusty relics hanging on an aristocrat's wall, and the experience you so longed for is ever fleeting...until now!

"You see, my friend Abdul Hamid is a traveler as well. He understands the romance that fuels such excursions, and as he visited my homeland he had his own vision—why not use all of this industry, all of this progress, to make a new thing of beauty? To make a new experience for the worldly traveler? To keep the East as it was without having to stay stuck in the past! His vision —the Şehrazatın Diyoraması!

"What you see before you is the marriage of art and science— the brainchild of some of the best minds in both the East and West. He hired me to oversee the Şehrazat's design and construction. Osman Hamdi Bey, the Turkish painter who was one of the first here to embrace the French techniques and was so well acquainted with the style we needed, curated and created the synthesized images you will shortly see. Louis Majorelle, the French furniture maker who can often be found in a Constantinople café, was commissioned to design her body, but would you believe the Sultan himself—a great carpenter— constructed it!" He pulls her flowing costume away from her abdomen to reveal the elaborate Marjorelle cabinet made of juniper wood inlayed with beech and ivory crocuses. Although it is shaped in the voluptuous style of a de Milo torso, its realism is blemished by two oblong doors inlaid with bronze knobs, which von Froeschner opens to reveal the contents within: a plethora of mechanical intestines that intertwine so densely that one cannot fathom what any of it is for.

Smiling at the quizzical expressions of those who gaze inside the cabinet, he closes her up. "You see, inside here is the *karanlık oda*—the darkroom—the camera obscura that projects this tour. This," he knocks on the torso, "this is the pride of the Ottoman Empire, for the diorama was devised and constructed by the Sultan's favored photographer, Bora Fahir Çağlar." He lets the skirts fall over the cabinet-torso and walks behind the Şehrazat with a melancholic expression. "Sadly, he disappeared before he could see his genius realized. No doubt, he would have marveled at the illusion he helped create."

On that somber note, the waifs pull shut the black curtains. Someone from the audience exclaims: "Professor, you have evaded explaining how she works."

Von Froeschner wags a finger. "Yes I have. With all due respect, ladies and gentlemen, if I explained how this marvel works, I would destroy the illusion you came here to enjoy. We, here, are not interested in bragging about our scientific discoveries, although we easily could do so and change the world.

No, we are here to provide you with an experience—so please, worry not on technicalities, just enjoy your holiday." He bends back down behind the Şehrazat, fumbling with her back as the room turns to pitch.

The tourists hold their breaths as a loud humming begins and exhale in delight as light composing the pale yellow and Prussian blue of Cappadocia shoots from her eyes and fills up the room. They forget about von Froeschner and the inner-workings of the machine, and journey forth into the fantasies of poets and painters.

In the Turkish Bath, grossly modeled after the infamous Ingres image, ladies and gentlemen are witness to voluptuous women lounging, dining, wading, and ultimately having their decadent ablutions tended to by maids.

Most all of the audience respond in wonder at the scene, some a little abashed to be witnessing it in mixed company, but there is one—there is always one—who mutters: "But that maid there with the perfume. She isn't Moorish like the other maids in the scene." And before their eyes, the blonde maiden who had been powdering another's hair darkens. Other comments follow: "That eunuch's hair is too auburn, and her skin still pale."

"Why don't they look us in the eye?"

"They seem too thin. Not voluptuous like the Venus."

And with every comment and observation, the image shifts, hair and skin brightens or fades, and the turbaned lute-player who faced away from the tourists now boldly strums while staring them all in the eye.

These effects are so subtle and undisruptive that the tourists who speak out are unsettled at first that the machine seems to hear them, while simultaneously pleased that the machine obeys them.

A group jester exclaims: "Perhaps there is a human brain tucked away in her bronze-casted skull of hers, hey, von Froeschner?"

"If that were true," von Froeschner retorts, "she'd still have human thoughts. Were that so, of what do you think they'd be?" The rhetorical question sinks into the merry group who are quieted by awe as the projection exits the Bath and enters onto a bustling marketplace, crosses the street, and enters a café filled with dozens of young bearded men in turbans and fezzes huddled to discuss news of the day in a great vaulted marble establishment with the walls decorated with *Iznik* tiles in the tulip fashion.

The shift is so seamless that the tourists are enthralled once again, and forget that with each critical utterance the projection changes into a more ideal vision—it is so imperceptible they forget they had even thought it, much less muttered it out loud. None of them consider that the image they see may be more romanticized now than it was before, and that the experience they are having is a false one. No, they came here to be comfortable. They especially disregard von Froeschner's retort and have no more notions of the dark rumors that were broached in jest.

Had von Froeschner equipped the Şehrazat with a voice box, she could have addressed the jester herself. She—he—may no longer be able to see or speak, but he can hear and think. He dreams what he can no longer experience. Sometimes, when he hears the tourists ask von Froeschner whether he—she—is "quite the storyteller like her mother, Scheherazade?" an allusion much encouraged by the scientist, he thinks his retort: *my mother died of consumption in Girit and told Christian stories to her older children while bedridden, and she named me Nikos Antonakis, not Bora Fahir Çağlar, not Şehrazat.*

But he cannot tell the tourists that Bora Fahir Çağlar was a deceit, and instead continues to project the falsehoods that most interest them.

The Sultan was interested in lies as well. They were a grand distraction from rumors, and the Ottoman Empire was becoming full of vile and horrid ones.

But behind every rumor is a semblance of truth. Nikos Antonakis learned this when he went to work as one of the myriad photographers called upon by the Sultan to document the Ottoman Empire with their lenses. Many of these photos became official tourist propaganda and souvenirs, but none of Nikos' images would be found in foreign scrapbooks, even less likely upon the gallery wall.

He began taking images that showed the classical grandeur and status of the Empire, but rumors of an uprising in his home village in Girit made him aim his lens beyond empirical glory and towards some unacknowledged Ottoman truths. He heard of other incidents and revolts in Armenia, and took his lens there.

The Photography Project had little tolerance for journalism, so Nikos sent his tintype testimonies to certain liberal reform newspapers under the Turkish name Bora Fahir Çağlar, thinking a proper Turkish name would give his work more credit. Even with the pseudonym, he knew he'd be found out and arrested.

So it was no surprise that, a fortnight after the photographs were published, police stormed his home, beat him unconscious, and burned down his hut along with his darkroom, and carted him off to Constantinople to a dirty jail cell.

But he did not awaken in a jail. He found himself on a straw mattress shoved in the corner of a stonewall laboratory, his right foot chained to a ball. Standing over him was von Froeschner, with a reassuring smile and a lab coat splattered in oil. He spoke to Nikos in Turkish:

"You don't know me, my friend, but I know you. While it has earned you the Sultan's disfavor, I admire your work and have heard much about your methods. In fact, it is my admiration that has kept you alive; it can keep you alive if you will help me."

Nikos spat at his shoes. Von Froeschner nodded and gestured for the guards to unchain him.

"See, already you are freer than before. Please, let me show you something; it may change your mind." He held his hand up to the guards to give Nikos over and he led the photographer-prisoner over to a slab where lay the Şehrazat.

She was undressed, with her skull and cabinet-torso open. Nikos could see how her appendages were attached to her torso-cabinet via bronze-wired knitting. The inner workings that would confound the tourists when she was displayed were pulled away, and Nikos could see deep inside her guts were three tiny gas lights sputtering cobalt flame, a slanted mirror that optimized and directed the lightening, and a spool on a rotating mechanism. Von Froeschner rummaged in the cabinet, connecting and attaching various things, and pointed to what Nikos would later learn was Bey's tableau scroll on an adjacent table.

"I think you know how to install that here." He watched Nikos place the scroll on the spool and came up behind him to ensure it was aligned. He closed her up, and walked to her skull. He gestured for Nikos to stand next to him. Nikos glimpsed the inside and saw that the skull housed a small brain connected to various internal prongs. The sight startled him, and von Froeschner placed a hand on his shoulder. "Ah, yes. It is disconcerting at first. It was generously donated to us from the Sultan, whose pet capuchin was ravaged by a tiger last week."

Where matter and metal met, blue sparks exploded when von Froeschner pulled a lever beside the slab. A soft hum emanated from her, and a bright light projected from her eyes to the ceiling, creating the pale yellow and Prussian blue of Cappadocia.

"There. You see?" Nikos marveled with mouth agape as the diorama became animated on the ceiling. The image was as clear and sharp as a photograph, but rendered in the palette of the Orientalists, making it the most realistic image he had ever seen. The image itself moved, not by rotation, but zoomed in and out of the scenery like binoculars. As amazing as that was, Nikos couldn't help but think: *it is inaccurate, like most paintings. It isn't real; it isn't truth.*

"What...what is this? A diorama?" he asked.

"Yes, for now she is a diorama, but she has the potential to become much more. The Sultan terms her a truth machine. People will believe what they see—it will be real to them. It will become memory—like a visceral dream."

"But it isn't true," Nikos muttered.

"The Truth is not real unless it can be seen—as you well know, a picture never lies."

Nikos stared up at the projection as it entered the Turkish Baths. "It depends on the picture. Many pictures lie."

Von Froeschner chuckled. "And there are many truths. There are harmful truths, just like there are beneficent lies. All are just means to an end."

"Whose end?"

"That is a good question." Von Froeschner turned off the machine and walked around the Şehrazat, running his hand down her cabinet-torso. "We are learning that the brain's capacity is grossly under-utilized. It is much like a difference engine, you know. It has electrical impulses that process and synthesize information at an uncanny rate, and yet we only use it for quotidian tasks, and it could be argued we barely use it for that. I want to test it—to challenge it. With constant stimulation, its capacity for performance could in theory double exponentially, to eventually maintain a tintype-like memory that could store and recall information and perhaps eventually become clairvoyant based upon patterns and probabilities it perceives."

Nikos could not comprehend what von Froeschner blathered about, but he knew it was momentous, and the excitement of the new, of the truly revolutionary, welled inside him. It made him forget that he was a prisoner and why he had been imprisoned.

"All of that from the brain of a monkey?" Nikos looked away from the diorama to meet von Froeschner's lachrymose smile.

"Perhaps it could," he said. "But I am not speaking of this there." He pointed to the beating rose matter. "I am speaking of that here." He gently placed his pointer finger on Nikos' temple. "This is what I need to help me."

Excitement gut-soured into trepidation within Nikos. "Help you? I am just a photographer. What does this have to do with me?"

Von Froeschner nodded with a frown. "You are aware of the extreme disfavor you've garnered yourself? The Sultan wants your head, but he has no use for it other than to make it an example to others. But I have use for it, and so have asked him to give it to me. I admire your mind, you see? I want it to live, to share many truths."

Nikos looked von Froeschner in the eye. Von Froeschner nodded and then turned away. Before Nikos could ask von Froeschner his meaning, he felt a cold prick at the base of his head and entered an unknown darkness.

The café scene is now a distant one. The image pans over the hundred or so men sitting and discussing politics in traditional costume, and goes beyond the city passing the Basilica Cistern and flying over the slate domes and white spires of Topkapı Palace, soaring over the three courtyards until landing on the Bosporus shore.

Underneath the current of the projections, Nikos dreams of his homeland. Eventually, after being encased within von Froeschner's contraption of charms for several months, he was able to achieve what von Froeschner had predicted, and under the constant stimulation and processing of tourist information, which included learning their languages, his mind developed the ability to multi-task, to dream and inhabit his internal world of personal memory while continuing to project the *faux monde* for the tourists, all while processing their cues to synthesize and revamp the diorama.

The Bosporus sea reminds him of the shore where he was born, and he thinks of his mother wasting away.

He is distracted from the dream by the tourists' gasps—not of the usual astonishment—but of distaste and disappointment. The sea's flawless view is obstructed by a consumptive Magdalene, who leans over a bed of sand and seaweed and spews sputum from behind her long stringy hair.

"Why, that woman is dying!" a matron proclaims, and Nikos holds onto the image to make it clearer. The tourists see the shore disappear behind barren stone walls and several newly-orphaned children tugging at their lost mother's soiled skirts.

Several of the female tourists wail at the pathos, upsetting their men.

"Von Froeschner!" a male tourist bellows. "This is grotesque. What is the meaning of this?"

Von Froeschner feigns ignorance and asks the audience to bear with what must be a glitch.

To their relief, they are lead out of the woeful house and into an image of a white stone church on the shore, the azul water lapping the pale yellow sand.

"Now that's more like it," says the bellowing Brit. Just then, the image becomes crowded with Turkish soldiers slicing *kilijs* into Cretan women and children; the church is engulfed in flames. The chiaroscuro haze is so realistic that the tourists panic, and some seek the doors. In response, the image leaves the Cretan massacre and enters the door of the church. The entire room darkens for a moment, and the complaining tourists quiet.

Slowly, a stonewall laboratory fades into their vision. Once the image is fully developed, they see von Froeschner standing in-between two operating tables. On his right they can make out the Şehrazat, her head unbolted, brain exposed and blue-sparking. It takes several moments for the exposure to reveal the other slab, but eventually the tourists make out the chiaroscuro depth of an open and empty human skull.

The tourists become frantic. The atramentous curtains are ripped from the rods, making the horrid image fade.

Those who haven't fainted or sought escape stare at von Froeschner and the orb-shining Şehrazat. The joke made fifteen minutes ago now hangs in the air like a noose.

Ignoring the tourists, who are demanding to be let out of the locked room, von Froeschner grins and saunters over to shut the Şehrazat down. She returns to her default position, her arm gesturing at the triumphant scientist musing over the mob scene unfolding before him.

The Constantinople street is drenched in pure sunlight, saturating almost all color from the scene. The tall, alabaster stone building that zigzags and narrows the passage casts a Payne's grey shadow onto the ocher cobblestones. Despite its disparity in hue, the street is made interesting by the people who populate it. Several dozen panting and pale Western tourists, sweating in their grey and pastel wools and cottons, faint and gesture wildly at shrouded women who ignore them, dazed by the seen and unseen of their dreams, bewildered by the scenes of Bora Fahir Çalğar and the truths of Nikos Antonakis.

The Emperor Everlasting

Nayad A. Monroe

September, 1914

With one day left until the Sapa Inca's meeting with emissaries from the Unified States of Ameriga, Ilyapa had no idea how to salvage the situation. The Emperor was still broken, and to the minds of anyone whose opinions mattered, it was her fault.

The Sapa Inca Ninan Cuyochi, Son of Sun, Emperor of Viracocha's Land, rested in a musty bundle in the corner of Ilyapa's temporary workshop, his four-hundred-year-old mummified body wrapped in a gold-embroidered cloak trimmed with hummingbird feathers and turquoise, and his glorious face hidden from the gazes of ordinary people by a translucent cloth.

"How will you demonstrate your superiority to the Amerigans now that you are broken, Powerful Lord? Was it worth the trouble to acquire one thousand wives?" Ilyapa asked him, staring at the metal mechanisms that usually made the Sapa Inca function. Even she, the First Deviser of his court, was now a wife of the Emperor, despite not being noble by birth. Newly and unwillingly wed as an old woman, aged forty-three. She might now have the right to see his face, but she felt no urge to do so.

For the dozenth time that morning, she lifted her gaze from the stone work surface to look out at the distracting view: the modern city of Cuyochitampu, with its driven professionals scurrying along the river-side streets in this wealthy section near the ocean, more colorfully dressed than the workers one might see on the other side of the city, closer to the overpowering Wall of Inti which separated Viracocha's Land from the strange little country called Panama. Cuyochitampu's hard edges were so different from the rustic, weathered stone of Ilyapa's normal surroundings in the University District of ancient Machu Picchu. She wondered if she would be allowed to return to her own small house, or be forced to move into some sort of wives' dormitory in one of the palaces. The oligarchy would at least permit her to continue running the royal workshops; they had promised.

All promises would be forgotten if she failed to restore the Sapa Inca. She couldn't see why the upgrade had ruined his answering system, his Voice. The old system had worked for centuries: on the rare occasions when the Sapa Inca was consulted in public, for the good of all, the designated supplicant would ask him a question. His machinery would randomly knot a cord into the numerical code for one of a series of programmed answers: *yes, not at this time, I will consider it further, I forbid it, I appreciate your good citizenship, you will become an honored sacrifice to the gods*, and so on, expressing the will of the gods through the Emperor. The wide range of these answers was not permittable for the mass wedding. Answers other than "yes" would have contradicted the Powerful Lord's previously-stated wish to have one thousand wives. It would have wasted a great deal of time, and would likely have aroused the suspicions of anyone who heard the same phrases repeated nonsensically. So, following the oligarchy's instructions, Ilyapa had finally upgraded the Sapa Inca's system to the new answering method of punching patterns into thin metal plates instead of tying knots into cords, which she had wanted to do long before. With the new system, certain preset response patterns—such as "always yes"—could be set with a dial on the mechanism. The conservatives in the secret ruling group wouldn't hear of the upgrade until it was too late to test the system properly, at which point they demanded it.

At least the upgrade held out until after all the brides were accepted, but that was her only consolation. Ilyapa had to fix the malfunctioning device immediately, or become known as the person responsible for destroying an entire continent's leadership. The Amerigan contingent, waiting on the other side of the Wall of Inti in nearby Panamatampu, would see their advantage and glide over the Wall with their strange, rounded flying devices, not afraid of either the gods or the technology of Viracocha's Land.

She turned from the window to glare at the disassembled gears and parts another time, and one of them glinted strangely at its edge, highlighted by the afternoon light's angle. Picking it up, Ilyapa examined a subtle crimp in the metal, just enough to intermittently throw the device's works out of alignment if it were jarred at all. "How could this happen, Sapa Inca?" she wondered aloud. "Your new gears were molded perfectly—I checked them. I checked *all* of them before I put them together. And they were only used a few times...."

The Emperor declined to comment.

The obvious first choice would be to replace the gear, but it was a non-standard size—a bothersome choice that Ilyapa would not have made herself. It had been chosen by her predecessor before his death. She checked her case of spare gears, but the space where she would keep that size was empty.

Luckily, Ilyapa had the perfect tool to fix the existing gear. Her anxiety lifted. The damage was certainly a concern, and she would have to analyze the new system's workings later to discern the cause, but for the short term, a small repair would solve everything.

The chest containing her own private tool set, a gift from her university mentor at graduation, sat in its place of honor in a protected corner. She rarely used the finely-made tools, preferring to protect their stone-inlaid handles, but she brought them out for special jobs. The tray of miniature tools held a set of pliers that would do exactly what she wanted without the risk of damaging the gear further.

She knelt and opened the llama-skin upholstered trunk, lifted the top tray of full-size tools from its support ledges, and started to reach into the small compartment beneath, but then pulled her hand back and stared. The lower tray was missing.

It had been there at the start of her journey to Cuyochitampu. She had checked and re-checked, unable to bear the thought of making a careless mistake with this set.

She stood and rushed from her workroom to the larger staff workshop. "Supay! Where is Supay?" she called out. Several devisers turned sharply, startled. Ilyapa rarely raised her voice. "Anahuarque, where is Supay? This is urgent."

The young woman pointed. "I think I saw him go toward the diplomacy gift stations," she said. "What is it? Can I help?"

"I'm missing important equipment," Ilyapa replied. "I need you to attend the Sapa Inca while I find it."

"But First Deviser, I can't, I'm not..."

"I authorize it. I'm his wife, after all."

Ilyapa strode away, ignoring the shocked looks her employees exchanged. "I'll be back soon," she called over her shoulder, trying to shake off her guilt at making Anahuarque go near the Sapa Inca. Most people were terrified of him and what he represented: the power of the gods and the dead. Ilyapa thought of him as a sad bundle of remains, and only feared the oligarchy. The living people who controlled her world were fearsome enough on their own. She had to find her assistant and her tools.

In the next devising room, teams worked in stations along the walls, each set of people completing gifts meant to impress and awe the visiting Amerigans without giving them anything particularly useful. The oligarchy wanted to impart the grandeur of Viracocha's Land, but not compromise its power. A difficult balance.

Supay was at the far end of the large room, conferring with the group responsible for a tricky decorative entertainment device, a jeweled column that could quietly beautify a corner when at rest, but open outward into spinning displays that, when lit properly, would reflect throughout a room to create a festive environment. The Amerigans were known for liking parties and dances. Frivolous, but easy to indulge.

She broke into the conversation without acknowledging anyone but her assistant. "Supay, my miniature tools are missing, and I need them immediately. Do you know where they are?"

The tan of his face turned reddish. "I forgot to tell you. I'm sorry. Second Deviser's assistant came for them. The Coya has a special project, and Second Deviser needed the tools quickly."

So quickly that he couldn't ask permission to borrow my personal set? Ilyapa thought. *And now I can choose to offend the Emperor's first wife, or cause an international incident.* She wasn't sure which would be worse.

"You *must* tell me when things like this happen, Supay. I'm offended."

"I am so very sorry," Supay replied. "I meant to tell you immediately, but then people kept asking me for help, and...."

She relented. "I understand. And you couldn't deny Khuno's request, of course. I will have to go and get the pliers I need, assuming they aren't in use."

It really didn't matter if they were in use or not, since she had to have them. Ilyapa started the walk to Khuno's workshop. Their division of labor had been established for years: he worked on transportation, where less subtlety was required to make devices work, and Ilyapa, while actually in charge of all devising, focused her attention on the more difficult, intricate work. This allowed the two of them to hate each other quietly, at a distance. She wondered why, given their usual division of assignments, he hadn't asked her to use her own tools on whatever was so dainty about the Coya's project.

When she entered Khuno's realm, a young apprentice sitting on a stool near the entrance hopped down and dashed away. She held back a smile at his nervousness about being caught sitting. Khuno, of course, was nowhere in sight. She would have to cross yet another oversized space to get to his private workroom; the relentlessly new buildings here were not of the intimate scale she was used to. The smells of metal and oil, stone dust and sweat still managed to fill the room's large volume. Khuno strangely preferred working with men, saving women for romance, so his area boomed with too many low voices and made her edgy.

Ilyapa had passed only half of a long row of new riding carts when Khuno's assistant approached. She could never remember the man's name.

"Welcome, First Deviser," he said.

"Hello. I am looking for Khuno," she said. "Or, at least, the tools he had you take from my workshop without my permission."

"He regrets that," the assistant said smoothly, not seeming flustered at all. "The Coya was impatient."

"Well, I wouldn't want to inconvenience the Coya," Ilyapa said, "but I will need to take back my pliers, for emergency repairs on the Sapa Inca's Voice. You understand the urgency."

"Of course, First Deviser."

"Then I'll go and see Khuno now."

"Unfortunately I am not allowed to let anyone visit his workshop, on the Coya's orders. He is not to be interrupted."

"Do you comprehend that I am repairing the Coya's husband, *my* husband, the *Son of Sun*? Whose ability to communicate with the Amerigans is surely more important than the uninterrupted workflow of the *Second* Deviser?"

"First Deviser, please, I do understand. But the Coya Pachama assigned guards, and runners to report on any unauthorized activity...."

The boy beside the door. "Thank you for your help," Ilyapa said stiffly. "Please have the tools returned as soon as Khuno is finished."

Fuming, she left, turning toward the building's side exit. It was impossible. She needed those pliers. Anything else would be too big and clumsy, and they were *her own pliers*, given to her long ago, not even paid for by the court! Having met the Coya through her role as First Deviser, however, Ilyapa knew what the woman was like. An elderly former beauty long married to the Sapa Inca, celibate for life and making up for the sacrifice with her brittle and temperamental demands, she would not be denied. No matter how frivolous her wishes.

In the courtyard outside, Ilyapa paced, irritated further by the humid, briny air, which was worse in the sunlight than inside the building's cool stone. The frantic activity level of preparation was not reduced outdoors. People rushed past talking rapidly, gesturing and bickering. Two women stopped in a corner full of lush plants and hot pink flowers to whisper fiercely at each other.

A llama trainer came through with an immense, freshly-groomed auburn creature wearing superlative ornamental armor of silver, gold, and copper worked intricately together. The battle llamas were scheduled for a parade, she had heard; if this was the standard, it would be glorious.

She stopped pacing.

The llama outfitters had tools. Good ones. Possibly better than hers. She hurried toward the nearest runner stand and hailed a cart.

Fading light accompanied Ilyapa back from her failed errand. She hadn't eaten since morning, and her stomach snarled as ferociously as she would if she ever got her hands on Khuno. He had beaten her to the llama outfitters, too, and claimed every piece of equipment she could hope to use for her project, as well as the ones she might turn to in desperation. She snapped her fingers at the lightbringer as she passed the fire pit, and the girl followed with a torch to light the ones set in mountings on the walls in her workshop. Ilyapa hated working after sunset, as her eyes didn't focus well in low, flickering light at her age, but she had no choice.

In the near-darkness of the unlit room, Anahuarque sat in the farthest corner from the Emperor, with her arms wrapped around her knees, wide-eyed and tear-streaked.

"Oh, gods," Ilyapa said. "I forgot that I left you here. Are you all right?"

Anahuarque shook her head.

Ilyapa forced her crankiness down. "I am sorry. I'm sure that the Sapa Inca must appreciate your loyalty, though. Please, go home. Rest and eat."

Anahuarque fled.

When she was alone again, Ilyapa reexamined the damaged gear. It was amazing: the bend amounted to the minimum damage that could possibly break the device. *Exactly* the minimum. The crimp didn't look like damage from use and wear; with her suspicions sharpening her thoughts, the bend's even line suggested the edge of a tool. At minimum, Khuno was working against her, and she wondered if others were involved. Had the Coya really ordered any of it, or was that a ruse of Khuno's, who knew how hard it would be to ask the Coya for verification? Khuno had always been jealous of her position, but what would motivate the Coya to destroy the power of Viracocha's Land?

"Khuno thinks I won't ask the Coya, Sapa Inca, but I will."

She was glad she had chosen to live in the workshop instead of being assigned to a household elsewhere in the city. The tiny adjacent room intended for storage suited her for its convenience and privacy. She wouldn't have to go somewhere else to change clothes before the visit. To show respect she would discard her usual simple attire and wear her most colorful *ascu*, long and made of alpaca wool, with her best bracelets and sandals. She would still look relatively shabby compared to the Coya, but that would be appreciated.

Preparing to leave, Ilyapa gave a final look around the workshop and nearly choked when she saw the Emperor in the corner. Despite her odd habit of talking to him, she hadn't really thought about the fact that he was still there. She couldn't leave him unguarded and she had already dismissed Anahuarque, so she had to find someone else. *Who can I trust?* she thought. Just outside her door, she surveyed the people at work. Someone solid and calm, unlikely to argue... "Supay!" she called.

He was at a nearby work station, kneeling as he made adjustments to a project that couldn't possibly be as important as hers. She waved him over, explained, and rushed out. "I'll be back soon," she said for the second time that day. "I promise!"

Outside, smoke from the walkway's torches kept the mosquitoes back, mostly, but Ilyapa could sense thousands of them just above in a buzzing, whining chorus, and she hoped the bats were feasting. Cockroaches skittered away from her feet with every step she took along the path. At least she wasn't the only one out by night, as frenzied work continued, but walking in the dark made her nervous. As she approached the main street, someone called her name and she twitched, startled.

It was a man she didn't recognize. "You *are* Ilyapa, the First Deviser?" he said.

"Yes. Who are you?"

"I'm directing the procession. I'm so glad I didn't miss you out here. I was on my way to find you," he said, gesturing toward the building she had just left.

"Oh. Well, I'm sure my assistant can help you. He's still inside," Ilyapa said, turning to leave.

"No, he can't. This is about the *procession*. I obviously can't replace you with your assistant!" the man snapped.

"What procession? What are you talking about?"

"The Emperor's wives! You're to be shown to the visitors. It was the Coya's idea. You should have been told already."

"The visitors won't be here until tomorrow. I will be there for whatever is required, but I have urgent work to do. For the Emperor himself."

"You don't understand. You and all of the other wives are to spend the night in fasting and preparation for the procession. This is mandatory. The Coya Pachama has ordered it."

"I'm just on my way to see her about my work. I'm sure she'll understand that her husband must be in his best condition before the visitors arrive."

"You may send her a message if you like, once you're where you're supposed to be," the man said, "but you're late already and everyone else is waiting for you, so you will come with us right now." He beckoned, and two guards emerged from nearby shadows.

On either side of her, holding her elbows, the guards marched her toward a waiting cart, big enough to hold two people and a driver, one of the rare ones with a team of two llamas. A second large cart and team sat behind the first. The guards split, one to each vehicle, with Ilyapa in the first and the procession director in the second. It was an ostentatious display of wealth and force.

The Coya doesn't want the Sapa Inca to be fixed, Ilyapa thought. *But why not?*

The wives were sequestered in possibly the most austere building Ilyapa had ever seen. It was certainly modern, with the high ceilings and echoing spaces of the newest buildings in Cuyochitampu. It was so new that it lacked furnishings, decorations, and all forms of charm. The wives were to sleep on the cold stone floors, naked, exposing themselves to the gods for judgment. Ilyapa began to perceive a calculating, punishing hatred in the Coya's design for the night's activities.

But before the sleep, there would be intensive bathing, grooming, and rituals. After the first ritual, Ilyapa was assigned to a group of twenty-five women. "Go through that passage to the baths," their leader told them. "Leave your clothes in the dressing room, and make sure to submerge yourselves completely and cross to the other side of the pool."

They filed through, entering the water one at a time. Not a single one of the women failed to gasp at its temperature. The man-made waterfall filling it drew from an icy spring: refreshing if wanted, intolerable if not. Painful cold shocked Ilyapa's skin and sank into her bones as she sloshed through the pool, moving as quickly as she could against the chest-height water's resistance and saving full immersion for the moment before she could climb out on the other side.

They were ushered into a cool underground room where they sat, shivering, and waited as a few women at a time had their hair twisted into hundreds of tiny braids, so that they would all look as similar as possible.

The intensive schedule of activities went on late into the night, including a long practice for the morning's procession, and all the while Ilyapa's stomach burned and raged with hunger. Finally, they were arranged in rows to rest for a few hours, but she couldn't allow herself to sleep.

It didn't matter why the Coya wanted her to fail. She simply refused to do so.

The cold, hard floor worked in her favor, but Ilyapa still had to dig her fingernails into her palms and bite the insides of her cheeks to stay awake. She had not slept well for the past several nights due to the stress of her job. Exhaustion fought with rage over her ill-treatment. She had never felt any ambition to marry a dead body, but after being forced into this bizarre position, she was now kept from her work and tortured, for what? The Coya's jealousy? The unfairness tore at her, adding to her array of discomforts.

Finally, the silence indicated that everyone was asleep, including her group's leader. Ilyapa rolled over silently, rising to her hands and knees and then to her feet. She crept down the corridor between the splayed bodies of her co-wives, gritting her teeth, so tense that she thought she might lose control of herself and scream.

But she didn't. She passed silently behind the guards as they joked around the fire. Around a corner, she stole a torch from a sconce and found her way down to the bathing pool, where she held the flame above her head as she crossed through the water, which seemed even icier than before. Her clothes and jewelry were where she had left them. No one was watching the building's entrance; all of the guards were stationed inside.

Once outside, she had to choose between risking a witness to her absence and taking too long to get back to her workshop, so she hired a small llama-pulled cart, handing its sleepy driver one of her silver bracelets.

At her work building, Ilyapa circled around toward a back entrance. Off the main walkways, the distance between torches scared her. In the darkness she ran her left hand nervously against the building's stone wall as she walked, flinching with every change in the surface's texture. She imagined spiders lurking on it, waiting to creep across her skin. The small portal she wanted was also dark, but once inside she found that enough low fires had been left glowing to let her navigate to Khuno's workroom.

She wanted her pliers.

The area was shockingly unguarded. Was this really the same place she'd been warned out of earlier in the day? *Maybe their project is finished now*, she thought. *But then why did they block my repair of the Sapa Inca?*

She took a torch from the wall closest to Khuno's private space, and slipped into the room. It was a risk to have the light, but there was no other way to find her pliers. At first, she couldn't take in the specifics of the cluttered space, but as she sought the work ledges where tools would most likely be left, reflections flickered from a large, shiny thing at the room's center.

The project? She couldn't tell what it was. Lifting the torch, she stepped forward and looked down at the thing, which had legs, a torso, a head...It was a giant metal man, twice the height and width of an ordinary man. A device, clearly meant to move and function. The impressive llama armor she had seen earlier would look like the work of clumsy children next to the grandeur of the metal man's lavish decorations, so ornate as to stop just short of gaudiness. Every surface glittered with inlays of amethyst, mother of pearl, lapis lazuli, citrine, and more, the abundant gemstones made into patterns in the device's gold exterior. Ilyapa wished desperately to examine it—to open it up and see the inner workings and deduce what it could do. Clearly this was the project, but to leave it alone here? Unbelievable. She had to be missing something. A trap of some kind? Hidden guards?

Then she heard voices nearby, a man and a woman laughing in sensual tones. The voices sounded familiar. Khuno and...? She knew the woman's voice.

She ran to the nearest workbench, crouching behind it. If they came into the room, they would see her light. The only way to put it out would be to take off her ascu and smother the fire, leaving her naked and the room full of burnt wool smoke. She didn't know where they were, so running away would be difficult. Rising to a half-crouch, she looked for possible exits. There was the door she had entered, and another door on the side, closed with a hanging reed mat, which, she now realized, had a slight glow around the edges. She crouched again.

I am an idiot.

With her heart stuttering, she considered her options. Khuno clearly felt secure enough to leave the Coya's project here with no one watching it. Why? Why would he take even the slightest risk of displeasing the Coya by neglecting the project for sex?

Another burst of laughter from the next room answered her question, as she recognized the woman's voice.

The Coya was in there with him.

Ilyapa had to leave immediately. She stood, taking a breath to prepare herself for the escape and trek to her workshop, and saw that a leather tray sat on the ledge by her right hand. Her tools. If she took the whole tray it might be missed, but by the gods she would have her pliers. She snatched them up and left, trying not to picture what Khuno and the Coya were doing to each other behind the reed mat.

Supay was dozing in Ilyapa's workshop, loyal enough to stay despite her broken promise to return soon. Ilyapa hated to wake him, but there was too much to do and discuss, and she had only a few hours left before someone might find that she was missing. She shook him.

After some grumbling and muttering, he opened his eyes. "Wha'd you do to your hair?" Supay murmured.

She scoffed. "That's the least of my worries. Wake all the way up, and I'll tell you what I know."

While giving Supay a few moments to follow her instructions, Ilyapa began to unpack the pieces of the Sapa Inca's old Voice. If they wouldn't let her fix the new system, she would restore the old one.

The next morning, Ilyapa rose from the cold, hard floor with the other sequestered wives in her group, after sneaking back in and snatching a brief, turbulent sleep. Her neck was so stiff and sore that she could only turn it halfway to the left and a quarter to the right. Although she had tried to hold her hair up out of the water on her return, the lower halves of her long, skinny braids were still wet. She hoped no one would notice. Luckily, between being rushed into matching outfits—she wondered how many people had been pressed into making them—and lectured repeatedly on the way they were to behave in the procession, her wet hair was the last thing anyone wanted to think about.

Then the Coya arrived at the front of the great room where all of the wives were gathered, so thoroughly bedecked with precious metal and jewels that seeing her in sunlight might hurt. The procession director clapped his hands above his head, and his assistants made shushing noises.

The Coya spoke. "Honored sisters, I welcome you to my family." Her face, cold and remote, looked anything but welcoming. "Today you represent Viracocha's Land to the foreigners allied with the dirty Spanish and their weak pawns in Panama. We have long held the Spanish and their diseases away from our land, so our strength is unquestionable, but you must make them know the value of our precious Sapa Inca, who even from beyond death is denied nothing. He who has as many warriors, as many llamas, as many wives as he requires. He who decides our destiny. The Emperor Everlasting."

The Coya looked around the room. "I hope you are all worthy of such a powerful lord." With a sour expression on her face, she left.

Ilyapa still could not imagine the woman's plan. If the Sapa Inca couldn't speak, it would be an embarrassment for all. What was the Coya trying to do? And Khuno? How did they intend to use the metal man?

Well, they wouldn't get their way, she hoped. She and Supay had returned the Sapa Inca and his workings, fully functional, to his oligarchy attendant—generally known as his "advisor." Bachue didn't care for the solution of restoring his old-fashioned Voice, but she agreed that it was better than no Voice at all. Concerned about plots, loyalties, and repercussions, Ilyapa and Supay had decided not to mention their suspicions about the Coya, but they both intended to watch as events played out, and report on the situation if necessary.

Ilyapa paced up the ramps toward the broad expanse atop the Wall with the wives, between two narrow columns of battle llamas in their sparkling light armor. Ilyapa was near the front due to her position, only outranked and preceded by the few teenaged noblewomen who had been available for marriage to the Sapa Inca when it was called for. The rest, behind her, were mostly country girls. They had all been instructed not to talk, and that was the one thing about the situation which suited her well. The Coya didn't have to walk with them, of course, and she would arrive separately.

The sky full of ominous clouds didn't help Ilyapa's mood or her energy level, but she pushed on, keeping in step with the others. She glanced upward frequently as they reached the top and filed into position, expecting the perfect final touch of drenching rain at any moment, and it was during one of those glances that she saw the massive shape in the air above the Wall, emerging from the clouds, followed by another, and another. Her involuntary yelp earned sharp looks from the irritable wives around her, until they noticed the ships—*dirigibles*, the Amerigans called them—and reacted even more strongly by clutching at each other, pointing, and embarrassing themselves with babbling and tears. On the terraced walkways and streets below, waves of reaction rippled through the crowds. Even the well-trained llamas, despite being accustomed to battle chaos, began to groan fearfully in the strange tension.

And that was when the metal giant appeared, striding mechanically toward them from the opposite end of the Wall with the Coya's own cart following close behind him. He wore a tall royal headdress, made of metal feathers instead of real ones, and he carried a colorful bundle in his arms: the Sapa Inca, Ninan Cuyochi, cradled within the device which served as his Voice.

The members of the oligarchy, known to the public only as high advisors and honored citizens, had been arranged in a semicircle facing the approaching dirigibles, but now they all turned to watch as the Coya was helped down from her vehicle, followed by Bachue, Sapa Inca's attendant and interpreter. The two women preceded the metal man, walking toward Villac-umu, the high priest. He greeted the Coya as usual, while the advisors shuffled and hesitated as Ilyapa had never seen them do before. The crowd began to settle, curiosity overtaking fear.

Villac-umu, in his rich speaking voice, called out, "I welcome Yupanqui Capac, the son and heir of the Sapa Inca Ninan Cuyochi and the Coya Pachama!"

The metal giant raised his free left hand to wave, still holding the Sapa Inca in his right.

"The gods have informed me that this modern age requires a young, vigorous, and powerful new Emperor. They have placed the spirit-son of Ninan Cuyochi and Pachama in this metal vessel to create our new Sapa Inca, Yupanqui Capac. The Coya will now ask the Emperor if he wishes to object."

Ilyapa's understanding clicked into place. She stepped forward, watching avidly, not caring a bit for the rank of other wives.

The Coya said, loudly, "Ninan Cuyochi, do you wish to object to this transition?" She reached up to push the button on his device that would prompt an answer, and Yupanqui Capac leaned down to allow her access.

How does the device work? Ilyapa wondered. *How does it know what to do?*

The Emperor's Voice whirred into operation. The Coya jerked back, looking to Villac-umu, who shrugged slightly. A cord began to emerge from the device, displaying a short sequence of knots. Bachue hurried forward to examine the cord.

"You will become an honored sacrifice to the gods," she stated in a carrying voice.

The Coya shrieked. She turned on Villac-umu furiously, gesturing with both hands as she launched into a series of curses and insults. He stepped backward, holding up his hands in front of him. The Coya turned to the giant metal man and spoke. Ilyapa couldn't tell what she said, but he began to walk toward the Panama-side edge of the Wall and the dirigibles that hovered above it. Ilyapa could see pale faces watching through the clear walls in the nearest one's riding section. No one had tried to come out yet; she wondered what they were waiting for. Yupanqui Capac stopped in front of it and tilted his head to look up, surprisingly lifelike.

The metal giant raised his arms to lift the Sapa Inca over his head. Slowly, he pulled his hands backward. For a long moment he paused there, and Ilyapa thought, *No, he wouldn't.* But then the giant flung the Sapa Inca Ninan Cuyochi and his Voice with enough force that the apparatus hit and cracked the dirigible before dropping to the ground far, far below, in Panama.

All sanity broke down. The Sapa Inca's wives turned to run away, screaming. Llamas fought their handlers, braying their anxious noises again and spraying spit in all directions. Shoving, shouting, and shrieking erupted. Ilyapa put all of her remaining energy into standing still and watching, despite the battering of frightened women pushing past.

The Amerigans, clearly agitated, seemed to be arguing behind their cracked wall. Some peered through what she thought were the seeing tubes she had heard about at university. Maybe she could examine one when they landed, she thought. But then the lead dirigible began to move up and backward, away from Viracocha's Land, and the others went with it.

Ilyapa found widowhood to be tolerable. She thought of her late husband fondly, but without regret, as he had lived an extraordinarily long life. Immediately after the Coya was sacrificed, it became apparent that performance evaluations would be necessary in Ilyapa's department. Khuno received an evaluation so unsatisfactory that the oligarchy sent him to work on the maintenance of mining devices far away, in the southernmost gold mine of Viracocha's Land.

The new Sapa Inca wasn't terribly complicated. His giant size allowed one of his specially-trained "brothers" to climb inside and operate his body when necessary. Although the Amerigans didn't return to visit for a long time afterward, Ilyapa thought her step-son was much more handsome than his father had been, and she enjoyed working on his Voice.

Mary Sundown and the Clockmaker's Children

Malon Edwards

I reach thirty-five miles an hour the moment I see the pinprick of light leading to the surface. My stride is smooth; my clockwork is fluid.

And then, I stumble. Another explosion has rattled the north passage of the LaSalle Street Tunnel.

It takes me just a fraction of a second to recover my balance and regain my speed, despite the incline and the sifted dirt and flakes of concrete shaken loose. It's a treacherous floor. The Chicago River has found its way in, too. One misstep, and I won't ever run again.

As the tunnel mouth looms large, I accelerate piti a piti—little by little. I hit forty-five miles an hour when I burst into the daylight and my feet touch the cobblestones on Kinzie Street.

I'm out! I almost shout to Marie-Louise through the aetherlink we once shared, but then I remember: she's dead. Broken. Crushed by Zonbi Robot.

The very same Zonbi Robot leveling its Dahlgren guns at me now.

Lè Marie-Louise te eseye fè m fache—.

Ah. Excuse me. I apologize. Allow me to say that again.

When Marie-Louise tried to piss me off, which was often, she would say I killed papa nou—our father, the Clockmaker— because he built me last and I was the most difficult of his children to assemble.

Sometimes, when she said that, I would remind Marie-Louise papa nou crippled his once strong brown hands and blinded his once sharp brown eyes fashioning the fine springs and small gears he gave my three hundred ninety-nine brothers and sisters. Long before he built me.

Other times, I would answer Marie-Louise by showing her how long and shiny my middle finger is.

Like I show Zonbi Robot now. It doesn't seem too happy about that. But then, neither was Marie-Louise.

It takes less than half a second for me to realize I'm not the target of Zonbi Robot's Dahlgren shell guns. It's aiming behind me, at the rebuilt Chicago Board of Trade Building.

Maybe Zonbi Robot thinks that's where the Lord Mayor Jean Baptiste Point du Sable is hiding. Maybe it perceives the building as a symbol of our city-state wealth. Or maybe it just gets off on wanton destruction. I wouldn't be surprised. Papa mwen, my father, built me to get off on speed.

But no matter what the building means to Zonbi Robot, I have sworn to protect the Lord Mayor. Until I am broken. Until this war ends. Or until I wind down.

I promised papa mwen.

Kounye a, I am all that stands between the jealous might of the State of Illinois and a living, breathing, functioning Sovereign State of Chicago. If the Lord Mayor dies, so does everything he's given us. Freedom. Prosperity. Kreyòl.

So I do what I do best to ensure he does not die. I challenge Zonbi Robot to a race.

Marie-Louise first called it Zonbi Robot. The Illinois National Guard calls it Big Boy. Fè sans. Makes sense.

One hundred feet tall, it's a massive coal-fired boiler with a Bonnet stack for a head, two soda-pop-shaped IX-inch Dahlgren shell guns for arms, and two 4-8-8-4 Union Pacific Big Boy steam locomotives for legs.

Every fifth step Zonbi Robot takes, black smoke belches out of a smaller diamond stack set in the middle of its back. I can only imagine the amount of coal and steam power it needs to ambulate.

As Zonbi Robot stomps with toddler fury around River North and Old Town and the Gold Coast, wispy, thin smoke wafts up from the deep, jagged footprints it leaves behind. When the rains come, those footprints will become miniature ribbon lakes matching the Great Lake to the east.

Zonbi Robot might be big and strong, and it might be able to stomp more than just mud holes in the earth, but I'm faster. Even faster than Marie-Louise was.

That used to be all that mattered to me. But now, I realize: ou pa ka mare pye lanmò.

You can't outrun death.

But you can give her a hell of a race.

Bonjou, Zonbi Robot! I shout, throwing back my head and craning my neck to the sky. Do you want to race?

Zonbi Robot doesn't answer. I'm not surprised. It's not as sophisticated as I am.

Sa pa fè anyen. It doesn't matter. It's also not as fast as I am. Watch. I'll show you.

Tankou moun fou, like a crazy person, I run right at Zonbi Robot. In six strides, I hit fifty-five miles an hour. In ten strides, I hit seventy-five miles an hour.

I am swift. I am deft. I am fleet. I've never run this fast before from a standing start.

I just hope I don't wind down before I reach Lake Michigan.

I could never just leave it at the middle finger. Marie-Louise always pissed me off. She knew how to get my gears.

It was how papa nou made us. He built us in pairs. We always ran together.

Marie-Louise was my counterpart. She was my competition. She was my rival. Even when we delivered messages and packages west of the Mississippi River.

That had been our original purpose. We'd been built to bring word and comfort to the few remaining people between the Mississippi River and the West Coast after the bombs dropped.

It is a noble task, papa nou had told us, as he wound Marie-Louise and me for departure. He'd made sure each and every child of his was aware of the gravity.

Before each run, he made us recite:

We are the Clockmaker's Children.
We deliver throughout the scorched land.
We are swift. We are fleet. We are cunning.
Our days are nights, and our nights are endless.
Yet, we run fast and nimble, guided by the faint, daemon-light of the glowing ashes.
We are the dawn on the horizon.
We are the hope of despair.
Four hundred strong, we are brothers and sisters of the gear.

But now, we are one.

It's quite easy to avoid the slow-motion stomps of Zonbi Robot. I also have no trouble navigating the craters it leaves behind. I long jump those with quick-smart grace.

But each stride, as I now move at eighty miles an hour, could be my last.

The two wind-up keys in my shoulder blades, and the two keys in my hips, spin like mad. But my clockwork is still fluid.

For now.

One of the reasons papa nou built us in pairs was to ensure we had a partner who wound us before we ran down. He also made certain to assign us destinations not too far from one another.

If I delivered to San Diego, Marie-Louise delivered to Los Angeles. We would meet in Oceanside to wind each other before the run home.

I would always need far more time to wind Marie-Louise than she would need to wind me. It may have been wretched of me, but I couldn't resist teasing her about it.

Fè vit! I would yell into the aetherlink wired inside my mouth and left cheek when I saw Marie-Louise approaching in the distance. Hurry up!

Fèmen dyòl ou! she would yell back at me. Shut up!

Once Marie-Louise made it to my side, I would tell her: I've reached the rendezvous point before you because I am younger. Because I was built long after you.

Non, Marie-Louise would respond, se pa vre. You know that's not true, at all. Papa nou always sends me on the most difficult route because I am stronger. That's why I take longer.

She was right, of course. But I refused to admit it.

Then, let's race, I would say to her, as she wound me.

Se dakò, she would answer. Fine. But not here. Wait until—

But I never waited. I was off, ak tout vitès—like a shot—before Marie-Louise could finish her sentence.

The survivors out West would always laugh at that. You are both graceful, they would tell us. You both run like the wind on a fierce day of endless storms. You are greyhounds.

Non, Marie-Louise would tell them. We are dogs, sent to fetch.

Zonbi Robot is frustrated. The stack in the middle of its back now belches with every stomp. It has laid waste to much of the Near North Side.

The smoke drifting up from the new landscape it has wrought curls about its legs, clinging, wanting to tag along. It's darker. More acrid. Within some of the craters Zonbi Robot has stomped, I can see the soft glimmer of fire.

If Zonbi Robot continues on like this, all of Chicago will be ablaze in no time. And I'm only halfway to Lake Michigan.

The survivors out West used to call me Mary Sundown. They used to call my slower half, my twin, my sister, Mary Midnight.

Damn Westerners! Marie-Louise had said about that. Always changing things! I'm certain behind our backs they call us dogs!

I'd been surprised by her bitterness. I didn't know where it had come from. I'd thought greyhounds were regal dogs. Beautiful. Graceful. Very much like Marie-Louise and me.

It was obvious to me that when papa nou built us—and all of his children—he'd had that particular breed of dog in mind.

Just look at me. My build is lanky and slim, like theirs had been. My legs are long and powerful, like theirs had been. And my spine and hips, though copper-laced, are flexible, like theirs had been.

Vrèman vre—truth be told—I'd thought it was a compliment to be compared to a greyhound. But for Marie-Louise, it was an insult.

Now that I think about it, Marie-Louise's bitterness could have stemmed from the reasoning behind the nicknames the survivors had given us.

They called me Mary Sundown because I always arrived on time, the moment the sun dipped down below the horizon. And they called Marie-Louise Mary Midnight because she always arrived at the rendezvous point in the dark of night. Well after me.

Every single time.

I suppose I would be bitter, too, if I always lost to my twin sister.

Speaking of bitter, Zonbi Robot seems a bit rancorous about losing this fight with me right now.

Its frustration turns to anger, and it's not long before it has its Dahlgren guns going full on. The explosions are much louder above ground.

And much more violent.

I falter and stagger every time Zonbi Robot's missed shot slams into a structure—sometimes, a burgeoning skyscraper, sometimes, a house. Concrete and wood and steel go flying, end over end. I have to reduce my speed down to twenty-five miles an hour.

I'm not happy about that.

And then, the lethargy sets in.

The herky-jerky movement. It's as if I'm running with a bear on my back.

Fout.

Before papa mwen died, desan rekòt kafe pase—two hundred coffee harvests ago—he told us how the land came back after the bombs dropped.

Each night, he would wind all four hundred of his children before bed, deep down in the tunnels under the city. His gnarled hands pained him much, but he would still smile as he recounted how Bèl Flè—his beautiful flower—gave birth to Chicago again.

Bèl Flè had been a sickly child, he would begin, wincing as he reached up to wind the keys in each of our left shoulder blades. One by one, we stood in a line, and one by one, he wound us.

Polio had ravaged her organs, he would continue. Manman li, her mother, took Bèl Flè to a steam surgeon, which was quite fortunate. This particular steam surgeon happened to know metallurgy and glasswork.

Here, papa mwen would pause, and try to massage the arthritic pain from his left hand with his right one. My brothers and sisters and I would stand silent in the dim underground hangar, waiting for his next words, with patient obedience. We knew the story. And yet, we enjoyed it. Bèl Flè had birthed us, as well.

Manman li, papa mwen would continue, begged the steam surgeon to fix ti pitit li, her little one. And, oh, did he fix her.

The steam surgeon put Bèl Flè into a deep sleep, and then removed all her dying organs. But don't fret, pitit cheri mwen yo. Gone was her sickness.

Again, papa mwen would stop to rub his left hand. If he'd had a good day, he would be more than halfway finished winding our left shoulder blade keys. But if his body was feeling its age, he would have shuffled through only a quarter of us.

But always, he pressed on. We had packages and messages to deliver to survivors in the morning.

Unbeknownst to Bèl Flè ak manman li, papa mwen went on, the steam surgeon had, days before, built a steam clock heart. He'd been saddened by the children whose hearts had weakened from the polio epidemic sweeping Chicago.

By this time, papa mwen would have finished winding our left shoulder blade keys and moved on to the right ones. And still we stood, listening.

Oh, pitit cheri mwen yo, my dear little children, the steam surgeon placed that steam clock heart into Bèl Flè with the utmost care. Tapping our chests with a crooked finger, papa mwen would then smile and say, It was very much like the one you have now.

But that wasn't all he gave Bèl Flè, papa mwen would say, his eyes sparkling with delight as he told his tale. To ensure cheri mwen and her steam clock heart worked, he also gave Bèl Flè a compost boiler, fed by the highest quality coal dust. And to protect it all, he bound her entire torso with unbreakable glass.

Papa mwen would pause again to rub his right hand with his left, but he shuffled faster. The best part of the story was coming soon.

It's unmistakable now. My gears, my cogwheels, are slowing. I'm winding down. I can run no more than a few steps.

But this is good. I've reached the shores of Lake Michigan.

Zonbi Robot lumbers after me. Its Dahlgren shell guns are spent. Chicago burns behind it.

The city is lost. But Jean Baptiste Point du Sable will be safe. I have kept my promise.

A few more stomps, and Zonbi Robot shall blunder neatly into my trap.

That steam surgeon was a very clever man, papa mwen continued, as he wound the keys in our left hips. Every three weeks, Bèl Flè's compost boiler would produce the most pristine, rich and loamy soil this green Earth has ever seen.

But even cleverer than him was Bèl Flè mwen. My beautiful flower.

Papa mwen would smile with pride as he told this part.

For days on end, Bèl Flè mwen spread that purified soil from her chest upon the scorched lands and glowing ash, never tiring. Day after day, she did this. And when those long days turned to years, she still did not tire.

Not even when the green grass grew and the plants and trees sprouted. Or when the storm clouds gathered, and the rain fell from the sky, and the fish swam again in Lake Michigan.

Non, petit cheri mwen yo, papa mwen would murmur, exhaustion deep down in his voice, unlike me, Bèl Flè never tired. And how blessed we are now because of her endurance.

I hadn't planned on losing to Zonbi Robot.

I hadn't planned on getting stomped by it, either.

I suppose those two things are one in the same now.

But I did plan on Zonbi Robot, in its haste to stomp me flat, stepping into the muck and morass just off the shores of Lake Michigan.

And I planned well.

One leg stuck fast, Zonbi Robot tries to free itself. Its stack belches furiously . It struggles harder.

And then, like a toddler true, it topples over. Into the swampy lake mire. Boiler extinguished. Thick, black smoke rising. Body still.

Never to stand again.

Oh, how Bèl Flè loved her dear Chicago! papa mwen would go on to say, now winding the keys in our right hips. Not only did Bèl Flè mwen seed her city and nurture her city and grow her city healthy again, he continued, but Bèl Flè mwen gave her city beauty, as well. On the inside. Where it counts.

Papa mwen would tap our chests again with his crooked finger, and then wind us some more.

Bèl Flè mwen placed copper and uranium, and gold and diamonds—and every other precious metal she could think of— far beneath Chicago's surface. She wanted pitit cheri li—her dear child—to thrive. To live long. To excel.

And the State of Illinois was jealous of her for that.

Here, papa mwen would lose his smile, and his voice would change as he played the role of the State of Illinois.

The bombs scorched our lands, too! he would whine, thin and reedy. We want to be beautiful, too! he would beg, like the childish, no-good brat the State of Illinois had become.

So, papa mwen would continue in his normal, but frail voice, Bèl Flè sent frè mwen—my brother—Jean Baptiste Point du Sable, to the governor in Springfield bearing gifts. She sent him with copper and coal and uranium and steel. She even sent him with that rich, loamy pristine soil.

But the State of Illinois was not satisfied. This is not enough! they told frè mwen. Give us more! Give us the diamonds! Give us the gold!

One last time, papa mwen would massage his right hand and gather his remaining strength as he wound the last of us.

But frè mwen refused, papa mwen continued. He was steadfast. He was Lord Mayor. You have what you need, Jean Baptiste told them. You have more than enough to succeed and become a strong state again. But that was not what the State of Illinois wanted to hear.

But at long last, papa mwen collapsed into his huge, leather wingback chair, and he finished his story.

So the State waged war against Bèl Flè's child, Chicago, he would whisper, sleep coming on him. They built huge, horrible robots and huge, horrible bombs with those precious metals Bèl Flè gave them.

Frè mwen, Jean Baptiste, seceded Chicago from the State and declared it sovereign. But, by then, it was an empty gesture.

Here, we would lean forward as one to catch Papa's last few words.

Many people died. Much of what Bèl Flè mwen nurtured was lost. Including our love.

But not her love for frè mwen. She loved his strength. She loved his tenacity. She loved his leadership.

She loved him more than me.

And then, papa mwen would snore until dawn.

I can see what little of Zonbi Robot the lake cannot swallow. My head is twisted at an odd angle. I am crushed and broken, like Marie-Louise.

And still, I lie here, yet.

Perhaps, the Lord Mayor will find me. Perhaps he will wind me. Perhaps, he will tell me stories of Bèl Flè ak papa mwen.

He must. Bèl Flè has gone out West. I am all he has now.

One of my first visual memories is of Marie-Louise. She is the first one I saw when I opened my eyes.

She had been so excited when papa nou was building me. She begged him to be present when he finished me.

She was beautiful. I remember the shape of her head. It was sleek. It was sexy. It was aerodynamic.

(Unlike mine now.)

She was a shade of copper that shone like gold when papa nou polished her.

(Unlike me now.)

She was so vibrant. So full of life. Her windup keys whirred with so much energy.

(Unlike mine now.)

Oh, those first few days! We were fast. No one could beat us. Not even the wind down.

Or so we thought.

How naïve we were. We didn't know. How could we know?

Ou pa ka mare pye lanmò.

You can't outrun death.

Good Hunting

Ken Liu

Night. Half moon. An occasional hoot from an owl.

The merchant and his wife and all the servants had been sent away. The large house was eerily quiet.

Father and I crouched behind the scholar's rock in the courtyard. Through the rock's many holes I could see the bedroom window of the merchant's son.

"Oh, Hsiao-jung, my sweet Hsiao-jung..."

The young man's feverish groans were pitiful. Half-delirious, he was tied to his bed for his own good, but Father had left a window open so that his plaintive cries could be carried by the breeze far over the rice paddies.

"Do you think she really will come?" I whispered. Today was my thirteenth birthday, and this was my first hunt.

"She will," Father said. "A *hulijing* cannot resist the cries of the man she has bewitched."

"Like how the Butterfly Lovers cannot resist each other?" I thought back to the folk opera troupe that had come through our village last fall.

333

"Not quite," Father said. But he seemed to have trouble explaining why. "Just know that it's not the same."

I nodded, not sure I understood. But I remembered how the merchant and his wife had come to Father to ask for his help.

"How shameful!" The merchant had muttered. "He's not even nineteen. How could he have read so many sages' books and still fall under the spell of such a creature?"

"There's no shame in being entranced by the beauty and wiles of ahulijing," Father had said. "Even the great scholar Wong Lai once spent three nights in the company of one, and he took first place at the Imperial Examinations. Your son just needs a little help."

"You must save him," the merchant's wife had said, bowing like a chicken pecking at rice. "If this gets out, the matchmakers won't touch him at all."

A *hulijing* was a demon who stole hearts. I shuddered, worried if I would have the courage to face one.

Father put a warm hand on my shoulder, and I felt calmer. In his hand was Swallow Tail, a sword that had first been forged by our ancestor, General Lau Yip, thirteen generations ago. The sword was charged with hundreds of Daoist blessings and had drunk the blood of countless demons.

A passing cloud obscured the moon for a moment, throwing everything into darkness.

When the moon emerged again, I almost cried out.

There, in the courtyard, was the most beautiful lady I had ever seen.

She had on a flowing white silk dress with billowing sleeves and a wide, silvery belt. Her face was pale as snow, and her hair dark as coal, draping past her waist. I thought she looked like the paintings of great beauties from the Tang Dynasty the opera troupe had hung around their stage.

She turned slowly to survey everything around her, her eyes glistening in the moonlight like two shimmering pools.

I was surprised to see how sad she looked. Suddenly, I felt sorry for her and wanted more than anything else to make her smile.

The light touch of my father's hand against the back of my neck jolted me out of my mesmerized state. He had warned me about the power of the *hulijing*. My face hot and my heart hammering, I averted my eyes from the demon's face and focused on her stance.

The merchant's servants had been patrolling the courtyard every night this week with dogs to keep her away from her victim. But now the courtyard was empty. She stood still, hesitating, suspecting a trap.

"Tsiao-jung! Have you come for me?" The son's feverish voice grew louder.

The lady turned and walked—no, glided, so smooth were her movements—towards the bedroom door.

Father jumped out from behind the rock and rushed at her with Swallow Tail.

She dodged out of the way as though she had eyes on the back of her head. Unable to stop, my father thrust the sword into the thick wooden door with a dull thunk. He pulled but could not free the weapon immediately.

The lady glanced at him, turned, and headed for the courtyard gate.

"Don't just stand there, Liang!" Father called. "She's getting away!"

I ran at her, dragging my clay pot filled with dog piss. It was my job to splash her with it so that she could not transform into her fox form and escape.

She turned to me and smiled. "You're a very brave boy." A scent, like jasmine blooming in spring rain, surrounded me. Her voice was like sweet, cold lotus paste, and I wanted to hear her talk forever. The clay pot dangled from my hand, forgotten.

"Now!" Father shouted. He had pulled the sword free.

I bit my lip in frustration. *How could I become a demon hunter if I was so easily enticed?* I lifted off the cover and emptied the clay pot at her retreating figure, but the insane thought that I shouldn't dirty her white dress caused my hands to shake, and my aim was wide. Only a small amount of dog piss got onto her.

But it was enough. She howled, and the sound, like a dog's but so much wilder, caused the hairs on the back of my neck to stand up. She turned and snarled, showing two rows of sharp, white teeth, and I stumbled back.

I had doused her while she was in the midst of her transformation. Her face was thus frozen halfway between a woman's and a fox's, with a hairless snout and raised, triangular ears that twitched angrily. Her hands had turned into paws, tipped with sharp claws that she swiped at me.

She could no longer speak, but her eyes conveyed her venomous thoughts without trouble.

Father rushed by me, his sword raised for a killing blow. The *hulijing* turned around and slammed into the courtyard gate, smashing it open, and disappeared through the broken door.

Father chased after her without even a glance back at me. Ashamed, I followed.

The *hulijing* was swift of foot, and her silvery tail seemed to leave a glittering trail across the fields. But her incompletely transformed body maintained a human's posture, incapable of running as fast as she could have on four legs.

Father and I saw her dodging into the abandoned temple about a *li* outside the village.

"Go around the temple," Father said, trying to catch his breath. "I will go through the front door. If she tries to flee through the back door, you know what to do."

The back of the temple was overgrown with weeds and the wall half-collapsed. As I came around, I saw a white flash darting through the rubble.

Determined to redeem myself in my father's eyes, I swallowed my fear and ran after it without hesitation. After a few quick turns, I had the thing cornered in one of the monks' cells.

I was about to pour the remaining dog piss on it when I realized that the animal was much smaller than the *hulijing* we had been chasing. It was a small white fox, about the size of a puppy.

I set the clay pot on the ground and lunged.

The fox squirmed under me. It was surprisingly strong for such a small animal. I struggled to hold it down. As we fought, the fur between my fingers seemed to become as slippery as skin, and the body elongated, expanded, grew. I had to use my whole body to wrestle it to the ground.

Suddenly, I realized that my hands and arms were wrapped around the nude body of a young girl about my age.

I cried out and jumped back. The girl stood up slowly, picked up a silk robe from behind a pile of straw, put it on, and gazed at me haughtily.

A growl came from the main hall some distance away, followed by the sound of a heavy sword crashing into a table. Then another growl, and the sound of my father's curses.

The girl and I stared at each other. She was even prettier than the opera singer that I couldn't stop thinking about last year.

"Why are you after us?" she asked. "We did nothing to you."

"Your mother bewitched the merchant's son," I said. "We have to save him."

"*Bewitched*? *He*'s the one who wouldn't leave *her* alone."

I was taken aback. "What are you talking about?"

"One night about a month ago, the merchant's son stumbled upon my mother, caught in a chicken farmer's trap. She had to transform into her human form to escape, and as soon as he saw her, he became infatuated.

"She liked her freedom and didn't want anything to do with him. But once a man has set his heart on a *hulijing*, she cannot help hearing him no matter how far apart they are. All that moaning and crying he did drove her to distraction, and she had to go see him every night just to keep him quiet."

This was not what I learned from Father.

"She lures innocent scholars and draws on their life essence to feed her evil magic! Look how sick the merchant's son is!"

"He's sick because that useless doctor gave him poison that was supposed to make him forget about my mother. My mother is the one who's kept him alive with her nightly visits. And stop using the word *lure*. A man can fall in love with a *hulijing* just like he can with any human woman."

I didn't know what to say, so I said the first thing that came to mind. "I just know it's not the same."

She smirked. "Not the same? I saw how you looked at me before I put on my robe."

I blushed. "Brazen demon!" I picked up the clay pot. She remained where she was, a mocking smile on her face. Eventually, I put the pot back down.

The fight in the main hall grew noisier, and suddenly, there was a loud crash, followed by a triumphant shout from Father and a long, piercing scream from the woman.

There was no smirk on the girl's face now, only rage turning slowly to shock. Her eyes had lost their lively luster; they looked dead.

Another grunt from Father. The scream ended abruptly.

"Liang! Liang! It's over. Where are you?"

Tears rolled down the girl's face.

"Search the temple," my Father's voice continued. "She may have pups here. We have to kill them too."

The girl tensed.

"Liang, have you found anything?" The voice was coming closer.

"Nothing," I said, locking eyes with her. "I didn't find anything."

She turned around and silently ran out of the cell. A moment later, I saw a small white fox jump over the broken back wall and disappear into the night.

It was *Qingming*, the Festival of the Dead. Father and I went to sweep Mother's grave and to bring her food and drink to comfort her in the afterlife.

"I'd like to stay here for a while," I said. Father nodded and left for home.

I whispered an apology to my mother, packed up the chicken we had brought for her, and walked the three *li* to the other side of the hill, to the abandoned temple.

I found Yan kneeling in the main hall, near the place where my father had killed her mother five years ago. She wore her hair up in a bun, in the style of a young woman who had had her *jijili*, the ceremony that meant she was no longer a girl.

We'd been meeting every *Qingming*, every *Chongyang*, every *Yulan*, every New Year's, occasions when families were supposed to be together.

"I brought you this," I said, and handed her the steamed chicken.

"Thank you." And she carefully tore off a leg and bit into it daintily. Yan had explained to me that the *hulijing* chose to live near human villages because they liked to have human things in their lives: conversation, beautiful clothes, poetry and stories, and, occasionally, the love of a worthy, kind man.

But the *hulijing* remained hunters who felt most free in their fox form. After what happened to her mother, Yan stayed away from chicken coops, but she still missed their taste.

"How's hunting?" I asked.

"Not so great," she said. "There are few Hundred-Year Salamanders and Six-Toed Rabbits. I can't ever seem to get enough to eat." She bit off another piece of chicken, chewed, and swallowed. "I'm having trouble transforming too."

"It's hard for you to keep this shape?"

"No." She put the rest of the chicken on the ground and whispered a prayer to her mother.

"I mean it's getting harder for me to return to my true form," she continued, "to hunt. Some nights I can't do it at all. How's hunting for you?"

"Not so great either. There don't seem to be as many snake spirits or angry ghosts as a few years ago. Even hauntings by suicides with unfinished business are down. And we haven't had a proper jumping corpse in months. Father is worried about money."

We also hadn't had to deal with a *hulijing* in years. Maybe Yan had warned them all away. Truth be told, I was relieved. I didn't relish the prospect of having to tell my father that he was wrong about something. He was already very irritable, anxious that he was losing the respect of the villagers now that his knowledge and skill didn't seem to be needed as much.

"Ever think that maybe the jumping corpses are also misunderstood?" she asked. "Like me and my mother?"

She laughed as she saw my face. "Just kidding!"

It was strange, what Yan and I shared. She wasn't exactly a friend. More like someone who you couldn't help being drawn to because you shared the knowledge of how the world didn't work the way you had been told.

She looked at the chicken bits she had left for her mother. "I think magic is being drained out of this land."

I had suspected that something was wrong, but didn't want to voice my suspicion out loud, which would make it real.

"What do you think is causing it?"

Instead of answering, Yan perked up her ears and listened intently. Then she got up, grabbed my hand, and pulled until we were behind the buddha in the main hall.

"Wha—"

She held up her finger against my lips. So close to her, I finally noticed her scent. It was like her mother's, floral and sweet, but also bright, like blankets dried in the sun. I felt my face grow warm.

A moment later, I heard a group of men making their way into the temple. Slowly, I inched my head out from behind the buddha so I could see.

It was a hot day, and the men were seeking some shade from the noon sun. Two men set down a cane sedan chair, and the passenger who stepped off was a foreigner, with curly yellow hair and pale skin. Other men in the group carried tripods, levels, bronze tubes, and open trunks full of strange equipment.

"Most Honored Mister Thompson." A man dressed like a mandarin came up to the foreigner. The way he kept on bowing and smiling and bouncing his head up and down reminded me of a kicked dog begging for favors. "Please have a rest and drink some cold tea. It is hard for the men to be working on the day when they're supposed to visit the graves of their families, and they need to take a little time to pray lest they anger the gods and spirits. But I promise we'll work hard afterwards and finish the survey on time."

"The trouble with you Chinese is your endless superstition," the foreigner said. He had a strange accent, but I could understand him just fine. "Remember, the Hong Kong-Tientsin Railroad is a priority for Great Britain. If I don't get as far as Botou Village by sunset, I'll be docking all of your wages."

I had heard rumors that the Manchu Emperor had lost a war and been forced to give up all kinds of concessions, one of which involved paying to help the foreigners build a road of iron. But it had all seemed so fantastical that I didn't pay much attention.

The mandarin nodded enthusiastically. "Most Honored Mister Thompson is right in every way. But might I trouble your gracious ear with a suggestion?"

The weary Englishman waved impatiently.

"Some of the local villagers are worried about the proposed path of the railroad. You see, they think the tracks that have already been laid are blocking off veins of *qi* in the earth. It's bad *feng shui*."

"What are you talking about?"

"It is kind of like how a man breathes," the mandarin said, huffing a few times to make sure the Englishman understood. "The land has channels along rivers, hills, ancient roads that carry the energy of *qi*. It's what gives the villages prosperity and maintains the rare animals and local spirits and household gods.

Could you consider shifting the line of the tracks a little, to follow the *feng shui* masters' suggestions?"

Thompson rolled his eyes. "That is the most ridiculous thing I've yet heard. You want me to deviate from the most efficient path for our railroad because you think your idols would be angry?"

The mandarin looked pained. "Well, in the places where the tracks have already been laid, many bad things are happening: people losing money, animals dying, household gods not responding to prayers. The Buddhist and Daoist monks all agree that it's the railroad."

Thompson strode over to the buddha and looked at it appraisingly. I ducked back behind the statue and squeezed Yan's hand. We held our breaths, hoping that we wouldn't be discovered.

"Does this one still have any power?" Thompson asked.

"The temple hasn't been able to maintain a contingent of monks for many years," the mandarin said. "But this buddha is still well respected. I hear villagers say that prayers to him are often answered."

Then I heard a loud crash and a collective gasp from the men in the main hall.

"I've just broken the hands off of this god of yours with my cane," Thompson said. "As you can see, I have not been struck by lightning or suffered any other calamity. Indeed, now we know that it is only an idol made of mud stuffed with straw and covered in cheap paint. This is why you people lost the war to Britain. You worship statues of mud when you should be thinking about building roads from iron and weapons from steel."

There was no more talk about changing the path of the railroad.

After the men were gone, Yan and I stepped out from behind the statue. We gazed at the broken hands of the buddha for a while.

"The world's changing," Yan said. "Hong Kong, iron roads, foreigners with wires that carry speech and machines that belch smoke. More and more, storytellers in the teahouses speak of these wonders. I think that's why the old magic is leaving. A more powerful kind of magic has come."

She kept her voice unemotional and cool, like a placid pool of water in autumn, but her words rang true. I thought about my father's attempts to keep up a cheerful mien as fewer and fewer customers came to us. I wondered if the time I spent learning the chants and the sword dance moves were wasted.

"What will you do?" I asked, thinking about her, alone in the hills and unable to find the food that sustained her magic.

"There's only one thing I *can* do." Her voice broke for a second and became defiant, like a pebble tossed into the pool.

But then she looked at me, and her composure returned. "There's only one thing *we* can do: Learn to survive."

The railroad soon became a familiar part of the landscape: the black locomotive huffing through the green rice paddies, puffing steam and pulling a long train behind it, like a dragon coming down from the distant, hazy, blue mountains. For a while, it was a wondrous sight, with children marveling at it, running alongside the tracks to keep up.

But the soot from the locomotive chimneys killed the rice in the fields closest to the tracks, and two children playing on the tracks, too frightened to move, were killed one afternoon. After that, the train ceased to fascinate.

People stopped coming to Father and me to ask for our services. They either went to the Christian missionary or the new teacher who said he'd studied in San Francisco. Young men in the village began to leave for Hong Kong or Canton, moved by rumors of bright lights and well-paying work. Fields lay fallow. The village itself seemed to consist only of the too-old and too-young, their mood one of resignation. Men from distant provinces came to inquire about buying land for cheap.

Father spent his days sitting in the front room, Swallow Tail over his knee, staring out the door from dawn to dusk, as though he himself had turned into a statue.

Every day, as I returned home from the fields, I would see the glint of hope in Father's eyes briefly flare up.

"Did anyone speak of needing our help?" he would ask.

"No," I would say, trying to keep my tone light. "But I'm sure there will be a jumping corpse soon. It's been too long."

I would not look at my father as I spoke because I did not want to look as hope faded from his eyes.

Then, one day, I found Father hanging from the heavy beam in his bedroom. As I let his body down, my heart numb, I thought that he was not unlike those he had hunted all his life: they were all sustained by an old magic that had left and would not return, and they did not know how to survive without it.

Swallow Tail felt dull and heavy in my hand. I had always thought I would be a demon hunter, but how could I when there were no more demons, no more spirits? All the Daoist blessings in the sword could not save my father's sinking heart. And if I stuck around, perhaps my heart would grow heavy and yearn to be still too.

I hadn't seen Yan since that day six years ago, when we hid from the railroad surveyors at the temple. But her words came back to me now.

Learn to survive.

I packed a bag and bought a train ticket to Hong Kong.

The Sikh guard checked my papers and waved me through the security gate.

I paused to let my gaze follow the tracks going up the steep side of the mountain. It seemed less like a railroad track than a ladder straight up to heaven. This was the funicular railway, the tram line to the top of Victoria Peak, where the masters of Hong Kong lived and the Chinese were forbidden to stay.

But the Chinese were good enough to shovel coal into the boilers and grease the gears.

Steam rose around me as I ducked into the engine room. After five years, I knew the rhythmic rumbling of the pistons and the staccato grinding of the gears as well as I knew my own breath and heartbeat. There was a kind of music to their orderly cacophony that moved me, like the clashing of cymbals and gongs at the start of a folk opera. I checked the pressure, applied sealant on the gaskets, tightened the flanges, replaced the worn-down gears in the backup cable assembly. I lost myself in the work, which was hard and satisfying.

By the end of my shift, it was dark. I stepped outside the engine room and saw a full moon in the sky as another tram filled with passengers was pulled up the side of the mountain, powered by my engine.

"Don't let the Chinese ghosts get you," a woman with bright blond hair said in the tram, and her companions laughed.

It was the night of *Yulan*, I realized, the Ghost Festival. *I should get something for my father, maybe pick up some paper money at Mongkok.*

"How can you be done for the day when we still want you?" a man's voice came to me.

"Girls like you shouldn't tease," another man said, and laughed.

I looked in the direction of the voices and saw a Chinese woman standing in the shadows just outside the tram station. Her tight western-style cheongsam and the garish makeup told me her profession. Two Englishmen blocked her path. One tried to put his arms around her, and she backed out of the way.

"Please. I'm very tired," she said in English. "Maybe next time."

"Now, don't be stupid," the first man said, his voice hardening. "This isn't a discussion. Come along now and do what you're supposed to."

I walked up to them. "Hey."

The men turned around and looked at me.

"What seems to be the problem?"

"None of your business."

"Well, I think it *is* my business," I said, "seeing as how you're talking to my sister."

I doubt either of them believed me. But five years of wrangling heavy machinery had given me a muscular frame, and they took a look at my face and hands, grimy with engine grease, and probably decided that it wasn't worth it to get into a public tussle with a lowly Chinese engineer.

The two men stepped away to get in line for the Peak Tram, muttering curses.

"Thank you," she said.

"It's been a long time," I said, looking at her. I swallowed the *you look good*. She didn't. She looked tired and thin and brittle. And the pungent perfume she wore assaulted my nose.

But I did not think of her harshly. Judging was the luxury of those who did not need to survive.

"It's the night of the Ghost Festival," she said. "I didn't want to work anymore. I wanted to think about my mother."

"Why don't we go get some offerings together?" I asked.

We took the ferry over to Kowloon, and the breeze over the water revived her a bit. She wet a towel with the hot water from the teapot on the ferry and wiped off her makeup. I caught a faint trace of her natural scent, fresh and lovely as always.

"You look good," I said, and meant it.

On the streets of Kowloon, we bought pastries and fruits and cold dumplings and a steamed chicken and incense and paper money, and caught up on each other's lives.

"How's hunting?" I asked. We both laughed.

"I miss being a fox," she said. She nibbled on a chicken wing absent-mindedly. "One day, shortly after that last time we talked, I felt the last bit of magic leave me. I could no longer transform."

"I'm sorry," I said, unable to offer anything else.

"My mother taught me to like human things: food, clothes, folk opera, old stories. But she was never dependent on them. When she wanted, she could always turn into her true form and hunt. But now, in this form, what can I do? I don't have claws. I don't have sharp teeth. I can't even run very fast. All I have is my beauty, the same thing that your father and you killed my mother for. So now I live by the very thing that you once falsely accused my mother of doing: I *lure* men for money."

"My father is dead, too."

Hearing this seemed to drain some of the bitterness out of her. "What happened?"

"He felt the magic leave us, much as you. He couldn't bear it."

"I'm sorry." And I knew that she didn't know what else to say either.

"You told me once that the only thing we can do is to survive. I have to thank you for that. It probably saved my life."

"Then we're even," she said, smiling. "But let us not speak of ourselves any more. Tonight is reserved for the ghosts."

We went down to the harbor and placed our food next to the water, inviting all the ghosts we had loved to come and dine. Then we lit the incense and burned the paper money in a bucket.

She watched bits of burnt paper being carried into the sky by the heat from the flames. They disappeared among the stars. "Do you think the gates to the underworld still open for the ghosts tonight, now that there is no magic left?"

I hesitated. When I was young I had been trained to hear the scratching of a ghost's fingers against a paper window, to distinguish the voice of a spirit from the wind. But now I was used to enduring the thunderous pounding of pistons and the deafening hiss of high-pressured steam rushing through valves. I could no longer claim to be attuned to that vanished world of my childhood.

"I don't know," I said. "I suppose it's the same with ghosts as with people. Some will figure out how to survive in a world diminished by iron roads and steam whistles, some will not."

"But will any of them thrive?" she asked.

She could still surprise me.

"I mean," she continued, "are you happy? Are you happy to keep an engine running all day, yourself like another cog? What do you dream of?"

I couldn't remember any dreams. I had let myself become entranced by the movement of gears and levers, to let my mind grow to fit the gaps between the ceaseless clanging of metal on metal. It was a way to not have to think about my father, about a land that had lost so much.

"I dream of hunting in this jungle of metal and asphalt," she said. "I dream of my true form leaping from beam to ledge to terrace to roof, until I am at the top of this island, until I can growl in the faces of all the men who believe they can own me."

As I watched, her eyes, brightly lit for a moment, dimmed.

"In this new age of steam and electricity, in this great metropolis, except for those who live on the Peak, is anyone still in their true form?" she asked.

We sat together by the harbor and burned paper money all night, waiting for a sign that the ghosts were still with us.

Life in Hong Kong could be a strange experience: from day to day, things never seemed to change much. But if you compared things over a few years, it was almost like you lived in a different world.

By my thirtieth birthday, new designs for steam engines required less coal and delivered more power. They grew smaller and smaller. The streets filled with automatic rickshaws and horseless carriages, and most people who could afford them had machines that kept the air cool in houses and the food cold in boxes in the kitchen—all powered by steam.

I went into stores and endured the ire of the clerks as I studied the components of new display models. I devoured every book on the principle and operation of the steam engine I could find. I tried to apply those principles to improve the machines I was in charge of: trying out new firing cycles, testing new kinds of lubricants for the pistons, adjusting the gear ratios. I found a measure of satisfaction in the way I came to understand the magic of the machines.

One morning, as I repaired a broken governor—a delicate bit of work—two pairs of polished shoes stopped on the platform above me.

I looked up. Two men looked down at me.

"This is the one," said my shift supervisor.

The other man, dressed in a crisp suit, looked skeptical. "Are you the man who came up with the idea of using a larger flywheel for the old engine?"

I nodded. I took pride in the way I could squeeze more power out of my machines than dreamed of by their designers.

"You did not steal the idea from an Englishman?" his tone was severe.

I blinked. A moment of confusion was followed by a rush of anger. "No," I said, trying to keep my voice calm. I ducked back under the machine to continue my work.

"He is clever," my shift supervisor said, "for a Chinaman. He can be taught."

"I suppose we might as well try," said the other man. "It will certainly be cheaper than hiring a real engineer from England."

Mr. Alexander Findlay Smith, owner of the Peak Tram and an avid engineer himself, had seen an opportunity. He foresaw that the path of technological progress would lead inevitably to the use of steam power to operate automata: mechanical arms and legs that would eventually replace the Chinese coolies and servants.

I was selected to serve Mr. Findlay Smith in his new venture.

I learned to repair clockwork, to design intricate systems of gears and devise ingenious uses for levers. I studied how to plate metal with chrome and how to shape brass into smooth curves. I invented ways to connect the world of hardened and ruggedized clockwork to the world of miniaturized and regulated piston and clean steam. Once the automata were finished, we connected them to the latest analytic engines shipped from Britain and fed them with tape punched with dense holes in Babbage-Lovelace code.

It had taken a decade of hard work. But now mechanical arms served drinks in the bars along Central and machine hands fashioned shoes and clothes in factories in the New Territories. In the mansions up on the Peak, I heard—though I'd never seen—that automatic sweepers and mops I designed roamed the halls discreetly, bumping into walls gently as they cleaned the floors like mechanical elves puffing out bits of white steam. The expats could finally live their lives in this tropical paradise free of reminders of the presence of the Chinese.

I was thirty-five when she showed up at my door again, like a memory from long ago.

I pulled her into my tiny flat, looked around to be sure no one was following her, and closed the door.

"How's hunting?" I asked. It was a bad attempt at a joke, and she laughed weakly.

Photographs of her had been in all the papers. It was the biggest scandal in the colony: not so much because the Governor's son was keeping a Chinese mistress—it was expected that he would—but because the mistress had managed to steal a large sum of money from him and then disappear. Everyone tittered while the police turned the city upside down, looking for her.

"I can hide you for tonight," I said. Then I waited, the unspoken second half of my sentence hanging between us.

She sat down in the only chair in the room, the dim light bulb casting dark shadows on her face. She looked gaunt and exhausted. "Ah, now you're judging me."

"I have a good job I want to keep," I said. "Mr. Findlay Smith trusts me."

She bent down and began to pull up her dress.

"Don't," I said, and turned my face away. I could not bear to watch her try to ply her trade with me.

"Look," she said. There was no seduction in her voice. "Liang, look at me."

I turned and gasped.

Her legs, what I could see of them, were made of shiny chrome. I bent down to look closer: the cylindrical joints at the knees were lathed with precision, the pneumatic actuators along the thighs moved in complete silence, the feet were exquisitely molded and shaped, the surfaces smooth and flowing. These were the most beautiful mechanical legs I had ever seen.

"He had me drugged," she said. "When I woke up, my legs were gone and replaced by these. The pain was excruciating. He explained to me that he had a secret: he liked machines more than flesh, couldn't get hard with a regular woman."

I had heard of such men. In a city filled with chrome and brass and clanging and hissing, desires became confused.

I focused on the way light moved along the gleaming curves of her calves so that I didn't have to look into her face.

"I had a choice: let him keep on changing me to suit him, or he could remove the legs and throw me out on the street. Who would believe a legless Chinese whore? I wanted to survive. So I swallowed the pain and let him continue."

She stood up and removed the rest of her dress and her evening gloves. I took in her chrome torso, slatted around the waist to allow articulation and movement; her sinuous arms, constructed from curved plates sliding over each other like obscene armor; her hands, shaped from delicate metal mesh, with dark steel fingers tipped with jewels where the fingernails would be.

"He spared no expense. Every piece of me is built with the best craftsmanship and attached to my body by the best surgeons—there are many who want to experiment, despite the law, with how the body could be animated by electricity, nerves replaced by wires. They always spoke only to him, as if I was already only a machine.

"Then, one night, he hurt me and I struck back in desperation. He fell like he was made of straw. I realized, suddenly, how much strength I had in my metal arms. I had let him do all this to me, to replace me part by part, mourning my loss all the while without understanding what I had gained. A terrible thing had been done to me, but I could also be *terrible*.

"I choked him until he fainted, and then I took all the money I could find and left.

"So I come to you, Liang. Will you help me?"

I stepped up and embraced her. "We'll find some way to reverse this. There must be doctors—"

"No," she interrupted me. "That's not what I want."

It took us almost a whole year to complete the task. Yan's money helped, but some things money couldn't buy, especially skill and knowledge.

My flat became a workshop. We spent every evening and all of Sundays working: shaping metal, polishing gears, reattaching wires.

Her face was the hardest. It was still flesh.

I poured over books of anatomy and took casts of her face with plaster of Paris. I broke my cheekbones and cut my face so that I could stagger into surgeons' offices and learn from them how to repair these injuries. I bought expensive jeweled masks and took them apart, learning the delicate art of shaping metal to take on the shape of a face.

Finally, it was time.

Through the window, the moon threw a pale white parallelogram on the floor. Yan stood in the middle of it, moving her head about, trying out her new face.

Hundreds of miniature pneumatic actuators were hidden under the smooth chrome skin, each of which could be controlled independently, allowing her to adopt any expression. But her eyes were still the same, and they shone in the moonlight with excitement.

"Are you ready?" I asked.

She nodded.

I handed her a bowl, filled with the purest anthracite coal, ground into a fine powder. It smelled of burnt wood, of the heart of the earth. She poured it into her mouth and swallowed. I could hear the fire in the miniature boiler in her torso grow hotter as the pressure of the steam built up. I took a step back.

She lifted her head to the moon and howled: it was a howl made by steam passing through brass piping, and yet it reminded me of that wild howl long ago, when I first heard the call of a *hulijing.*

Then she crouched to the floor. Gears grinding, pistons pumping, curved metal plates sliding over each other—the noises grew louder as she began to transform.

She had drawn the first glimmers of her idea with ink on paper. Then she had refined it, through hundreds of iterations until she was satisfied. I could see traces of her mother in it, but also something harder, something new.

Working from her idea, I had designed the delicate folds in the chrome skin and the intricate joints in the metal skeleton. I had put together every hinge, assembled every gear, soldered every wire, welded every seam, oiled every actuator. I had taken her apart and put her back together.

Yet, it was a marvel to see everything working. In front of my eyes, she folded and unfolded like a silvery origami construction, until finally, a chrome fox as beautiful and deadly as the oldest legends stood before me.

She padded around the flat, testing out her sleek new form, trying out her stealthy new movements. Her limbs gleamed in the moonlight, and her tail, made of delicate silver wires as fine as lace, left a trail of light in the dim flat.

She turned and walked—no, glided—towards me, a glorious hunter, an ancient vision coming alive. I took a deep breath and smelled fire and smoke, engine oil and polished metal, the scent of power.

"Thank you," she said, and leaned in as I put my arms around her true form. The steam engine inside her had warmed her cold metal body, and it felt warm and alive.

"Can you feel it?" she asked.

I shivered. I knew what she meant. The old magic was back but changed: not fur and flesh, but metal and fire.

"I will find others like me," she said, "and bring them to you. Together, we will set them free."

Once, I was a demon hunter. Now, I am one of them.

I opened the door, Swallow Tail in my hand. It was only an old and heavy sword, rusty, but still perfectly capable of striking down anyone who might be lying in wait.

No one was.

Yan leapt out of the door like a bolt of lightning. Stealthily, gracefully, she darted into the streets of Hong Kong, free, feral, a *hulijing* built for this new age.

*...once a man has set his heart on a*hulijing, *she cannot help hearing him no matter how far apart they are...*

"Good hunting," I whispered.

She howled in the distance, and I watched a puff of steam rise into the air as she disappeared.

I imagined her running along the tracks of the funicular railway, a tireless engine racing up, and up, towards the top of Victoria Peak, towards a future as full of magic as the past.

About the Authors

New Zealand born fantasy writer and podcaster **Philippa (Pip) Ballantine** is the author of the *Books of the Order* and the *Shifted World* series. She is also the co-author with her husband Tee Morris of the Locus best selling, *Ministry of Peculiar Occurrences* novels, which have all appeared in the top 10 science fiction titles of the Goodreads Awards for the year they were published. Her other awards include an Airship, two Parsecs, the Steampunk Chronicle Reader's Choice, and a Sir Julius Vogel. She currently resides in Manassas, Virginia with her husband, daughter, and a furry clowder of cats.

Alex Bledsoe grew up in west Tennessee an hour north of Graceland (home of Elvis) and twenty minutes from Nutbush (birthplace of Tina Turner). He's been a reporter, editor, photographer and door-to-door vacuum cleaner salesman. He now lives in a Wisconsin town famous for trolls, writes before six in the morning and tries to teach his three kids to act like they've been to town before. He is the author of the Eddie LaCrosse series (most recently *He Drank, and Saw the Spider*), the Tufa novels (*Wisp of a Thing* and *The Hum and the Shiver*) and the Firefly Witch ebooks.

Emily Cataneo is a dark fantasy and horror writer based in Boston, Mass. Her short fiction is forthcoming from the *Chiral Mad 2* anthology and from the online magazine Kaleidotrope. She is a 2013 graduate of the Odyssey Writing Workshop and a member of the online Codex Writers Group. Her stories usually involve winter, bones, female friendships, the Victorian occult, anxious characters, and the darkly beautiful. When she's not writing fiction, she's a freelance journalist for the paper of record in the Greater Boston area.

S. J. Chambers is the Hugo and World Fantasy nominated co-author of the best-selling *The Steampunk Bible* and *The Steampunk Bible 2014 Calendar* (Abrams Image). Her fiction has appeared in a variety of venues, including *Mungbeing* magazine (where her story "Of Parallel and Parcel" was nominated for a Pushcart prize), *New Myths*, *Yankee Pot Roast*, as well as in anthologies like the World Fantasy nominated *Thackery T. Lambshead's Cabinet Of Curiosities* (HarperCollins), *Zombies: Shambling Through The Ages* (Prime Books), and the Spanish steampunk anthology *Planes B*. She has stories forthcoming in *Starry Wisdom Library* (PS Publishing), *Acronos II* (Tyrannosaurus Books), and in *The New Gothic* (Stone Skin Press) the latter which features her collaboration with writer extarodinnire Jesse Bullington.

Lillian Cohen-Moore is an award winning editor (Indic RPG Awards, Origins Award, for *Do: Pilgrims of the Flying Temple*), and devotes her writing to fiction, journalism and game design. Influenced by the work of Jewish authors and horror movies, she draws on bubbe meises (grandmother's tales) and horror classics for inspiration. She loves exploring and photographing abandoned places. She is a member of the Society of Professional Journalists and the Online News Association.

Indrapramit Das is a writer and artist from Kolkata, India. His fiction has appeared in publications including *Clarkesworld Magazine, Asimov's Science Fiction* and *Apex Magazine*, as well as anthologies such as *The Year's Best Science Fiction: Thirtieth Annual Collection* (St. Martin's Press), *Aliens: Recent Encounters*(Prime Books) and *Mothership: Tales from Afrofuturism and Beyond*(Rosarium Publishing). He has written reviews of film, books, comics and TV for *Strange Horizons* and *Slant Magazine*. He is a grateful graduate of the 2012 Clarion West Writers Workshop and a recipient of the Octavia E. Butler Scholarship Award to attend the former. He completed his MFA at the University of British Columbia and is currently in Vancouver working as a freelance writer, artist, editor, critic, TV extra, game tester, tutor, would-be novelist, and aspirant to adulthood.

Malon Edwards was born and raised on the South Side of Chicago, but now lives in the Greater Toronto Area, where he was lured by his beautiful Canadian wife. Many of his short stories are set in an alternate Chicago and feature people of color. Currently, he serves as Managing Director and Grants Administrator for the Speculative Literature Foundation, which provides a number of grants for writers of speculative literature.

Jaymee Goh is the postcolonial steampunk writer of Silver Goggles, a blog that focuses on postcoloniality, anti-racism and the meaningful participation of people of color in steampunk beyond tokenism. She has been seen on the Apex Book Company Blog, Racialicious.com, and Tor.com. Her non-fiction has been published in *Steampunk III: Steampunk Revolution, The WisCon Chronicles*, and *Fashion Talks: Undressing the Power of Style*. Her previously published short stories take place in the same steampunk 'verse as this one. Currently she is a Comparative Literature PhD student at UC Riverside.

Jay Lake is the award-winning author of ten novels, five collections, and over 300 short stories. He was the winner of the 2004 John W. Campbell Award for Best New Writer. He has been nominated for the Hugo, Nebula, and World Fantasy awards. He has been published by Tor Books, Night Shade Books, MonkeyBrain Books, Fairwood Press, Wheatland Press, and Subterranean Press. He is also a cancer survivor who blogs about politics, technology, and health.

Ken Liu is an author and translator of speculative fiction, as well as a lawyer and programmer. His fiction has appeared in *The Magazine of Fantasy & Science Fiction, Asimov's, Analog, Clarkesworld, Lightspeed, and Strange Horizons*, among other places. He has won a Nebula, two Hugos, a World Fantasy Award, and a Science Fiction & Fantasy Translation Award, and been nominated for the Sturgeon and the Locus Awards. He lives with his family near Boston, Massachusetts.

Rochita Loenen-Ruiz is an essayist, a fictionist and a poet. A Filipino writer, now living in the Netherlands, she attended Clarion West in 2009 and was a recipient of the Octavia Butler scholarship. In 2013, her short fiction was shortlisted for the BSFA short fiction award. Most recently, her fiction has appeared in *We See a Different Frontier, Mothership: Tales from Afrofuturism and Beyond, What Fates Impose, The End of the Road* anthology, and as part of Redmond Radio's Afrofuturism Event for the Amsterdam Museumnacht at FOAM museum. She also has upcoming work in *Clarkesworld Magazine*.

Nayad A. Monroe is an editor and short-story writer. She read over 5,000 submissions for the Hugo Award-winning semiprozine, *Clarkesworld Magazine*, before she became an editor with her anthology of divination stories, *What Fates Impose*. Several of her short stories have been published in various anthologies, such as *Space Grunts: Full-Throttle Space Tales #3;*

Space Tramps: Full-Throttle Space Tales #5; The Crimson Pact: Volume Two; and *Sidekicks!*. Her sidekick story, "Quintuple-A," is scheduled to be made into a short film by Wild Hawk Entertainment. Nayad has also contributed an interview with Tim Powers to Writers Workshop of Science Fiction and Fantasy. You can find her making odd remarks on Twitter as @Nayad.

Balogun Ojetade is author the Steamfunk novel *Moses: The Chronicles of Harriet Tubman*, the Sword and Soul novel *Once Upon A Time in Afrika* and the Urban Fantasy novel *Redeemer*. He is contributing co-editor of the anthologies, *Steamfunk* and *Ki-Khanga: The Anthology*. Finally, he is screenwriter and director of the action film, *A Single Link* and the Steamfunk film *Rite of Passage*.

Diana M. Pho (Ay-leen the Peacemaker) is a scholar, activist, blogger, and general rabble-rouser. She earned her B.A. from Mount Holyoke College and her M.A. from New York University. Awards given for her work include the Steampunk Chronicle Reader's Choice Awards for "Best Politically-Minded Steampunk" (2013 & 2014) and "Best Multicultural Steampunk" (2012 & 2013) as well as "Best Blog" and "Best Feminist Steampunk" in 2012; the SteamCon Airship Award for "Community Contributor" in 2013; the Last Drink Bird Head Award for "Gentle Advocacy" in 2010. About her work, *New York Times* bestselling author of the Leviathan trilogy, Scott Westerfeld has said, "I always point to her to rebut the genre's haters." Diana currently lives and works in New York City for Tor Books & blogs for Tor.com. You can follow her academic work on Academia.edu.

Nisi Shawl's collection *Filter House* was a 2009 James Tiptree, Jr., Award winner; her stories have been published at *Strange Horizons*, in *Asimov's SF Magazine*, and in anthologies including *The Year's Best Fantasy and Horror*. She was the 2011 Guest of

Honor at the feminist SF convention WisCon and 2014 co-Guest of Honor for the Science Fiction Research Association. She co-authored the renowned *Writing the Other: A Practical Approach* with Cynthia Ward. Shawl's Belgian Congo steampunk novel "Everfair" is forthcoming in 2015 from Tor Books.

Lucy A. Snyder is the Bram Stoker Award-winning author of the novels *Spellbent, Shotgun Sorceress, Switchblade Goddess,* and the collections *Orchid Carousals, Sparks and Shadows, Chimeric Machines,* and Installing*Linux on a Dead Badger.* She will have two new books out in 2014: *Shooting Yourself in the Head For Fun and Profit: A Writer's Guide* will be released by Post Mortem Press, and her story collection *Soft Apocalypses* will be released by Raw Dog Screaming Press. Her writing has been translated into French, Russian, and Japanese editions and has appeared in publications such as *What Fates Impose, Strange Horizons, Weird Tales, Hellbound Hearts, Dark Faith, Chiaroscuro, GUD,* and *Best Horror of the Year, Vol. 5.*

Lucien Moussa Shukri Soulban is an author from Montreal, Canada. He was born in Saudi Arabia, but grew up in Houston, Texas. He has lived in Montreal for 16 years. Lucien Soulban is his real name. As well as numerous credits, both role-playing and fiction, with White Wolf, he has written for Dream Pod 9, AEG, WizKids and Guardians of Order, and has also worked on video games with Relic and Artificial Mind and Movement, among others.

Benjanun Sriduangkaew enjoys writing love letters to cities real and speculative, and lots of space opera when she can get away with it. Her works can be found in *Clarkesworld, Beneath Ceaseless Skies, The Dark, GigaNotoSaurus, The Mammoth Book of Steampunk Adventures, Upgraded,* and *Solaris Rising 3.* They are also reprinted in *The Best Science Fiction and Fantasy of the Year Vol. 8, The Year's Best Science and Fantasy 2014* and

The Mammoth Book of SF Stories by Women. Her novella *Scale-Bright* is forthcoming from Immersion Press.

Tade Thompson's roots are in Western Nigeria and South London. His short stories have been published in small press, webzines and anthologies. Most recently, his story "Notes from Gethsemane" appeared in *The Afro SF Anthology*, and "Shadow" appeared in *The Apex Book of World SF 2*, and "120 Days of Sunlight" appeared in *Mothership: Tales from Afrofuturism and Beyond.* He lives and works in South England. He creates under a unified influence field comprised of books, music, theatre, comics, art, movies, gourmet coffee, and amala. He has been known to haunt coffee shops, jazz bars, bookshops, and libraries. He is an occasional visual artist and tortures his family with his attempts to play the guitar.

A Note From the Publisher

Dear Reader:

I hope you enjoyed this book. I did, and that's why I helped it become a reality. Too many big publishers are more concerned with cash instead of characters, stories, and ideas. They care more about their bottom line instead of what you really want.

That's not how I work. I want to bring you awesome characters and stories from authors that *you* enjoy.

So I have one small favor to ask of you.

Leave a review for this book. Loved it, hated it - just let the author and I know what you thought of it. What you liked, what you didn't like, and what you *loved*.

A short honest review will help me—as a publisher—know what you what to read... and it will help other readers like you find this book.

To help make it even easier for you, there's a full list of my publications at http://alliterationink.com/pubslist.html so you can easily review them.

I look forward to hearing what you thought of the book!

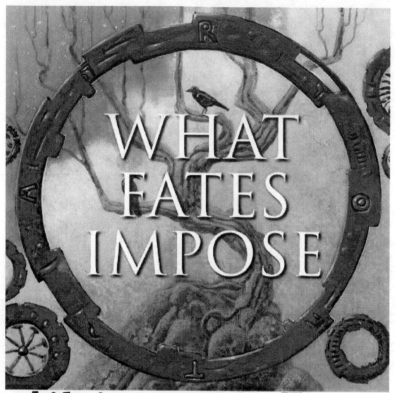

WHAT FATES IMPOSE

Life is uncertain. The chance to peek into the future is tempting. But is it a good idea to look?

fates.alliterationink.com

AN
INHERITANCE
OF STONE

"Some poems in this book gallop and kick. Some swerve elegantly like an escape pod caught in a gravity well. Other roll quiet as a child's blanket. The words in these pages won't seem the same each time you read them. They will be just what you were looking for, but nothing that you expected."

- Lucy A. Snyder, author of the Bram Stoker Award-winning poetry collection *Chimeric Machines*

inheritance.alliterationink.com

Heroes and heroines perform world shaking deeds, but sidekicks? Sidekicks are the unseen glue holding those powerhouses together. They are the backbones. They are the voices of reason.

It's long past time for them to shine.

Let the heroes sit this one out. Celebrate the Sidekick!

sidekicks.alliterationink.com

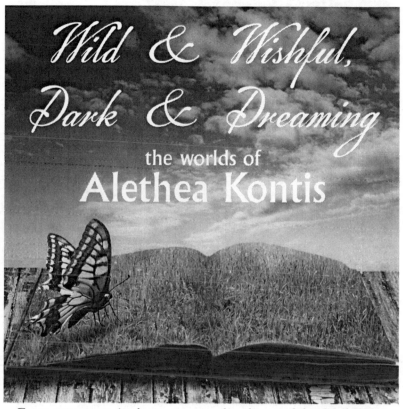

On his late-night radio show *The Red Eye*, Sam Brody pulls back the curtain on paranormal hoaxes, exposing the charlatans posing as psychics, vampires, and alien messengers. Sure, he started out hoping that someone would prove that there was something "more," but after all the con artists and fakes, that hope's gone.

Sam Brody definitely doesn't believe in the supernatural.

But with one phone call, he discovers that the supernatural definitely believes in him.

redeye.alliterationink.com

We thought we defeated the demons.
We were wrong.

"Almost 30 years later The Crimson Pact supplants Clive Barker's Books of Blood series as the modern compendium of fantasy horror short stories." Lance Roth

thecrimsonpact.com

He can save his partner, his son, his marriage... or the world. But he can't do it all.

"This is a spy novel that intersects with the world of MMORPGs and combines a set of topics I haven't seen before. It is a bit of The DaVinci Code with some James Bond and a modern virtual reality spin."

-Game Knight Reviews

netimpact.alliterationink.com